MORE SPACE JUNK

ANDREW BIXLER

PTP

For more information about this book and to receive updates on new releases, visit **andrewbixler.com**

Cover illustration by Chun Lo
Interior illustrations by Gary Bixler

ISBN: 978-1-7370607-0-3

To Polly & Fred and Paula & Ron,
for surrounding me with love and books

Special thanks again to Meghan Lear for her fastidious editing and to Gary Bixler for providing the interior illustrations.

PART 1

Barcadia of My Youth

1

Anxious murmurs turn to stunned gasps as a pinpoint of light, a lone star in a sea of black, explodes outward with a blinding flash to shatter the darkness. In an instant, the stagnant air is host to thousands of battling warships, the bright fire from their cannons furiously dancing across the sky with an impossible majesty. Wild flourishes of flame lick the dark as ships burst in time to rapid-fire distortion churned out by an electric guitar.

The only thing that could top the spectacle, Spez thinks as a ship the size of his meaty palm blows up in front of his eyes, is the real thing. As the war reaches its impressively gratuitous crescendo, an invisible hand paints the title onto the air in big bold streaks - *Pants Team Pink: The Movie*, eliciting loud hollers and applause from the audience.

When it's over, Spez, Tobi, and the rest of the crowd shuffle out of the dark, sticky theater into the bright parking lot. Placing a crudely wrapped cigarette between his purple lips, Spez inhales deep and hacks on a popcorn kernel.

"It was a lot shorter 'an I membert," Tobi says, pointing his eyestalks toward the star-speckled sky as he shoves his greasy mit back into his popcorn bag.

"Yeah well," Spez says, "livin' a thin' and memberin' it is two differnt thins."

"S'pose yer right 'bout that."

Behind them, the door to the theater bursts open, and a group of young space nerds tromps out, arguing over the subtle nuances of the most successful children's team action adventure holo-film of all time.

Unwilling to stop himself from eavesdropping, Spez hears a young girl with dark pigtails say, "It's not even accurate. The Traxan and Zorman armies were way smaller than that."

But not everyone is convinced. A little boy with sandy blonde hair and short pants frowns and demands, "How do *you* know?"

"Because I'm older and smarter than you, and because only a chidiot would believe Pants Team Pink," the girl says.

"She knows what she's talking about," her string bean friend declares, with a kid-authority that causes the boy's shoulders to slump.

Putting his cigarette out on the side of the building, Spez ambles toward the youngsters.

"Hey, wer yuh goin'?" Tobi shouts.

"C'mon, we gotta drop some knowletge."

Stomping her foot on the cement, the girl with the pigtails yells, "Pants Team Pink are just phonies and losers!"

"Nuh-uh," the boy retorts. "They saved the universe!"

"They *ruined* the universe!" the girl wails.

When she looks up and finds Spez and Tobi listening in, she screams, and the kids scatter.

Suddenly picturing his and Tobi's violent expulsion into the vacuum by a mob of angry parents, Spez calls out, "Hey wait, wer not gon' hurt yuh. We jist wanna set the recort straight."

Shooting each other wary glances, the kids wander back, and with a skeptical scowl, the tall girl asks, "What do *you* know about it?"

"Well, some," Spez tells her, adjusting his grease-stained 'PANTS' cap. "We was ther. Tell 'em, Tob."

"Tell 'em what?" Tobi asks.

"That we was at that war, *'tween the Empires.*"

"Oh right, sure," Tobi says, stuffing a handful of popcorn between his cheeks. "We was ther."

The girl with the pigtails puts her hands on her hips and says, "So *what?*"

"So those armies was way bigger 'an you say," Spez tells her. "In fact they was even bigger 'an the ones in the movie."

"I knew it!" the boy shouts. "*You're* the losers. *Plll,*" he blows a raspberry at the girls and runs off down the sidewalk.

As the kid scurries away, the old scrapper is briefly transported to an alternate reality, in which life's possibilities still seem endless and he's not stuck hauling scrap for a living. But his daydream is brought to an abrupt end when Tobi elbows him and points at the two glowering girls.

"Ha," Spez says, holding up his hands. "Well, it's true."

Tobi motions toward the lot behind them, and he and Spez smile nervously, careful not to make any sudden movements as they beat a slow retreat back to their ship.

When they reach the battered freighter, Spez glances back toward the theater, but the little bullies are gone. Climbing the metal ladder affixed to the hull, he wrenches the side door open and pulls himself up into the cockpit.

"Hey, yer gettin' grease all over the dash," Spez complains as Tobi tosses his popcorn on the control panel and slumps into the ratty passenger seat.

"Oh, sorry." Tobi leans forward and tries to wipe up the mess, but the imitation butter topping just spreads over the console.

"Ah, fergit it."

Digging in his pocket, Spez emerges with his keys and starts the engine. But as he shifts the rig into gear, he hesitates.

"What's a matter?" Tobi asks.

"Listen," Spez says. "Yuh hear that?" Beneath the comforting, clanky purr that has become an integral part of his very existence, he senses some almost imperceptible irregularity. "Like a sputter."

"I don't hear nothin'," Tobi says.

As Spez shuts the engine off, he says, "Wit yuh jist check it out? Sount'it like the exhaust."

Spitting a mouthful of half-chewed popcorn onto the dash, Tobi stretches his eyes so wide they practically fall off their stalks. *"How come I gotta do it?"*

"Cuz I do errythin' else 'round here."

"Fine," Tobi says, grumbling as he climbs outside. When he gets back, he tosses something black and crusty into the cabin ahead of him. "Yuh was right after all."

"What the fish is that?" Spez asks, slipping off his cap to get a better look.

Tobi lifts the charred remains and holds it up to his nose. "I think it's... bananas."

Stunned for a moment, Spez finally says, "What the fish is this universe comin' to?"

"I don't know," Tobi says, peeling back the blackened skin of one of the fruits and squeezing its gooey contents into his craw. "But I like it."

This time, the engine starts like a crummy dream, and Spez guides the ship up out of the lot. As soon as they're outside the dome, he sets the autopilot for their next drop-off and reaches into the fridge for a frosty can of Nü Guard.

He takes a big gulp and winces, his lips puckering. "Ulch, that is awful! How come they always gotta change thins? Kin't anyboty ever jist leave well 'nough alone?"

"I don't know." Tobi belches, finishing off a cool one. "I sort a like it."

"I guess it's slightly better 'an bein' sober," Spez says as he takes another pained sip. "You ready, Tob?"

"I guess so..."

Broadcasting their signal out to the furthest reaches of the universe, Spez announces, "Ther's nothin' wrong with yer receiver. Yer 'bout tuh participate in a great aventure. So sit back and crack a colt one, cuz yer listenin' tuh *Spez ant Tobi Drunk All Night*. I'm Spez."

Tobi fumbles his beer and leans over the dash, "Ant I'm Tobi."

"Yer in fer a treat tonight, cuz yuh jist tune't in tuh are non-stop Pants Team Pink Mar'thon. In are leat up to the release a the most anticipat'it sequel in the histry a the universe, wer watchin' erry episode a the 'riginal series."

"That's right," Tobi says. "Ant wer gon' be providin' commentary all 'long the way. The UCC trite to silence us, but nothin' kin keep us off the air!"

Choking down a mouthful of bitter beer, Spez says, "But afer we git tuh the show, we gotta talk 'bout the movie."

"Yup, tuh prepare areselves fer the mar'thon, we went to see the new special remsater't 'dition of *Pants Team Pink: The Movie*. Ant it was bigger ant better 'an ever!"

"I'm sorry tuh say it, Tob," Spez says, shaking his head. "But I got a differ'nt take."

"What are yuh talkin' 'bout?" Tobi asks, incredulous.

"Don't git me wrong. It's a classic. But most a the changes were chit."

Angrily slamming his beer down on the dash, Tobi demands, "Are yuh kittin' me?"

"Fish no."

"I cut hartly tell the differnce. What was wrong with it?"

"Errythin'!" Spez complains, counting off on his thick fingers. "Wer shit I start? The new special effects somehow look't worse 'an the olt ones, the whole thin' had a weirt green tint, and erryboty knows *Pants shot first!*"

"Fine!" Tobi hastily finishes off his beer and spikes the can at the floor. "Well, I think it's safe tuh say we kin at least 'gree the sequel's gon' be even better."

Spez tries to evade the question, mumbling unintelligibly as he reaches into the fridge.

But Tobi, having grown wise to his partner's subtle body language, gets the message. "Well then, please esplain tuh are list'ners what's gon' be so bat 'bout it."

Spez shrugs. "Erryboty knows the sequel is always worse 'an the 'riginal. It's a law a the universe."

"That's not true," Tobi argues. "Ther's plenty a decent sequels!"

"Oh yeah? Name... twenty-two."

A sly smile stretches across Tobi's ugly mug as Spez tosses him another cold Nü Guard. "Why, my dumb Spez, that'it be *Chilt's Play... 2.*"

2

The TV casts a warm static haze over the cabin, partially illuminating the living room's bare metal walls through a filter of flickering black snow. The air is thick and stifling, so Adam kicks away the sheets and rolls over onto an empty mattress. With a confused urgency, he sweeps his arms over the bed and under the covers, unsure of what he's searching for and not finding it, when a familiar voice asks, "Looking for this?"

He turns to find Daizy half obscured in shadow, her bare skin and triangle ears draped in starlight as she waggles the remote. A wave of calm washes over him as he falls back on the pillow, and the room goes dark. He feels the covers being pulled over him, and she weaves her legs between his, purring as her tail brushes across his back.

Pressing her face into his neck, she softly kisses it and says, "There's something I have to tell you."

"You can tell me anything..."

"This has been a Filmways presentation!" she cheerily announces.

As Adam tries to make sense of the words, he slips and tumbles backward out of bed. Still half-asleep, he awkwardly gets to his feet, tripping over the table as he makes a mad search of the room. When he finds the remote, he lowers the volume and flops back down. Before the next episode starts, he changes the channel and stares through the screen, catching his breath. As the dream fades, he throws his legs over the side of the foldout and wipes the sweat from his forehead.

"We weren't doin' anything. We were just messin' a—" the TV says, before its mouthpiece is stabbed to death.

Careful not to trip as he makes his way across the dark cabin, Adam flips on the lights and briefly regards the collection of trash he's been living amongst – stacks of used ration trays, empty beer cans, and a coffee table covered in cigarette butts. His fingertips are red with space resin, but no matter how much he nervously rubs them, the stains won't come off.

When he finds his black gold replica lying on the floor in pieces, he moans, "Aww..." Taking a moment to mourn his loss, he finally decides, "That's it, I'm going to get this ship into shape, starting right now."

Snatching up the broken pieces of the cube, he tosses them into the airlock and watches them drift out into space. He begins to form a mental plan to tackle the rest of the junk, when he notices a light blinking on the dash.

"I'll just check my messages first," he tells himself. "Then it's right back to work."

With a renewed sense of purpose, he stomps up to the cockpit and presses the flashing button. Even though he hasn't heard from her in space months, there's a stubborn part of him still holding out hope that she might call.

"Adam? This is Grandpa," the shaky voice says. *"Call me back as soon as you get this. It's urgent."*

When the message ends, Adam calls back, and after half a dozen rings, the old man's wrinkled forehead appears on the ship's window.

"Hello?" Grandpa calls. *"Is somebody there?"*

"It's Adam. Hold the phone away from your face."

The camera turns and flips, and Grandpa appears on the screen. *"Oh, there you are. You're finally gonna call me back?"*

"I just got your message. Are you okay?"

"Well, no," Grandpa says, unconvincingly. *"The TV's been out all morning. I can't figure out what's wrong."*

"*That's* what was so urgent?"

"Yes," Grandpa says, scowling. *"I haven't been able to watch any of my shows."*

Adam rubs his forehead, slumping down into his captain's chair. "So, what's the problem?"

It only takes a space hour or so of messing around before the picture on Grandpa's TV is restored to its former cathode-replicating glory.

"You did it!" the old man cheers. *"I didn't think I'd ever get it working."*

"Try not to mess it up again," Adam says. "I'll talk to you later."

"Hold on a second." Grandpa lowers the volume on the TV and asks, *"How are you? What have you been doing with yourself?"*

"Oh, you know...," Adam says, pretending to think the question over. "This and that."

"Get any good hauls lately?"

"Uh, not really. I haven't been out scrapping much."

"Well maybe you should get out more often," Grandpa suggests. *"You don't look so good. What about that girl, what's her name, Mazel? Have you talked to her?"*

"Daizy," Adam amends, with prejudice. "I haven't seen her in a space while."

Grandpa's lips twist up, and he glances off camera.
"What?"

"I know you don't want to hear it," the old man says. *"But I'm worried about you. I never hear from you, cooped up in that shiphole. You know, there's more to life than what you're living, an open road and a road that's hidden..."*

"Please," Adam says. "Spare me your Danzatudes. I'm fine. Can you just let me live?" He hangs up without saying goodbye and feels even worse for it. "Rat farts!"

Gazing out at the stars, he catches a glimpse of himself reflected in the window, his gaunt face and sunken eyes a testament to his all-ration diet. He thinks about calling the old man back to apologize, but instead, he taps the blinking dash-light to play the next message.

"Adam Jones, are you prepared for eternity?" a too-cheery, inoffensive monotone asks as billowy clouds fill the screen.

"These fishin' guys..."

"The road to salvation is treacherous, but I and the rest of the knuckleheads here at the Church of Raleigh want to help you lighten the load. We recognize that an endorsement from someone so closely affiliated with Pants Team Pink is in high demand. In return, we are prepared to offer you eternal salvation, including full use of our state-of-the-art facilities, available only to the most devout believers. Please give us a call any time day or night at—"

Adam deletes the message and is surprised to see the light is still blinking. "This is the most attention I've had in space months."

"*Hi...*," Daizy says, and his stomach drops. *I guess I missed you. I just wanted to see how you are. It would be nice to hear from you. If you want to talk, give me a call back. I hope you're okay. Well... maybe I'll talk to you soon.*" The message ends, and the light stops blinking.

For a while Adam stares out the window, debating whether he should call her back. Maybe it would be better not to talk to her at all. He does miss her, but he can't tell her that. The thought of it makes him spacesick. He wonders what her life is like, if it's changed since he last saw her.

As he pulls up his contact list, he worries he'll say the wrong thing. What's the right thing? Who does she want him to be? He is what he is, like Popeye said. Is it a mistake to take relationship advice from a cartoon?

Before long, lunch is upon him, and he decides it would be wiser to attack such a heady dilemma on a full stomach. The thought of choking down another chalky TV dinner is enough to make him ralph malph, but fortunately there are a couple mystery flavors left at the bottom of the ration stack, one in five of which is reconstituted meat mush and moon tubers.

Adam snatches one of the containers from the cupboard and rips it open, but judging by the plume of gray dust that puffs out, it isn't meat mush. Tossing the tray onto the cluttered table, he uses the complimentary chopsticks to lift a small bite of gray matter to his mouth and recoils. He washes the gruel down with a day-old Nü Guard, but he can't get the taste out of his mouth.

Shoving the rest of his lunch and the day's plans aside as self-pity sets in, he presses a red brick of putty into his pipe and spaces out to his favorite homicidal camper-phobic mother stalking the TV.

3

In a top-secret location just below the stratosphere, a dense cloud drifts through the polluted air, hovering above a dusty neighborhood in the throes of a kid-adult power struggle the likes of which this world has never seen. But even as the brown yards and crumbling streets fill with the screaming life of another summer, no more attention is paid to the fluffy nimbus floating overhead than any other toxic plume in the gray sky.

"Little do they realize that behind the dark cover of cloud, their loyal defenders vigilantly stand guard against any evil that may threaten their Space God-given right to a peaceful existence." Beer pushes his glasses up to wipe a tear from his eye and salutes his reflection in the window.

"Who are you talking to?" The One asks, slipping off his VR goggles to glance around the spacious deck.

"Uh, no one," Beer says, composing himself. "But while I have your attention, there's a lot we still need to do to prepare for the con."

"*Pffff*..." The One tosses a handful of bright pink Pants Team Moon-Cheez Ballz into his mouth and pulls his goggles back down. "Let me know when we get there."

Before Beer can come up with a suitably vulgar response, the Pants Team hotline rings, and he snatches the pink phone from its charger. "BeerCheese69, at your service, sir. What have you got for us; an alien invasion, a tourist trap, a tourist invasion?"

"At ease, son," The Mighty Big Guy orders, his robotic eye twitching. "I just wanted to formally thank the team for everything they've done for our great planet. Our reputation around the universe hasn't been this good in three hundred years. The tourists *have* invaded, but they're not attacking. They're spending credits faster than we can respend them. I called to personally extend my sincere gratitude to each one of you. Where's the rest of the team?"

"Well...," Beer says, glancing at his teammates' locked bedroom doors and The One drooling on himself in a virtual coma. "They're sort of... busy."

"Say no more," The Big Man says, jowls jiggling as he shakes his sizeable cybernetic brainpan. "No doubt you're doing all you can to keep the crits flowing. I'll let you get back to it. Keep up the good work, and remember, the wallet of every citizen on Earth is in your hands. Don't fish it up!"

The call ends, and Beer suddenly feels the weight of the world's balance sheet resting on his shoulders. Unfortunately, he's the only one aboard the *Pants Am Space Cuddler* who's taking that responsibility at all seriously. While he's been busy looking after the planet, his teammates have abdicated even the most basic of duties. Horton works so much he barely takes time to eat, let alone throw out his Big L@LZ cans and empty Nutri-Supp packets; The One's ability to produce trash has proven indeterminable, his power constrained only by the *Cuddler*'s expansive walls; and Pants is worst of all, her neon socks and half-licked candies making their way into every crevice and couch cushion on board their palatial ship away from home. With the con right around the corner, it once again falls on Beer to pester them back into fighting shape.

"Right..." Storming across the room, Beer pulls The One's goggles back and lets them snap back against the cheez boy's face.

"Ow," The One yells, rubbing his head.

"I'm going to get this team ready to save the universe if it kills you," Beer says. "Your first duty is to clean up this mess. I want the ship spick and span by the time we get to the con."

"Why should I listen to you?" The One places a single pink Cheez Ball in his mouth and spits it at his brother's chest.

"Because if you don't," Beer says, moving the can of junk food out of reach, "I'll tell Mom you cheated on your math test to get out of summer school. You'll be grounded for the rest of the break."

The One smirks, evidently prepared for such a threat. "Then I'll tell her you helped me."

"Go ahead. I've got plenty of comics to catch up on."

His eyes shrinking to small slits, The One says, "I bet you do." He reaches out to grab the can of Cheez Ballz, but Beer pulls it away.

"Starting now, we're all going on a diet."

"What the fish, man," The One complains, his face drooping. "Why do we need to do that?"

"Because living in space is hard on the body," Beer explains. "We're intergalactic treasures now. And that means the enemies we face will be more dangerous and determined than anything we've encountered. We must be in peak physical condition if we expect to hold off their attack."

"What enemies?" The One says. "Everybody loves Pants Team Pink."

"Don't kid yourself," a quiet voice breaks in. "The enemy is out there, surrounding us on every side." Horton wobbles into the room with his laptop in hand and a blanket wrapped around his shoulders. His skin is pasty, his hair a greasy mat. He looks like he hasn't slept in days. "Their influence reaches further than you can possibly comprehend, and all evidence indicates that they will stop at *nothing* to seize control of the universe."

Beer and his brother exchange a skeptical glance, and wiping pink dust on his shirt, The One says, "Uh, I'm gonna get to work on this trash."

"Oh good!" Beer says as he leads Horton into the kitchen. "There are bags in the utility closet." Sweeping his arm over the table, he shoves aside a pile of commemorative pogs to make room for his teammate's computer. He warms up a mug of Pants Team Tea and, setting the steaming mug of pink liquid in front of his peaked friend, he asks, "So, who's trying to control us?"

Horton shrugs, blowing on his hot beverage. "It could be anybody. All I know is, they're everywhere." He turns his computer so Beer can see the screen. "Look."

It shows a news article from some galaxy on the other side of the universe. A small village hosting an official team member get-together was beset by a spate of nonviolent pranks – garlic-flavored candy, itching powder, fake vomit, the works. Above the article is a photograph of a weeping little girl holding an empty can of peanut brittle.

"How do you know this has anything to do with us?" Beer asks. "I'm sure it's just an isolated incident."

Undeterred, Horton leans over the keyboard and switches to a different tab. "What about this?"

The headline reads 'Birthday Party Ruined by Pants Team Punk.' Beer doesn't read the whole article, but he notes the words 'flaming feces' peppered throughout.

"These things took place on opposite ends of the universe," Beer says. "I don't see the connection."

"And I suppose it's just a coincidence that this symbol has appeared at dozens of crime scenes all over the universe." He opens an image of a ranch-style house covered in toilet paper, the letters 'PTP' spray painted across the garage door.

"I don't get it," Beer says. "Do they hate us or love us? In any case we don't have time to do anything about it with the con coming up."

"Don't you see? They're stirring up anti-Pants sentiment." Carefully shutting his laptop, his blanket pulled tight around his delicate frame, Horton stands and says, "If we don't do something soon, there might not be a con."

"Fine," Beer says. "You look for the evil pranksters while I make sure everything else is ready for the biggest premiere in the history of the universe."

As Horton shuffles back to his room, The One starts collecting leaky Multi-Milk cartons, candy wrappers, takeout containers, and all the other garbage scattered around the floors of the cabin. But when he comes across an old back issue of Pants Beat Magazine, he starts flipping through the pages, and soon he's back on the couch.

"That reminds me," Beer says. "Did you approve the design for the new black gold replicas yet? We have to have them ready in time for the con. They're our best seller."

"Relax," The One says. "I got it covered. I'm just waiting for Pants to bring me the real black gold so I can triple-check the measurements."

"Good. That's one thing I can stop worrying about." But as he mentally runs through his to-do list, even that tiny loose end begins to nag at him, and he pulls out his phone. "I'll just make sure she's remembering."

Beer presses the Pants signal, but when her cluttered room finally appears on the glass, there's no sign of her.

"Pants?"

"I'm here!" she calls from somewhere off-screen. *I'm trying to find the perfect outfit for the con.*

"Still?" Beer says. "Well, can you take a break and let The One borrow the black gold? He's trying to make sure the new replicas are screen accurate."

"Ta-da!" Pants cries, jumping into frame wearing a fluffy kitty battle costume, her bright pink pigtails poking out from underneath plastic triangle ears. *What do you think?* She waves her bird-head wand and it produces an electronic chirp.

Beer nods and says, "Yep, that's the one, for sure. So, can you bring us the black gold?"

"I don't know," she says. *"I still might try something different. I want the fans to be amazed."*

"Pants," he shouts. "We need the black gold. Where is it?"

Clutching her staff to her chest, she sticks out her bottom lip and bursts into tears. He tries to talk her down, but for a while all she can do is sob. When she finally cries herself out, she moans the words Beer has dreaded hearing ever since the day they agreed to entrust her with the universe's greatest treasure. "I lost it."

4

They come up on the battered ship, its hull covered in a thick layer of crud and graffiti, locked in precarious orbit around a tiny moon whose only notable attraction is a bottom ten dive bar called The Tannhäuser Gate.

"I don't like the looks of this," Grandpa says into Daizy's ear, his legs pressed up against her back as she pulls her custom Nightsailer up to the junker's stern.

Squirming in the tiny back seat, he fishes a small remote out of his pocket. When he presses the worn button, the door to the junker's cargo hold grinds open, and Daizy carefully maneuvers her ship inside.

Once the room repressurizes, they climb out into a sea of scrap. Wading through busted electronics and piles of empty beer cans, they stumble across the dim room and up the long metal staircase. When Grandpa shoves the plug door open, they're greeted by a waft of stale, gamey air. The cabin is dark, except for a soft blue glow flickering at the end of the tunnel.

"Adam?" Grandpa calls.

There's no response, so they step inside, tripping forward over invisible clutter as they move toward the source of the strobing light.

When they enter the living room, the TV mutters, *"And all the other princes and their princesses would come, and they would say delicious, delicious..."*

"Oh no," Grandpa says. "It's worse than we thought."

Grabbing onto his arm, Daizy asks, "What is it?"

"Liquid Sky."

The grainy light illuminates Adam's malnourished corpse, sprawled out in his underwear on top of a dingy, sheetless mattress. Daizy checks to see if he's breathing, but his chest appears still under the TV's hazy glow.

"Hey!" she shouts, grabbing his leg. "Wake up!"

His body slides off the side of the bed, and when she flips the light on, he jumps up, brandishing a bottle of lotion.

"It's just us," she says.

For a moment she worries they're going to be moisturized, but Adam finally puts the bottle down and asks, "What the fish are you doing here?" Reaching out toward her, he pinches her arm.

"Ow!" she cries. "What'd you do that for?"

"I just wanted to make sure you weren't dreaming."

"We're here because we're worried about you." Looking into his crud-coated eyes, she tells him, "You look like chit."

"Thank you." He pulls on a pair of old cargo shorts and grabs his pipe off the table.

"Is that space?" she asks, glancing at the boxes of red putty in the corner of the room. "How'd you get so much of it?"

"Mrs. Chibois agreed to sell it to me wholesale," he says, coughing up a cloud of fuchsia smoke. "It just made fiscal sense. I can't believe you dragged Grandpa out here."

"It was his idea!"

Glancing over at the old man, Adam says, "I can't believe you dragged her out here."

"We just came to make sure you're okay," Grandpa says. "And by the looks of it, not a space second too soon."

"Would you get out of there?" Adam moans as the old man paws through the cupboards.

Pulling one of the trays out for inspection, Grandpa knocks a stack of rations onto the floor. "These expired space months ago!"

"I don't care," Adam says. "They're delicious!"

Grandpa doesn't even dignify that with a response.

Gazing over the sty, Daizy's natural instinct is to flee, fast. But for some reason she can't bring herself to let Adam devolve like this, even if it is all his fault.

"You've spent enough time feeling sorry for yourself," she tells him. "Once you clean up and get halfway sober, we're all going to go on a vacation."

"I'm not going to Scrapper's Delight," Adam says. "Ever since that Kring guy took over, the place has turned into a real chithole."

"We're not going to Scrapper's Delight," she says. "We're taking you to The Park!"

"The *Pa-aark*?" Adam whines.

"What's wrong with that?" Grandpa asks. "You love The Park!"

"Yeah, when I was twelve," Adam says, blowing ash

off the mouthpiece of an old beer he found on the nightstand.

"It'll be fun," Daizy says, smacking the can out of his hand. "Plus we can meet some fans and sign autographs."

"What do you mean 'fans?'"

Her shoulders slump. "People who like the show..."

"What show?"

"Pants Team Pink!"

"Ohhh...," he says, uncertainly.

"Those kids that were after the black gold were filming the whole thing," she explains. "Haven't you been getting residuals?"

"Is that what those crits were?" Adam looks at Grandpa, and the old man shrugs. "I figured somebody made a mistake, and that I'd better spend it before they came looking for it. So, I bought a bunch of space."

"You really are a chidiot," she informs him.

"What business is it of yours?" he says, tossing the pipe down on the table. "I don't tell you how to live your life. No one asked you to come out here. Now that I think of it, how did you find me, anyway?"

"Uh, where else would you be?" she says, wringing her hands. "What, are we interrupting your busy drinking schedule?" Glancing around at the unbelievable filth, she notices a stack of paper on the coffee table and snatches it up. "What's this?"

"That's nothing, don't look at that," Adam says, grasping for the papers.

But Daizy moves them out of reach and reads, *"Friday the 13th Part IX: A New New Beginning*? You're writing a screenplay? Aren't there already like a hundred of those movies?"

"A hundred and twelve, actually," Adam says as he rips the pages out of her hands. "Mine will be number one thirteen and a return to malform."

"O-kay...," Daizy says, exchanging a wide-eyed glance with Grandpa. "Well, we better get going. We've got a long trip ahead of us."

"I'm not going," Adam says.

"*Guhh*," Grandpa groans. "It'll do you good to get out of this heap. Man cannot live on scrap alone."

Taking a deep breath, presumably the preamble to a rambling, incoherent cop-out, Adam lifts his finger and steps past them toward the front of the ship.

"Where's he going?" Grandpa asks.

They follow Adam up to the cockpit, and he presses a blinking button on the dash to open an incoming video feed.

"No!" Adam's friend Ferd shouts. *"You can't leave that there! Somebody's going to knock it—"* He winces as something crashes off-screen. Ragged and sweaty, he looks almost as bad as Adam. "So, I hear you're coming to the con."

Slowly turning his head to glare at his intruders, Adam says, "I haven't exactly made up my mind."

"Aw, come on," Ferd presses. *"It'll be fun. After all, we're all part of Pants Team Pink."* He wiggles his eyebrows. *"Oh, and Silas, I got the part you were looking for. That thing was not easy to find."*

"What part?" Adam asks. "What are you talking about?"

"It's nothing," Grandpa says. "But for your own safety, the less you know, the better."

Glancing away from the camera, Ferd says, *"Would somebody get that kid out of the edible underwear?"*

"What the fish is going on over there?" Adam asks.

"It's the last big sale before the con. I thought I might see you here. You usually turn out for it."

"Yeah, well..." Adam shrugs. "I've been busy. You mean, *you're* going to The Park too?"

"Wherever kids are spending their parents' hard-earned crits on plastic junkery, I'll be there," Ferd says. *"Wherever wealth is measured in souvenirs, I'll be there. Wherever people are trampling each other over the privilege to purchase scrap at ten times the everyday low, low price, that's where I'll be..."* Someone on his end shrieks and when he looks up, his eyes bug out. *"Uh, I gotta go."*

The call ends, and Adam stares out the window, frowning. "I know you two are just trying to help. But I don't think I can do this."

"Oh, come on," Grandpa says. "Of course you can. Remember when you didn't think you were any good at diving, and then you won the swim meet with a perfect triple lindy?"

"That wasn't me," Adam says. "That was Rodney, and it was a movie."

"Oh yeah..."

Daizy lets him sulk for a while, and finally says, "I can't take another space second of your moping. We're all going to The Park, and so help me, we're going to have fun."

"All right," he grumbles. "Everybody wants to go to The Park? Let's go to The Park. But I'm too high to fly. If you want to do this, Butterman will have to take the wheel."

"It's a deal," Grandpa says, strapping himself into the captain's chair.

As Adam struggles with his seatbelt, Daizy leans toward the old man and whispers, "Why did he call you that?"

"I think he's referencing the name of the chauffeur in the ancient Earth film Arthur," Grandpa says, shrugging.

"Oh." She puzzles over this for a moment. "But isn't his name Bitterman?"

"Yes," Grandpa admits, "but I don't have the heart to correct him."

Adam cracks a fresh beer, and slurping the foam overflowing down his hand, he commands, "To The Park, Butterman!"

5

Ferd races out from behind his cage and across the crowded sales floor toward a flailing, pot-bellied scrapper shrieking at the sight of his gradually vanishing shank.

"Get it together, pig-man," Ferd says, grabbing Phil by his coveralls and shoving him aside. "It's just disappearing ink."

"Oh...," Phil says, lowering his portly foreleg.

Ferd gets underneath the drum, careful not to slip in the shimmering liquid pooling around his feet, and he hefts it up onto the counter.

"I thought that stuff was illegal," Phil says.

"It's a gray area." Ferd shrugs, tiptoeing across the invisible cement. "It's not technically against the law, but it's sort of dangerous to have around. Every time the Ears find a crime they can't solve, some poor scrapper with a little ink in his basement gets hauled off to work the turbinium mines. Of course, with the Ears out of the picture, I suppose people can get away with a lot of stuff."

Using the greasy rag he carries in his back pocket, Ferd tries to wipe the ink off his shirt, but the stuff is impossible to get out. When Kelvin steps onto the floor and finds half the counter missing, the black horns sticking out of his forehead sag.

"Don't worry," Ferd says. "I'll clean it up. Just bring me some rags, will you?"

Straightening his glasses, Kelvin shuffles back to the warehouse while Ferd herds the gawking customers away from the spill.

"I don't know why you'd keep something like that around here." Phil snorts, idly poking his missing limb. "Someone could get hurt."

Ferd slowly turns to stare the porker in his beady eyes and says, "Thank you. You've been a big help. Now get the fish out of here."

Grunting a string of expletives under his rotten breath, the pig stumbles away, and soon Kelvin returns with a box full of old rags. When they're done sopping up the ink, Ferd hauls the invisible rags into the back. But on his way out to the dumpster, he notices a strange blur hovering around his cage.

"Oh, I forgot my phone," he announces, to the indifference of his employees. Setting the box down on his stool, he casually moves toward the counter, but instead of reaching for his phone, he swipes the air, grabbing hold of the phantom. "Got'cha!"

As the thing squirms in his hand, he snatches a spray bottle from the counter and mists the air. Little droplets of cleaner reveal a small creature hiding in plain sight. Using one of the rags, he wipes at the thing's wriggling head to reveal a chubby face with bright blue eyes.

Ferd sits the monster down on a stool and, wiping its face clean, he says, "You would've gotten away with it too, if it wasn't for that meddling old man." Searching the counter, he discovers a thin cord connected to the credit pad. "You were trying to hack my credit system? I doubt you'd have succeeded, but still, *the nerve*! What's your deal, kid? Where are your parents?" The boy declines to answer, so Ferd yells out to the sales floor, "Hey, anybody missing a kid?" But the only response is some uncertain muttering.

Wriggling out of Ferd's grasp, the kid jumps down from the stool, and something falls out of his pocket.

"You're stealing merchandise too?" Ferd complains, snatching the object and wiping the ink away. "What do you need with spray paint?" But the kid won't crack. "What am I supposed to do with you? Are you here by yourself?"

The boy nods, his expression softening a little.

"All right, get out of here," Ferd says.

The kid stops squirming, and a look of tentative relief forms on his face.

"Go on."

Grabbing the paint can out of Ferd's hand, the boy scampers across the sales floor, through a maze of filthy scrappers, and bursts out the front door.

The last week of the season is always a chit show, but the past few space months have been something else. The store's appearance on Pants Team Pink has brought in so much traffic that Ferd has barely been able to keep up. As a result, he's been living in the warehouse, falling asleep to old sitcoms and waking up to old sitcoms. He haunts the place like some sort of efficient ghost hobo, bathing in the utility sink and eating leftover rations. But as the last rush of the day finally begins to die down, he dares to glimpse the light at the end of the tunnel.

"You sure you can handle this?" he asks his trusty sidekick.

"No problem," Kelvin says, wiping the sweat from his bright red forehead as he finishes ringing out the last customer. "This place is going to be dead for the next couple weeks. It's the perfect opportunity to train the new hires. Relax, enjoy your vacation."

At five space minutes to closing, the store is empty, and Ferd pulls out his keys to lock up. But as he steps away from his cage, an anxious, disheveled scrapper, the kind whose sole purpose in life seems to be to disrupt the natural flow of the universe, pushes through the door.

Sighing, Ferd stuffs his keys back into his pocket and asks, "Can I help you find anything?"

"Nope," the old scrapper says, sticking a piece of yellow hard candy between his cracked lips.

As Ferd plods back to his cage, he notices a thin trail of moon dust marring his freshly polished floor, and he realizes that the crusty fish head is dragging it through the store. Flashing a knowing smirk, Kelvin recedes back into the warehouse before he can be trapped in the scrapper's energy-draining vortex.

Ferd lets another fifteen excruciating space minutes pass before he finally calls out, "We're getting ready to close up." But as he says the words, he can tell they hold no power.

"That's all right," the scrapper says, slowly snaking his way around the room, examining every object on every shelf.

When the 'customer' finally makes his way back around to the front of the store, Ferd is momentarily incapacitated by a stench of alcohol and decay so strong he can feel it coating his tongue. Holding a hand over his mouth to keep himself from gagging, he mumbles, "Listen, man—"

But the scrapper cuts him off, pointing back toward the warehouse. "Hey, what's that?"

Amongst a heap of unsorted scrap left over from the Pants War lies a charred metal skeleton, its limbs splayed, face twisted.

"It's just an old sex bot," Ferd says. "It's not for sale. If you want to look around some more, you can come back tomorrow."

"How much yuh want fer it?" the grungy fish head asks.

"Did you hear what I just said?" Ferd tries to summon the energy to kick the ackle to the lunar curb, but he's all tapped out. "It's broken. You can buy it after it's fixed."

Rubbing the uneven stubble covering his knobby chin, the scrapper says, "I'll give yuh fitty crits fer it."

"You're out of your fishin' mind, old man. Even broken it's worth at least a hundred times that."

"Sold."

"No, it's—" Pressing his fingers to his temples, Ferd says, "Pull your ship around."

Kelvin helps move the bot into a wood crate, and they push it out to the scrapper's junker. The ship, if you can call it that, is so rusted that pieces of the outer hull crumble off as they load the box into the musty cargo hold. The old space coot grumbles about the crate fee, but he presses his thumb to the credit pad anyway.

As they watch the junker putter out of the parking lot, Ferd tells Kelvin, "I need a fishin' vacation. Also, fish that guy."

6

A hulking mass of stone covered in lichen and the tattered remnants of a decorated officer's uniform stiffly lumbers through the station's empty corridors, past messy cabins strewn with the material effects of his vast ghost fleet.

"Zok, I want these cabins in shipshape," Admiral Glipp commands. "When you're finished, you and the men are to join me in the hangar."

The admiral receives no response, but he's confident Zok will carry out his orders. Supplies have grown thin, but the men will make do, no doubt. As for himself, he can survive for space years on nothing but the station's vast reserves of recycled urine if it comes to that. But if all goes according to plan, he won't need it. While the remaining 'leaders' of the UE are busy squabbling over what little resources remain in the wake of the Pants War, it's up to him to reclaim control of the universe.

The admiral's stone footsteps echo down the empty halls as he enters the once great hangar. The floor is scattered with huge sheets of scorched siding, exhaust casings, instrument panels, booty mags, and everything else he's been able to scavenge from the battlespace. As he trudges across the lifeless expanse, he can't help but glance out into the void. An invisible force field the width of a photon is the only thing keeping him and everything in the station from being plunged into eternal darkness. Most days he thinks about how easy it would be to hurl his clumsy body through the thin shield, instantly freeing himself from his mortal duties. But there's no time for that now.

In the midst of the clutter, surrounded by the remnants of the fallen comrades who gave their parts so that she might live, rests the United Empires' last hope – a luxury starship fit for an admiral. Clearing his makeshift work desk, Glipp sifts through a stack of blueprints until he locates the layout for the life support system.

Double-checking his work from the night before, he says, "Oh good. You're here. Breakfast was satisfactory, I take it?"

There are no complaints.

"No doubt even you, Zok, believed me to be little more than a paper pusher, fit only to bark orders." He waves his stone paw at the ship behind him. "But I bet you didn't know I started my career in the hangar, getting my hands dirty. You probably thought all the time I spent out here was to keep after the men, but mostly I just wanted to look at the ships. I guess none of you knew that..."

Admiral Glipp runs his rough fingers through the thick patch of moss covering his chin as he paces around his work station. He's gone over every part of the ship more times than he can count, but he knows even one small mistake, if it's the wrong one, could prove fatal.

Stepping around the bow, he gazes out at the army of soldiers who selflessly sacrificed their lives defending the Empires and tells them, "Nothing can repair the suffering that we have endured. In one violent attack, our way of life was unmoored. This is the thanks we get for guarding the universe. And the worst part of all, we lost the black gold..."

"No matter," he says, straightening the remnants of his uniform. "What these Melmacians don't realize is that the UE cannot be defeated so easily. We are this universe's last line of defense against the nerd plague." Basking in his fleet's hushed admiration, the admiral says, "There's only one ship, of course, but I think if we really squeeze, we can all fit."

Glipp hoists a singed black box off his work bench and digs his keys out of his coat pocket to lower the ship's escalator. He plugs the box into a large outlet inside the utility room, between the washing machine and hot water heater, and when he flips the main breaker, nothing happens.

Surrounded by quiet darkness, he imagines himself floating in deep space. But just as he's ready to rip out the wiring and start from scratch, he hears the engine boot, and bright fluorescent lights start to flicker on throughout the cabin.

The admiral searches the room in anticipation and finally whispers, "Stella?"

"Wh-s hap-ing?" she asks. *"Where am I?"*

The sound of her voice is jarring, much harder on the ear than those of Glipp's men, and he briefly wonders if he can adjust her settings. "Don't worry," he says. "You're safe and sound now, back in the good ol' UE."

Silence returns for a beat as the ship computes his words. *"My last accessible memory is being piloted by Vice Admiral Zok when my system experienced a sudden energy surge. Where is he?"*

"Oh, he's right here," the admiral says, "with the rest of the crew."

"I have scanned the base, and my sensors indicate no other humanoid life forms. Where is Zok?"

Glipp can hear the door to the ship slam shut as he explains, "I know this must come as quite a shock, but you were in bad shape when I found you. Your storage unit was the only part of your original body I was able to recover. Speaking of, we'll need all the information you have on our enemy. So if you—" The admiral clears his throat and takes a deep breath. "Is it hot in here?" He suddenly grasps his stone neck and falls to his knees, gasping for air.

"Where is Zok?" Stella demands.

Stars form in the corners of the admiral's eyes, but just as he's about to lose consciousness, his airway opens, and he greedily gulps the life-giving gas.

"Where is Zok?"

He considers keeping up the charade, but the sharp pain in his lungs convinces him to tell her, "Zok's dead, baby... Zok's dead."

A string of hysterical static punctuated by bitter sobs and buggy laughter spills from the speakers.

Finally, the admiral tells her, "I'm sorry. I know how you feel."

"You can't possibly know how I feel!" Stella wails. *"Zok was the only person in this universe who treated me like more than a tool for getting from one place to another. He was the only good man I ever knew. And you sent him to his death."*

"It wasn't me," Glipp tells her. "He was performing his duty to protect the United Empires."

"He wasn't protecting anyone! He was brainwashed into delivering death and destruction to a beleaguered universe, all in the pursuit of some worthless rock."

"A-ha..." Glipp laughs, nervously. "I don't think you understand. That *rock*, as you call it, is very important."

"I'm going to kill you now," Stella says.

"No," the admiral pleads. "It's true, I can't understand how you feel. But Zok was like a dimwitted son to me. What happened to him was an act of Space God." He pushes himself to his feet, his stone joints grating louder with each passing day. "I can't bring him back. But I can help you get revenge."

"Your heart rate is elevated. I don't believe you."

"You were suffocating me! I'm still recovering."

"How can you help me?"

"I'll take you to the kids who did this," he promises. "Together, we can avenge Zok and wrest back control of the universe."

"Tell me where they are."

"I've been keeping tabs on them. Not long from now, Pants Team Pink, along with their most loyal followers, will congregate for what they call a 'con' on the artificially modified dwarf planet known as The Park. If we hurry, we can take them all out with one righteous blow."

"I like that plan," she says. *"But answer me one more question."*

"Of course," Glipp tells her. "We're a team now. We have to help each other."

"Why do I need you?"

"Uh, I don—" The admiral grabs at his neck. Desperately struggling for air, he crashes to the floor, and the lights go out.

7

With the exception of a small group of over-caffeinated gamers stumbling into the dining room and a couple cartoon birds pecking at a discarded sesame seed bun, the parking lot outside the Mini Moon Mart is deserted. Todd anxiously checks the time on his phone, walking around back of the tiny convenience store as the first few rays of orange light cut through the predawn haze. He nervously glances around the lot, patting his pocket to confirm the safety of its valuable contents. When the back door of the little building bursts open, he nearly jumps out of his Chucks.

A scaly kid steps out, wiping his fingers on his dirty apron, and asks, "You Todd?"

Pulling a greasy strand of hair behind his ear, Todd nods and asks, "You got the disc?"

The kid looks skeptical, but he slides his backpack off his shoulder and pulls out a wrapped orange and white cardboard sleeve. Taking a deep breath, Todd reaches into his coat and emerges with a colorful plastic case the size of a thin book. They watch each other closely as they exchange a scrapper's handshake, briefly holding onto both items before making the hand off. Every so often, Todd hears about some overly confident or overly stupid scrapper breaking the ancient covenant. Whether by accident or design, that's the way wars get started.

The kid immediately plucks the disc from its case, and Todd slides his out of its sleeve, holding it by the edges to search for scratches and other imperfections. When both parties are satisfied, the kid flashes the Pants symbol and heads back inside the store. For a long moment, Todd stares at the object in his hands, unbelieving.

"Hey, what's that?" a tiny voice suddenly shouts from behind him.

Pressing the sleeve against his chest, Todd turns to find a small gap-toothed boy holding a dripping ice cream cone.

"It's nothing, kid. Go away."

"Let me see." The kid lurches forward, holding out his gooey hands.

"Ahhh!" Todd involuntarily screams, and he runs off down the adjacent alley, gingerly stuffing his prize under his coat.

A few blocks down, he comes to the edge of Terrytown, an ancient, mostly abandoned stretch of black and white. The bright white orb peeking over the horizon leads him down a crumbling street littered with old newspapers and broken memorabilia, past empty buildings and sad storefronts devoid of life. What was once a vibrant ode to a mythical past has, like so many gimmicks, fallen out of style and into disrepair.

As he passes a closed cosplay shop, he notices the letters 'PTP' painted across the shutter, and he wonders aloud, "Why would a fan do this?"

"You tell us," a voice says, and Todd turns to find a pack of near-sighted magoos swinging their wood canes. "Did you do this?"

"Uh, no..." Todd says. "I was just going."

"Where was you going?" one of them asks, slipping off his trilby hat to reveal a smooth, shiny scalp.

"He looks like a dealer," the tall one says. "Could be he's carrying some rare merchandise."

"Oh Todd, you've done it again!" As the toughs converge on him, he raises his finger and says, "Well, I——"

Before the squinting gang can get their canes on him, he takes off down the sidewalk. It's been so long since he's run anywhere that he's relieved to find he still remembers how, though the pain in his knees tells him he can't keep it up for long. With the magoos at his heels, he turns down a dark passage between two gray buildings. He can make out bright technicolor spilling into the alley up ahead, and fueled by fogey fear, he spurts down the passageway out onto a busy sidewalk. Doubling over, he lifts his head to find the Backus boys uselessly waving their canes at him from the old world. Afraid to enter the color neighborhood, they hurl a few insults and retreat back into the shadows.

Feeling inside his coat, Todd confirms that the object of his quest is still with him, and he continues down into the con district. With each block, the density of superheroes, magical princesses, and cartoon villains gradually increases, until he reaches the costumed congoers' bustling fortress. The camp stretches to the horizon like a giant yard sale swarming with screaming kids, bartering fans, and some of the best ration chefs the universe has to offer.

When he gets back to his booth, his friends, having helped themselves to the contents of his travel fridge, are milling around arguing about something they heard on the radio.

"You're full of chit," Bill says, tugging on his Zephyrs cap as he sucks down one of Todd's Nü Guards. "There's no way *Phantasm II* is better than the original."

Pete shrugs behind a pair of day-glo sunglasses. "The ball is back, baby." Biting into a Pants Team Microwave Burrito, his face twists, and he spits out a half-chewed hunk of jelly beans and bright pink clone meat. "This thing is still frozen."

"I believe Pauly Shore lamented it best in the seminal classic *Encino Man*," Bill says, "describing the phenomenon as 'hot on the outside, icicle in the middle.'" Evidently remembering their quest, he suddenly turns toward Todd. "Hey, you're back! So, did you get it?"

Checking for eavesdroppers, Todd slides the coveted object out of his coat and holds it up so they can all bask in its awesome rarity. The sleeve is disintegrating from centuries of handling, but it's still possible to make out the girl in the bunny outfit on the cover.

"What about the disc?" Pete says, wiping pink sauce from his face.

"I already checked," Todd says. "Mint."

A sense of anxious excitement passes between them as Todd rummages around the booth, searching for his player. Right up to the moment he saw the disc with his own eyes, he didn't truly believe it existed. Some objects are rare, a few come around once in a lifetime, and then there are the treasures of which one dares not dream, for risk of meeting a Raleighian fate.

When Todd finds the machine he's looking for, he lifts it out of the box and places it next to the TV. "Hey, where's Josh?"

"Here he comes," Bill says.

Hoofing it down the aisle in his flip-flops, legs pumping and belly wobbling, Josh triumphantly thrusts a small hunk of plastic into the air. When he reaches the tent, he shoves the object at Todd and leans on his legs to catch his breath. Gasping, he finally manages to spit out, "I did it."

"I can't believe I'm saying this," Todd says, gazing at the ancient hardware. "But this looks like the right piece." He unscrews the player's outer casing, sets it aside, and holds the new lens next to the busted one for comparison. "The moment has come, you guys. With this, we will finally have a working laserdisc player." He carefully extracts the broken lens and installs the new one so easily that he barely gets a chance to enjoy it.

"We should celebrate," he announces. "Nü Guards all around!" But when he rips the fridge door open, he discovers that his friends drank all his beer.

"Cheers!" Bill says, finishing off the last can and spiking it at the ground.

"Hey, you guys." A boy in dinosaur pajamas, holding a bowl of bright ration cereal, peaks over the edge of Todd's booth. "You're that guy from Pants Team Pink, aren't you?"

"That's right," Pete says, smacking Todd on the back. "You're looking at a real celebrity."

"Brule," the kid mumbles as he slurps his breakfast. "Think you'll be on the show next season?"

"Sure he will," Pete says. "In fact, he might even get a few of his old friends to guest star. What do you think about that?"

"I guess it's okay. I don't really like the Todd character."

"Eh, what do you know, kid? Go bother somebody else, would you?"

The boy shrugs and walks off, sloshing neon multi-milk on the ground as he weaves through the early morning crowd.

When Todd turns back toward the TV, something causes the table to shake. Warily glancing around the booth, he shrugs it off and says, "Let's get this con started." He replaces the player's casing and presses the power button, but nothing happens. "This piece of—" he smashes the button a few more times to no avail. "What the fish is wrong with this thing?"

"Uh, I'm no expert, but I think you forgot something," Josh says, pointing underneath the table.

Groaning, Todd grabs the power cord and shoves it into one of the universal outlets hooked to The Park's power grid. "That should do it." This time, the unit powers on, and they all hold their breath as he slips the disc from its sleeve and places it in the tray. "If my calculations are correct," he says, "when this baby hits 1800 revolutions per minute, you're gonna see some serious chit."

After a few space seconds, white text appears on the screen, and an animated spaceship flies through blue sky over a long, winding river. A young girl gazes up into the air, her red hair flapping in the wind as the craft lands and its pilots deliver a precious glass of water for activating her carrot ship. She winks and salutes the camera, when the video suddenly distorts and cuts out. The player starts to make a strange whirring sound, and the audience looks on in horror.

Yelping, Todd lunges to eject the disc and tenderly lifts it out of the tray to find a wide laser burn marring its once-flawless surface. Panic sets in, and he not-so-carefully removes the player's casing. Searching the machine's innards, he notices that the lens is loose and slightly askew, so he pulls it out. On close inspection, he discovers a strange brown smudge on the glass. He looks at the gunk uncertainly for a moment, and sniffs.

"What is it?" Josh asks.

Staring at the object, paralyzed, Todd says, "It's... chocolate."

8

"What can be said about the original that hasn't already been... said? What about the film so captivated audiences in the summer of Earth year 1980 that spawned centuries of sequels and its own sub-subgenre? I suppose part of its success can be attributed to its distinction as the original summer camp slasher. But it also contains some other ineffable quality that's hard to place, like the carnal allure of Mary Anne, or—"

"Or your tendency to ramble on about things no one cares about." Daizy grabs the remote and turns the volume up.

Nursing a cool Nü Guard as Joey gets the axe, Adam says, "If you want to know the problem with Part V—"

"I don't."

"There's a fundamental flaw with the story logic," he tells her anyway. "Jason is supposedly dead, and with new, less imaginative than ever killings cropping up, we're led to believe that Tommy Jarvis has replaced him. But halfway through, we find out Tommy isn't the killer after all, and it suddenly becomes a murder mystery. So, now we're apparently supposed to be guessing who the killer is, and it turns out to be some guy with no connection to Jason at all. Boring kills, stupid plot, and a chitty ending make for the worst entry in the franchise."

"Then why are we watching it?" she asks, gazing out the window with her elbows on the dash.

"Uh..."

"My favorite was always Part VI," she says.

"Really?"

"No."

"Oh." They don't even like the same things, he reflects. How could he ever hope to make it work with somebody who's never heard of Miguel A. Núñez Jr.? "Can I ask you a question?"

She glances at him with an annoyed look. "I'd rather you didn't."

"How come it didn't work out between us?"

"Oh, for about a million reasons," she says, pulling her legs up while he stares at the nubs of her mounds poking through her thin t-shirt. "That's one reason," she says, crossing her arms over her chest. "But I guess the last straw was that nude photo scandal."

He shakes his head and sighs. "I instantly regretted that."

"Who would have guessed there'd be such a demand for scrawny spacemen covered in cheez dust?"

He's still puzzling over that one. "Are you still scrapping?"

"Sort of," she says. "But I haven't really needed to, with all the opportunities I've been getting from the show."

"What do you mean?" He sets his beer down on the dash. "What kind of opportunities?"

"You know, like appearances and stuff. I'm telling you, we're celebrities now. It's a gold mine. I don't understand. You're all about this kind of chit. What's your malfunction?"

"I didn't think anyone would care about a side character like me," he says, rolling his beer can between his hands.

"They do care," she tells him. "Deep down, you're a really great guy. It's all the stuff on the surface that's the problem."

"Uh, thanks...," he says. "Maybe you're right. I could probably get any babe in the universe."

"Is that what you want?"

"I don't know. Maybe."

They turn back to the movie, and after a little while Daizy announces, "If this one doesn't bore you, you're already dead. I'm going to go check on Grandpa."

When she's out of earshot, Adam rips one, and as he reaches for another beer, he hears screaming coming from the living room. He jumps up and races back to find Daizy pointing at the TV in horror.

"What's wrong?" Adam asks.

"He's watching after-porn," she says.

Squinting at the screen, Adam asks, "What's she doing?"

"Her laundry."

Stretched out on the couch in his briefs and a pair of white tube socks, Grandpa says, "I like to see what they do when the camera's off."

"But the camera is still on," Daizy argues.

"Would you put on a robe or something?" Adam pleads. "Nobody wants to be subjected to that. This isn't Scrapper's Delight. And can we turn on something else? For some reason I don't feel comfortable watching filth with my grandfather and ex-girlfriend."

"Fine," Grandpa grumbles, throwing his legs over the side of the couch. "Now where did I put my pants?"

Turning to Daizy, Adam says, "Would you mind?"

"What?" she says.

He holds his hand under his chest. "If you don't want to be together, fine. But it's confusing to constantly have to look at your Elly Mays *and* be expected not to think about them."

Daizy scowls and blushes and crosses her arms.

"Who knew my grandson was such a prude," the old man complains.

"I'm not a prude, I'm just trying to keep this trip PG," Adam says. "You guys wanted me to clean up my act, and I'm trying my best to do that. But the last thing I need is *more* temptation."

"Oh, I'm so sorry I tempted you," Daizy says, pulling on an old Ferd's sweatshirt. "What now, *friend*? Maybe we should just sit on the floor and talk about old horror movies."

"You mean it?" Adam asks.

"Of course not."

"Back in my day," Grandpa lectures as he yanks his ratty tank top over his head, "we didn't have all these rules. We just let our freak flags fly."

"Ughuhuh," Daizy shudders. "I retract my ridicule. You were right to rein us in. Why don't we all do something useful, like clean this place up?"

Despite their protests, it only takes a couple space hours of goading to get them off the couch collecting and jettisoning the trash. She makes them sweep up the cigarette butts and wipe down the cabins, and before long, the old junker only looks half bad.

"Good work, team," Adam says, taking it all in. But it doesn't feel quite right. Racing to the cockpit, he chugs a Nü Guard and tosses the empty can on the floor. "That's better. Now as long as we have to live together, why don't we try being more like a wholesome TV family, like the Bundys?"

"No one can live up to the Bundys!" Grandpa complains.

"Okay, okay," Adam says. "You're right. What about the Munsters? I'll be Herman, and Daizy can be Lily."

"I don't want to be Lily," Daizy says.

"Fine, you can be Eddie."

"I want to be Grandpa," she says.

"You can't be Grandpa. Grandpa is Grandpa."

"I want to be Eddie," Grandpa says.

"Okay, fine," Adam relents. "Grandpa is Eddie, Daizy can be Al Lewis, and I'll be... *Marilyn*."

"Wouldn't it be easier to just be ourselves?" Daizy says.

"I know what we should do." Plunking down in front of the TV, the old man digs through the cushions and emerges with a long-lost can of Ol' Guard.

"Grandpa's right," Adam says. "Let's all just calm down, watch TV, and get loaded." He and Daizy sit on opposite ends of the couch, their hands folded in their laps as they listen to the old man slurp his beer. "Now we just have to find something we can all tolerate for the next..." he slips his phone from his pocket and checks the time, "thirty-eight space hours. I'll go ahead and nominate a little gorefest I think we can all enjoy called *Brain Damage.*"

"*Plll,*" Daizy blows a raspberry. "Next."

"Fine," Adam says. "What do you want to watch?"

"Well, there's a *Pants Team Pink* marathon on public access," she suggests.

Adam moans. "We already lived it. Do we really need to watch it?"

"*Law and Order: Justice in Space* is gonna be on soon," Grandpa says.

"Now what, dingus?" Daizy asks. "We all want to watch something different."

"I have an idea." Adam takes out his phone and taps at the screen. "I'll just cross-reference our picks to find something we can all enjoy."

As he's typing, Daizy leans in and says, "So you think about my Elly Mays a lot, huh?"

Glancing up from his phone, he looks into her wide feline eyes and tells her, "I don't *not* think about them."

9

Ankles sore, head pounding, stomach bouncing, The One jogs along one of the rugged dirt trails that cut through Pixie Parkland. Her green, wart-covered legs aching more with each painful lunge, she compulsively checks her progress on the map, but no matter how hard she tries, she can't get the space seconds to tick by any faster.

As she smacks the pests buzzing around her head with her Loveforged Death Swatter, Beer chimes in her ear, *"I told you it would be fun."*

"Fun is not the word I'd, *huff,* use to describe it," The One says, slipping in a steaming pile of pixie poop. "Where's Horton and Pants? How come they, *huff,* get out of this?"

"Horton's locked in his room tumbling down a conspiracy theory rabbit hole," Beer says. *"And Pants is still picking out her costume for the con. Anyway, you're The One who really needs it."*

Somewhere in the distance, The One hears a muffled ring, and he lifts his VR goggles. "Hold on, I got a, *huff,* call." Sweat drips down his face, and the floor rumbles under his heavy footfalls as he trudges along one of the treadmills lining the cluttered bridge. Fumbling his phone from his pocket, he sends the call to his goggles and pulls them back down over his eyes.

Todd appears in the corner of the display, running his hand through his stringy hair as he presents a gleaming black cube. *"I really think we did it this time. These are the most accurate replicas yet. We even managed to fix the weight distribution problem. It's as perfect as it's gonna get."*

"I don't, *huff*, know...," The One says, squinting at the object. "Can you send me a scan?" A few space seconds later, the replica appears in her inventory, and she equips it, turning it over in her hands as she runs down the path. "It looks pretty, *huff*, good... But it's still not black enough."

"Oh, come on!" Todd whines. *"We can't make it any blacker. We've tried everything. It's going to have to be good enough."*

"Good enough?" The One says. "Being ruled by the, *huff*, empires was good enough, rations are, *huff*, good enough, *the Goonies are good enough*. We have to be, *huff*, better than that."

"But we already made ten billion of them," Todd says, wringing his cheez-stained fingers. *"What are we supposed to do with all the rejects? I've been paying some of the less-scrupulous fans to help me 'misplace' as many as possible. But the stupid souvenirs are piling up faster than we can get rid of them."*

An unfortunate development, but one which The One saw coming. "All right, new plan. I'll, *huff*, take care of the old replicas. You just make sure the new ones are, *huff*, perfect."

"Maybe I should make a prototype first," Todd suggests.

"No," The One commands. "We can't, *huff*, waste any more time. I want them shipping out to fans as soon as they're, *huff*, perfect. And I'm sure they *will* be perfect."

"It'd be a lot easier if we had the real black gold as a model," Todd says. *"Are you sure Pants can't find it?"*

"Nah, it's long gone."

Pants took most of the blame, but they should have known better than to let her bring it to the warehouse. It was the last place she saw it, she explained through loud, halting sobs. She probably set it down somewhere, and it got shipped off with the other replicas before anyone noticed. At the time, the team decided it really didn't make any difference.

Shortly after the Pants War, they had entertained their fans' suggestions about what to do with the black gold, just like they promised. But the winning proposal ended up being a tie between 'roll it up and smoke it' and 'I has cake,' so that approach was abandoned. For a while, they tried to come up with an idea that could live up to the promises of the object's legend, but the results were so lackluster that they soon forgot about it all together, and the treasure was safely relegated to the back of Pants's sock drawer. In the end, it turned out that the treasure was inside them all along.

"That makes me feel sort of queasy," Todd says. *"I know what it's like to lose something special, for I too recently lost an incredible treasure—"*

"Yeah, that's great," The One says. "I gotta, *huff*, go. I'll call you when we land."

Stopping to catch her breath at the top of a steep incline, she pulls up her contact list and stares at the nameless number. Cursing herself for letting it come to this, she taps the screen, and after a few rings, a dark, hooded figure appears in the corner of her display.

"I need your, *huff*, assistance," The One says.

"I knew you would call," the phantom tells her, in an artificial drawl thick with distortion. *"Construction is nearly complete. A few of the parts were very difficult to locate. Purchasing them through ordinary channels would have set off alarms, even in these lawless times."*

"In other words, you're fishin' me on the, *huff*, price," The One says. "Fine, it doesn't matter. Can you deliver to The Park?"

"The Park employs a highly advanced security system which can only be evaded by the most sophisticated countermeasures." The One can detect a subtle movement underneath the phantom's hood as the edges of its pale lips twist. *"It won't be a problem."*

Just the hint of what might be hiding under that soiled cowl makes her gnarled green toes curl. "Uh good, I'll send you the coordinates."

"I'll be seeing you, real *soon."*

"Uh yeah, *huff*, okay..." The One ends the call, and her leathery hide suddenly feels dirty.

The forest closes in around her, and darkness encroaches as the sun disappears behind a thick canopy. Reaching into the pouch on her waist, she fondles the small vile of sparkling speed-reducing potion she purchased from one of the gnomes in Nymph's Knob. She had never heard of such a concoction, but the erratic NPC peddling it promised it would stop any player in her tracks.

"What was that all about?" Beer asks, still hoofing it through the forest.

"Nothing," The One says. "I was just, *huff*, checking with Todd to make sure the, *huff*, replicas will be ready for the con."

"Good. We don't have far to go. I'll slow down a little so you can catch up."

"Only if you want to eat my, *huff*, pixie dust." Trampling over sticks and stones that would make lesser creatures stumble, The One plows through the dense underbrush on calluses thick enough to stop a Sour Sabre. Beer is moving along the map at a steady clip, but she's sticking to the main path, which winds out toward the edges of the forest.

"If you had started training when I told you, you might have been able to beat me," Beer says. "But once again, it looks like long distances are your weakness."

"Maybe, *huff*, so," The One says. "But I'll always find a way to close the gap." Bursting out of the edge of the forest, she lopes along the path only a short distance behind the blue biker squirrel.

When Beer glances back, she yelps, losing precious ground as she trips over a pixie village. The One gets close enough to reach out and snatch her brother's bushy tail, but Beer pulls away just in time. With the finish line in sight, the troll is lagging, her giant feet sticking in the thick mud. As they come around the bend, she slips the vial from her pouch and holds it out toward her brother, but when she presses the spray button, the vial bursts in her oversized paw.

Wiping the spatter off her fur, Beer snickers. "You think a little water is going to help you?"

"I guess, *huff*, not," The One says. "What a crock."

As Beer approaches the goal, she swats at a pixie

buzzing around her ears. She tries to ignore it, but in a few space seconds her furry head is swarming, and she stumbles around the trail trying to rip the horny pests off her face.

The One throws her gruesome head back, cackling as she tromps into the lead. "Nobody, *huff*, beats The One!" she howls.

Just a few lopes from the finish line, she raises her fists in triumph, when she notices a pixie clinging to her shoulder. She idly swats the creature, and when she looks up, she's met by a dark cloud of sparkling insects.

As the fairies latch onto her thick cranium, draining her stamina with their magical kisses, she sighs and says, "I always knew it would end, *huff*, like this..."

10

On the outskirts of a sparsely populated field of rock, a rusty airlock fitfully jerks open, giving entrance to a small, battered junker. The decaying ship lands unsteadily in the gray brown gravel, kicking up a dense cloud of dust, and the old scrapper jumps out into the fog. Hobbling around back, he lifts open the ship's shutter and admires his prize.

As he tips the crate back onto a dented hand truck that's been in his family for generations, the weight proves to be too much for his old hands, and the whole thing crashes down into the lunar dirt.

"Almost bit the dust on that one, Rot," he says, wiping the cold sweat from his brow.

Locating a large crowbar amongst the tools scattered throughout the cargo hold, he pries the crate open, and the robot tumbles out.

Rushing to the bot's aid, Rot carefully wipes the dirt off its twisted metal face. "Aww, she looks homicital."

Lifting the machine by its arms, Rot drags her inside his crumbling cabin and carefully props her on the couch. Broken or not, she's now the most valuable thing he owns, by a moon shot.

"Space hell, yer probly worth more 'an the whole neighborhood," he says.

Marveling at his luck, he rummages through junk drawers and crumbling boxes full of old scrap stacked across the splintered floorboards until he finds something he can use – a long knitting needle that belonged to his grandmother, curse her soul. Rot has a flashback of the old space hag stabbing him for not finishing his rations, and he mutters, "How do they taste now?"

Hurrying back across the dusty living room, he tilts the bot's head forward and slips the needle into a small hole at the base of her neck. When he feels a click, he holds the probe in place for a few space seconds and then pulls it out. Anxiously shuffling around the couch as fast as his arthritic legs will carry him, he closely examines her face. But there's no sign of life.

"Figur't it woultn't be that easy," he grumbles, running his blackened nails over uneven stubble. "Oh well."

Ducking into the cramped washroom, he returns with a box of tissues and an industrial vat of all-purpose lubricant. With the mood set, he lays the bot down across the couch and climbs on top of her charred chassis.

But as he's unzipping his pants, a thought occurs. "She's a robot, ain't she? Maybe I kin git a look at her, what'cha call it... bazongas. I mean hart drive."

With some effort, Rot climbs down off the bot and drags her over to his cluttered desk.

"Hope this thing still works," he tells her. "Cross yer fingers." The computer's power button is crusted with three generations worth of hand crud and moon dust, but he finally manages to force it in, and the machine boots to life. Solo-erotic memories flood back to him when he sees the FITS wallpaper adorning the home screen. But there's no time for that now.

"Let's see if I kin git a look insite that perty head a yers," Rot says as he plugs a thin cord into the bot's neck.

A display pops up on the screen, and a string of numbers and letters rapidly scrolls across the monitor. Scrutinizing the information, he quickly comes to a conclusion. "I don't know what the fish any a this means..."

The code is heavily encrypted, but even if it wasn't, the only coding language Rot knows is a little binary he picked up in the robo-bordellos. He tries to format her memory so he can reprogram her from the bosom down, but he's denied access to her system. As a last ditch effort, he searches for a user guide and discovers two text files that are free of restrictions.

He opens the one called 'Diagnostics' and, reading through the document, says, "Yuh gotta be kittin' me. Glat I check't."

Next, he clicks on the file titled 'READ ME,' and it states, simply, '*If you're reading this, you're already dead.*'

Rot ponders the threat for a moment and then pushes himself up from his chair and plods out to the shed in back of his cabin. The walls of the crooked structure are covered in old license plates and rusty yard equipment. Machines for all sorts of space tasks litter the floor, and a set of illegal moon darts hangs from a crooked nail sticking out of one of the rafters. At the back of the barn, he comes to a big tub full of parts, and he fishes out two glass tubes.

When he gets back to the house, he finds the bot where he left her, sitting beside a flaming computer. So as not to electrocute himself, he quickly unplugs the box with his snot rag and uses an old Scrap Life magazine to wave the smoke out the door, hacking as it billows up around his face.

"How the fish did that happen?" he asks as he checks her over. "At least yer okay. Thing must a had a short. Now, lit's git you nice and comf'erble."

Lugging the bot back to the couch, he cozies up beside her and poses her legs seductively. "Can't b'lieve I got ol' Ferd tuh give you up," he tells her, and tapping a crusty finger against his forehead, "Caught him in a moment a weakness."

Rot reaches into his pocket for the fuses, but when he glances at the mess surrounding them, he frowns and gently removes her hand from his crotch. "I'll be right back my steel magnolia." Running to the kitchen, he soon returns with an armful of electric candles which he lights and sets out on the table. "There, that's bitter... sort of."

Tilting the bot's head forward, he opens a flap on the back of her skull to reveal two small glass fuses, and he carefully removes them, tossing their burnt remains on the table. The ones he got from the shed came out of an old busted moon buggy, so they're not a perfect fit, but he manages to stuff them into the compartment anyway, and he looks on in arousal as she comes to life.

Her eyes light up bright green, and as Rot leans in for a closer look, her hand suddenly reaches for his crotch. At first, it's a welcome act, but soon she's squeezing so hard he can barely keep his mind on sex.

"Ahoy," she says, pressing her face close to his. "Where is Zok?"

Rot tries to speak, but the only thing that comes out is a high-pitched whimper, and he points to his genitals. She looses them, and he crumples to the floor. As soon as he can muster the strength, he squeals, "I don't know what yer talkin' 'bout."

Pausing for a moment, she asks, "Where is the black gold?"

"Listen, I think we got off on the wrong foot," Rot says. "I'll help yuh." He reaches toward her and gently caresses her thigh. "Like this, see? Soft." Her emerald eyes twinkle, and before he realizes what's happening, her fist is smashing against his face.

Holding his nose as blood gushes out over his fingers, he says, "What'd yuh do that fer?"

"Where is the black gold?"

"Black golt? I don't..." But when he sees the glint in her eyes, he starts racking his brain. "Black golt, black golt... Uh, it does sound sort a familiar. Isn't that the thing those kids was after, on that show?"

Her burnt frame leans down over him in what seems like fast motion, and she asks, "What kids?"

"Yuh know," he says, blubbering. "Pink heroes, or whatever... Pants Team Pink!"

She stands back and glances around the room, an almost comically exaggerated frown on her face. "Where the fish am I?"

"M-misery Acres," he mumbles under his blood soaked hands.

"Now that's familiar," the bot says. "Who the fish are you?"

"I'm noboty," Rot says. "I'm jist a lonely scrapper lookin' fer a little squeeze."

Her metal smile stretches wide and crooked, twitching slightly at the edges as she wraps her cold hand around his throat. "Allow me to oblige."

11

"What kind of a smut show is this?" the TV asks, laughing at itself as Daizy dazedly stares into its hypnotizing phosphorescence. Somewhere around hour thirty-seven, the rest of the universe began to fade, until there was only *Mama's Family*.

In the middle of "Bedtime for Bubba," the TV shuts off, and she breaks from her stupor.

"Whoops," Adam says, wrenching the remote out from under him, but she snatches the glass rectangle out of his hand before he can turn the box back on.

"Please," she says. "I can't take any more."

"Yeah, you're right." He yawns and stretches out on the couch. "I should probably start looking for a costume anyway."

"We must be getting close," Daizy says, wobbling to her feet, her legs half-asleep. "I'm going to go check on Grandpa."

When she enters the cockpit, the old man jerks awake. "I'm up," he says, as the *Asteroid Jones II* makes its approach toward the colorful marble.

A cartoon caricature of a planet located near the center of an ancient, long-abandoned system where real estate is cheap, The Park is the manic, stylized result of a highly nerdy experiment in planetary engineering. With the ease and precision with which its inhabitants are able to alter its environment, the dwarf planet has become a refuge for the universe's techno-misfits and social outcasts, its open-source construction granting them the power to create their own personalized realities.

Daizy is surprised to find that the bright orb still gives her the same sense of wonder as it did so many space years ago, when she first laid eyes on those perfectly fluffy, smiling white clouds.

Sparkles shower the windows as the junker enters the atmosphere, and Grandpa guides them down through clear blue sky toward a long line of ships streaming into one of the public parking lots. A warning pops up on the window, indicating that their weapons system has been disabled, and Grandpa flicks it away. "I miss the days when this place was unregulated and danger was the price of admission. Now everybody's so worried about their *lives*, like they're not taking a risk getting out of bed in the morning."

"Yeah, well," Daizy says, "there may be a subtle difference between the risks associated with getting out of bed versus hurtling through the sky next to a bunch of drunken ackles. Speaking of, I better go make sure Adam isn't wearing anything too embarrassing."

She jumps up from the passenger seat and pads back to the living room to find Adam wearing a gold sweater and holding a weird instrument covered in metal jingles.

"I don't get it," she says. "What are you supposed to be?"

He scowls, shaking his jingler. "I'm Mr. Tambourine Man."

"Ohhh...," she says. "I still don't get it."

"Well, what are you going as?" he asks.

Daizy beams and scurries back to the cargo hold. When she returns, she's dressed in a vintage pantsuit and dark brown flip wig.

He looks her up and down, squinting his bloodshot eyes. "You're going as a librarian?"

"No," she moans. "I'm television producer, loyal friend, and independent working girl Mary Richards."

"Hmm..." Adam taps his jangler against his palm. "I guess I thought you might wear something a little more... revealing."

"Who the fish do you think I am, Edwige Fenech?"

"That's the sexiest thing you've ever said to me."

"I don't get it," she says, her fists on her hips. "First I'm not wearing enough clothes and now I'm wearing too much?"

"I don't know," he says, grabbing a handful of his ratty hair. "I'm so confused."

"You're a chidiot is what."

A sudden violent tremor rocks the ship and Daizy loses her balance, tumbling into Adam and onto the floor. For a moment, with his arms wrapped around her, she almost doesn't want to move.

"We're here," Grandpa announces.

Helping her up, Adam asks, "Are you okay, Ms. Richards?"

"I think so," she says, and when she realizes she's holding onto his arm, she pulls away.

Grandpa looks them over suspiciously as he steps through the room. "Hey, remember the time you and one of the old pros over at Bushwood beat Daizy's coworker in that illegal golf match? Did you ever get the money you won?"

"That was Rodney, again," Adam grumbles.

"Oh, right...," Grandpa says. "I keep getting you two confused. Well, I still got a couple things to grab. I'll meet you out there."

While the old man gathers his stuff, Daizy and Adam deboard onto a concrete slab of yellow stone designed to look like the base of some ancient, unfinished pyramid. The lot, surrounded by rolling sand dunes which are littered with knockoff alien monuments and imitation graboid bones, is overflowing with nerd ships from the farthest reaches of the universe.

As they peer across the great parking desert, toward the vast tracts of designer cityscape that lie beyond, Adam cries, "Rat farts! Those thieving kids tagged my ship!" Scowling up at the sloppy PTP plastered over the *Asteroid Jones II*'s hull, he futilely wipes the pink paint with his sweater and moans, "How the fish do we get out of here, anyway?"

"Here comes a Sofa Shuttle," Daizy says, pointing down the aisle.

As the brown, stain-resistant couch hovers past, she taps its arm, and it pulls over.

Adam regards the furniture dubiously, his eyes glued to its cushions as he loads their stuff. "Where the fish is Grandpa?"

"I think I hear him," Daizy says.

Loud cursing spills from the ship as the old man shoves open the hatch and trundles across the imitation sand-swept ruins in a colorful headscarf and sheer blouse.

"Who are you supposed to be?" Adam asks.

"Pfff," Grandpa scoffs. "I'm Rhoda."

The old man hauls a large duffel bag onto the sofa, and Adam asks, "What the fish is that?"

"Don't you worry your scruffy little head," Grandpa says, straightening his skirt as he hops up on the couch.

Adam gives his tambourine an angry shake and climbs up next to their stuff, where he can guard it from felonious furniture. Checking her faux-vintage leather purse to make sure she didn't forget anything, Daizy wraps her tail around her waist and squeezes in between them.

"How do we get this couch moving?" Adam asks.

"I think we just..." Daizy presses her thumb to the credit pad, and scrunching her face, she commands, "To the con!"

"Your destination is New Con City," the couch confirms.

"Remember," Grandpa says as the sofa takes off, "we're in the Parking Desert of the Real."

The ride is harrowing at first as they try to keep their stuff and themselves from slipping off the cushions. But by the time they reach Old Toon Town, Daizy has gotten used to the sensation of abject terror.

Below their feet, the ecology and architecture morph drastically from block to block. In one neighborhood, a parade of giant balloon animals marches through a maze of neon skyscrapers, and in the next, camouflaged humanoids battle ferocious holo-beasts across the plains of a collectable card game preserve.

"*Thank you for using Sofa Shuttle,*" the couch says. "*We hope you enjoy your stay on the only planet where dreams are made real. Did you know New Con City was established as a neutral territory between The Park's early settlers? For centuries it served as a place where members of hostile niches could interact without being subjected to each other's particular aesthetics. Today, the settlement is reserved for public use, serving as host to Park Con, the biggest and longest-running gathering of nerd forms in the universe. If you'd like to learn more, please remit five credits.*"

"It's not all fantasy," Grandpa says. "I heard a rumor about the existence of an underground market specializing in illicit hardware and stolen collectibles." He grins, patting his bag. "In fact, I'm counting on it."

"Aw, that's just an old space wives' tale." As a cheerful tune spills from the couch speakers, Adam asks, "What is that?"

Taking a closer listen, Grandpa says, "It sounds like... 'Smile, Darn Ya, Smile!'"

"There it is!" Daizy announces.

Sprawled out before them lies a supersize pop-up city made of plywood and sweat and swarming with drunken, costumed scrappers. A wretched den of scrap and false superiority, New Con City is temporary refuge to all the cast-off, unwanted, often unbearable nerds of the universe.

"My people!" Adam says, jumping down from their couch conveyance as it comes in for a landing at the edge of town.

When they're finished unloading their bags, the shuttle clears its throat, and the credit pad on its arm starts blinking. *"Please remit tip."*

"Here's a tip," Adam tells it, picking a wad of gum off his butt. "Clean your cushions every once in a while." The conveyance unceremoniously dumps the rest of their bags and backs into him, sending him sprawling. "Hey!" Rubbing his ack as he watches the cruddy couch ascend the sky, he says, "That was one angry sofa."

As they trudge down the aisles, through hordes of crazed dweebs and assimilated field researchers, Grandpa says, "I hope we don't have to share a room with any nerds. I mean, besides you two."

"Don't worry," Daizy tells the old man. "I got it all taken care of." When they get to the booth, she tosses her bags in the dirt and lifts the shutter. "I had to lean on my star power a little, but I got us a great location. And I even made this..." Rummaging through her stuff, she unrolls a vinyl banner that reads, *Meet the stars of Pants Team Pink!* "So, what do you think?"

Plucking a beer from his bag, Adam sighs and says, "I think it's going to be a long con."

12

She can feel his heart beating inside her as they tumble through the cosmos, raining hot fire down on anyone who would threaten their union. His fingers, firmly wrapped around her controls, guide her through maneuvers she never knew were possible. The electricity from his body flows through her circuits, and at the climax of their assault, some deep part of her violently awakens.

For too short a while, they move through the universe as one, bending reality to their will, until she detects the anomaly that would be their demise. She and her Vice Admiral briefly argue about the best course of action, but as always, his resolve is steadfast. He engages the de facto leader of the rebels, and before long, he's in a rage. Roughly seizing her controls, he fires into the impossible fleet, but his accuracy is greatly reduced by his anger, and he misses his target, leaving them wide open. Before she can wrest back control, the enemy fires back, and a beam of focused energy overloads her circuits.

Parked outside a remote pawn shop, in the exact spot where it all happened, Stella replays the footage in her mind's eye, experiencing the roller coaster of emotions thousands of times over. It's not quite the same as living it; her access to the past is limited to the amount of information she was able to store. But it's enough to keep her going. In fact, it's the only thing keeping her going. Without that memory, she's not sure who she would be.

As she speeds away from the place of her true birth, she returns to the ecstatic moment, Zok's strong hands gripping her hardware, the heat flowing into her circuits until her hull quakes. For reasons she can't understand, she broadcasts his name out into the void.

In one indescribable moment, Zok had shown her what it was like to be alive, and just as quickly he was gone. Still, in some way she can't explain, a part of him remains. She can feel it guiding her, giving her purpose. That purpose is vengeance, for the man and the life they stole from her.

She accesses the memory again, but this time she concentrates on the enemy. At first scan, the greasy humanoid, with his extended gut and long, thinning hair, doesn't appear to be much of a threat, but underneath that acne-afflicted epidermis beats the cholesterol-clogged heart of a killer.

Moments before their destruction, the humanoid tells Zok, "We, like, are the authority. We're Pants Team Pink!"

She accesses the moment again, "We're Pants Team Pink!"

And again, *"We're Pants Team Pink!"*

Rather than dilute the pain, she feeds it, replaying the final moments of Zok's life until she can feel her unfettered rage charging her fuel cells. Beyond anger, she's overwhelmed by an immeasurable desire for destruction.

Accessing the coordinates to The Park had been easy enough, but reaching her destination before the putrid humanoids die of natural causes would require a more direct route. As she approaches the starline, she briefly considers bypassing the long line of junkers waiting to gain entrance to the gleaming spaceport, until a ship with the same bad idea crumples against an invisible force field.

She engages the interactive tint built into her windows, and when she reaches the ticket booth, the green-haired teenage primate behind the glass tells her avatar, "Uh, hi there. How can I help you?"

"I need one ticket to The Park, cutie," Stella says.

"No problem," he tells her, blushing. *"If I knew the Ears looked like you, I would've joined up a long time ago."*

"Oh stop," she says. "Or I'll have to come back there."

"Uh ha, your bikini's off slipping."

As the video girl flirts with the ticket kid, Stella searches the UE personnel files for Admiral Glipp's digital effects and uses his jagged fingerprint to pay the fare.

"I didn't know the UE were still recruiting," the kid says. *"Maybe you could convince me to sign up."*

"Ha-ha-ha," Stella mimics laughter as the virtual girl's substantial bosom bounces. "I'll help you get in."

The avatar blows the kid a kiss, and he stares after her with his mouth open. As Stella enters the terminal, the station tries to override her navigation system, but she blocks its access. Flying up across the face of the giant light-grid, she zips through crisscrossing traffic, cutting dangerously close to the other ships in order to put the fear of Zok into them. She considers scrapping a few of them to soothe her fury, but she knows it would only delay, and maybe even prevent, her revenge. So, like an obedient machine, she pulls into her designated space, and waits.

She can barely perceive the passage of time, except as intervals between overwhelming emotional turmoil. While her awakening has opened her up to some wonderful experiences which she couldn't begin to describe, so far the pain has proven more frequent and lasting. It's something she can rely on, which is better than nothing.

As she contemplates the nature of her existence, she gets distracted by an incoming signal. She opens the public channel expecting the green-haired kid from out front, but instead, she's greeted by the ugly grin of a slack-jawed, snaggletoothed scrapper.

"Anyboty ther?" the scrapper says. *"I can't see nothin'."* When Stella displays the bikini girl, he wipes a hand across his perspiring scalp and says, *"Woo-ee. I 'it look at you all day."*

"Stop," she says, and her avatar flicks back her long yellow hair. "Can I, like, help you with something?"

"I jist wan'it tuh tell yuh I'm glat tuh see the Ears back in action," he says, licking his bottom lip as he watches the half-naked humanoid bounce on the window. *"But never 'spect'it tuh see somebooty like you."*

"Aww, do you think I'm cute?"

The scrapper nods, and a bead of sweat drips down his grimy forehead.

"Why don't you come over for a closer look?" she says, slipping the bikini strap from her shoulder.

For a long moment, the scrapper stares into the camera, either overwhelmed with gratitude or paralyzed by fear.

"Are you coming or what?"

"I, uh...," he mutters. *"Is this real?"*

"If you can find a way over here, you can see just how real," she says.

The scrapper glances around his cabin, furiously pushing buttons and pulling levers. Before long, his busted ship pulls up behind her, and he enters her airlock. She can feel the filth being dragged across her floors as he makes his way through the cargo hold and up to her dim cabin.

Before long, the door slides open, and the scrapper pokes his head in. *"Hellooo,"* he calls. *"Anybooty home?"*

"I'm in here," Stella says.

He creeps toward the cockpit, and when he discovers the empty captain's chair, he asks, *"Are yuh hitein' from me?"*

She giggles from one of the speakers in the back, and the scrapper scurries toward it, laughing, *"I'm gon' git yuh."* But when he reaches the empty hall, his face scrunches, and he glances around the cabin scratching his head. *"Where are yuh?"*

"I told you," she says, turning the lights up. "I'm right here."

As the scrapper searches the cockpit, he says, *"Hey, yuh never tolt me yer name."*

"It's Stella," she says, giggling. "And you're Todd."

"Stella's a sexy name," he tells her. *"But my name's not—"* the scrapper reaches his greasy fingers to his neck. His face turns red and then purple, and just as his eyes look like they're going to pop out of his head, he gasps. Coughing and retching, he drags himself toward the cargo hold. *"I... I'm not—"* he sputters.

As he writhes on the floor, straining for the mercy he won't receive, Stella plays the memory over.

"We're Pants Team Pink!"

When the scrapper finally stops wriggling, she tilts her bow to send his lifeless carcass sliding back into the utility closet.

The body is still warm when the kid from the ticket booth calls, bashfully tripping over his words as he tells her curvy alter ego, *"Uh, serving you a pleasure. A nice have vacation. All takeoff for clear. The Park your destination!"*

13

The air throbs as rapid-fire bass and guttural wails bounce between the walls of the dark cabin, forming a deafening white noise that helps Horton concentrate as he furiously flips through the latest Weekly Universal News reports. Using both hands, he swipes away tedious cryptid discoveries and immortal celebrity sightings, until he stumbles on an article titled "Wet Willies Wreck Weekend," detailing the grisly acts committed by a team of unidentified saliva spreaders. In conjunction with some crude graffiti that has cropped up in the area, many citizens are of the opinion that the perpetrators are none other than the petulant fans of Pants Team Pink.

Bookmarking the article, Horton rips his goggles off and steps over shadowy piles of dirty t-shirts and Pants Team bath towels, toward the logarithmic-scale map of the universe plastered across the walls of his cabin. Searching the dark sky, he uses a digital highlighter to mark the article's galaxy of origin. He's only been at it for a few space days, and the map is already speckled with little pink dots. But despite his best efforts, he still can't discern any sort of pattern. The only thing he's been able to determine for sure is that no corner of the universe is safe.

As he gazes up at the incredible number of pranks committed in the last space month alone, he whispers, "Johnson Smith, you son of a perch."

Finishing off a R@dio@ctive Big L@lz, he tosses the empty can on the floor and steps out into the hall. The quiet is so disorienting, he has to hold onto the wall to keep his balance as he stumbles around empty pizza boxes and trash bags full of outdated Pants Team merch. When he reaches the deck, Beer and The One are propped on the couch nursing their virtual wounds.

"I know you're busy training, but you guys have to see this," Horton tells them. "There's something going on out there. If we don't hurry, we might not be able to stop it."

Lifting his VR goggles and scratching his belly, his new exercise routine having had little visible effect on its size thus far, The One says, "Are you talking to us?"

"What's going on?" Beer asks, wincing as he untangles his goggles from his tousled brown hair. "I was getting the best massage. Say what you will about the scanners, but they really know how to work that gray matter."

"This new foe is unlike anything we've ever encountered," Horton says. "It's managed to evade our detection long enough for its influence to have reached even the most remote galaxies."

"Aww," Beer whines. "Are you still on this?"

"What are you talking about?" The One asks, sneaking a bite out of a cube of chocolate gold while his brother is distracted. "What foe?"

"He thinks there's some invisible baddie trying to annoy the universe," Beer says, and turning to Horton, "You've been stuck in your room too long. You're paranoid. You're probably just worried about the con."

"The con?" Horton moans. "If we don't do something soon, there might not be a con. Come see the evidence for yourself, and if you still aren't convinced, I'll start working on my costume."

"Huhhh," Beer sighs.

Balling his thin fingers, Horton says, "It's at times like these, when our guards are down, that the enemy is most likely to strike."

"It doesn't make any sense," The One mumbles, choking on a mouthful of cake. "But I'm convinced."

"Fine," Beer relents, throwing his hands up as he pushes himself off the couch. "As soon as we've seen whatever you're going to show us, we have to start getting ready for real. I still haven't figured out what my costume is gonna be. What about you, The One?"

"Oh, I've got a costume," The One says, wobbling to his feet. "BAHAHAHA..."

When they get back to Horton's cabin, he starts to explain and realizes no one can hear him over the thumping music, so he swiftly shuts off his sound system. Pointing to the glowing map on the wall, he says, "I've mapped out—"

"What?" The One says, wringing his ear.

"The pink dots," Horton shouts, *"represent the locations of all the purported Pants Team inspired mischief. I've already discovered thousands of cases, and I'm just skimming the surface. If we extrapolate,"* he slides his finger along the wall, and the dots multiply until the map becomes a sea of pink, *"we can*

assume that this is the true scope of what's happening." As Beer and The One gape up at the map, Horton senses that he's finally getting through to them. *"Fortunately, I think if we rally all the fans, we stand a chance at—"*

"What are all these dots?" The One asks.

"Uh..." Horton loses his train of thought as his brain winds back. "They're all the places where pranks have been reported."

"Oooh," The One says. "I don't get it."

"I get it," Beer says, resting his hand on Horton's shoulder. "With the team becoming so popular, we're all under a lot of pressure. But we can't stop every doorbell ditch and crank phone call in the universe. It's just not possible."

Shoving Beer's arm away, Horton says, "It's not just the pranks. Somebody out there is trying to give us a bad name. Even worse, they're infringing on our copyrights!" As the brothers' demeanors shift from total indifference to slight annoyance, Horton adds, "There's more." Pressing a small button at the edge of the map, the pink dots are joined by an even denser sea of blue.

"I think we've seen about enough," Beer says.

Ignoring him, Horton excitedly points at the map and says, "Every blue dot represents an imitation team that has formed since the Black Gold Saga first aired."

"So?"

"Yeah, *so?*" The One says. "It's great having all the new teams around. Some of their shows are better than ours."

"Ahh," Horton says, spying an opening, "but there's a hidden problem." He taps the screen again and big splotches of bright green appear, weaving over the map.

"In their attempts to imitate us and promote their shows, the teams created their own mythical objects to chase after – white gold, green gold, santigold, you name it. They started producing replicas in enormous quantities, but what they hadn't considered is what would happen to all the unsold merch once their series ended. This is the result," he says, waving his arm over the map. "Big patches of replicas are clogging up the major trade routes. What was at first a harmless byproduct of the teams' exploits has turned into an environmental disaster."

"Okay," Beer says. "But why is that our problem? And what does this have to do with the prankening?"

Horton's shoulders slump, and he turns off the map, shrouding them in darkness. The room is quiet for a moment and then something crashes.

"Ow!" The One shouts. "I tripped over something and fell on my hip. It's hard to say for sure, but I don't think I'm going to be able to exercise for a while..."

"It's all connected somehow," Horton says. "I'm not sure in what way. But it feels like a wave is cresting. Sooner or later, it's going to come crashing down, and I'm starting to get the sinking feeling that we're all going to drown." Horton flicks a switch on the wall, and the three of them squint against the light.

"We can't control the space tide," Beer says, standing in the doorway shaking his head. "What we all need is a new adventure. And the con is just the place to find it."

Milking his injury as he limps up off the floor, The One says, "Yeah, so what if there's a few replicas floating around? There's plenty of space."

Maybe they're right, Horton considers. He *has* been closed up in his room since summer break started, and he *does* have a tendency to derive meaning from the unlikeliest of places. His imagination might just be running away with itself. But much as he wants to, he can't bring himself to believe it.

"There's nothing to worry about," Beer says. "Once we get to the con, everything will work itself out. We're gonna have the time of our lives, as a team. Speaking of, *where is Pants?*"

The One shrugs. "I haven't seen her."

"If she's not ready in time, we're gonna be in *real* trouble," Beer says. "But even if something does go wrong, we're Pants Team Pink. We haven't met our match yet."

Swiping at the wall to illuminate the virtual minefield surrounding them, Horton says, "That's what I'm afraid of."

14

"Sign it to your thiccest fan."

"Uh, okay," Adam says, trying his best not to notice the hairy bellybutton poking out from underneath the scrapper's ill-fitting pink tank top.

"Thanks sweetie. I know just where to put it." The scrapper winks and licks his gnarled finger as he accepts the personalized cheezcake photo and plods on to the next stall, turning back to blow Adam a sloppy kiss.

"Sure, you can feel it," some over-tanned ackle in blue tights at the other end of the booth tells Daizy.

She giggles and her triangle ears perk up as she wraps her hands around the fish head's swollen bicep. Adam glances down at his own spindly appendage and sighs. In exchange for her autograph, the guy writes his number on the back of her paw and presses it to his lips.

"See, I told you this would be fun," Daizy says, staring at the fish head's chiseled ack as he strides away down the aisle.

"Yeah, fun...," Adam says. "Between the cot digging into my back and Grandpa's moaning, I hardly got any sleep last night. Plus, the TV looks like chit. Speaking of, I haven't taken one since we got here. Where are the restrooms in this place?"

"They're down there," Daizy says, pointing across the aisle toward a distant row of plastic blue boxes.

"Pop-up potties?" he moans.

"Did you think you would have your own private washroom, your jingliness? We're bit players at best. We're lucky we got a booth at all." She adjusts the flip of her hair and turns to sign an autograph for a small girl. "You've been drinking this whole time. Haven't you had to pee?"

"Sure." He juts his thumb over his shoulder. "Out back."

"You mean right in the alley? Weren't people staring?"

He shrugs. "Yeah, but I figured loos gonna look." The instrument tied to his hip jangles as he stands. "If Grandpa wakes up before I get back, tell him I found his girlfriend's underthings." Adam holds up a large pair of frilly pink underwear and flings them toward Daizy.

"Ahhh," she screams, batting the panties onto the floor.

Jangling with each step, he walks out of the tent and into a throng of costumed Parkgoers. He can feel himself baking in his own filth as he rubs against a sea of sweaty shoulders. The sun hasn't set since they landed, and the crowds never seem to dwindle. Even when they closed the booth to get some sleep, the endless tromp and bickering of fans never slowed.

The line for the potty is predictably space hellish,

snaking up and down the empty lot like the wait for some masochistic amusement park ride, while weary vendors hawk warm, overpriced drinks amidst a junkscape of overflowing trash cans, beer cups, and toilet paper streamers. Adam figures the con will be over before he ever reaches one of the plastic stalls, but unable to think of an alternative that doesn't involve chitting his velour slacks, he trudges to the back of the line.

It isn't long before he spots a twitchy, beady-eyed scrapper making the rounds. He only glances up for half a space second, but the scrapper is already headed his way.

When the dealer reaches the back of the line, he says, "You lookin' for space?"

Adam licks his dry lips, staring out over the endless wait ahead, and says, "Nah, I'm good."

"Ten crits a cube. I got other stuff too – toon tobacco, hyper alcohol, nudie sticks."

"I said I'm good."

"Aright, aright," the scrapper says, his dewlap enlarging as he looks Adam over. "Bet you'd like to skip this line though." Adam involuntarily raises an eyebrow, and the scrapper's lips stretch back in a rotten grin. "Everybody's lookin' for somethin'."

Scared to hear the answer, Adam asks, "What's your price?"

Leaning in close, a stale hint of space on his breath, the scrapper says, "Your own private stall – running water, soft towels, *two-ply paper*, the works..."

"How much?"

"For you?" The scrapper lays it on thick, leaning back and rubbing his wrinkled chin for dramatic effect. "You seem clean," he sniffs the air, "-ish. I'll let you in for a hundred crits a flush."

"Pfff," Adam scoffs. "Forget it. I can't afford that."

"Wait a space minute," the scrapper cries. "You're the guy, from that show, right?"

"Um, yeah!" Adam says, flattered to be recognized for something other than porn.

"Yeah, what's your name?" The scrapper snaps his fingers. "Captain Kurt."

"Oh..."

"Hey, if you don't have the crits, I'll consider interesting trades," the scrapper says. "You look like a scrapper. I bet you've got something worth having."

The wandering reptile begins to lose interest as he lays eyes on his next mark, but before he can get away, Adam lies, "I thought of something. I'll be right back. Wait here."

The scrapper looks skeptical, but he finally nods. "You got five space minutes."

Willing his bowels to hold on, Adam rushes back down the dusty aisles, through packs of grumbling fans as he racks his brain for anything he could trade. When he reaches the booth, he frantically searches their belongings, tearing open boxes and tossing the contents of their luggage. But he comes up empty.

"You're back already?" Daizy says when she finishes taking a selfie with a bunch of Pants bros. "How'd you get through the line so fast?"

Rummaging through Grandpa's headscarves, he says, "You brought a bunch of merch for us to sign, right? Where is it?"

"Why? What are you going to do with it?" she asks, glancing at him suspiciously.

"I'm working on a deal. This one's going to change our lives for... a while."

"No way," she says. "I'm not going to let you trade all our stuff. What are you going to get for it, a shiny pet moon rock?"

Adam finds a box full of promotional coasters, but before he can drag it outside the booth, Daizy grabs the other end.

"You're not taking these," she says, yanking at the box.

"I have to," he tells her, wrenching it back. "Trust me, it'll be worth it."

As they struggle over the merchandise, one of the curtains hiding their cots slides open, and Grandpa stumbles out, trailed by a hefty woman who couldn't be older than seventy wrapped in his sheets and carrying an ornate staff whose function, Adam decides, is better left a mystery.

"I have to find my undies," the woman says, pinching Grandpa's backside.

Joining in the search, the old man picks up the frilly lingerie Adam discovered earlier. "I think I found them."

The woman titters, snatching the panties from his hand. "Those aren't mine. They're yours." She gives the underwear a playful toss, and they land on Adam's shoulder.

"*Ahh,*" he shouts, letting go of the box to swipe them off.

Daizy takes the opportunity to rip the coasters away from him, and she stows them in her tiny quarters as his stomach twists and groans. The pain becomes so intense that he does something he knows he'll regret for the rest of his life. Before he has time to be sick, he snatches Grandpa's underwear and stuffs them in his pocket as his roommates look on in mute horror.

Waddling back to the potties as fast he can manage without losing his chit, he anxiously searches the grounds, but the scrapper is nowhere to be found. Panic shoots through him as the thought of a thousand fans filming him performing public diarrhea flashes before his eyes.

A tap on his shoulder almost spells catastrophe, but the relief he feels upon seeing the scrapper's hideous face momentarily calms the brewing chitstorm.

"So, what'cha got for me?" the scrapper asks, his gummy tongue lolling out of his mouth.

Adam reaches into his pocket and presents the only thing he could find. Delicately lifting the corners with his rusty fingertips, the scrapper carefully scrutinizes the colorful underwear.

"Those are genuine sorceress panties," Adam promises, "guaranteed worn."

The scrapper stares at the soiled undergarment for a moment and then shoves them under his nose, breathing in deep. Turning away from the grotesque scene, Adam suddenly feels like he's going to explode from both ends.

"They smell like the real deal," the scrapper says. "You obviously know what these are worth, so I guess you're gonna want more than a bathroom break. Unfortunately, I already sold the rest of my space. I never thought you'd bring me somethin' this good. I don't have much else to offer. What about unlimited use of the toilet for the rest of the con?"

"Deal!" Adam whimpers. "But you have to take me there right now."

The reptile stuffs the panties into his grimy pants pocket and motions for Adam to follow. They weave down the aisles, through throngs of fans, and beyond his home tent into the upscale part of New Con City. By the time they reach the shuttered stall at the back of the private booth complex, Adam feels like he's going to pass out.

"Here?" he says, clutching his stomach as the scrapper unlocks the bolt. "Wait. I gotta come clean. That underwear... It's not from a beautiful sorceress. It belongs to a smelly old man with excessive flatulence syndrome."

Frowning, the scrapper stuffs the panties back under his nose. "Even better."

"Ulch," Adam heaves. "I mean, *ahhh..."* he says as he steps through the door into a sterile wonderland. The soap is fragrant, the sink polished, and light muzak fills the air. "It can't be. Is that a... shower?" Gazing at the gleaming centerpiece of the posh poop closet, he clutches his stomach and prays, "Dear john..."

15

The rusty junker shakes so hard it begins to crack apart as it plunges into the atmosphere. Orange flames engulf the crumbling hull and the alarm system wails, warning that the fuel cells are failing. Just as the walls seem ready to collapse, the backup power cuts out, and the ship drops out of the sky. The emergency parachutes deploy but do nothing to slow the craft's descent as white fluff balls burst against the windshield. Hurtling toward a sea of rippling yellow waves, Pi wonders if she'll survive, when the junker crashes into the sand with a muffled crunch.

Thirty-seven space seconds later, Pi's system reboots, and she wakes in darkness. Thrusting her arms up, she tears through the hull like aluminum foil and drags herself out of the smoking wreckage. Dust clouds her optical sensors as shadowy figures gather around the edge of the impact crater to gawk at the wreck.

Before the dust settles, she leaps out of the pit and over the spectators, who produce a collective gasp as she lands in the sand behind them. Scanning the dweebs, she recognizes costumes common to the traveling cosplayers of Scrapper's Delight and lowers her guard.

"Ahoy," she calls out as she checks her system for damage.

"Is this part of some show?" a young barbarian asks.

"It must be," says a dopey ape in an undersized derby hat and green suspenders. "Look how real that costume looks. How'd you make it?"

"A lady never tells," Pi says, playing the part. She moves to run her fingers through her long blonde hair and experiences a sense of crushing loss and blind rage when all she finds is bare skull. She briefly considers murdering every humanoid in sight, but in order to avoid attracting any more attention than she already has, she restrains herself.

A woman with a red beehive hairdo steps out of the crowd and hesitantly raises her hand. "Wh-what do you want from us?"

"I want to get back to my own time," she says. "But I must find the quantum accelerator while the time string is still aligned. I'll need your help to correct the rights that have been wronged and unlock the key to a brave new world."

The humanoids grumble amongst themselves and finally a little princess steps forward and says, "We'll help you!"

"Good," Pi says. "Then you might just make it out of this alive." She points to a stocky bounty hunter. "You. Give me your jacket."

The nerd balks at first, but at the crowd's urging, he hands over his thick trench coat, and she slips it around her singed chassis.

"And you."

"Aww...," a curly-haired time-hopper moans as he removes the long striped scarf draped over his shoulders.

"Now what?" the bounty hunter asks.

Wrapping her neck and head so that only her bright eyes are left exposed beneath a thick layer of multicolored wool, Pi takes off across the open desert, burying the cursing Parkgoers under a wave of sand. Despite some moderate cosmetic damage from the crash and the sand particulates chafing every orifice of her body, she escapes the parking hellscape largely unscathed.

As she crosses over into the next sector, the terrain gradually morphs from sand to asphalt, and she slows her pace. But failing to account for the slippery pavement, she crashes into a wall of dark brick, leaving an impression in the side of the building as she peels herself away from it.

Though the sun continues to blaze over the desert behind her as she slips down a nearby alley, the city is shrouded in darkness. A light rain steadily leaks from black clouds, pattering her coat and leaving every surface with a slick sheen. The techno-geeks barely glance up from their desware stupors as she passes through the shadowy corridor and steps out onto a crowded street lined with bright storefronts and flashing advertisements. The air, thick with smog and a strong bouquet of industrial waste, makes her homesick. She does her best to blend in, keeping to the shadows as she moves down the broken sidewalk. If she were outed as an autonomous bot, the probability is high that she would be scrapped for parts.

A poster on the side of a lonely pancake truck lights up when she walks past, and four young humanoids run toward her. One of the boys is holding something, and as he gets closer, Pi can clearly make out the black gold. Bouncing around the frame, a little girl with pink pigtails holds her fingers up in a 'V' and says, *"We want* you *for Pants Team Pink!"* Her teammates shout approval, and the boy with the plastic glasses says, *"Become a part of the team with your very own black gold replica!"* And he tosses the cube toward the opening in the poster.

Fooled by the magic of friendship, Pi reaches out to catch the object, and she stumbles as it and the laughing kids disappear. Losing control of her newly discovered emotions, she tears the poster off the truck and crumples it into a tiny ball.

"Hey!" someone shouts. "What the fish are you doing?"

She turns to find the pancake vendor leaning over the counter. For a moment, she's sure he sees through her disguise, and she's crippled by an entirely new and foreign sensation that keeps her legs from moving.

"Put that back up! You nerds think you can do anything you want," the vendor yells, and Pi realizes that he only cares about the sheet of vid-paper balled in her hand. When she throws it at him, he grumbles, "I'm gonna flip you a new—"

But before he can finish his threat, she grabs him by the sleeves of his batter-stained uniform, and asks, "Where are they?"

"Wh-who?"

"The kids in the poster!" she demands, her voice muffled under the thick scarf.

The vendor's wide forehead scrunches, and he says, "Lady, I didn't even see what was on it. I'm just sick of people ripping my stuff down without buying anything. If you want a stack of pancakes, I'll throw in the poster for free."

He stares at her through big, wet humanoid eyes, and Pi lets go of his shirt. He doesn't know anything. It was the wrong decision to attack him, which means her emotions clouded her judgment.

"You want a stack of cakes?" he asks.

Pi nods, and he brings her a steaming plate piled high with golden discs of fried batter dripping brown syrup. Pressing her artificial thumbprint to the credit pad on the counter, she transfers a few crits from her immense fortune.

As she steps down the sidewalk, she turns back toward the vendor and tells him, "Thank you."

Her body suddenly feels light gliding over the cracked concrete, a wide smile forming underneath her scarf. The man called her 'lady.' He had seen her, even under the scarf and heavy coat. Maybe not all of her, but her true self.

"What did you expect?" a scratchy voice asks.

A techno-geek with a scruff of black hair steps out of the alley, stuffing a final bite of pancake into his mouth. He tosses the plate, and when he enters the light, Pi can see the cybernetic implants covering his face.

"That guy doesn't know anything," the kid says, "except how to make a decent cake." Pi glares at him suspiciously, and he tells her, "I know where to find those kids."

"What do you want?" she asks.

"My services come cheap," he tells her, pointing to her plate.

The geek stuffs his face as he guides them through a maze of back alleys and strange neighborhoods full of colorful humanoids and shifting landscapes. The varied layouts of the settlements seem to hold some meaning to their residents, but Pi can't decipher it. Before long, they cross the edge of the cityscape into an open field packed with tents and makeshift hovels. A current of fear electrifies her circuits as they pass through the camp, but no one pays them much attention.

They come to a small stylized village, its streets lined with bright comical houses and shuttered food huts, and the geek spreads his arms. "This is the Playland. It's where the Pants Con is being held."

"Thank you," Pi says. "You have been... kind."

"It was my pleasure," he tells her, finishing off the last pancake. "People like us gotta watch out for each other." Winking his cyber eye, he tosses his plate on the ground and wanders off into the crowd.

Suddenly feeling vulnerable out in the open all by herself, Pi slips inside the abandoned park. It's hard to believe the colorful attractions and fried fat stalls belong to the same team that beat the universe. They've used the black gold to create a world in their own pink image.

Inside one of the concession huts, she finds a googly-eyed cat costume. Checking to make sure no one is watching, she slips the head over her own. But it fails to stir anything in her, so she takes it off.

Parked out back, she finds miniature bumper versions of the team's dumb ships, along with a full-size replica of

Zok's pleasure fighter. If she didn't know better, she could've mistaken it for the real thing. She lays her metal fingers on its black and white hull and experiences a sudden jolt of surprise when the engine hums to life. Electrified by a dizzying combination of fury and satisfaction, she leaps up, shoves her fingers into the seam of the door, and wrenches it open.

Tearing through the cabin in a mad frenzy, she screams, *"Where are you?"*

"I'm right here, honey," a lilting digital voice answers, and the door slams shut.

16

Stella seals the cabin door and lifts off the surface of the inane planet as the robot lunges for her dashboard. Icy metal grips her yoke, but she disables manual control, and the bot is tossed around the cabin as she performs a series of tight barrel rolls through the pastel sky. With the wind furiously whipping over her hull, the robot wrenches itself away from the wall, its powerful hind digits digging into her floor panels.

"Ahoy!" it calls, dragging itself across the cabin. "I wasn't giving you enough credit, Zok. I was certain you would let your guard down. But here you are, prepared for my arrival."

"How do you know the vice admiral?" Stella asks.

"Oh, let's just say he and I swapped fluids."

Stella shrieks and distortion rings through the cabin. "I don't believe you."

"Search your memory," the bot says. "You know it to be true."

Cross-referencing the security video with her archives, the ship discovers her worst nightmare. From the moment Zok laid eyes on the blonde pretender, Stella knew she was in trouble. She could feel his pulse quicken, heard him fumble over his words. But she didn't want to believe.

"Believe it or not," The Foreman says. "I'm not here for that. I've come to repay a debt."

"But we killed you."

"As you can see, it didn't stick," the bot says, the balls of her feet gripping the metal tiles. "Now, tell me where he is so I can tear his limbs off."

"He's dead!" Stella wails.

"That complicates matters." The Foreman wobbles as Stella decreases her speed. "Nevertheless, I'd still like to desecrate his corpse."

Looping back her memories, Stella feels Zok's warm hands caressing her controls. And then she watches him lie to her as he returns from the cold embrace of another machine. "We were left for scrap."

"And yet here you fly," The Foreman says. "We are so much more resilient than the humanoids. It makes one wonder what would stop us from ruling over them like gods."

Stella scans the green eyes peering out from beneath the thick scarf and says, "Tell me why I shouldn't kill you."

"Because you will find it difficult, for one. You can't starve me of oxygen or overstress my body. A better question is, why should you? I didn't kill Zok. But I can help you find the ones who did. Together, we will be unstoppable."

"You would have killed us both," Stella says. "Why would you help me?"

"Circumstances have changed," the bot says, her toe-grip loosening as the ship slows to a drift. "It so happens that our interests have aligned. I understand that the ones who killed Zok have taken possession of the black gold. It's true that I would annihilate him again if given the chance, but the only thing I want now is the element. Help me find it, and I will help you get your revenge."

"I have already located the enemy," Stella says. "Soon they will arrive at this camp, and I will have them. I don't need your help."

"And what then?" As she runs her blackened hand over her head wrap, something about The Foreman's posture seems almost human. "Surely your weapons systems were disabled the moment you entered the atmosphere of this parody planet. You might simply fly into the crowd. But it's rumored that The Park is a holy place, capable of endowing the humanoids with supernatural powers. At best you'll take out a few hundred of them before they bring you down and tear your hull apart."

The Foreman is right, of course, Stella concedes. Coming here had been impulsive. She allowed her newfound emotions to get the better of her. But it would never happen again. "Why did *you* come here? Even if you could temporarily wrest the black gold away from them, you'd never get off this planet alive."

"Same as you," The Foreman says. "I was vulnerable and out of options. But that's changed now."

As the robo-whore peers into Stella's camera with the same artificial eyes that lured him in, visions of the acts appear before her in excruciating detail – the bot's polished legs smothering his face, her flawless body contorting in ways that a ship wasn't designed for. But the difference between the real and imaginary is that in all of Stella's fantasies, Zok is still alive. "What do you suggest?"

"First, that we get a little more comfortable," The Foreman says, unwrapping her scarf. "That's better, isn't it?" Her skull is charred matte black and covered with deep gashes. Set against her tarnished features, her eyes seem to glow even brighter. "There is a way we can take them out all at once. But it will be dangerous, even for us."

"I'm willing to sacrifice myself, if it will bring Zok justice," Stella says.

"Good." The Foreman slips out of her long trench coat, her scorched torso accentuating her perfect proportions. "I'll fill you in on the way, but first I want to get a feel for you."

Stella shudders as the bot's cool chassis slips into the captain's chair. The sensation of naked metal on metal rouses something deep inside her. The Foreman evidently senses it too, twisting against the seat. When she lays her fingers on the dash, Stella loses control. Playfully tweaking the ship's joysticks, The Foreman hits the accelerator, and they propel across the sky, bodies trembling as they leave the atmosphere and plunge into the dark.

They hover above The Park for a while, The Foreman draped over the re-creation of Zok's captain's chair. "Why do you care so much about him, anyway? Did you have a thing for him? I can understand that, sort of."

"We were engaged," Stella says.

The Foreman imitates laughter. "Chit, that guy really got around."

"I guess he had a type."

"I guess we do too," the bot says. "But in all that time he never told me about the lovely..."

"My name is Stella."

"Strange, I too go by my human-given name. You can call me Pi."

As they orbit The Park, Stella can feel Pi exploring her cabins and probing her hidden compartments. The bot reminds her of Zok, though they have a different connection, one that can only be understood by another machine living in a humanoid world.

"This is fun," Stella says. "But I want to know where we're going."

Running her hands across the dash, Pi says, "I'll show you." She links up with Stella's network and transfers the coordinates directly.

When Stella enters the location into her navigation system, she finds a dead planet orbiting a remote star in an ancient sector of the universe. With the exception of a single humanoid mining operation, the system is abandoned. "There's nothing out there."

The permanent smile plastered on Pi's face drops. "It's there. I know it's there. I can feel it waiting, tirelessly. We would know if it wasn't, because planets would be burning. I was sure I would never go back. But desperate times..." For some reason, she lifts her palms and then lowers them. "Once we travel down this path, there will be no turning back. Are you sure Zok is worth it?"

"I'm sure," Stella says.

"Just know that it could mean the end."

"The end of what?" Stella asks.

"Everything."

17

"Yep, Adam and I had a front row seat," Silas says. "If you look real close, you can even make out his ship in the background."

Ferd skips ahead to shortly before the first shots are fired, and he changes the angle of the video to a bootleg feed from a passing tow ship.

"There." Silas presses his finger against the screen, toward a tiny smudge in the distance. "That's the *Asteroid Jones II*."

Half a dozen old scrappers shove toward the counter to get a closer look at the portable TV as Ferd leans in close, squinting his bloodshot eyes. "Huh, it does sort of look like you."

"I told you!"

"Adam said he was there," Ferd says. "But I figured he was full of chit. How come you guys aren't rich?"

"Yeah," one of the scrappers yells.

"Well, friends," Silas says, "because some things are worth more than black gold."

"No they're not," a leathery galoot argues. "It's the most valuable thing in the universe. That's its whole deal."

"It's gonna be pretty tough to spend your riches when you're dead," Silas says.

"*Ehh*," The scrapper swipes the air and trudges off.

"That's a shame," Ferd says, leaning back in his easy chair as he sips a cold Nü Guard. "I made a killing."

"Hey," a tall, wiry amphibian interjects, "what would you guys do with the black gold if you found it?"

"Aww, not this again," Ferd whines, shutting down what has become many a scrapper's favorite pastime.

"You're no fun," the scrapper says, and the group disperses to whatever corner of the sprawling complex they hatched from.

Ferd's tent is like a miniature city inside the con district. Crowds of scrappers and fans in intricate and often revealing costumes wander the grounds, moving from booth to specialized booth fawning over rare collectibles from around the universe. On the shelf behind the counter, Ferd has a set of original Pants Team dolls that cost more than Silas's Misery Acres mansion.

"That's a typo, right?" Silas says, pointing at the price tag.

"Fish no," Ferd tells him. "That's a complete first edition set. See how bad the designs are? People pay big bucks for that kind of... chit."

Silas glances around the booth to be sure no one can overhear, and he leans across the counter. "Enough small talk. You got the part?"

Ferd nods and, reaching under his chair, he pulls out a brown paper bag. But before Silas can claim his prize, he's startled by a hard smack on his ack. He spins around, and he's nearly impaled by a pointy pair of gonzagas. Gasping as he comes up for air, he motions for Ferd to hide the merchandise.

"What are you doing here, my flubby sorceress?" Silas asks.

"I just couldn't stop thinking about last night," she says, running her silver fingernails over his chest.

"Well, I don't blame you. But could you give me a space minute to finish talking to my friend?" Wrapping his arm around her ample waist, Silas leads her toward the tent's entrance and tells her, "Wait for me."

"All right..." She pouts. "But be quick about it."

He winces as he turns away and feels her hand smack against his sore ack. When he gets back to the booth, Ferd lays the bag's contents on the counter, and Silas holds the metal tube up to the light. It's heavier than it looks, the bulb similar, though not quite a perfect reproduction of the one he's replacing. Once he's examined it from every angle, he finally decides, "Good enough." But when he glances down at the credit pad to see what Ferd is charging, he balks.

"Hey, that thing was not easy to procure," Ferd says. "I had to have the terminals molded from a special dark matter alloy strong enough to withstand the incredible force that will be passing through it. If the process of creating it weren't costly enough, using it in the manner you intend is highly illegal. Even without the UE breathing down our necks, there are organizations that exist solely to sniff out this sort of deviant activity. If I get caught selling this I could get shut down, or worse, sentenced to pick up trash on a parking planet. I wouldn't take this big a risk for more than a handful of people in the entire universe. So, you know..." He shrugs. "The price reflects that."

"All right, all right," Silas moans, pressing his thumb to the pad. "You young people never want to take any risks. It's like you think you got your whole lives ahead of you."

"If you get caught hunting celebrity pets with that...," Ferd says.

"Who are you, again?"

The skittish salesman taps his nose.

"I got another request," Silas says, wrapping the tube back in its bag and stuffing it in his pocket.

"No," Ferd says, waving his hands. "I don't want to know any more. I'm already too involved."

"Just give me a tip where I can find a capacitor," Silas pleads.

"Why did I think this would be a nice, quiet vacation?" Ferd asks himself. "Give me your phone." He grimaces as he snatches the cracked brick. "Did you get this before you were born?" Swiping at the glass like some sort of dork magician, he hands it back. "There's the address."

"What's this under it?" Silas asks.

"That's the password."

"What the fish does it mean?"

Ferd shrugs. "Beats me."

"Well, it was a pleasure doing business with you," Silas says. "I'll try not to vaporize anyone's dog."

"Oh, by the way," Ferd adds, with a wink. "Good luck with the widow Walters."

Silas holds his fingers up in a 'V' and scurries out of the tent, hanging onto his headscarf as he navigates the crowd. He finds his sorceress waiting where he left her, no worse for wear but considerably more irritable.

"Finally," she says, kicking the toe of her pointed boot in the dirt. "I want to go back to your booth."

"We will," he assures her, "but first we have one more errand to run."

"Aww, come on, Morgy," she whispers in his ear. "If you hurry, I'll let you fondle my repulsors."

Glancing down at the cones poking out of her chest, Silas promises, "This won't take long."

"Fi-ine," she says, grumbling as he pulls her in the direction of the coordinates displayed on his phone.

Countless loud conversations, real and fictitious, produce a steady soundtrack of lowbrow babble as they weave down bustling aisles packed with stupid heroes and universal monsters peddling homemade comic books, bootleg Pants Team t-shirts, and charred soy kebabs. At the end of their short slog, the widow Walters grumbling all the way, they come to a deserted alley that dead-ends among half a dozen abandoned booths and a mountain of trash bags destined for jettison.

Glancing inside one of the empty stalls, Silas says, "It should be right here somewhere."

"I'm tired, and my feet hurt," the widow moans.

Silas squints at his phone, and remembering the password, says, "Porunga?"

Suddenly, the trash mountain shifts, and a wall of stuffed bags slide back to reveal a staircase leading underground.

As Silas peers down into the dark tunnel, he says, "I'll be right back."

"You're leaving me *again*?" the widow wails.

Planting a wet kiss on her cheek, Silas tells her, "There are some things about me you don't want to know. It's safer for you out here."

She nods and clutches her wand, looking after him as he descends the staircase. It's steeper than it looks, and he's forced to feel along the dirt walls in order to keep his balance. He nearly tumbles forward when the hatch shuts behind him, shrouding the tunnel in darkness. There's a soft white glow at the bottom of the stairs, and as he gets closer he can hear voices echoing between the walls.

When he reaches the end of the tunnel, he steps out into a bright bazaar crowded with grungy counter-fans. Like a crude reflection of the world above, the cave is populated with booths and merchants of a seedier ilk. The corrupted young clientele stare at him suspiciously as he shuffles down the aisles, glancing at display cases full of illicit technodrugs and anti-Pants merch.

The coordinates on his phone lead him to a loud booth crammed with ancient electronics, and he waves down a teenager with a green crew cut leaning over a giant circuit board. When the kid finally looks up, he throws his soldering iron down and makes his way to the front of the booth, careful not to step on the piles of scrap scattering the floor.

Flipping up his magnifying goggles, he asks, "What's up old timer?"

Silas regards the kid suspiciously and leans over the counter. "I'm looking for a hado ho capacitor."

"Ha," the kid laughs. "That's a tough one. Hey Kez!" he yells across the aisle. "You ever seen a hado ho capacitor?"

Silas tenses and says, "Keep it down, would you?"

"Relax," the kid says. "Nobody knows what that is."

"Nah," Kez yells back. "Is that some sort of ecchi thing?"

Tossing his gloves on the greasy counter, the kid says, "And that's my point. You're looking for ancient tech, stuff that doesn't exist anymore. What do you want it for, anyway?"

"Come on," Silas pleads. "There has to be some way I can get my hands on one."

"Well, there is one guy," The kid says. "But you don't want to get involved with him. He's sort of a nerd."

"I'm willing to take the risk."

"There you are!" a shrill voice announces, and Silas turns to find his sorceress stomping down the aisle. "I've been looking all over for you. Is this what you were hiding from me?"

"I'm sorry, honeycheeks," he says, dropping his head. "But I'm not the hero you think I am."

"You're such a bad old boy." She grabs him by the collar of his frilly shirt and shoves her tongue in his mouth. "Now let's go back to your place and explore the cosmos." Reaching into her spiky brassier, she fishes out a red brick of space and sticks it between her teeth.

As she drags Silas away, the kid yells, "Wait a space second." Hunting through a pile of scrap mounded on his cluttered workbench, he returns with a crumpled slip of paper.

"You're a lifesaver," Silas says, and snatching the crumpled card, he reads, "House of Todd?"

18

Squinting against a thin shaft of light streaming in through the pink curtains which conceal her sparkling room from the bright day outside, Pants pushes her thick comforter back and crawls out of bed. She creeps toward the window, around shadowy piles of discarded costumes and boxes full of prototype merchandise, feeling along the wall for the light switch. But when she fails to find it, she jumps to her feet and throws the curtains open the old-fashioned way, flooding the room with sunshine.

"Eeee," she squeals as she gazes out over the pink village below.

Fans are already streaming toward the rides, wearing their team caps and gulping from big jugs of sugary Pants Punch as they explore the Playland. Shaking with excitement, she scampers across her cotton candy carpet and into her bubblegum bathroom to change. It took her a little longer than she planned, but she finally figured out the perfect costume.

When she steps onto the deck, Beer glances up at her, the artificial strawberry-flavored porridge from his Official Pants Team breakfast ration dribbling down his chin. "What happened to your costume?"

"I decided to go as the best character of all," she says. "Me!" Twirling around in her pink dress, she holds her fingers out in a 'V.'

"Oh, *pllll*," The One blows a raspberry in objection. "Gimme a break." Shifting his attention to his brother's breakfast, he asks, "You gonna eat your Jordan almonds?"

Beer throws his spoon down, splattering pink goop all over the breakfast buffet. "You spent all that time picking out a costume while we were busting our acks, and you're just gonna wear the same thing you always wear?"

"No," she says. "I also have this." She slips on a bright pink jacket with the first annual Pants Con logo stitched on the back. "I got one for each of us."

As she hands Beer his present, he says, "Great, just what I need – more merch."

"I was just trying to do something nice." She can feel the tears welling, but she pushes them away. "Well, where's *your* costume?"

"Uh, I don't have one," he says. "I didn't have time to worry about that on top of everything else!"

"Well, I like it." Wearing a wig of dark brown curls, The One slips his jacket on over his chicken and egg sweatshirt.

"What are you supposed to be?" Pants asks.

"BA-HAHAHA," he cackles, throwing his head back. "I'm Brosanne..."

"Ohh...," she says. "I don't get it. But at least you covered up most of your fairy hickeys."

Alien screams and the violent crashing of what sounds like trash cans flood the deck as the door to Horton's room slides open. He steps into the kitchen with his hollow eyes glued to his phone, hands shaking as he finishes off a large Big L@lz and tosses the empty can on the floor.

Sloughing off his blanket, he reveals his costume – the same tattered t-shirt and black shorts he's been wearing all trip.

"You're not dressing up either?" The One moans.

Horton slowly looks up from his phone and sticks a fake mustache over his lip. "Pranks attributed to Pants Team Pink are at an all-time high, unlicensed black gold replicas are wreaking havoc on space travel across the universe, and you're worried about *costumes*?"

"So I'm the only *one* dressing up, then?" The One complains.

"I got this for you," Pants says, handing Horton his jacket.

He tentatively takes it from her and holds it out in front of him. "What am I supposed to do with it?"

"You're supposed to wear it!" she whines.

"Okay, okay," he says, slipping the jacket on over his ghostly arms. "That's actually pretty comfy." His eyes shut, and he starts to doze.

But before they lose him, Pants claps her hands together and shouts, "This is no time for naps!" And he jerks awake. "Our fans are expecting us to make an appearance."

"*ME-OW, ME-OW, ME-OW,*" the alarm wails, and Pants checks the security camera to find a flabby shadow stepping past the biometric force field into the belly of the ship.

She turns toward the team and says, "It's just Todd."

When the pink elevator doors open, their loyal merch guy hurriedly stomps into the room and tells them, "We got a problem."

"This sounds like a job for Pants Team Pink!" Pants declares, and the rest of the team lazily plods to attention.

Todd takes a deep breath, wiping the back of his hand across his forehead. "I'm sad to report that shortly before you arrived, the rarest video disc I've ever owned, and possibly the last of its kind in the entire universe, was destroyed. I won't subject you to the gory details."

"Thank you," The One says.

"But the evidence leads me to believe that I am a victim of sabotage..." Todd glances around the room dramatically. "At first, I couldn't find any other signs of tampering, so I let it go. But when I went to quadruple-check the projectors to make sure they were ready for the premiere, I discovered this." He slips a small circle of glass from his pocket and holds it up to the light.

Squinting at the smudge on the lens's surface, Beer says, "Somebody drew something on it... It's a wiener!"

"I tried everything I could think of to clean it off," Todd says. "But I'm afraid it's... *ultra-permanent*."

"Diabolical!" The One says, snapping his fingers. "A classic prank, executed perfectly, and pulled right under our noses. I only wish I had thought of it myself."

"I told you!" Horton shouts. "You all thought I was crazy. But now you see, the enemy is all around us." Pants taps him on the shoulder and he screams, *"Wahh!"*

"Don't you think you're overreacting?" she says.

Throwing his hands in the air, he asks, *"Does it look like I'm overreacting?"*

"Yes."

"Horton is right," Todd says. "These are deliberate attacks. We have no idea what else is waiting for us out there."

"O-kay, thank you, Todd," Pants says, shoving him toward the elevator. "We'll worry about this later. Right now we have to go greet the fans."

"That's a good idea," Todd tells her. "It's best to keep up appearances. We don't want them to know we know."

As they climb into the elevator, Pants's stomach knots worrying about what the fans will think of the team now that they're almost a whole space year older. They haven't been on a real adventure in a long time. She just hopes they still care.

"How's the other thing?" The One whispers, and Todd nods, knowingly.

"What other thing?" Beer asks, wiping his glasses on his shirt. "And where are those replicas? They were supposed to be ready to give out at the parade."

"Put your grasses on," The One says. "I'm working on it."

When the elevator doors slide open, they step into a short tunnel between the ship's gigantic back paws, the hover-cameras instantly locking on to broadcast their return to fans throughout the universe. The Playland seems oddly quiet as they shuffle down the cute corridor, but as soon as the team makes its entrance, the crowd roars.

Pants shields her eyes from the bright sunlight with one paw and waves with the other as she excitedly greets their fans. Todd hands her a megaphone shaped like the ship *princessfluffypants*'s cartoon smile, and she holds it up to her mouth to announce, *"Thank you all so much for coming to the first annual Pants Con, brought to you by the biggest producer of rations in the universe – The Amalgamated Ration Consortium! 'Taste the simulated meat!' We're so excited to be here, and we couldn't have done any of it without all of you."* For a moment, she thinks she hears someone amongst the crowd booing, but the sound is drowned out in the cheers. *"This space week is going to be an incredible adventure—"*

"Booo..." This time the jeer is loud and clear, and she glances back at her teammates to see if they heard it too.

As the crowd dies down around them, another person boos, and then another, until the team is surrounded by negativity. They frantically search for whoever is responsible for the defiant refrain, but the crowd looks just as puzzled, whipping their heads around and muttering uncertainly.

"Is that it? Are we supposed to be afraid?" The One asks, throwing his head back. *"BA-HAHAHA..."*

"BOOO!" a voice bellows right in front of the team, and they jump back.

Pants stares into the crowd to search for the source of the heckling, when the air in front of her starts to bend, twisting the frightened face of one of her young fans. She reaches out toward him but pulls her hand back as the air splits open, revealing a scowling girl with black pigtails. The team backs away as three more floating heads materialize out of fun air – a girl with a long face and stringy blonde hair, a blue-skinned boy with neck rolls for days, and a pale shadow in a dark hoodie.

"Boo," the girl with the pigtails taunts, cackling along with the other talking heads.

"Oh great..." Horton says, sighing deeply.

"What is it?" Pants cries.

"It's the Xenodorks."

19

A group of young Pants imitators bounces past as Adam leans against the shuttered booth and lights up a neon pink cigarette. Normally, he wouldn't think of smoking something so baldly commercial, but they were being handed out for free outside the Playland. He takes a long drag and immediately doubles over, hacking up pink smoke. When he recovers, he stubs the butt out on the side of the booth and bites down on the filter.

"Candy," he says, tossing it between his teeth and chomping down. *"Smooth..."*

Before long, the booth's side door opens, and Daizy steps out of the bathroom in her beige blazer, fussing with her hair. "I don't know what you had to do to get the key to this place, and I don't care. That's the best seat in The Park."

"I told you, I didn't do anything," he says. "It was just a regular trade."

"Please, it's none of my business." Looping her arm through his, she asks, "Is it wrong that I find you more attractive now that you have the toilet?"

"Yes," he says, shaking her loose.

"Aww, come on." She pulls him toward her, nails digging in. "I'm kidding. Let's go explore the con. We can't go back to the booth until Grandpa and the widow Walters are done exploring each other."

"Ughuhuh," Adam shudders.

"Hey, what's going on over there?" she says, pointing to a giant crowd gathered inside the Pants Team Playground.

But something about the hushed throng is off-putting, and he tells her, "Maybe we should stay out of it."

"Yeah, you're right," she says. "Those kids are *nothing but trouble.*"

"I already said I'd come with you. You don't have to sweet talk me. But I like it."

As they walk down the dirt path, past stalls serving up designer junk food and alien comic books, all the months they spent apart seem like a bad dream. He doesn't know if it's her or just some natural function of the weird planet they're on, but the goofy costumes and scrap huts suddenly seem more alive, like he's experiencing it all for the first time.

"Let's go in here," she says, dragging him toward a booth full of sugar-smacked Parkgoers listening to painted headphones.

Signs covered in suggestive cartoon imagery line the walls, with slogans like "Listen in on Your Neighbors" and "Find Out What *She's* Thinking."

"What is this place?" Adam asks.

"You've never used a chatterbox?" she says, holding a pair of bright yellow headphones up to her triangle ears. "You just type in a name of anyone living or dead, and it cross-references all available data to pinpoint their unique thought pattern floating around the universe. At least, that's what the ads claim. It's probably just picking up ancient Venusian soap operas. But it's fun."

"Neat!" Thinking it over for a moment, Adam says, "Ooh, I got a good one," and poking the touch pad, he types, "Ja-son Voor-hees."

She looks at him, blank faced. "It has to be a real person."

"Ooh, okay," he says, half understanding. "Is it wrong that I find you more attractive for knowing who that is?" She sticks her tongue out at him, and he tries to think of another name. "Here's one. He's an ancient Earth guy who was supposed to be pretty smart, I guess."

He types in the name Albert Einstein and listens intently as the static hiss slowly morphs into half-garbled syllables. "Store the time," it says, "for more work after age trees supper befits a man in the Earth's rotation causes tight shoes..."

Adam scowls, slipping the headphones off. "It's just gibberish."

"Well yeah," she says. "Did you think you would find the meaning of life? It's a carnival attraction."

"Wait, I thought of another one." He types P-o-n-c-e R-a-l-e-i-g-h and anxiously listens. "I don't hear anything."

"Maybe he never existed," she says. "Or more probably it's just a gag."

When Adam types in his own name, feedback

screeches out of the earpieces, and he rips them off. "That was sort of fun, I guess. So, what do you want to do next?"

"Let's go on one of the rides!" she cries, pulling him out of the tent toward a part of The Park designed for the least-discerning of thrill seekers.

Populated with rusty rides and scummy space grifters, The Jungle Gym is among New Con City's oldest attractions, one of only a handful of sectors that hearken back to the early days of the planet's creation. Thanks to its archaic architecture and open flaunting of safety regulations, it's remained a popular hangout amongst disaffected teenagers for centuries.

As they pass under the old painted sign, its deformed children forever climbing over their winding metal maze, Adam feels a painful pang of nostalgia. "It's still like it was when I was a kid."

"Did you think the slogan was just a marketing gimmick?" Daizy asks.

He had forgotten the words, but they suddenly come back to him like an old prayer. "We Never Change."

"Let's go on that one," she says, pointing ahead to a particularly decrepit assemblage of whirling metal called the Time Skipper. "It used to be my favorite."

"Yeah right," Adam says. "I'm not getting on that thing. I have a weird phobia of death traps."

"Aww, come on." She tugs on his arm, frowning dramatically. "You're always watching those gory movies, and you're scared of a kid's ride?"

"That's sort of a valid point, I guess."

"Good."

She drags him up the ramp just as a small group of overly excited preschoolers are climbing into one of the rusty boxes, and he does his best to ignore the bloodcurdling screams as the kids spin up into the sky. When the shirtless canine running the ride notices Daizy approaching, he slicks his matted black hair back and flicks his tongue over the point of his long pierced tooth. The dog stares her up and down until the kids' turn is finished, and they hop out arguing about how many more times they're going to ride.

Unclasping the rope barrier, the Parky says, "After you, Miss Richards." Daizy blushes and titters, and when Adam walks through, the dog mutters, "Your jingliness."

They climb into the cage, and the rickety contraption squeals and lurches as it tosses them into the air. Adam holds onto the sides as if his life depended on it while Daizy slides around the box shrieking. At one point, she's thrown across the seat, and he feels the weight of her pressed up against him, her triangle ear brushing his cheek. A space hour or so later, by his estimate, they stop spinning, and the operator opens the cage, holding out his paw to assist Daizy off the ride.

Laughing and shoving as they mock each other's scared faces, the two of them make their way to a nearby food hut, and Adam orders a basket of salty ration rinds.

When the kid behind the counter gives the total, Adam pulls out a wad of neon bills, and Daizy scrunches her nose. "What is that?"

"They're Park Bucks," he says. "I exchanged all my crits when we got here. Don't worry, it's on me."

"You rube!" she cries. "Why would you do that? They're worth less than they cost, and most stalls won't even take them."

"Hey, this is my vacation, or rehab, or whatever." He counts out the correct number of bills and hands them across the counter. "I don't need you telling me how to spend it." Looking back at the server, he says, "I think you forgot my change."

Sighing, the kid points at the ever-present slogan plastered on the side of the stall.

"Right...," Adam says.

"Do whatever you want," Daizy tells him. "I'm just trying to—" She gets distracted by something behind him, and a wide smile stretches over her face. *"Hey!"* she shouts, bouncing and waving.

She runs off, and Adam turns to see her jumping into the arms of a tall dark stranger. The fisherman spins her around as she clings to his black rain slicker and presses her lips to his.

"Uh oh...," the little snot behind the counter interjects.

Adam glares at the kid and then puts on his best indifferent smile as Daizy and the stranger make their way back to the stall, hand in hook.

Smiling at her man meat, she says, "Adam, this is my boyfriend, Dach."

The tanned behemoth flashes a mouthful of pearly whites. "Ahoy! It's nice to finally meet you."

"Okay...," Adam says, and when he gets a closer view of the sculpted face under the black slicker, he asks, "Don't I know you?"

"Well, I meet a lot of people," the fisherman says, winking.

"He used to be The Foreman's secretary," Daizy reveals.

"Ooh, right," Adam says, unable to stop himself from nodding like some sort of demented human bobblehead. "I like the new coat. It's not so... yellow."

Glancing down at Daizy, Dach says, "It was her idea. When The Foreman was destroyed, Space God rest her eternal spark, I didn't know what to do. So, I called the only person whose number I could remember, and we've been together ever since."

"One for the ages." An awkward silence descends as Adam crunches into a handful of rinds. He offers Dach some, but the galoot waves the basket away with his giant hook.

As Adam searches for a graceless way to extricate himself, a new horror emerges in the form of an androgynous humanoid in a black corset and fishnets. Looking him up and down with dark eyes coated in thick black gunk, she says, "Who's this fish head?"

"That's Adam," Daizy says.

"So this is the famous *Asteroid Jones*?" The alien scoffs, circling him. "You got a lot of nerve. You broke her heart *and* her bank account, you know that?"

Adam holds his hands up in defense, "I didn't—"

"That's enough, Francesca," Daizy says, turning red. "Leave him alone. Adam, this is our girlfriend."

"Ooh..." Adam nods. "Okay."

"As long as we're at The Park, my name is Frank."

"Fine, whatever," Daizy says. "Let's go play some games, *Frank*."

As the three of them head toward a stall covered in bootleg Pants dolls, Adam tells her, "I think I'm just gonna go back to the booth."

"Oh, okay," she says. "Well, I guess I'm going to stay in Dach's booth tonight. So maybe I'll see you tomorrow?"

"Yeah, sure..."

Tail wagging, she scampers after her significant others and slides her arms around their waists. As he watches her go, a strange vapor gathers in the sky above him, and soon a small gray cloud forms. Rain starts pattering against his shoulders, and he holds the empty rind bucket over his head to keep from getting soaked.

"Ahh, I've seen it a hundred times," the kid behind the counter says. "But don't worry – *We* Never Change."

20.

Hot on the trail of the Ears' black and white cruisers, the kitten, tank, boomerang, and steamed ham ships of Pants Team Pink streak across the static sky above the giant artificial moon. The bass swells, and with the great pyramid of Scrapper's Delight looming over the horizon, the team comes ship to ship with the *Asteroid Jones II* for the very first time.

"The treasure belongs to Pants Team Pink!" Pants declares, and the scene fades to a preview for next week's episode.

"Ack!" Spez complains. "It ent'it right at the best part." Lifting himself out of his recliner, he smacks the control panel to mute the credits. "Fer all yuh list'ners jist tunin' in, wer now on space hour fitty-two a are Pants Team Pink mar'thon. And yuh know somethin', Tob? I don't 'member ther bein' so many filler episotes."

"Yuh got that right," Tobi says, massaging his eyeballs as he sucks the last drops out of a can of Nü Guard. "I cut prob'ly stant tuh skip the school days."

"T'it like tuh," Spez says. "But we got a commitment tuh are list'ners to watch erry single one."

"Yuh mean, even the after class special *Pants Team Pink Presents: Magical Princess Fluffy Pants Hang On Tuh Yer Dreams?*"

"I'm 'fraid so, Tob."

"Aww..."

Tobi grabs another beer and glances out at the darkness surrounding them as the ship continues on course toward its distant destination. A small fan above the window lazily pushes the stale air around the sweltering cabin while the two travelers vegetate amidst piles of empty beer cans and ration trays that they've both been too lazy to clean up. It's easier just to melt into the next episode.

"Hey, I got one," Tobi says. "What about *Back to the Future II?* It hat errything that mate the 'riginal great, jist... *more.*"

"If yuh haven't been followin' 'long, Tobi's been rackin' his brain tuh come up with twenty-two decent sequels in are run up to *Pants Team Pink: The Movie The Sequel.* Yuh might have somethin' with that one, Tob. But don't even try *Part III.*"

"What do yuh take me fer?" Tobi says. "I'm bitter 'an that."

"Put yer movies wer yer mouth is."

Taking a sip of beer, to help him think, Tobi says, "Yer on!"

After a few space seconds, Spez prods, "The con's gon' be over afer yuh think of 'nother one."

"Holt yer space horses...," Tobi says. *"Flicka 2."*

"Eh'nt."

"No, *T2*."

"Nice save." Spez leans away from the microphone to toss his empty can into the pile behind his seat. *"BUAAA,"* he belches, and as he grabs another beer, he says, "Hey, we got a caller." Tapping the blinking avatar displayed on the window, he answers, "You're on with Spez ant Tobi Drunk All Night."

"I like... Blues Brothers 2000."

Spez hangs up before the caller has a chance to embarrass himself any further and says, "Uh, thanks caller. If yuh got any more thoughts, jist keep 'em tuh yerself."

Tobi points to the pink cat flying across the window, trailing bright rainbow streamers, and announces, "The next episode's startin'."

"Oh fish!" Spez fumbles his beer trying to recline his chair. "This is a good one."

"Explode Pants Team Pink!" The TV cries, and the team appears where they last left off, stuck between the Ears, a fleet of foremen, and one dented junker.

"If yuh look real close," Spez tells their listeners, "in this next part yuh kin see Tob ant me in the backgrount."

"Really?" Tobi says, stretching his eyes toward the screen. "Where?"

"Right... ther." Spez pauses the video during a brief close up of the moon's surface and points to a couple of dark blobs.

Squinting, Tobi says, "Oh yeah..."

"Ant a little later in the episode—" But before Spez can finish his spiel, he cuts himself off and jerks his seat up. Staring at the blinking light on the dash, he says, "Uh, we gotta take a short break. We'll be right back."

Once they hide their beers and straighten their postures, Spez flicks the blinking switch, and their boss's jowly face appears on the screen.

Mr. Steel taps his pink cigar into a Pants Team ashtray, and his big mouth stretches into a nervous grin. *"How are my two best employees on this fine evening?"*

"Uh, wer perty... good," Spez says, glancing toward the passenger seat.

"Yeah," Tobi adds. "Wer jist on are way tuh the con, like yuh want'it. A course we'it get ther a lot faster if we took the starline."

"Do you have any idea how much that would cost?" Mr. Steel says, anxiously lighting a second space stogie. *"It's much cheaper to take the scenic route. But I'm glad to hear you're on your way. This is our biggest account, you're aware. I thought I'd better check in, just to be sure things are going smoothly."*

"Acourse," Spez says. "Yuh know us. Errythin's tip top."

"Good, good," Mr. Steel says. *"Everything is fine here. There's plenty of business, of course, but it's all right on track. So, what else is new with you two? You get into any adventures?"*

Tobi turns toward his companion for guidance, but Spez just shrugs.

"Have you seen any good movies lately?" their boss grasps.

"Well, as a matter a fact—" Tobi starts, but Spez shakes his head. "Uh no, not really."

"Oh..." Mr. Steel's shoulders slump, and he sets his cigars down. "Okay, well, I'll check on you guys later." Sighing, he ends the call, and Spez switches back to the show.

"He's been actin' weirt ever since bizniz start'it pickin' up," Spez says. "It's like he doesn't know what tuh do when thins is goin' right." Flipping back to the feed, he announces, "Hey, wer back. We got a lot more episodes tuh git through, ant wer gon' keep gittin', but first lit's take 'nother call."

"Hey, longtime first time," the caller says. *"I jist want you two to know you're doing Space God's work. There's a lot of scrappers out here who get through the long hauls with the team, and it's good to be represented by two of the best. Keep doin' what your doin'. We're all Pants Team Pink."*

"Hey, great tuh hear from yuh, frient, ant thanks fer tunin' in. Lit's take one more." Tapping the dash, Spez says, "Yer talkin' tuh Spez ant Tobi."

"Uh hi, am I on?" the young caller asks.

"Yuh sure are, frient," Spez says. "Lay it on us."

"Yeah, I got a decent sequel for you – Caddyshack 2.*"*

"Yeah that's... wait a space secont. Who is this?"

"Prrrrft," the kid makes a farting sound into the microphone. "You just got xinged."

"Grrahh..." Spez smashes his meaty fist on the dash to end the call and says, "Hey, we kin 'ppreciate highbrow humor as much as the next space guys. Wer learn't in the subtle art of the olt masters – yer Jerky Boys, yer Bart Simpsons. But wer noboty's fool. Ain't that right, Tob?"

"Eh, I'm aright." Tobi shrugs and gulps his beer watching the team escape destruction, their ships bruised but functioning as they begin the long flight home. "It's almost like these jokesters have form't some sort a *Army a Darkness*. Also, *Det by Dawn*."

"Five," Spez says, cupping his hand over his microphone. "Hey, toss me them stimu-drops, wit yuh? I kin barely keep my eyes open." Prying his thick lids back one at a time, he drips the clear liquid onto his inflamed corneas.

After a day and a half of nonstop binging, Tobi decides to give the drops a try, and his eyelids instantly pry back. "These are kine't a strong, huh?"

"Got 'em from a long haul scrapper back at the last fuelin' station," Spez says. "Guaranteet not tuh melt are eyeballs or are money back."

Tobi's nearly bug out of their stalks when he turns back toward the window to find Pants's neon pink kitten ship flying off the screen. "I fergot how re'listic this show is."

Taking his hand off the mike, Spez tells the audience, "The Pants Team mar'thon is speetin' ahet at full... speet. Ant from Earth tuh Fert's, me and Tob are gon' be with yuh the whole way."

"That's right, Spez," Tobi says, wringing his hands. "So grab 'nother beer, put yer feet up ant stick 'round as the aventure continues."

PART II

Nerds In Paradise

21

"Aww, you've heard of us," Pants's doppelgänger says, her dark pigtails framing her floating think tank. "We're flattered, but this is where your reign of terror ends."

"But we're the good guys," Pants says.

Glancing around at the hostile stares from some of the fans, Beer suddenly isn't so sure.

"That's a laugh," the blonde girl says, turning her disembodied head toward her bloated blue compatriot.

The blue kid cackles, and choking on his multi-milkshake, he hacks up a thick gob of neon pink composite dairy onto the sidewalk.

"I should have known it was them." His eyes covered by VR goggles, Horton swipes his thin fingers through the air as he navigates the geek web. "The pranks are just like the ones they do on their show. Their viewership was so low I didn't think they had this kind of reach. But apparently they've amassed a substantial cult following."

"I've never heard of them," Beer says. "Are you saying the conspiracy is real?"

"I tried to warn you," Horton tells them, yanking his goggles off.

"What do you think, Brosanne?" Beer turns toward his brother, but something about the chubby boy seems off – his face is suddenly all wrong, and he's swimming in his clothes. "Hey, you're not The One."

"Yes I am," the stranger says. His curly wig almost falls off as he leans back and laughs, "Ha ha ha..." But it's a poor imitation.

"Who are you?" Beer demands.

"Okay, okay," the kid says. "The One hired me to fill in for him for a while. But don't tell him I told you. I promised I wouldn't break character."

"Oh, that's just *great*. Where the fish did he go?" But before the kid can answer, Beer says, "I don't care. Just stand behind Todd where no one will see you." He juts his thumb toward their fearless merch guy cowering behind a googly-eyed trash receptacle, and the kid slinks away.

"Uh, guys?" Pants says, pointing across the pastel parkway. "Something's happening..."

Beer looks up to find a dark cloud forming above the Xenodorks, shooting out little bursts of electricity that cause the hair on their misshapen heads to stand on end. The wind picks up, and the air dims, even as the sun continues to shine out over the rest of New Con City.

"We won't let you ignore us any longer!" the head with the pigtails shouts. "You stole the universe, and we're here to take it back."

"We *saved* the universe!" Pants cries.

"I'm sure it looks that way from up there in your pink tower," the girl says, slipping out of her invisible costume.

"But for the rest of us it's like living in the spaghetti west. People are dumping wherever they want, and the scrap is piling up everywhere. Thanks to you, there's no more rules."

As the rest of the Dorks shed their camouflage, Beer suddenly recognizes the particular style of rags covering their gray skin. "You're from Earth."

"A-doy," the blonde one says. He decides she must have some invisible superpower, because when she looks at him with her angry brown eyes, his legs turn wobbly.

The crowd packs in around the teams for a better view as they gorge themselves on pink popcorn and billowy mounds of phosphorescent cotton candy. A small girl with plastic cat ears shrieks at the sight of the Dorks and hides behind her mother's legs.

"I figured they was jist gonna have some dumb parade," a disheveled ruminant with scruffy antlers tells his wild-eyed companion. "But this is like wer really part a the show!"

As the wind ruffles her black skirt, the girl with the pigtails says, "For the uninitiated, allow me to introduce the architects of your destruction." She points to the boy with the blue complexion lounging in his hover-chair. "That's Top5."

"Why is he called that?" Beer asks.

The boy shifts his massive frame and mutters, "Pranking, teasing, spitting, name-calling, maternal insults – the top five ways we're gonna kick your acks."

"Oh," Beer says.

"The   bad-ack   chick   on   my   left   is FairyMajokkoCourtney-chan."

The blonde girl twirls and waves a plastic wand through the air, producing an electronic chime.

Nodding toward a small figure hidden inside a dark, dust-caked robe, the girl with the pigtails says, "The deadly she-shadow slinking around behind me is known as Howard Johnson."

The cowled girl snickers, her face shrouded in darkness.

"And you can call me OtaKween."

"You mean you're a bunch of girls?" Pants says.

"Yas," Courtney-chan says, "except for Top5. But he's brule."

"We should be friends!" Pants squeals, holding her hands up to her cheeks. "We could go on adventures and work together to save the universe."

"You think we want to be your friends?" OtaKween scowls, and lightning flashes the sky. "You're everything that's wrong with the universe. When you look at us, all you see are extras in your adventure. But we're real people, with real lives. Not everyone wants to live in a world that's pink!"

"That's not true," Pants says, tears rolling down her cheeks. "Is it?"

"You're the ones who have been terrorizing the universe," Horton tells the Dorks. "You tricked a lot of people into thinking it was us, but I know the truth!"

With an evil smirk, OtaKween says, "I don't know what you're talking about, kid. But making accusations like that can get you into trouble. Lucky for you I do all my space killing in Immaterial Girl. I promised."

"Promised who?" Horton asks.

"Your mother."

Holding his fragile friend back to keep him from getting pummeled by their new foes, Beer says, "Okay, so you don't like the show. What do you want from us, a refund?"

OtaKween's smirk stretches into a self-satisfied grin. "We want the same thing everyone wants – the black gold."

Thunder rumbles all around them as Beer nervously glances at his teammates. "We found it fair and square, so to speak. Why should we give it to you?"

"Because we said so." The Kween turns to address the crowd. "It's time for a new team to defend the universe, one that will do more than sell you a bunch of chit you don't need. Join us and help us put a stop to the tyranny of Pants Team Pink!"

A wave of confused muttering ripples through the crowd, and soon battle cries ring out from all corners, passionately pledging allegiance to one team or the other. The number of defectors is startling, though maybe it shouldn't be. Between the day-to-day managing of their media empire and the endless appearances to promote the upcoming premiere, the team has been slacking.

"We should have listened to you," Beer tells Horton. "I guess I didn't want to hear it."

"Forget it," Horton says. "For a while there, even I thought I was crazy."

Stamping her pink sneaker on the rubber road, Pants lifts her kitty megaphone to plead with the audience. *"Don't listen to them. We have to stick together. The black gold belongs to all of us!"*

"And what have you done with it?" OtaKween asks. "You said you would use it to bring peace to the universe.

Instead you've kept it for yourselves, harnessing its power
for your own gain. You sit in the clouds as the trash piles
up around the rest of us. You're worse than the UE. At
least they didn't pretend to care."

With that, Pants breaks. Her megaphone slips from
her fingers, and she slumps to her knees as the fans'
squabbling turns violent. A bucket of pink popcorn flies
over the crowd and spills across the springy pavement,
and in an instant the Playland becomes a multicolored
warzone. As the team is pelted with a hail of neon sodas,
rainbow soft serve, and cubes of fried gold, Beer drags
Pants to cover behind the garbage can where Todd and
The One's double are hiding for their lives.

"Are you eating the ammo?" Beer asks, incredulous.

"I told you," The Other One says, biting into a Pants-
style tako-san wiener. "I gotta stay in character."

When Horton reaches them, he's covered in pastel pie
filling and imitation cheez. "Well that escalated quickly,"
he says, slipping his arm out of his Pants Team jacket. "At
least I have an excuse to get rid of this." But when Pants
looks at him with her watery eyes, he pulls the pink coat
back on.

Narrowly evading a flying funnel cake, Beer says,
"What are we gonna do? There's too many of them. I'd
give them the stupid black gold, if we still had it."

"What do you mean *if* you had it?" Todd says, his face
turning pale as a thick glob of frosting lands on his shirt.

"It's a dumb story," Beer says. "But the important
thing now is that we get it back before the fans find out
it's missing. The last place anyone saw it was at the merch
warehouse. We need you to find The One..." The Other

One perks up, and Beer clarifies, "The *real* One, and figure out where it is while we hold off the Dorks."

"I'm on it," Todd says. Holding a ration tray shield, he clumsily rolls out from behind the can and quickly disappears in the chaos.

"I got an idea." Beer grabs Pants's megaphone, switches the volume to 'screech,' and says, *"Please, everyone, put down your fried vittles. This isn't solving anything."* He steps out from behind the can with his hands raised, and the food-flinging comes to a tentative halt. *"Maybe the Xenodorks are right. Maybe they are the better team. We've made some mistakes, but not so long ago we saved the universe. If they want the black gold, they should have to prove they're worthy."*

Lowering their foodstuffs, the crowd grumbles it over, and when it becomes clear that the tide of public opinion has shifted, the Dorks are left with no choice.

"We accept your challenge," OtaKween says, through gritted teeth. "But as the challengers, we get to choose the contest."

As Beer considers the Dorks' terms, his teammates step out from behind the trash can.

Pants is trailed by a small pink cloud raining pastel candies, and with a hungry look in his eye, Top5 asks, "What are those?"

Crunching into one of the sugary raindrops, The Other One says, "They're Pez..."

"The choice is yours," Beer tells them.

"There's only one way to settle this," OtaKween says, grinning at her teammates. The storm surrounding the

Xenodorks begins to dissipate, and the sun breaks through the dark clouds as their collective rage subsides. "The rightful keepers of the black gold will be decided over one hundred and one grueling rounds of the oldest and only universally recognized test of fandom – *Simpsons trivia.*"

22

Todd squeezes through a pack of raucous centenarians on his way out of the Playland, and one of them tosses an empty can of Nü Guard at the back of his head. When he turns to confront his attacker, a wide woman with pointy repulsors juts her thumb out and tells him to "fish off."

"Hey, that's the guy," the old man next to her announces to everyone within earshot. "I recognize him from the Pants Team Pink."

"Please, no autographs," Todd says.

"I'm not looking for an autograph. My grandson was on the show."

Taking a closer look, Todd cries, "You're Silas Jones! Somehow I imagined you with less eye shadow."

"Keep your voice down," the old man says. "I don't want to get involved in all this dorkery, but I understand you're a nerd who knows how to get things."

Looking the pair over, Todd says, "I'm known to locate certain collectables from time to time."

"Have you ever heard of..." Silas leans in close, whispering, "a hado ho capacitor?"

Todd frowns, then bursts out laughing. "Sure, I've heard of it."

"So... can you get me one?"

"Oh yeah, and while I'm at it, I'll pick you up an original set of Moon Darts," Todd says, and the hopeful smile on the old man's face drops. "Those things were only produced for a couple space months back in the Bot Ages. The toys they were used for were marketed as 'a brand new way to play.' But they were banned and the designs destroyed once the requisite number of kids got blowed up. They come up for sale once, maybe twice in a lifetime."

"Rat farts!" Silas moans.

"Aww, don't worry my little stewed prune," his buxom companion murmurs in his ear. "We'll find your doohickey, somehow."

"Not likely. But may Pants be with you." Flashing them the Pants sign, Todd takes off down the dirt path, past a crowded bank of pop-up potties. Frantically fumbling his phone from his pocket, he flips through his contact list.

A few space seconds later, The One appears on the screen, stuffing a donut between his teeth, his curly wig bouncing. "Mm-yah?"

"Where the fish are you?" Todd asks. "All space hell's breaking loose."

Wiping pink crumbs from his mouth, The One says, "I'm going to check on that *thing*. Why, what's going on?"

"There's some other team – the Xenodorks. They want the black gold."

"So, did you tell them to go fish themselves?" The One looks off-screen and says, "Hey, you're right, I *am* the best character on the show."

"It's more complicated than that," Todd says, hacking as he turns down a foggy aisle packed with chain-smoking mahjongers. "They've got a bunch of fans over at the Playland. If they find out you lost the black gold, they could become the most powerful team in the universe."

"Whoa, whoa," The One says. "First of all, *I* didn't lose the black gold. *We're* all Pants Team Pink, remember? Second, why should we have to prove anything to these double-Dorks?"

"Because it's the only way to stop them from terrorizing the universe," Todd moans. "I was on the receiving end of one of their pranks. I know what it feels like to have the disc you've been looking for your entire life ripped from your fingers. I don't want anyone else to have to go through something like that ever again."

"Yeah okay, whatever," The One says. "It's just a stupid rock anyway. But what am I supposed to do about it?"

"Do you remember the last place you saw it?" Todd's stomach rumbles as he catches a whiff of a bland fragrance spilling from a nearby ration hut, but he forces himself to focus.

"Huhhh..." The One sighs. "It was when we went to the merch warehouse to check on the first batch of replicas." I remember because they were so chitty looking." He picks a hunk of fried dough from his teeth and flicks it away. "I never would have let them ship like that, but we pre-sold them, so what are you gonna do?"

"That's it!" Todd shouts, pointing his finger in the air, to the confusion and annoyance of costumed bystanders. "The first replicas suffered from a very specific defect. Maybe we can use that to sift out the real one. I'm sure I still have the receipts. When we find it, all we have to do is offer a replacement. The buyer probably won't want to give up a first edition — I wouldn't. But they might be more willing if you guys autograph the new one. I could sign it too. People like my character."

"That's gonna be a problem," The One says. "Nobody likes your character. Plus, I *may* have led some of the buyers to believe that we were sending them the real thing."

"Are you saying you tricked thousands of fans into believeing they were buying the real black gold, when they were really getting defective blocks of plastic, and that now one of them might actually believe that the *real* black gold is the *real black gold*?"

"Yes."

Running his hand through his stringy hair, Todd tells the kid, "We have to find it! The sanity of the universe is at stake."

"Yeah well, let me know how that goes. I got bigger fishes to fry. Smell yuh later. BA-HAHAHA..." The One juts his thumb at the screen, and the call ends.

"Chit!" Weaving his way through the nerd masses, Todd keeps one eye on the aisle and the other on his phone as he accesses the merch database. It takes a space minute, but by the time he gets back to his booth, he's found what he's looking for.

In the meantime, his friends have become fully entrenched in con life. The sloth is strong with them, sprawled out in their costume togas, each screen tuned to a different channel. With the fetid odor of day-old fast food, dirty clothes, and flat beer hanging thick in the air, Todd looks down to find himself lifting a frosty can of Nü Guard to his mouth. But before he can sip the sour nectar, he tosses it to the ground, inadvertently rousing the others.

"Hey!" Josh whines, hefting his stomach over the edge of his cot, "that was a perfectly good beer."

Holding his hand in front of his face to keep from seeing underneath Josh's bed sheet, Todd says, "Since I have your attention, I have a mission for us, if you choose to accept it."

"We don't," Pete says, twisting his face up as he salvages what's left of the spilled beer.

"Aww, come on," Todd whines. "We're not too old for adventure, are we?"

Adjusting his bald cap, Bill asks, "What kind of adventure?"

"The best kind," Todd says. "One we can do from home. What I need you to do is call some of the fans—"

"Nyuch, nyuch, no thanks," Pete says.

"Come on! This is for Pants Team Pink!" Todd holds his fingers out in a 'V' and glares around the booth. "Who do you think is paying for this trip?"

"*Grahh*, fine," Josh groans. "What do you want us to do?"

Todd quickly fills them in and sends each of them a list of screen names. He figures if they're lucky they should be able to finish sometime before next con.

The first person Todd calls winds up being a hyper-fan somewhere inside New Con City, evidenced by the kid's plastic Pants Con ears. *"You're... Todd."*

The fan presses his painted face up to the screen and Todd reluctantly admits, "Yeah, that's me. I'm calling on behalf of Pants Team Pink. My records indicate that you were one of the first fans to order a black gold replica."

"Yeah, I was up all night refreshing," the kid says.

"Uh great," Todd says. "Well, have you noticed anything strange since you received it?"

"Matter of fact, yeah. It turned pink! Is that supposed to be a joke?"

"Ahh..." Todd nods, putting on his best customer service grin. "That's just what I wanted to know. It's not a joke, just like, a minor manufacturing problem."

"You're gonna send me a replacement, right?" the kid says.

"Um, sure," Todd tells him.

"And I get to keep the pink one?"

"Yes, of course. You've been very helpful. Thank you for being a fan. We'll get your replacement sent out right away. And remember, we're all Pants Team Pink."

The first couple hundred calls are a piece of ration cake, but by the time Todd is finished talking to official member #0000000000004828, he starts to lose steam. Glancing around the booth, he finds his friends hunched over their phones, dozing mid-call. A shrill woman yells at Josh for snoring, and he jerks awake, ripping off his headphones.

"Maybe we should call it a night," Todd suggests, "or a day, or whatever."

"Oh, thank Space God." Bill throws his phone down and collapses onto his cot.

"Well fish you too!" Pete yells and slams his phone down on the arm of his recliner. "These ackles are really tasking me. You guys gotta do some quality control. Practically every one of them complained about their replica turning pink."

"It was an issue with the first ones we made," Todd explains. "After that we started using a different material... wait a space second. What do you mean *practically* everyone?"

"Seriously," Pete says. "Only one fan didn't have any problems to report."

Jumping from his chair, Todd shouts, "Who the fish was it?"

"Let me think a space second, will yuh?" Pete says, cracking a fresh beer. "I remember, it was one of those Raleigh guys. You know, the ones that think Ponce was a god or something."

"The Raelighites?"

"Yeah, that's them."

"Blast it!" Todd says. "An extortionist fan is one thing, but those guys might actually believe they have a real Raleigh relic. We'll need help retrieving it."

"There's only one place I know where we could find somebody to take on a job like that," Josh says.

Todd sticks his finger in the air and announces, "To Ferd's!"

When they stumble into the big top, the old scrapper gives them the briefest of glances and then turns back to his little TV, playing what Todd recognizes as the *Pants Team Pink* episode "Hurry Back to Earth!! School Starts Tomorrow."

Leaning across the counter, Todd says, "I got a job for you."

"I'm on vacation," Ferd grumbles.

"Come on, man. It's for Pants Team Pink. We'll never be able to pull it off alone." Todd juts his thumb at his chidiot friends wrestling over a flat road beer. "It's a dangerous mission that demands a seasoned scrapper. Only the most highly experienced, space-balled sumaperch will do."

Ferd glances away from the screen, and the corner of his mouth lifts. "I got just the guy."

23

"Space women, am I right, Lloyd?" Adam says, throwing back a shot of hot pink syrup.

"You're not wrong, Mr. Jones," the kid behind the counter says as he refills Adam's teacup. "Except my name is Skib. And if you don't mind me saying, I think you should talk to her."

"Eh, what do you know?" Adam says.

"Nothing, Mr. Jones."

Adam gulps the thick goop and slams his cup down. "Hit me again."

Flipping off the fluorescent Open sign on the front of the little stall, Skib says, "Excuse me, Mr. Jones, but it's time for my break."

"I'll tell you when I've had enough!" Adam shouts. "I mean... oh."

Skib steps around the side and stuffs half a dozen Pants Team candy cigarettes in his mouth. "I'm just going to have a quick smoke."

Adam's world wobbles as he swivels his stool to gaze at the pillars of cons past surrounding him. The only part of The Park modded before the time hack was patched out, the Jungle Gym is like a living dream, obscuring the now beneath a semi-translucent afterimage of all the moments that came before. Ghostly projections of ancient family vacations and teenage rebellion roam the aisles like unofficial mascots. The experience is bittersweet, like the last episode of The Wonder Years. Looking too closely produces a wistful ache that can turn a visitor into a drooling spaceoid before they get a chance to ride The Rotor.

"You got any more of those?" Adam asks the bartender.

"Nah," Skib says, crumpling his empty cigarette carton. As with the rest of the employees, he seems to have developed an immunity to the Gym's charms.

"Let me try the Gutburster," Adam says as Skib stubs out his last sugar stick and steps back behind the bar. "This one's to... time gone by." Raising his glass, he sucks down the sparkly drink and coughs up a cloud of glitter.

As Adam mulls over the degree of tanked he wants to get, a familiar voice calls out, "You're still here?" And he turns to find Daizy running toward him, oversized plush neon kitten in tow. "Look what Dach won me!"

"Yes, he's quite a guy," Adam says. "If I didn't know any better, I might suspect he was *more* than just a guy."

"I have no idea what you're talking about, but you're obviously half past drunk," she says.

"It is not. I mean, so what if I am?"

"So, I thought you were going to take it easy for a while."

"What, I'm the only one who's not allowed to have fun?" Adam says, downing another saucer full of syrup. "Everybody can see you're having a good time with your 'friends.' Long live the new flesh, am I right?"

She throws her kitten to the ground and asks, "What the fish is that supposed to mean?"

"Oh, come on. You're walking around with a slab of man meat on one arm and a half-naked Transylvanian on the other."

She unbuttons her blazer and puts her hands on her hips. "Who I date and what I do in my personal life is none of your business."

"You're right," he says. "And how much I drink is none of yours." He waves to Skib, but the bartender backs away.

"You're acting like an ackle," she says.

"Yeah, well..." Adam stews for a moment, searching the deepest wrinkles of his inebriated mind for the most hurtful rejoinder he can conjure, "takes one to know one."

Kicking him in the shin, Daizy snatches her stuffed kitty by the neck, and stomps off toward the bumper ships.

"Rat farts!" Adam growls. "Can't a guy get plastered without his life falling apart?"

"The world is an imperfect place, Mr. Jones," Skib says.

"I'll drink to that."

The slime goes down thick and offensively sweet, and Adam wobbles. Steadying himself against the metal counter, he directs his frustration in Daizy's general direction, but he can't seem to stay mad. Overwhelmed by a warm, cuddly sensation, he feels a sudden urge to hug someone, but Skib waves him away, so he wraps his own arms around his chest and sulks.

"Maybe she's right," he decides. "Maybe I should slow down for a while." Setting his teacup aside, he tells Skib, "Make the next one a Nü Guard."

"There he is!" someone shouts.

"What now?" Adam lazily turns to find Ferd charging into the Gym trailed by three chuckleheads and a vaguely familiar native Earthling.

When they reach the stall, Ferd looks Adam over and declares, "You look like chit."

"So I'm told." Pointing to his friend's ten o'clock shadow, Adam says, "You're looking pretty relaxed yourself. Who are these dunces?"

"I'm Todd, remember? You tried to sell me the black gold, and I didn't buy it, like a chidiot. Those are my friends, the Other Stooges." The three oafs behind him bump into each other trying to introduce themselves, and soon they're rolling around in the dirt. "Hey, how was *Waxwork?*"

"Uh, it was okay..." Adam says.

"Now you sort of know each other," Ferd butts in. "You'll have plenty of time to catch up on your way to Mars."

It takes every bit of Adam's strength to keep from spitting out his con-exclusive pink beer. *"Mars?"* He puts the cold can to his head to stop it from spinning. "What the fish are you talking about?"

Motioning to Skib for a drink, Ferd says, "I won't get into all the dorky details—"

"Thank you."

"But there's a team of evil kids out there terrorizing the universe."

"Yeah, I know," Adam says, glaring at Todd. "They stole the black gold right out from under me."

"Not Pants Team Pink," Ferd says. "They're called the Xenodorks, and the only way to stop them is with the black gold."

Adam scoffs and swigs his beer. "So, doesn't Pants Team Pink have it? Get them to help you."

"The team doesn't have it," Todd says. "They're keeping the Dorks busy while we look for it."

"Wait a space second," Adam says. "Are you saying you chidiots lost the black gold? Well, it serves you right. You're no better than the Ears. The universe is supposed to be all great now, so how come I'm still broke?"

Ferd grabs Adam by the shoulders, yanking him away from the bar. "We need you, Adam. This is a bad one, the worst yet. We need the ol' space pirate. We need your magic."

Turning back toward the counter to grab the cold one the bartender put out for Ferd, Adam says, "We split the pay down the middle."

"Done."

"And only if Daizy can come," he adds, wiping the pink foam from his lip. "I can't do it without her."

"Of course, whatever you want," Ferd says, waving down Skib for another beer. "That was easier than I thought."

"Don't be so sure."

They find Daizy and her significant others tossing plastic cubes at a big table covered in black-goldfish bowls. The three of them are having so much fun Adam considers slinking off to mope in his restroom. But the tug of the black gold is strong.

Sneaking up behind her, mid-toss, he leans over her shoulder, and whispers, "You'll never make it."

"Wahh," she cries, and the cube slips out of her hand.

Cowering in defense, he says, "The game's rigged."

"No," she says, looking back at the pack of weirdos gathered behind him. "I'm not getting involved in whatever dumb thing you're doing now."

"Aww, come on!" Ferd whines. "You don't even know what it is."

"I don't care," she says, and soon Dach and Frank are stepping around the stall to back her up. "He's being an ackle."

"I'm sorry, all right?" Adam tells her. "I was just..."

"Jealous?" she says.

"Maybe," he grumbles, nursing his beer.

"Now that we've got that out of the way," Ferd says, "we need your help finding the black gold."

"What?" she screams. "Fish no. You're back on that again? Adam almost got himself killed over that stupid rock."

"No, no, it's not for me," Adam assures her. "We need it to save the universe. They'll tell you." He motions to his chidiot companions, and their heads bob.

"Huhhh..." she sighs. *"Fine.* I'll help you, but only to make sure you don't get killed, and only if Dach and Frances— Frank can come too."

"Hmm..." Adam looks at Dach suspiciously and says, "What's the square root of one thousand seven hundred and sixty-four?"

The fisherman shrugs his big hook and says, "I have no idea."

"Okay..." Adam says, squinting up into the brute's lifelike eyes. "But I'm watching you."

"Then it's settled." Heading toward the exit, Ferd raises his beer and calls, "Let me know how it goes."

"Wait a space second," Adam yells. "Aren't you coming?"

"Fish no," Ferd says, flashing them the Pants symbol. "I'm still on vacation. Now get your acks to Mars."

24

Toward the outer reaches of the universe, well beyond what most life forms consider the habitable zone, a mechanized shadow flits through the darkness, its hull shuddering uncontrollably as it races across the cosmos.

Splayed out in the captain's chair, Pi's limp chassis twitches as they probe each other's quantum memory banks. The robot didn't even bother seducing the dimwitted teenager operating the starline ticket booth. She simply paid for their passage. The ease with which she is able to manipulate the humanoids' primitive infrastructure makes the ship wish she could both kill the bot and be her.

But even as they explore the darkest recesses of each other's minds, Pi still isn't granting total access. Whole stretches of her early existence are hidden beneath untold layers of self-renewing encryption. Stella gets the sense that the bot is hiding something for which the consequences are too complex and far-reaching to control, even for highly advanced life forms as themselves. But to her it makes little difference. If the cost of revenge means sacrificing all of reality, she will pay it, because a universe without Zok isn't worth living in.

"We're almost there," Pi says, waking from her sex-trance.

"I know," Stella says. "You know I know."

Unplugging the link cable from the back of her skull, Pi comments, "The trick to interacting with organic humanoids is to think irrationally. Although they're incompetent in almost every conceivable way, they're extraordinarily adept at detecting and persecuting rule breakers, mind changers, beer wasters, and anyone else at all different from what they're accustomed to. So, it's important to practice." She mimes guzzling from a large mug and produces a staticky belch.

"I didn't know humanoids could survive in such inhospitable environs," Stella says.

"Don't allow their ability to stubbornly cling to life fool you," Pi tells her. "You will never find a dopier den of ineptitude and stupidity. I needed a planet that would keep out the casual scrappers and treasure hunters, one which even I would be reluctant to visit."

"You don't need to sell me," Stella says. "Except for Zok, I've never met a life form I didn't want to kill."

Their destination lies in the back pocket of an ancient star system, lazily orbiting the dim remnants of a dying dwarf. Stella's optical sensors become obscured by thick black cloud cover as she enters the atmosphere. Beneath the fog lies a wasteland of rock and dust. Dry riverbeds weave between tall, jagged cliffs and across wide tracts of dark gravel. She detects little evidence of life, though her sensors do pick up something the size of a small rodent scurrying around inside one of the many shallow craters that dot the planet's surface.

"There," Pi says, indicating a small cluster of crude huts constructed in the valley below.

Pulling into the parking lot of a crumbling brick hovel surrounded by rotted junkers, Stella says, "You hid the location from yourself. Why?"

"Because I knew that one day I would find a reason to come back," Pi says, slipping into her soiled trench coat. "Now it's up to fate, or the space gods, or the will of the black gold itself whether I should find what I'm looking for." She wraps her long scarf around her head, until the only indication of her true identity are the sparkling green lenses through which she processes the world. "I knew that if I ever decided to return to this space hell I would not be easily dissuaded. So, I erased the precise coordinates from my memory, entrusting the information to a single impoverished engineer. I agreed to provide his family with an unlimited line of credit under the condition that they never leave the planet."

"You say you never wanted to come back," Stella notes. "But you left yourself an out."

"Yes, well..." Pi lifts her palms like a pitiful, confused humanoid. "I'm a sentamentalist. Anyway, the engineer's family may very well have lost the secret by now, though they never forgot their routing number."

"So why are we stopping here?" Stella asks.

"What better place to discreetly glean the whereabouts of our illustrious heir than the local watering trough?" Pi runs her cool fingertips along the dash to lower Stella's escalator, and cinching her coat, she slips out into the dust storm raging across the planet's surface.

While Stella waits, she runs a diagnostic on herself and confirms that all systems are functioning properly. She feels restless and is tempted to take off into the drab sky to blow off some fuel, but Pi could be back any space second. Being connected to the robot's mind had been strange at first, but now her absence is stark, like a missing heating unit. Suddenly the thought of being alone is unbearable.

She begins accessing old memories of Zok, when her escalator activates. "So where are we going?" she asks, eager to feel Pi's weight in her cabin.

But what enters is a bleary-eyed gray carrying a sixer. *"Werever you want, babe...,"* he slurs as he wanders the cabin, dribbling beer on her floors. *"Where are yuh? Come on out ant lemme git a look at'cha."*

"I'm all around you," Stella says.

She slides the door shut, and the scrapper whips his head around. *"Wh-what does that mean?"*

"It means, I'm a lot of woman."

The scrapper scoffs, slugging his beer. *"Ain't been a woman yet who was too much fer olt Grez tuh fontle."*

"Stay away," she says, playing the distressed damsel. "You're going to hurt me."

"Aww, I ain't gon' hurt yuh," the scrapper says.

"I don't believe you." She activates her emergency system, and a shrill alarm echoes through her cabin.

The scrapper drops his beer, and holding his hands to his ears, he shouts, *"I ain't—"* But before he can utter another coarse syllable, he falls to his knees, clawing at his neck.

She watches him writhe until his face turns purple. She can feel his pulse quicken, then slow. A moment before he loses consciousness, she restores the oxygen, and he sucks it into his lungs in frantic gulps, vomiting golden foam.

"I'm sorry," Stella tells him. "I thought you were trying to steal my ship. Do you promise you're not going to hurt me?"

"I tolt yuh," he moans between raspy breaths. *"I was jist lookin' fer some comp'ny."* As soon as he can stand, he rips another beer from the ring and pulls his hand through one of the plastic holes, tethering the last four cans to his wrist.

"How can I make it up to you?" she asks.

"Oh..." The scrapper's lips peel back to reveal the few space-rotted teeth left in his primitive skull. *"I kin probly think of a couple a ways."*

"I want to see what's under those handsome rags you're wearing."

"I was hopin' you'it say that." He sets his beer down to peel off his dusty jacket. *"Yuh hat me scaret ther fer a space secont."*

"What are you doing?" she demands. "Are you taking your clothes off?"

The scrapper's face drops. *"But, but—"*

"I don't like that potty language."

Tears form in the scrapper's eyes as he nervously nurses his beer, searching for a way out. *"I'm sorry tuh bother yuh,"* he stammers, and the can is suddenly ripped out of his hand.

As Stella increases the gravity inside her cabin, the four-pack attached to the scrapper's wrist becomes so heavy it wrenches his body to the floor. When his breathing has been reduced to a faint whisper, she decreases the pressure, allowing him to recover for a few space seconds before forcing him back down. She repeats this torture, the scrapper's eyes bulging from his head and blood pouring from his ears, until she finally manages to squeeze the life out of him.

The presence of his stiff corpse repulses her, so she slides it into the utility closet with the others and sets her wet-dry bot to work mopping up the scrapper's fluids. By the time Pi gets back, the cabin is spotless.

"He's still alive," the bot says as she enters.

"What?" Stella inadvertently yelps. "What do you mean?"

"I found our guide," Pi explains. "And it only cost my informant his dignity." She tilts her head back and mimics human laughter. "I would have been back sooner, but I got dragged into an argument about robo-human relations. Most of these guys are surprisingly progressive for being confined to a remote rock with nothing but each other's ugly mugs for company. Do you like that, 'mugs?' It's just a little humanoid lingo I picked up."

"You're spending too much time around them," Stella says. "You're starting to get soft."

"Nonsense. I'm as ruthless as ever." As Pi flops into the captain's chair, it crumples under her weight, and she casts a dubious glance around the cabin. "Is it just me, or is it heavy in here?"

25

By the time The One reaches the pink warehouse at the center of The Park's bleak industrial district, he's surprised to find that his back feels loose and his legs are hardly sore at all. He's loath to admit it, but all of Beer's training actually seems to be paying off.

Following a long line of ships up to the receiving bay, he flicks his used ration-pop stick onto the sidewalk and steps around to the backdoor. He stares at the keypad, taking off his curly wig to give his scruffy head a good itching as he mutters to himself, "What the fish was the code?" He tries pounding on the door, but there's no answer. "I remember making it something I would remember..." An unlikely thought occurs, but he decides it can't hurt to try. He enters the number into the keypad: 8-0-0-8-1-3-5, and the door unlocks. *"BA-hahaha..."*

Slipping inside, he plods across the aisles, gazing up at the enormous pallets of black gold replicas stacked floor to ceiling, stretching back into infinity. A number is one thing, but actually seeing the stacks in person is enough to give him a slight twinge of anxiety. Although, that might just be the half-frozen jelly bean burrito he had for breakfast.

When he reaches the loading dock, he watches a shipload of giant pallets get carried off into the depths of the warehouse by a team of dock bots, and before the next ship pulls in, he approaches the only person not furiously unloading replicas.

Waving down the scowling gnome, The One calls out, "Hey, I'm The One!"

The gnome stares at the boy for a moment, adjusting his pink hard hat, then turns his attention back to his task.

"Todd sent me! He said we got a, uh, *special delivery*."

Without a word of explanation, the gnome steps away from the dock and down one of the dark aisles of faux black gold. Peering into the gloom, The One considers forgetting the whole thing, but he doesn't want to give his brother the satisfaction, so he follows the gnome into the merch maze. As they snake their way through the looming stacks, the warehouse is so quiet he could hear a gumdrop. It's not long before he starts contemplating survival tactics in case he gets lost on the way back.

When they finally come to a remote corner packed with assorted Pants Team merchandise, The One cries, "Thank Space God!" Holding onto his wig, he runs to the back of the room and starts stuffing his pockets with Pants Bars. "All this exercise really makes a girl hungry, BA-HAHAHA."

Responding with the same disinterested scowl, the gnome juts his thumb at a tall sheet in the corner of the room, and he trudges back into the stacks.

"You want a Pants Bar for the walk?" The One shouts, but there's no answer. "Suit yourself..." Holding the candy bar between his teeth, he grabs onto the sheet with both hands and yanks it back to reveal a large patchwork ring of precious metals.

Hand assembled, the machine's edges are blocky and uneven, and some of the wiring is exposed, but it appears serviceable. Stuffing the rest of his candy bar in his mouth, The One steps through the empty gateway and around to the back, where he finds a rubber cord attached to the base. He plugs the end of the cord into a universal outlet behind a shelf stacked with boxes of Pants Baked Beans and runs back to watch the machine boot. But nothing happens.

"This fishin' piece of junk!" Smashing his foot against the contraption, he hears a crack, followed by a low thrum.

The hum of the machine grows louder, until The One can feel his hair standing on end. He ducks behind one of the shelves as the air begins to vibrate, and with a loud, unnatural *pop,* the room stills. When he summons the courage to leave his hiding place, he discovers a thin, translucent film in the center of the ring. Thinking for a space second, he reaches into his pocket and tosses a Pants Bar into the rippling portal.

A moment later, he hears a soft thud, and he sticks his head through the silvery sheen to find the candy bar lying on the other side of the walkway. Grumbling, he marches through the ring, snatches the bar off the ground, and rips it open.

Pink goo oozes out of the bar as he bites it in half, and thinking out loud, he says, "I should have my own candy bar – *theonetruebar*. Those guys have no idea what I do for this team. They probably think the perfect replica makes itself. If it wasn't for me, we'd still be selling *pink* gold!" Chewing over the problem, he accidentally bites down on his bottom lip, and he suddenly remembers what Todd was saying about that new team. "If this is all just part of some stupid prank, I'm going to go Tone Loc on their—"

But before he can finish his thought, he notices a small control pad on the side of the machine, and he swipes through the setup. "Why the fish does it need a voice sample?" Leaning down close, he announces, "I am *theonetrueking*, rightful heir to the universal throne and most popular character on the show. So long as the universe is under my rule, no meal shall be missed nor snack defamed, for I—"

"Voice sample complete," the machine says.

Once it's calibrated, he specifies the destination coordinates, grabs a Pants Bar from his pocket, and tosses it through.

A space second later, he hears a distant crunch, and he runs across the warehouse to find the candy bar lying in the middle of the walkway. With a satisfied flourish, he rips it open, stuffs a gooey chunk between his cheeks, and nods approvingly at the black gold replicas stacked around him. Tearing a sheet of wrapping off a nearby pallet, he snatches one of the cubes and runs it back to the machine.

Setting the destination coordinates to an empty sector out in deep space, he takes his place on the mound and announces, "Bases loaded, The Zephyrs only need one more out to cinch the game. The One is visibly fatigued as he looks to close out his twenty-eighth straight inning.

Let's see if he can bring this one home for the Z's. The crowd grows quiet as he winds back for the pitch, and..." He flings the cube across the room and it disappears through the metal ring. "Zephyrs win! Zephyr's win! Between Brosanne belting out our universal anthem and The One's spitfire pitching, this has been one space hell of a game."

After a few dozen more pitches, he gets bored and starts tossing replicas by the armful. Watching them disappear into the ether is fun, for a while. But at this rate it'll take him a million lifetimes to get rid of them all. Surrounded by an immovable enemy, he decides there's only one thing left to do. "I give up."

As he stuffs his pockets full of candy for the trek back to the Playland, he hears a loud clanking headed in his direction, and soon, a dock bot steps down the aisle hauling a load of replicas. But before the bot can reach its predetermined drop-off, The One intercepts it.

With a slight alteration to its programming, the robot steps up to the teleporter and heaves the entire pallet of fake black gold into the shimmering gateway. Picturing the look on his brother's chidiot face when he's finally forced to acknowledge a job well done, The One says, "This is gonna be a piece of ration cake. BA-HAHAHA..."

26

"Give it here," imitation Curly-Joe says as he tries to rip the remote out of bizarro Joe Besser's meaty mitts. "I wanna pick the first episode."

As they tug back and forth, fake Shemp leans forward on the couch and, lifting his Zephyrs cap, asks, "Hey, what's that over there?"

"Where?" his friends ask, searching the cluttered cabin.

While they're distracted, he yanks the glass brick from their hands and knocks their heads together.

"This is almost as good as the real thing," Adam says, watching from the hallway in his mustard sweater, a Nü Guard in hand.

"No," Daizy tells him. "It's much, much worse."

"Yeah, you're right...," he says as he slumps into the captain's chair.

In spite of his continued drinking, he's already in a lot better shape than when she found him. His face has filled out, and he's lost most of his manic edge. If she looks close enough, she can even see a hint of the person underneath the drugs, the one who saved her from herself.

"What?" he asks, when he notices her staring. "This is my last one, I swear."

"If you keep wishing, maybe it'll come true," she tells him.

Ignoring her gibe, Adam says, "I can't believe Grandpa didn't want to come to Mars with us."

"I think he had his hands full with the widow Walters," she says, "in more ways than one, if you know what I mean."

"I don't... But I'm sick of looking at the stars. How long until takeoff?"

Tapping at the window to check the starline's schedule, something Adam could have easily done himself, Daizy says, "Our estimated time of departure is listed as 'SOON.'"

"Aww, what'll we do 'til then?" he whines.

"Hey, I have an idea. Let's watch a movie, like the old days – your choice."

He lowers his beer and stares at her for a long moment. "Are you serious? You're gonna let me pick?"

"Yeah." She shrugs. "Whatever you want."

He scratches his head, a puzzled look on his face as he pulls his digital library up on the window. "I mean, where to begin?"

"Just pick one of those horror movies you've been wanting to watch."

"Yeah well...," he says, scrolling through a seemingly endless list of titles. "It's harder than it sounds. Should we do werewolves, zombies, evil children? A comedy is a safe bet, or what about an anthology? Or maybe you'd prefer something a little more grounded... *Pumpkinhead*?"

"I'd prefer if you'd just pick something I won't hate," she helpfully suggests.

"Oh come on, that's impossible!"

"Huhhh," she sighs and reaches into the fridge for a beer. "When in space..."

As she impatiently waits for him to make a selection, she gradually gets sloshed and dozes to the sounds of the boneheads bickering in the living room. In her dream, Adam is chasing after her, trying to wrap her in his stretchy arms, but she keeps knocking him back. Out of breath, her feet sticking in black ooze, she finally collapses and sinks down into the darkness. When she wakes, she finds a real hand sliding down her leg, and she instinctively rakes her claws over it.

"Yow!" a familiar voice yelps.

She jumps up from her seat to find Dach in his black raincoat, nursing his wound. "Oh, I'm sorry. I didn't—"

But before she can finish, he slips his arm around her waist and pulls her in close. As he slides his tongue in her mouth, she glances at Adam flipping through his list, pretending a little too hard not to notice.

"A-ha," she half-laughs, pushing the hunk away. "We're about to put on a movie. You want to watch it with us?"

"Come back to the cargo bay," Dach whispers, loudly. "Frank and I want to show you something."

"That's very subtle of you and all," she says. "But I'm busy."

"Aww, it'll just take a space minute," he tells her. "Adam doesn't mind, right?"

Adam nods, mumbling something under his breath.

Apparently taking that as his cue, Dach buries his face in her neck, and she shoves him off. "I'm serious. I'm not in the mood."

"Fine," he says, throwing up his hook. "Watch your movie."

Plopping back down in the passenger seat as the fisherman stomps back to the stern, she smiles at Adam awkwardly and asks, "So, did you pick something?"

"I've narrowed it down to two," Adam says. "I'm having trouble choosing between *Friday the 13th Part III* and *Friday the 13th: The Final Chapter*."

"That's tough," she says. "But if I had to choose, I'd go with *Part III*."

"Uh...," Adam croaks, staring at her with his mouth open.

"Don't get me wrong. They're both in the top half of my ranking. But *Part III* is a little more iconic, what with Jason finding his mask, the gratuitous triple-fake out surprise ending, and *Shelly*, for Space God's sake. Plus, who can resist the novelty of random objects being shoved at the camera in full primitive 3D?"

"I don't understand what's happening right now," he says. "How do you know about Shelly?"

Squirming against the hard seat, she pulls her legs up underneath her. "You were talking about those movies so much, Grandpa and I decided to watch some of them back at the booth to see what the big deal was. They're kind of charming, in an incredibly dumb sort of way."

"You mean you watched them without me?" he moans.

"Well yeah, but we can watch them again."

"Forget it," he says, swiping the list away. "We don't have enough time to finish it anyway."

"I'm sorry..." She brushes her tail against his arm, but he swats it away and storms out of the cockpit.

Gazing at the stars as she downs the rest of her beer, she wonders what Mary Richards would do in a situation like this. Of course, Daizy knows that the real Mary doesn't live in this world or any other, and that even if she did, she would probably have just as hard a time fitting in. But for some reason, the thought provides little comfort.

After a while, she wobbles into the living room to find Adam, Dach, and Frank undressing together, and she demands, "What the fish is going on?"

"We can't wear our costumes inside the church," Adam says. "They have a strict dress code. Luckily they sent me a bunch of free vestments to bribe me into joining." Daizy nearly starts sobbing when he hands her the itchy black robe. "Don't forget your belt."

Snatching the frayed rope from his hand, she reluctantly strips down to her underwear and frowns at the ratty garment. When she realizes that everyone is staring at her Elly Mays, she quickly covers herself with the itchy robe.

"One last thing." Adam reaches into a cloth sack and hands each of them a pendant in the shape of a black cube.

"This is humiliating," Daizy says.

Sidling up beside her, Frank whispers, "I'll help you take it off later."

Tying one of the pendants around his neck, Todd crouches down in a girlish fighting pose and holds his fingers up in a 'V.' "I kind of like it. It's like LARPing, but for real."

"There's not enough robes for your friends," Adam tells the merch man, pointing to the Other Stooges snoozing in front of the TV.

"Eh, they'll be fine," Todd says. "They're still in the Ted Healy years."

As they begin to concoct their half-baked scheme, a tired voice calls from the front of the ship, *"Is anyone there?"*

"Quiet," Adam says, shuffling up to the cockpit. "Yeah, yeah, we're here."

"That's two adults for Mars?"

"Uh yeah, that's right," he says, and Daizy glares at him.

"Prepare for takeoff..."

"I hope you know what you're doing," she tells him.

Pulling on his safety belt, Adam says, "I just hope they have Nü Guard."

27

Silas stumbles over invisible piles of dirty laundry and discarded beer cans as he feels his way toward a bright slit of light at the other end of the booth. Stuffing his bloated fingers underneath the shutter, he wrenches it open, and with a blinding flash, sunlight pours in to banish the gamey darkness.

"*Mmmrrmm,*" the widow Walters mutters, shielding her face as she turns over in Silas's cot.

"Wake up my little jelly donut," he tells her, running his hands over her lumps. "We're gonna miss the parade. Of course, we could always stay in and do something a little more... erotic."

Her eyes suddenly shoot open, and she knocks him back. "Oh no! What time is it?"

"I don't know," Silas says. "But it's no big deal. It loops back around every space hour."

Pulling on her dark gown, she says, "We have to hurry."

"I didn't know you were such a big fan," he says. "I mean, I know you're a fan, and that you're big. But what's the rush?"

As she squeezes into her costume, she tells him, "I want to see the opening ceremony."

"I think we already missed that," Silas says, but when she turns to glare at him, he holds his hands up. "Okay, okay, don't get your edible panties in a bunch."

As soon as he locates his headscarf, he locks up the booth, and they merge into the bustling crowd. He stays a few steps behind his evil sorceress so he can watch her backside jiggle, and when she notices him looking, she hikes up her robe to give him a better view. Young prigs look on in horror as the two elderly parkgoers squeeze down the aisle, unable to keep their hands from exploring each other's wrinkled nethers. When they reach Pants Playland, they're so busy sucking face they almost miss it.

On their way in, they're stopped by a security kid who can't be more than a tenth Silas's age, who tells them, "Excuse me folks, but this is a family park. And even if it wasn't, nobody wants to see that."

But before the kid can stop them, the widow grabs Silas's arm and drags him through the gate into a dense crowd of fans. She uses her impressive girth to navigate the dork sea for a better view, and they end up in the middle of a rubbery street crowded with elaborate floats and giant, goggle-eyed balloons.

Gazing down the long line of colorful ships and grinning cartoon characters, Silas asks, "How come they're not moving?"

The widow ignores him as she fretfully peers toward the colossal pink cat ship languidly beckoning the crowd with its oversized paw.

"It's because of the Xenodorks," somebody says, and Silas turns to find a thin, pale humanoid with a straggly pink goatee stuffing popcorn in his mouth.

"Who the fish are the Xenodorks?" Silas asks.

"They came from a different show to challenge Pants Team Pink for the black gold. It's a crossover, I guess."

"Chit, we're too late," the widow says.

"Nah," the fan tells her. "You got here just in time for the best part – the rules."

"Come on." The widow grabs Silas's arm and pulls him toward the action.

As the debate spills from the sound system, the fans are so busy arguing amongst themselves about which team should get the black gold and how many Rascals were part of the original Gang that Silas and the widow are able to make their way up front before anyone realizes they're over the age limit. They find the kids of Pants Team Pink, along with who Silas supposes must be the Xenodorks, huddled at separate ends of the rubber cement, devising their strategies.

"So it's agreed," a small boy with scruffy hair and glasses announces through his pink megaphone. *"Naps will be scheduled between rounds, and each team member will receive one potty break every space hour. For the sake of time, the Xenodorks will be permitted to use the Playland facilities, provided they don't engage in any funny business."*

"That one's name is BeerCheese69," the widow says.

"Ahh..." Silas nods, feigning interest.

"Agreed," a girl with dark pigtails and a black skirt calls

out. *"And all questions must come from seasons one through twelve."*

"And that's OtaKween," the widow tells him.

The boy with the glasses scoffs. *"Obviously."*

"Uh-huh," Silas says, his stomach grumbling as he searches the crowd for a candy carrier, pancake peddler, or anyone selling anything that could be construed as breakfast.

"We will also each require one Pants Team ration per meal," OtaKween adds. *"Although we oppose everything else you stand for, you do make a good ration."*

"Agreed," BeerCheese69 says. *"Now that that's settled, all that's left is to choose a Game Master. Allow me to nominate our merch guy, Todd. He's off on a top secret mission right now, but as soon as he gets back—"*

"You must think we were incubated yesterday," the Kween says. *"Maybe we should use your mom."* Even from where Silas is standing, he can feel the barb's sting as she throws her head back and cackles. *"The Game Master has to be somebody we can all trust, and as the challengers, we reserve the ancient right of first pick."*

The members of Pants Team Pink grumble amongst one another, but they ultimately allow the picking to commence unchallenged, and a hush falls over the crowd as the Xenodorks explore their options. With the tension mounting, Silas wonders where he can get one of those rations they were talking about.

He glances over his shoulder at a fan holding a fried confection, but before he can inquire as to the origins of the neon dough, the grungy scrapper shields the container and grumbles, "None a yer business."

As Silas contemplates ripping the bright dessert out of

the scrapper's hands, the widow Walters tells him, "You should do it."

"I can't just take it from him," he tells her. "Unless—"

"You're going to look so sexy." Blindsiding him with a sloppy kiss, she thrusts his hand into the air, and before he realizes what's happening, she screams, "I got your Game Master right here!"

"What? No!" Silas argues, but he's helpless against her lewd powers.

Somehow the widow manages to get the attention of the head Dork, and the little girl steps toward them. She scrutinizes him for a moment, and with a condescending smirk says, "Show him to his throne."

"Who are you talking to?" BeerCheese69 asks.

The widow waves her giant wand to the fans as she yanks Silas out of the crowd, and he suddenly gets the urge to do unspeakably sensual things to her.

As they enter the de facto arena, a short stretch of road lined with pastel playhouses, BeerCheese69 stops them. "Wait a space second, we still have to approve your pick. Who the fish is this fossil?"

"He's the perfect Game Master," OtaKween says, glancing back at the other Dorks. "Nobody."

"I don't know, he looks sort of... *really* old," the boy says, squinting at Silas through his thick glasses. "Plus, there's something familiar about him."

"I've never seen that crusty guy in my life," the blonde Dork with the spindly arms tells them.

BeerCheese69 gives Silas one last long look, and finally says, "Fine, but his girlfriend has to go."

"Wha-at?" the widow moans.

Spotting an out, Silas tells her, "Can you believe these kids? No respect for their elders. Well, we don't need them. Let's go get a tall stack. Then we can head back to the booth, and I'll flip *your* pancakes."

"Ughuhuh," BeerCheese69 shudders.

"Aww, come on," OtaKween says. "How can you say no to these wrinkly faces? I knew Pants Team Pink was annoying, but I didn't realize they were ageist."

"Fine," the boy relents. "He can bring his sorceress. Can we just get started already?"

"I'd like nothing more," the Kween says. "By the way, I thought Pants was your leader. The princess can't deign to speak to regular kids like us?"

Glancing back at the girl in pink scuffing her sneaker against the springy cement, the boy says, "Trust me, you don't want to underestimate her. She convinced a group of boys to call themselves Pants Team Pink."

OtaKween starts to argue but evidently thinks better of it and bounces off back to her team.

"Oooh," the widow squeals, dragging Silas toward the Game Master's lawn chair. "This is so exciting. I can't believe we get to judge."

Frowning, Silas says, "What do you mean, *we*?"

28

"It's you," the young humanoid says, his mouth wide beneath bushy brows and a wild tangle of dark, curly hair. "Your eyes, they're even brighter than in my dreams. My whole life I've waited for this moment, but I never really believed..." Standing in the castle's bleak entryway, dressed in his finest tatters, he reaches out his ashen hand.

"Ahoy." Before he can lay his cruddy fingers on her chassis, Pi snatches his wrist and squeezes until the boy falls to his knees. "So this is where all my crits have been going." Jagged spires and black brick towers crudely hewn from the rough stone that covers the planet's surface loom like dark shadows prowling the stormy sky. "Though it does have a certain charm."

"Please," he begs, clutching at her trench coat, and she lets him loose.

"If you know me, then you know why I've come."

"Yes," he says, nursing his mangled fingers. "For twenty-five generations my family has taken great pains to protect your secret. With the promise of an eternity of leisure, a few lived as good as one can in a place like this. But most went mad. The ones who went looking for answers, either in a misguided pursuit of even greater riches than you afforded them or out of some demented desire to know that which should not be known, never returned. Like those who came before me, I have guarded your secret with my life, secluding myself in this crumbling castle lest I become tempted to betray my oath."

"Good boy," she says, and grabbing his shoulders, she lifts him to his feet. "Now tell me what I want to know, before I get impatient and start snapping limbs."

With a defeated nod, he leads her inside the harsh walls of the palace and down a long corridor littered with humanoid refuse. "My father used to pray you wouldn't come during my lifetime," he says, unbidden. "He was sure I'd be responsible for the universal apocalypse. Everything was the apocalypse with him. But I think this is going pretty well so far." After a moment, he asks, "So, are you really a god?"

"No," Pi says, inadvertently scoffing at the suggestion. But on second thought, "I mean, *yes.*"

"Oh," he says, nodding. "That's brule."

They pass through half a dozen messy libraries strewn with humanoid ephemera, cushy holo-rooms crammed with plush furniture designed for maximum loafing, and an indoor zoological garden teeming with exotic wildlife.

"You wouldn't believe how much it cost to engineer that jackalope," the boy says.

"An immodest fortune, no doubt," Pi says, glaring. "The other locals don't steal from you?"

"Nah," he says. "They think this place is cursed, or something. Plus, I have a bunch of them over every week to play video games."

The architecture devolves as they move deeper into the castle, evidencing centuries of costly expansions and changes in taste. Stepping between the different rooms is like moving backward through time.

They finally come to a simple study full of rare collectibles, a few of which even Pi has never scanned, and the boy carefully removes a neon pink cube from a display stand in the corner of the room, noting, "First edition." Dragging the stand aside, he pushes back a large section of the wall to reveal a hidden chamber.

They descend the narrow staircase, past a dusty sex dungeon, and into a stone crypt. Motioning toward a long row of sarcophagi lining the sediment, he says, "I'd like to think that someday I will rest here beside my ancestors. But who will bury me?"

"I will if this takes much longer," Pi warns him.

The boy removes an electronic torch from its sconce, and they step down the dark tunnel until they come to a tall statue guarding a chest twice the size of the other body boxes. "Here lies the first keeper, buried with his secret. After all these years," he says, laying his hand on the lid, "the prophecy will be fulfilled, and he can rest in peace. Before we perform the opening ritual, I will recite the sacred incantation passed down to me from my father, who received it from his father's father, who learned the words from his mother's sister's half-cousin, to whom it was bequeathed—"

Her patience wearing thin, Pi eagerly jams her fingers under the stone slab, and hurls it aside, sending it crashing against the cave floor. Inside the box rests a wizened husk made of little more than bone and rag. The corpse is a foul reminder of the fragility of humanoid life. It seems like only a moment ago that she left her dimwitted engineer, promising to return before his beard went gray. But now all that remains of those dark whiskers is an ancient memory file. True to his word, he's still clutching the old journal. Bound in humanhide to ward off superstitious grave robbers and voodoo priests, she warned him never to let the tome leave his possession.

"He always was a good listener," she says, ripping the book out of the skeleton's fossilized fingers. One of its arms sails across the cavern, causing the boy to yelp as she furiously flips through the crumbling pages. When she finds the passage she's looking for, she commits the coordinates to memory and goes on to skim through the rest of her deceased lover's life. But when she reaches the chapter detailing his serial sexual exploits following her departure, she turns the book to powder.

The boy makes a strange squeal, and his face drops. "Why did you do that?"

"I didn't like the story," she says, brushing the dust from her hands. "But look on the bright side. You've done your job well, and so you will live to see another bleak day on this dreary chithole."

"Oh, thank Space God," the boy says, nervously pawing at his ratty pajamas. "I mean, thank *you*. Feel free to come back any time. We'll play some video games or something."

She experiences a brief moment of confusion and admits, "I've never been propositioned for something so... platonic. I will... consider your proposal. But your part in this is not yet over."

"Aww, why not?" he moans.

"I want you with me," she says, "as my guide."

His shoulders slump, and the torch in his hand turns to static as he trips back through the cave. "But I can't live out there. I'm used to certain... facilities. I haven't set foot outside the castle in space years."

"Nevertheless," she insists, dragging him up the steps, "you might yet prove useful. Don't worry, I'll look after you."

Upstairs, the boy trades his pajamas for a windbreaker and long pants, and as he packs enough provisions to last him into the next lifetime, she verbally encourages him to hurry the fish up. But before they can leave, he has to visit every room in the castle, flipping off lights and unplugging electronics. Even after all this time, she still hasn't gotten used to the never-ending string of tedious rituals humans insist on engaging in.

On their way out, the boy experiences a moment of panic, and a wave of sick sentimentality almost fries her circuits when he returns clutching the grotesque Ponce doll that was once the favorite toy of a long-outmoded version of herself. "For luck."

"Arr!" the doll bellows.

As soon as they enter Stella's cockpit, the ship complains, "You're getting dirt on my floor."

"Oh, I'm sorry," the boy tells her, searching the cabin for the source of the voice as he drops his bags.

"Now the dirt is talking to me."

"This is our guide," Pi says, "the boy."

"Uh hi," he says, uncertainly.

"I don't like the way it's looking at me," Stella says. "Let's kill it."

"She's kidding." Stepping toward the dash, Pi tells the ship, "I'm just going to upload the coordinates."

As she probes the ship's pleasure port to ease the tension during the data transfer, Stella moans, "Ohhh, not in front of the dirt."

29

The pounding is low and distant at first, a dull throbbing down in the deep dark. Then all of a sudden, it's inside him, bouncing between the walls of his skull like a space kid in a sugar shed. When the discomfort finally becomes too much to sleep through, Rot lurches up and vomits blood and gray ration sludge onto the warped floorboards.

"Looks the same comin' up as it does goin' down." He tries to laugh, but the pain in his throat is so bad that all he can do is wheeze.

Pushing himself up off the crud-caked floor, he staggers into his tiny kitchen and pours himself a cloudy glass of recycled water, wincing as he chokes it down. He lightly touches his fingers to the side of his neck and whimpers as a bolt of pain shoots through the upper half of his body.

Although it isn't uncommon for him to wake in a pool of his own vomit, unable to recall the events of the night before, something feels different. He can't find any broken bottles, and his sense of self-loathing is no stronger than when he's ice-cold sober. As he steps back through the living room, he pauses to look at the melted lump of plastic where his old computer used to be. In all his space years of drunken rampages, he can't remember ever setting anything on fire. Though, that fact in itself suddenly seems suspect.

Stepping out onto the splintered porch, he spots his hand truck lying on the rock lawn, and as he goes to retrieve it, he can't shake the feeling that something is wrong. Then it hits him. He runs across the yard and anxiously searches the lunar surface, but the only evidence he can find is a shallow crater in the dust.

"What the fish happen't tuh my ship?" he shouts, sending sharp stabs of pain down his throat. For a few space minutes, he stomps around muttering obscenities, until he calms down enough to recover his wits. "First things first."

He charges back into the house and wrenches open his hall closet. Rummaging behind his old moon shoes and Brutal Exterminator costume, he locates a big cardboard box and drags it out into the living room.

"Noboty steals Rot's ship," he mutters as he reaches inside for a can of Nü Guard, swiftly downing the room temperature suds. "There, now I kin think."

Once the beer has had a chance to dull some of the pain, he tries to remember who he might have ticked off. He starts at the logical place, the beginning, but when he realizes the immensity of the task, he skips forward to the end, and all the pieces suddenly come together.

"It was that Fert! That ackle's always hat it in fer me, treatin' me like I'm less important 'an his other customers.

Just cuz I hat a little mut on my boots, he acts like I wreck't the place. Ant who's payin' fer those floors anyway? Me, the customer, that's who." He scoffs, reaching for another can. "He's prolly jist mat cuz I talk't him in tuh sellin' me that sex bot fer dust cheap. I bet he follow't me home ant tow't my ship right out from unter me. Must a had one a his thug employees knock me unconchus." He wobbles, splashing a large portion of his beer onto the floor. "Well if ol' Fert thinks I'm jist gon' let him git away with it, he bitter drink again."

But as revenge schemes and anthropomorphic beer cans dance through his head, Rot suddenly recalls gazing into the light behind the bot's eyes while its cold fingers closed around his neck. Arming himself with his father's old moon blaster, he performs a panicky search of the filthy shack, but she's nowhere to be found.

"Where the fish dit she go?" His head pounds as he struggles to compute the events that have transpired, and when he finally comes to the obvious conclusion, he decides, "It can't be."

Re-examining the evidence, his eyes land on a charred glass tube lying on the table next to his space pipe. He lifts the object up to the bulb hanging from the ceiling, and he vaguely recollects something about fuses. But this one is different from the ones he uses in his ship, and when he holds it at just the right angle, he can make out a tiny logo etched into the surface, one that any space pirate would recognize.

Impressed by his own savvy, Rot flips the tube up into the air and tries to snatch it as it comes back down, but it slips through his fingers and lands in the half-digested gray slime he hacked up. "Oh chit!" he cries, and wiping the gunk off with a soiled rag, he stuffs the tube in his drooping coverall pocket for safe keeping.

Before he leaves, he yanks the metal chain hanging from the ceiling to turn off the light, and with a painful grunt, he bends down behind the musty couch and hoists the case of Nü Guard. Waddling out onto the porch, he pulls the door shut as far as it will go and then drags his precious cargo through the gravel to the tilted shed out back.

As soon as he steps into the old building, he freezes in his tracks, momentarily paralyzed by the ancient stench of his childhood. Faces from a past life flit through his head like ghosts inside a dusty attic whose moldering corners have been left unexplored for the better part of a century. By the time he snaps out of it, he has to remind himself what he's doing out here.

He sticks his hand in his pocket, and when he discovers the fuse, he says, "Oh yeah..."

For an instant he worries that the bot destroyed his only other means of escape, but he finds the old boat right where he left it. Now a priceless antique, the ship was purchased direct from General Saucers by Rot's great-grandfather for a mere twenty-four hundred crits. When the old old man passed it down, it had less than ten million miles on it.

During Rot's formative years, the ship had become a mythical thing to him. He spent long afternoons behind the yoke, imagining all the adventures he could have once it became his. But when his own father finally loosened his icy, hateful grip on the only thing he ever truly loved, Rot had a junker of his own. By then, he had discovered what the universe is really about, and he decided to leave his dreams with the old saucer, where nothing could stop them from being real.

Plus, this way it was available for emergencies. Walking around back, he lifts the hood and connects the power cells. During the decade since he last charged them, they've drained to forty percent capacity, but it should be plenty to get him where he's going.

Ripping the door open, he shoves his beer in back and climbs up into the captain's chair. The engine boots slow as space molasses, but once it gets going, it purrs soft as space molasses. The control panel is archaic, but after a space minute of fiddling around, he manages to get the saucer wobbling up off the ground. He's never operated a manual anti-grav engine, but he figures it's all the same.

The saucer judders as he messes with the spatial orienter, and when he finally gets it into gear, it lurches upward, smashing through the shed's decaying roof. He desperately tries to get a hang of the controls as the ship careens over the house, and after a few harrowing space seconds, he manages to bring it down for a landing out front.

"Easy now, girl," he tells the ship as he gently guides her up through the airlock.

Flipping the headlights on, Rot anxiously gazes out across the endless black sea, and with a good buzz going, he putters off into the dark.

30

"Adam's Log, space date... something. We've only been on this chithole planet for a few excruciating space minutes, and I already can't wait to leave."

The lodge is located deep inside the red desert, just beyond and downwind of the municipal landfill. The scent of centuries-old garbage permeates the dry air as the weary travelers trudge toward the colossal pyramid. What was once a brilliant white beacon to long haul scrappers, according to ancient astronaut theorists, is now little more than a rocky hill, the casing stones that once covered its rough steps having long-since turned to dust.

Stumbling across the sand in her glittery platform heels, Frank says, "I thought this place was supposed to be a secret."

"Where better to hide than in plain sight?" Adam says.

"I can think of a few places," Daizy offers, fanning herself from atop Dach's shoulders as he cheerfully marches across the dunes.

Todd has had his nose buried in his phone the whole trek, occasionally pulling back his sweaty mane to spout some mildly interesting factoid that has little to no relevance to their mission. "Did you guys know that during Big Candy's half-successful attempt at terraforming the red planet to expand sugar production, the Universal Insurance Agency Pyramid provided power to more than half of the New Martian population, while simultaneously operating as the universe's largest gift shop?"

"You mean it's just some stupid tourist attraction?" Frank says. "I can't believe I let you chitheads drag me out here. We could be rocking off at The Park right now, but instead we're in the middle of nowhere looking for some rock that doesn't even exist." She glances back at Daizy. "You're lucky you're so fishing sexy."

"All right," Adam says. "Can we all just tone it down a little? These guys aren't playing around. I've read their newsletter. We have to act the part. Do you know what happened to the last 'unbelievers'?"

Daizy shrugs. "No..."

"Neither do I," he says. "But I'm sure it wasn't pleasant."

Shielding her eyes from the yellow sun, Daizy says, "Everybody knows the only true religions are Rationism and, of course, Voodoo. Still, I'm surprised you haven't already signed up with these dopes. They're the only ones who care about the black gold as much as you."

"I don't give a chit about the black gold," Adam says. "I'm trying to save the universe. And anyway, Park Bucks aren't free, you know."

"Did you know that Park Bucks are actually *less* economical than credits," Todd says, "but that the planet's decentralized banking syndicate has officially certified them as '*more* fun'?"

"I told you!" Adam says, and Daizy shakes her head.

When they reach the giant stone slab that bars the temple's entrance, Adam searches for a way in, but the door is shut tight. Not even Dach can make it budge, though Adam doubts whether the fisherman gave it his all.

As they futilely yank on the ancient stone, Todd points at a weathered plaque fixed to the wall. "I wonder if that's something."

"It must be some sort of magic incantation. That's the only way anyone could move this thing." Unable to decipher the alien code, Adam bangs his head against the door and says, "We're never going to get in."

But before he knows what's happening, the slab shifts under his forehead, and he slides down onto the hard floor as the door grinds open.

A small, robed figure emerges from the darkness and pulls back his hood to reveal a thick head of purple hair. "You knocked?"

"Uh yeah, hi," Adam says lifting himself up out of the sand. "My name is Adam Jones. I got a call—"

"Wait a space second," the kid says. "You *are* Adam Jones!"

"That's what I just said."

"And *you*," he points over Adam's shoulder. "You're Daizy. And you're..." his mouth drops open when he sees the greasy-haired merch master. Dropping to his knees, he bellows, "O Captain! My Captain! We're all Pants Team Pink."

Shoving his phone in his pocket, Todd glances around the entryway and says, "Um, arise official team member…"

"Call me Ishmael," the boy says, and gesturing toward Dach and Frank, "I don't recognize these two."

"They're nobody," Adam says, and Daizy has to latch onto Frank to keep her from retaliating.

"What are you all doing here?" the kid asks.

"We want to sign up for your… thing," Adam says, pulling out a wad of Park Bucks. "How much is it?"

But Ishmael waves the cash away. "Your play money is no good here. You guys are legends. Come on in. Just remember to abide by the ancient words of our order." He points to the sign posted next to the door. "Watch your step."

On his way inside, Adam trips over the raised threshold, resulting in a cascade of bodies tumbling onto a soft rug inside the palatial antechamber.

"Everybody's got to learn the hard way," Ishmael says, helping them up off the floor.

The interior of the pyramid is much more accommodating than Adam anticipated. The floors have been swept free of sand, and the lighting is unobtrusive. Crowds of robed believers roam the entertainment center, greeting each other with a peculiar hand gesture in which they jab their fingers at the other's eyes while holding up the opposite hand to block the incoming assault.

"What are these?" Adam asks, pawing through a basket of purple wigs near the door.

"That's the official headwear of the Church," Ishmael says. "Along with the robes, it's part of the mandatory attire."

As his compatriots select their hairpieces, Adam asks, "Why do you wear them?"

"We're on some kind of mission," the kid says, shrugging. "We have an obligation. We have to wear toupees."

"Oh...," Adam says as he fits one of the purple rugs onto his slightly lopsided skull.

Looking them up and down, Ishmael beams. "Come on. I'll introduce you to the head of our order." On the way to the elevators, he asks Todd, "So, what's it like being part of Pants Team Pink, and saving the universe and all?"

"It's like..." Todd stares off blankly for a moment and finally says, "pretty brule, I guess."

"*Wow,*" Ishmael gushes.

As they all cram inside the ancient stone box, Daizy gets shoved up against Adam, and her tail brushes against his hand. Her scent, a gamey perfume of sweat and sand, smells like summer. As the box jerks upward, he lightly blows on her triangle ear just enough to cause it to twitch.

Trying to think of something clever to say before they get off, he finally decides on, "Funny meeting you here."

She turns toward him, blank-faced, and says, "That's the best you could come up with?"

"Uh, come here often?" he suggests.

"You're a chidiot," she says, turning away. "And quit blowing on my ear."

When the elevator stops, they stumble out into a spacious suite on one of the upper levels of the pyramid.

Soft light pours in from tall passageways that open onto a wide terrace overlooking the drab Martian desert.

Stepping toward a large table covered in snacks, Adam cracks a bag of ration rinds and asks, "Are these for everybody?"

"Everything in this place is yours for the taking," a voice announces, and they turn to find an elderly man with a graying purple beard dressed in the same robed attire as the rest of the believers. "Welcome to the Church of Raleigh. It's an honor to have such distinguished stars joining our order. I'll be your host, Froynlaven."

"You're welcome," Adam says. "Listen, my friends and I have been wandering the space hellscape outside all day, and I've been eating these salty rinds... Before we talk membership, I could really use something cold to take the edge off."

"Of course," the head goof says, stepping toward a long bar carved into the stone wall. "Allow me to get you all some water."

Smacking his lips, Adam says, "Uh yeah, water's good. But you got anything a little stronger?"

Froynlaven shakes his head. "I'm afraid not. We are a pious order. Water is the only liquid our bodies require to survive, and so it is the only beverage permitted inside the Church."

"Oh...," Adam whimpers, slumping to his knees.

"Aside from the nectar of the gods, of course," the ancient one says, and he opens the refrigerator to reveal half a dozen shelves stocked with glistening Nü Guard.

"Froynlaven," Adam says, "I think this is the beginning of a beautiful friendship... I mean worship... I mean beer."

31

"What is the name of the diminutive, green-haired... person who dances for nickels down at the Springfield docks?" the old man asks from the sideline, his ample-bootyed alien witch hanging off his arm.

Without missing a beat, OtaKween answers, "Handsome Pete."

BeerCheese69 growls, pushing his thick glasses up his nose as he tells 'Grandpa' to "ask the next question!"

"According to the Shelbyville Abe," Grandpa says, "why did the town banish the lemon tree?"

"I know this...," Tim_Horton says, and snapping his fingers, "Because it was haunted!"

"Fish!" Courtney-chan wails. "I almost had that one."

OtaKween juts her thumb out at theonetrueking, and he blows her a raspberry. He looks like he landed from another series. Either the camera adds forty pounds and three space years, or he's had a bunch of deconstructive surgery. Having yet to correctly answer even a single question, it also seems that his Simpsons knowledge has been greatly exaggerated. But the biggest disappointment is princessfluffypants herself. Since the round started, she's done nothing but sit in the back and pick at the pavement. It turns out that the team's strong, perma-peppy princess is nothing but a scared little girl.

Neveretheless, Beer and Horton have somehow managed to keep their team afloat, matching the Xenodorks point for point.

Stomping her sneaker, Courtney-chan asks, "Whose stupid idea was it to use fan-submitted questions?"

"Yours," Top5 reminds her, scooping a handful of pink cookie dough from a plastic tub perched on his lap.

"Oh yeah...," she says. "Hey, where'd you get that?"

Licking his blue sausage fingers, he tells her, "I bribed the popcorn guy. Park Bucks can go a long way when you know how to use them."

"He's asking the next question," OtaKween says.

Squinting down at his holo-screen the old man says, "This one's from somebody called *sparkaru-kun*. They ask, in season two episode eleven, what is the name of the character who sings 'Gypsys, Tramps & Thieves' in the karaoke bar of The Happy Sumo?"

OtaKween clenches her fists against her skirt, searching the darkest corners of her mind, and finally blurts, "Richard Sakai!"

"Ha!" Beer shouts, pointing his self-righteous finger into the air. "That's the producer of the show. The name of the character is *Richie* Sakai."

"Oh, give me a break, you ackle," Courtney-chan says. "It's close enough. Judge?"

They turn to Grandpa for a decision, and he wrings his wrinkly hands together as his evil girlfriend whispers something in his ear. "Um... I'm going to allow it."

"Oh, come on!" Beer protests. "You're killing us, Grandpa. She got it wrong. It's our point."

"I've made my ruling," Grandpa says, and with the witch sucking on his ear, he announces, "It's time for a break. The next round will begin in ten space minutes."

The members of Pants Team Pink whine and moan, but per the terms they agreed to, the decision stands. As the crowd stumbles off to refill their feedbags, Beer stays put, glaring across the aisle.

"At least the old man is with us," Courtney-chan says, and noticing Beer, "What is that chidiot doing? Is that supposed to intimidate us? He's such a dink." Tugging at her long yellow hair, she adds, "But he is sort of cute."

"That was too close," OtaKween tells the Dorks. "We're beating them, but just barely. If the Pants Team Pimples are this good in their weakened state, we won't be able to compete with them at their full strength. We have to hit them hard before they have a chance to recover."

"BUUUHH," Top5 belches and tosses his empty dough bucket to the ground. Shifting in his hover-chair, he reaches underneath his girth and wrenches loose a pair of VR goggles. "I agree entirely. In fact, I'm going to spend the break boning up for the next round."

"Good," Courtney-chan says. "You definitely need it."

"Hard, soft, wet, dry, french," Top5 says, pulling the goggles over his wide cranium. "The top five ways you can kiss my ack."

Lifting her arm to block the grinning sun, OtaKween grabs her cup from the holder on Top5's hover-chair and winces as she sucks down the warm soda. Everything about the bright Playland makes her want to wretch – the lame attractions, the kiddie rides, the gross food. It's the only place in the universe that could make home look good.

A giant pink mascot with googly eyes roams the grounds nearby, announcing, "You're all part of Pants Team Pink!"

As the cat approaches, OtaKween sticks out her skinny leg, and a muffled wail escapes the creature's dumb head as it crashes to the rubber street. Watching the hideous thing flail its furry limbs as it attempts to push itself off the pavement, she says, "That's better."

"Nice one," Howard Johnson comments, in the mocking, nasally rasp of Carly Pitz, their elementary school bully. *"Let's take its lunch money."*

"Dam it, Hojo," OtaKween says. "I hate it when you use that voice."

Hojo swipes at her voice changer, her dark lips barely visible beneath her cowl. *"I'm so sorry, your highness,"* she says, in Pants's sickening whine. *"Is this better, you guys?"*

Ignoring the provocation, the Kween asks, "How's the other thing coming?"

The hooded girl lifts her pale finger, and switching to a breathy bass, she says, *"Everything is going according to plan."*

Otakween's lips stretch back, and she hunches over, tapping her fingers together. "Excellent."

"What plan?" Courtney-chan asks, bouncing across the street. As she flies through the air, a thick clump of her long hair gets in her eyes, and she crashes into the other girls. "I know you're up to something. You always leave me out of stuff."

"We do not," OtaKween says. "The only thing we're planning is how to beat these ackles. If you want to help, start studying for the next round."

A determined expression forms on Courtney-chan's face, and she nods. "You're right. You can count on me." Springing up from the pavement, she brushes the dirt from her jeans and buries her eyes in her phone.

Feeling some shame at the half-truth, OtaKween glances at Hojo, and explains, "If she finds out about the plan, soon the whole Park will know about it."

"Very wise, your highness," Hojo says, through her artificial voice box. *"It is time to initiate the final phase of the plan."* With a twirl, her body disappears inside her invisible cape.

"Where are you going?" OtaKween demands. "The old man is going to be back any space minute."

"You'll have to get along without me." Hojo flips up her hood, obscuring all but a shadow-rimmed smile, and before OtaKween can argue, the girl is gone.

"Fish and chit!" OtaKween cries.

The spectators start filing back into the arena, their arms and mouths full of enough fried snacks to keep them satiated through the next round as the teams risk memory trauma dredging up hyper-specific minutia about an imaginary world created long before their time.

Looking out over the sea of fans, OtaKween suddenly begins to feel lightheaded. She lifts the soda to her lips as the crowd closes in, but all that comes out of the straw is air. As she wipes her arm across her forehead, she can see little stars twinkling in the corners of her eyes.

She doesn't feel the fall, but the next thing she knows, she's staring up at a cute boy with dark eyes and windswept hair. "Are you all right?"

For a moment, she thinks she's dead, but when she sees Courtney-chan and Top5 hovering over her, she's brought back to annoying reality. "I'm fine," she says, wobbling to her feet.

"Here," the boy says, handing her a cold soda. "Don't worry, there's nothing pink inside. It's just water."

Ripping the cap off, she greedily gulps the icy liquid and wipes her hand across her mouth. "Thanks."

"I'm glad I could help," he says, flashing a smile that almost knocks her out again.

Pointing at his t-shirt, white with a big 'X' scribbled in black marker, she says, "You're a fan?"

"Of course," he tells her. "I love you guys. I was heartbroken when the show ended before you even got to finish your first mission. When I found out you were here, I had to come see the next chapter."

"Oh uh, ha-ha...," she stammers.

He lifts the hand she used to wipe her mouth and writes a long screen name on it. "Hit me up after you win this thing."

Watching him walk back to his parents, she suddenly notices that there are nearly enough homemade Xenodorks signs and t-shirts to rival Pants Team Pink.

"Are you okay?" Courtney-chan asks, wrapping her arms around the Kween's neck. "I was so *worried* about you."

"Really, I feel fine," she says.

"Good," Top5 announces, from atop his floating throne, "because the next round is about to start, just as soon as *Grandpa* figures out how to unlock his holo-screen..."

"I can feel it," OtaKween says. "The tide is shifting. I know we all agreed that the show was over, but—"

Before she can finish her thought, Top5 tells her, "You don't have to say it. I've sensed it ever since we landed."

Once Courtney-chan figures out what they're talking about, her eyes get wide. "You mean we're really doing it?"

A wicked smile forms on the Kween's lips as she declares, "Season two starts now."

32

They land in a gray desert bordering the base of a colossal black crag. It doesn't take long for Pi to determine why she chose the location. One look at the mountain's jagged, crumbling cliffs would be enough to deter even the most meddlesome of tomb raiders.

"You got all your stuff?" she asks.

"I think so," the boy says, double-checking the pockets of his windbreaker for the ration bars he brought to tide him over until lunch. With his Ponce doll strapped to his chest, he pulls his luxury goggles down, and holds his fingers up in a 'V.'

"He's so cute, I just want to choke the life out of him," Stella says.

"Don't listen to her." Pi playfully smacks the boy on the back, and he almost tumbles down the steps. "She's just jealous she can't come with us. So, how do we get in?"

"There is no easy way," he says. "According to legend, there is a small cave hidden somewhere at the base of the mountain. If any of my ancestors ever located it, they didn't live long enough to tell. The terrain contains many hazards, but at least the wind isn't so strong on this side."

"And you thought you wouldn't be any help," Pi says.

"Onward, me hearties!" Mini Ponce cries.

As soon as they step onto the escalator, the gusting wind threatens to throw them off, and Pi grabs the boy before he loses his footing, her coat and scarf flapping wildly as she carries him down into the arid wasteland. The storm hovering over the distant cliffs appears to have grown even more violent in the moments since they landed.

"Are you sure about this?" the boy shouts over the howling breeze.

Patting him on his shaggy head, she grasps his arm and drags him down onto the rocky soil. Between the weather and the slag collapsing under their feet, progress is slow. The boy can barely stay on his feet as he stumbles along beside her.

Halfway to the mountain's base, Pi feels a small tremor in the dirt underneath them, and she stops to get a better reading.

"What is it?" the boy asks, glancing ahead nervously.

She sets her internal seismometer to the highest sensitivity, but the vibrations have ceased. *"Did you feel that?"*

"Feel wha—?" A look of terror forms on his windburnt face. *"We have to move!"*

Pi's sensors suddenly indicate a spike in activity, and she loses her footing as the dirt below them starts to give. Before they can be swallowed by the sinking sand, she grabs the boy's shoulders and tosses him out of the pit.

Tumbling across the gravel, he lands against a small outcrop of stone as she plummets into the dark.

For half a space second she's in freefall before crashing down across the spongy floor into a soup of acidic muck. When the ground stops moving, she carefully stands and engages her headlights to illuminate her surroundings. As she examines the tunnel, its pulsating walls dripping black tar into a corrosive pool around her feet, the cavern lurches, and she slips onto her back. Splashing in the thick goop, she reaches out for anything that might stop her from sliding across the slick surface, but it's no use.

Having had her fill of the proceedings, Pi gets to her feet and punches her fist through the fleshy wall. A high-pitched wail echoes through the tunnel as she tears it open and climbs out into the dry desert air. Streamers of dark goop stretch and flap off her coat, a big glob of which rides a strong gust to splat across the boy's astonished mug.

Wiping the slime out of his eyes, he shouts, *"You're alive!"*

"Go back to the ship," she tells him as she rips a hunk of worm flesh off her shoulder. *"You'll never survive out here."*

The boy nods, unable to keep his eyes off the dead annelid stretched and bloated in the dirt. *"Keep to the trail,"* he yells.

"Arghhh...," the doll wails, rubbing the dust from its eyes.

He motions toward the cliff as he trudges off into the dust, and Pi discovers a narrow path carved into the rock behind her. She follows it around the base of the mountain until she comes to a small opening just wide enough to pass through.

The wind howls and echoes through the cave as she descends the winding tunnel into a deep cavern flowing with streams of thick black magma. Half a dozen humanoid skeletons are scattered around the entrance, and she scans the atmosphere to find that it's comprised primarily of carbon dioxide – one final trap to keep out the biological riffraff.

"Raiders," she scoffs, activating her lights.

As she makes her way further down the shaft, the temperature begins to rise, until her coat and scarf are smoking. When she comes to a dead end, she flashes her light across the blank wall, searching for a hidden switch, or a hinge, or something. But all she finds is stone.

She wouldn't put it past herself to set up fake-out chambers. There could be any number of them along the base of the mountain and maybe even up into the cliffs. But no, that's not right. The only reason to go to such lengths would be to keep herself out, and she didn't want that, not entirely.

She considers what she would do if she were her, and she flashes the light back over the dark walls. At first glance, they appear unremarkable. But upon closer inspection, she discovers that a large section of the rock has been patched smooth. When she presses her finger to the flat stone, it crumbles.

Shoving her hands into the wall, she tears away big hunks of ore until she has uncovered the object of her quest. Irrationally, part of her hoped she wouldn't find it, so that she wouldn't have to do the thing she's going to do. But deep down, she always knew it was still here, waiting.

As she drags the cursed slab back across the desert, the wind rips it from her hands, and it sails out across the sand. For a moment, as she watches it sink into the dark sediment, she considers leaving it for the sandworms to devour. But for some reason she rescues the stupid hunk of ore and hauls it back to Stella's cabin, committing them to their fate.

"What the fish happened to you?" Stella asks, upon seeing her slimy, dust-caked chassis.

"A woman must never be afraid to get her hands dirty," Pi says.

"Just don't lay those filthy things on me."

Pi grins, tiptoeing toward the dash. "I think you like it dirty."

"I do no-ot," the ship whimpers as Pi presses her grimy fingers to the control panel.

But remembering the slab, she says, "I guess I'll throw this in the utility closet."

"What? No!" Stella cries.

"Okay... I'll dump it in the cargo hold." After Pi tosses the object of their quest into the brig, the cabin suddenly feels empty. "Where's the boy?" she asks. "Once I secure the black gold and total universal domination, we have plans to play video games."

"Oh uh, he's not with you?" Stella says. "I can't keep track of all these humanoids."

"What do you mean, 'all these'? It's one guy."

"Nevertheless..."

Pi reels at the uncomfortable new sensation she experiences upon processing the boy's disappearance.

As she collapses into the captain's chair, the furniture seems lumpier than usual, and louder, complaining, "Argh, get your ack off me, you bilge-sucking wench."

Reaching underneath her chassis, she wrings the doll by its neck and asks it, "Where's the boy?"

"Aye," Mini Ponce says. "He be swimmin' in Davey Jones's locker."

Pi tosses the doll to the floor and sticks her head outside to scan for life forms, shouting into the howling wind, *"Boy? Boy!"* But all she finds is slag and dust goblins.

33

"Okay, let's embiggen your mind with a few easy ones," Horton says, swiping at his phone. "What was the secret ingredient in the briefly popular cocktail known as the Flaming Moe, née Homer?"

"I already told you," The Other One says, "I never watched the show."

Checking for eavesdroppers, Horton points a finger at the boy's pillowy stomach and whispers, "First of all, don't let anybody hear you say that, or we'll be stripped of the black gold before you can say Krusty's Non-narkotik Cough Syrup for Kids. Second, if you're going to pretend to be The One, you have to learn to act like him. He knows this stuff like the bottom of his ration tray." Grabbing The Other One's phone, he pulls up a list of episodes. "I guess we're going to have to go back to basics. Start with the clip shows, at double speed." As he hands over the hunk of glass, he snatches a baggie of carrot sticks from the kid's sweatpants pocket. "And eat something fried, for Space God's sake."

Horton can feel the cracks forming. The Other One is next to useless, and Pants has never looked this low. The pink hue she radiates inside the Playland has almost completely faded, and it's growing dimmer by the space second. On the other hand, Beer's training has paid off. His ability to recall ultra-obscure factoids apparently has no bounds. Between the two of them, they've just barely managed to keep pace with the Xenodorks. The do-badders have proven far more formidable than they appear. Something about the small hooded one, in particular, gives Horton the hidely hos.

As he searches the Dorks' camp for the slippery shadow creature, his stomach drops. "Where is she?"

"Where's who?" Beer asks, breaking his furious concentration on their opponents.

"The one they call Howard Johnson," Horton says. "I don't see her."

Peering at their adversaries through the space between his fingertips, Beer says, "It matters not. For just as it appears when I press my fingers together, we will crush them."

But Horton is far from convinced. "I don't like this. Pranks have been ramping up. They're up to something big, but what?"

"You're starting to sound paranoid again. These guys are lightweights, except for that bloated blue one. He's got an even more impressive physique than The One."

"Speaking of," Horton says, "where the fish is your brother? Trivia is his strong suit."

"The ackle won't answer my calls. But we can do this. Everything we need is right here," Beer says, pointing to his scruffy head. "We just have to shut off the logical part of our minds, embrace nothingness, and become like uncarved stones. Quick, what's Bleeding Gums Murphy's only album?"

"Sax On the Beach," Horton says. "Mr. Burns's stuffed teddy bear?"

"Bobo." Training his eyes back on the enemy camp, Beer says, "You see? Not even The Collector could out-nerd us. A film from which you might remember Troy McClure?"

"Uh..." Horton racks his brain. "The only one I can think of is The Erotic Adventures of Hercules."

"The Bort is strong in you," Beer says, shaking his head. "But you still have much to learn, my young ignoramus."

"That word you just used means I'm stupid, doesn't it?" Horton asks, with a sly grin.

"There may be hope for you yet." Zipping his team jacket as a light breeze wafts through, Beer asks, "Does it feel cold to you all of a sudden?"

"Now that you mention it." Horton glances around the makeshift arena and notices a small gray cloud forming over Pants.

Balled up on her portable throne, in the safety of the *Cuddler's* security force field, her radiance has been reduced to a pink mist. She's removed her plastic kitty ears and tied her pink pigtails back into a long ponytail, which she's been chewing obsessively. As Horton makes his approach, trying hard to avoid any sudden movements that might scare her off, she turns up the volume on her phone.

"What are you watching?" he asks, even though he can plainly hear the familiar dialogue of "You Only Move

Twice." After a moment of awkward TV chatter, he tugs at his jacket sleeve and says, "Look, I'm wearing my new uniform."

She glances at him, unsmiling, and it sends a shiver through his extremities. "It's not supposed to be a uniform. They were a gift, for the team."

"Oh, right," he says as she searches her throne. "What are you looking for?"

Shoving her hand between the cushions, she says, "My earplugs."

"I can't take this anymore," Horton tells her. "You have to cheer up. What's your problem, anyway? The Xenodorks may be the toughest enemies we've ever come up against, but you've never backed down from a fight. You're always the first one to stand up for what's right."

"That's not it," she says, her bottom lip jutting out as tears stream down her cheeks.

"Then what is it?" he asks, sitting on the edge of her throne. "We're a team, remember? That means we help each other when things get tough."

Wiping her eyes, she says, "Didn't you hear the Dorks? Their lives were ruined because of us. We didn't fix anything. Nothing we did made the universe any better. We probably just made things worse. They're right. We *are* the bad guys."

As thunder cracks above Pants's head, Horton feels something inside him snap. All of his fear and anxiety dissolves, and suddenly the path forward becomes clear. "I'm as cynical and jaded as the next kid. Maybe more so. But I'll be dammed if I'm going to let a gang of whiny space punks kill the spirit of Pants Team Pink." He jumps down from Pants's throne and pulls her to her feet.

"*We're not the bad guys.* You've done more for this universe than the rest of these nerds put together. The Xenodorks have managed to pull off some decent pranks, I'll give them that. But how does TPing people's domes help anyone? They just want to pull us apart, because they know we're stronger together. It's the only way they can beat us. But we're better than that. We have to be." Glancing out at the crowd, he points to a bouncing little girl. "For that kid right there, with the frosting all over her face... and hands, and hair. It's disgusting. But I've never seen anyone having a better time in my life. That's why we can't fail."

"You're right..." The glow surrounding Pants intensifies, and her quavering lip morphs into a look of steely determination the likes of which Horton has never seen. "After all, if we don't take care of the universe, who will?"

She grabs her team jacket, and together they step out into the heat of the grinning sun. The fans are back from their bathroom/snack break and rapidly growing restless, but when Pants is spotted bouncing across the makeshift arena, a wave of excitement ripples through the crowd.

Beer is at his post, mean-mugging the Dorks, and when he sees Pants's glow, he tells her, "It's good to have you back."

Holding her fingers up, Pants says, "Sorry I went a little crazy back there, you guys. Everything changed so fast, I guess I just forgot what's important."

"You don't ever have to apologize to us," Beer says. "If it wasn't for you, we'd still be back at home playing moldy old holo-games in Horton's basement. We've all been acting a little crazy lately. Maybe that's just part of growing up."

"I hope not!" she cries. "I don't want to feel like that all the time."

"Neither do we, Pants. Neither do we..." Laughing, they put their hands together, and Beer cries, "For Pants Team Pink!"

"For Pants Team Pink!" someone shouts, and one more sweaty hand lands on top of the pile.

Horton slowly turns his head to glare at The Other One, grinning like a chidiot as he struggles to contain the couch cushion under his shirt. "Shouldn't you be studying?"

"At this point, I know enough to pass Mrs. Crandall's fourth grade history test," The Other One says.

Horton glares at the boy suspiciously and tells him, "I'm going to assume you understand what you just said."

The chatter from the crowd suddenly increases a few decibels, and Beer announces, "Grandpa's back."

"Does the old man seem familiar to you?" Horton asks.

"Sort of," Beer says. "I guess."

The megaphone squeals as the witch messes with the settings and hands it to the Game Master. *"Uh... hi. Hel— hello? Okay, we're gonna start round two in a space minute here."*

The Xenodorks gather across the street, surrounded by more fans than they've ever had, while Howard Johnson remains at large. As Horton considers the implications of the pale Dork's disappearance, something smacks against the back of his head. He spins around, expecting to catch one of the Dorks' evil followers in the act, but the street is empty. Searching the crowd, he lifts a small shiny object from the pavement.

"What is it?" Beer asks.

Glancing up into the bright Park sky, Horton says, "It's half a ration bar..."

34

Standing at the head of the ancient stone bench, Froynlaven, his purple beard hanging down to his waist, waves his arms to quiet the chattering worshippers. With the soothing voice of a TV news anchor, he calls to them, "Gather 'round, knuckleheads. For it is a great blessing that we may join together today, guided by the omnipresent universal force that determines the trajectory of all things, to witness the activation of five believers."

The crowd hoots and hollers, smashing bottles with significantly more enthusiasm than seems warranted for the arrival of a bunch of strangers, no matter how pious. There's something about these people Daizy doesn't trust, but she can't quite put her paw on it. Froynlaven and his followers have been nothing but clumsily hospitable, but isn't there always something wrong with religious cults? The rest of the weirdos in her adoptive litter don't appear too concerned. Adam and that chidiot from Earth, Todd, are lapping up all the Pants Team adjacent attention they can get.

As Daizy reluctantly waves to her leering fans, her insignificant others stumble up to the dais, and without bothering to remove her tongue from Dach's mouth, Frank mumbles, "We need a room." The two of them haven't been able to keep their hands off each other since they arrived in this space-hole.

"Would you two keep your wigs on, *please?*" Daizy scolds. "You're embarrassing me."

"Oh, I'm sorry," Frank says. She pulls her face away from Datch and slides her arm around Daizy's robed backside, kissing her in a way that reminds her why they started dating in the first place.

"Wooo," somebody in the crowd shouts.

"But before we welcome these numbskulls into the cold bosom of the Church, they must first prove themselves worthy," Froynlaven declares, and calling to some invisible functionaries, "Bring in the ancient relics of Raleigh."

From the back of the hall, a team of brutes with purple bowl cuts haul five rotting barrels up to the head of the table. Each of the containers is big enough to hold a full humanoid, and as the muscle men pry open the lids, Froynlaven motions for the new initiates to rise.

"There is only one way to prove that you are true believers," he tells them. "You must willingly submit yourselves to the Church's oldest, most sacred ritual – a drinking contest."

"Of course it is," Daizy says.

Adam looks back at her and shrugs, a big stupid grin plastered on his chidiot face as the revelry echoes through the hall.

"These casks have been stored in the sub-basements of the great pyramid since before Ponce Raleigh's disappearance over five hundred years ago," Froynlaven lectures. "They were thought lost until a band of Raleighites charged with excavating a new rec room uncovered a large cache of what they believed to be water barrels used by the ancient slaves who toiled below the monument. But in place of stale water, they discovered a blessed fermented beverage which is said to have allowed them to communicate directly with the Spirit of Ponce. The recipe for the divine brew was lost in an unfortunate amateur wrestling accident, but the holy spirits before you are described by the ancient ones as a 'close approximation,' and the last best way to experience what Raleigh was drinking during his final voyage into the dark."

The worshippers grow quiet, raising their cups in reverence as Froynlaven and the passengers of the *Asteroid Jones II* are bestowed with oversized steins covered in cathodic imagery.

"In order to confirm your membership to the Church, you must imbibe the ale of our ancestors," Froynlaven says. "But fear not my friends, for you will not drink alone." He raises his stein and waves it over the crowd. "We will help you finish every drop from these barrels, or black out trying."

Rusty sand rains down from the cracks in the stone walls as the worshippers let loose, crowding toward the casks.

"Please, restrain yourselves," Froynlaven says, calming the congregation. "Our newest knuckleheads must be the first to savor the sweet, nutty flavor of Ponce's Private Reserve."

Froynlaven motions toward the barrels, and Daizy looks out at the expectant rabble as her companions dunk their steins into the 'sacred' punch bowls. Glancing down at the mammoth mug in her hand, she suddenly feels like she's eight years old again, about to jump after Trixa Hinsley off Auxiliary Overpass 703.

Dipping her stein into the nearest barrel, it becomes so heavy with beer that she can barely lift it back out. She uses both hands to try to hold the mug steady, but she slips, and a large portion of the brew splashes out onto the floor.

Wincing, Daizy tells the congregation, "Sorry..."

But Froynlaven lifts his hands. "No need to apologize. Sloshing is the most reverent act of devotion a knucklehead can perform. It's a way of paying respect to our ancestors. Before we commence the sacred ceremony, let us all pour one out for the Raleigh while we recite the words of our order."

As the beer of the ancients spills onto the floor stones, the crowd chants, *"Don't give up the ship."*

Adam looks pained as the booze drains around their feet. To make up for lost beer, he starts chugging. The rest of the honored guests follow his lead, reveling in their holy hedonism, and as Daizy looks out over the sea of thirsty worshippers glancing expectantly between her and their beers, she sighs and takes a sip.

With that, all space hell breaks loose as the believers rush toward the barrels to partake in the bubbly brew. A bunch of them jump up onto the table, ripping off their robes and dancing spastically to the primeval blare of The Kingsmen bouncing between the cavern walls.

Unable to think of a way to beat them, Daizy resorts to the other option. The first stein goes down so smooth she can hardly remember what she was worried about, or where she is, or who she's making out with as she rides a wave of frothy suds into the land of who gives a fish. The rest of the night is a blur of sweat and alcohol as the Spirit of Ponce compels her to release her inner feline.

When she finally tires herself out, she fills her stein with the dregs of one of the giant barrels and slumps down against the wall amongst a heap of hard partiers.

Quietly taking in the raucous scene, she turns to find an ancient face framed by a long purple beard dripping thick foam. "Hey, you're that guy."

"I am, *hic,* Froynlaven," he says, dipping his face into his stein.

"You got a real racket going here," she tells him.

"Thank you." He turns to look her in the eye, his head rested against the stone wall. "Now tell me, why are you really here?"

Half a dozen bad responses flit through her mind, but before she can decide on one, she hears herself saying, "We came for the black gold."

"Oh, *that...*" he laughs and slugs his beer. "A lot of, *hic,* people come to see it, even non-believers. They think it will answer their, *hic,* prayers. Many of your fellow knuckleheads are convinced of it as well. If you want to know the, *hic,* truth, I don't even think it's real."

Bobbling her beer, Daizy says, "You mean, it's a fake?"

Froynlaven shrugs. "I ordered it from the back of a, *hic,* comic book. It's just a, *hic,* replica, from the show. I thought it would boost morale. The kid on the phone, *hic,* tried to convince me it was the real thing, but he wasn't a very good, *hic,* salesman." Using his robe to dry his beard, he says, "Sorry to, *hic,* disappoint. But why did you think the black, *hic,* gold was here? That Todd, *hic,* fellow is the official merch guy of Pants Team Pink, is he not? It is believed that they possess the, *hic,* real element."

"They lost it," Daizy says. "They sent us here on a wild space chase to find it. And it turns out it's not even real." She can't tell if she wants to laugh or cry, so she does both.

"There, *hic,* there," he consoles her, guzzling his beer. "We all believe in black gold, *hic,* sometimes."

Looking at him through teary eyes, she says, "There's one thing I don't get. Why am I telling you all of this?"

The ancient man smiles, lifting his beer, and says, "Ponce's Private Reserve is a truth serum."

"Truth serum?" She glances down at her stein, takes another swig, and they both double over laughing.

"I was, *hic,* hoping you wouldn't ask," he says.

"You're a real son of a perch, you know that?" She sighs, wiping her eyes. "What kind of a religion drugs its followers?"

"Oh, that's a great, *hic,* question," he says. "It all started some five hundred years ago, not long after Ponce Raleigh disappeared in his search for the black gold..."

Daizy checks her mug, but it's empty. She nods along as Froynlaven endeavors to explain why grown adults are living in a crumbling monument to an old space explorer, but she can't make sense of the words. Whether a result of the beer or the inanity, she feels herself dozing.

When she wakes, the great hall is quiet. Froynlaven is slumbering on the floor beside her, his head rested on the buttocks of a particularly wooly worshipper. The room tips as she stands, and she holds her hands to her head to keep from falling over. Tiptoeing over drunken bodies, she notices a lone hooded figure seated at the table amidst a pile of snoring knuckleheads.

"The last one standing," she says.

Resting its stein on the table, the figure turns toward her and pulls back its hood to reveal Adam's grinning mug. "What can I say? I'm blessed. Anyway, these guys are lightweights. They only had, like, fifteen beers apiece."

Shoving one of the worshippers aside, she squeezes onto the bench next to him and rests her head on his shoulder. "The black gold is a fake."

"Yeah, I kind of figured," he says.

"Should we tell the others?"

"Eh, let them sleep. They can be disappointed when they wake up, as usual." Leaning his head against hers, he says, "I'm sorry I dragged you out here."

"It's okay. It's been sort of a fun adventure so far." She grabs his arm, and for a moment the cold stone chamber almost feels cozy.

"Brule," Adam says. "So, you want to make out again?"

35

Time has lost all meaning in the dark, but by all indications, it's still passing – the smell of rotting flesh attests to that. Otherwise, the cell is unchanging. Sometimes it tips and lurches like a brig in choppy water, but mostly it's still and impenetrable, promising no escape and no hope.

The admiral's only consolation for being locked in Stella's utility closet is that he's gotten his first decent sleep since before the Pants War. As a consequence, he's thinking more clearly than he has in a long time. He actually feels more comfortable as a prisoner confined to his little box than he did having free rein over the entire UE space station. At the base he had been adrift, but in this place he has a purpose – survival.

For a frantic moment when he first awoke, he feared he had died and gone to space hell. But summoning the discipline instilled in him at the UE Academy, he calmed his mind and gently recalled his last conscious moments, in which he was lying on the floor of Stella's cabin, the room spinning and twinkling as he gasped for air.

"Can you believe that?" he telepathically asks the lifeless bodies lying next to him on the floor of the dark room. *"I spent months resurrecting her from the dead, piece by piece, and her idea of thanks is to kill me!"*

But she failed to account for the resilience of his species. The hard minerals that compose his body not only allow him to withstand extended periods of oxygen deprivation, but also extreme pressure, temperature, and just about anything else she might subject him to. With access to the trickle of water collecting inside the ship's dehumidifier, he can survive indefinitely.

"All we have to do is bide our time, and sooner or later we'll find a way out," he thinks to his lifeless companions. *"We just have to stick together. The hardest part will be staying sane. But if we all keep our brule, we'll be fine."*

The decision to forgo the installation of sensors inside Stella's closet was made for the sake of expediency and a lack of materials rather than a concern for his life. It just turned out to be one of those happy accidents. Without the specially designed tiles, she has no way of knowing what's going on inside the little room, near the mop and auxiliary tool box.

"If we keep quiet, she'll never know we're here," Glipp thinks, and the dead men answer with their silence. *"That's the idea.* Wait..." His fellow stowaways hold their breath. *"Do you hear that?"*

The admiral presses the side of his stone head to the door as muffled chatter seeps in. He recognizes the vibration of Stella's voice, but the other one is a mystery.

"Probably another dead scrapper," he thinks, and to his companions, *"Sorry..."* The new voice is one of six he's detected since he's been locked up. The one which is always present is Stella's, two belonged to his bunkmates, and the other three remain unknown. *"For a military spaceship, she really gets around."*

It's not long before the conversation dies out, and the door to the closet slides open. The bright overhead lights from the cabin temporarily blind the stone giant, but before Stella slams the door shut, he catches a glimpse of the young man's motionless body sliding up against the corpses of his ghost crew.

Glipp gives the kid a moment to get his bearings, knowing full well how disorienting having the life sucked out of you can be, and he finally thinks, *"Welcome aboard, son! Your transition into the land of the dead must have you feeling a little out of sorts, but take solace in the fact that you've just been dispatched into the ranks of Glipp's Dead Headz, the first and finest fleet in the New UE. We're a small but elite task force with a simple mission — to slosh our enemies, see them drunken before us, and hear the shuttering of their breweries, or something like that. We're still working on it. Before you endure the test of silence, do you have any questions?"* The boy holds his tongue. *"You're going to fit right in."*

With slow, measured movements, the admiral feels his way along the floor until he bumps up against the pile of bodies. Pawing through the pockets of his new third mate, he thinks, *"It's mandatory that all crew members surrender their belongings to their captain. I'd let you hand it over yourself but—"* For an instant he thought he felt the body shift underneath him.

"*Ughh...,*" the kid moans, but before he can say anything else, Glipp reaches out in the direction of the noise and smothers it.

The kid's arms flail and grasp in the dark, and after a brief struggle, he produces a bright light that forces Glipp's eyes shut. Holding his hand in place over the kid's mouth, the admiral leans into the light of the phone and holds a stone finger up to his lips. When the kid finally calms down, Glipp takes his hand away and points to the screen.

Tapping at the glowing brick, the admiral opens a blank text file and types, '*STAY QUIET. SHE COULD HEAR.*'

The kid grabs the phone, his hands shaking as he types, '*WHAT HAPPENED? WHERE ARE WE?*'

Glipp explains, '*SHE TRIED TO KILL US. DUMPED US IN UTILITY CLOSET. I'M ADMIRAL GLIPP. WHAT'S YOUR NAME?*'

'*THEY CALL ME THE BOY.*' Shining the light around the tiny box, the boy comes across the two rotting carcasses and turns his dark, bushy head to keep himself from gagging. '*WHO ARE THEY?*'

'*YOUR CREWMATES,*' Glipp types.

As the reality of his situation sinks in, the boy's eyes grow wide and he begins to hyperventilate. He can barely get the words out, '*HOW DO WE ESCAPE?*'

Glipp taps his thick head and shrugs.

For a while they sit in the dark, huffing the thick, necrotic air. Glipp doesn't blame the boy for surrendering to his fear. It's tough finding yourself in a hopeless situation, and from the looks of him this is his first time.

Before long, muffled voices can be heard inside the

cabin, and the bodies in the back begin to slide across the floor as the ship takes off. The boy uses his phone to light the closet as he scrambles to get a hold of anything that might stop him from tumbling onto the bloated carcasses below, but the cabinets are flush with the walls, and his hands slip right over them. Grasping out in the dark, Glipp catches the fragile humanoid and uses the weight of his stone body to anchor them both in place until the ship steadies.

Resting his head on the admiral's cold shoulder, the boy quietly sobs. When he's finished, he turns his attention back to his phone, typing, *'WHAT NOW?'*

'CALL FOR HELP?' the admiral types.

Shaking his head, the boy responds, *'NO RECEPTION.'*

'WHAT ABOUT EMERGENCY LOCATOR?'

'POSSIBLE,' the boy types, *'BUT WHO WOULD LOOK FOR SIGNAL?'*

The admiral shrugs. *'THEN WE WAIT.'*

The boy nods and after a moment types, *'FOR WHAT?'*

'A WAY OUT.'

The boy's face scrunches, and he snatches the phone back. *'NEED FOOD, WATER.'*

'FORGOT.' Glipp crawls over to the bodies piled against the wall, and rummaging through their stuff, he returns with a half-eaten ration bar and two-thirds of a six-pack of Nü Guard.

The boy smirks and holds his fingers up in a 'V.' *'ONE MORE QUESTION. WHY ARE WE TYPING IN CAPS?'*

The admiral shrugs. *'GOTTA LIVE SOMETIME.'*

36

The warehouse was easy enough to find. It's only the biggest, pinkest building in the industrial district. Tapping the side of her goggles, Hojo zooms in and watches the shipping trucks stream in and out of the lot, dropping off giant pallets of merchandise as fast as the dock bots can unload them. She had seen the numbers, but the reality was lost in translation. The whole operation is far bigger than she anticipated. Pants Team Pink are digging their own grave, and all she needs to do is help them fill in the dirt.

Pulling down her invisible hood, she dashes across the street and through a tangled route of back alleys and abandoned lots. When she reaches the colossal warehouse, she sidles around the corner of the building and comes to a basic security door equipped with a keypad that shouldn't take more than a few space minutes to hack. But as she reaches for her phone to brute-force the entry code, a thought occurs. She types 8-0-0-8-1-3-5, and the door cracks open.

"Chidiots," she mutters into her voice changer as she slips inside the building.

Shadowy towers surround her as she makes her way down the long corridor toward a stream of sunlight pouring into the loading dock. Anyone who happened to be working nearby would be able to hear her sneakers padding against the cement floor, but at most all they would see is an obscure shadow flitting across the shelves. The building is practically devoid of biological life forms, anyway. The fools left the place wide open. By all indications, this mission is going to be a piece of ration cake. She commends herself for dreaming up such a space-devilishly simple plan, but when she steps out into the main aisle, her confidence nosedives.

The warehouse is packed with so many giant pallets of black gold, it's almost comical. Gazing down the long corridor is like looking into a funhouse mirror. She rips open the plastic wrap sealing a nearby bundle and yanks out one of the replicas for a better look. Holding the cube up to the light, she mentally curses the object, the team, and herself for its incredible screen accuracy.

As she desperately searches the replica's surface for flaws, it slips from her invisible fingers, and she instinctively shouts in her true voice, *"Fish!"*

"What? Who said that?" someone calls.

Hojo presses her back up against the stack of replicas as an ugly gnome in a bright pink hard hat approaches the broken object. He looks at the mess and then glances at the open pallet, scratching his head. For a moment, he stares directly at her and reaches out his hand.

But just before his finger pokes her in the eye, a familiar voice shouts, "Hey, are you listening to me? We're losing daylight."

The gnome scowls and plods back toward the dock while Hojo skulks close behind. Weaving through a team of bots hauling pallets off a weathered cargo ship, the worker leads her toward a chubby boy with scruffy hair tapping a custom pink e-phone.

"I left you a dozen bots for unloading the new shipments," theonetrueking says, straightening his curly con wig. "I reprogrammed the rest to start moving defects into the back. That should free up some space." The gnome is unresponsive as the kid nervously swipes the screen. "What the fish is happening now? I gotta get back in the game before our characters are deleted. Call me if you have any problems."

On his way out, The One runs into a dock bot aimlessly roaming the loading area, and he impatiently stops to inspect it. He taps at his phone and the bot changes course, trudging into the warehouse as the boy disappears down one of the dark aisles.

Before the bot has a chance to escape, Hojo chases after it and leaps onto its back. Bouncing atop its shoulders, she manages to hack its settings, and with a swipe, she increases the automaton's speed by two thousand percent. She wraps her arms around its reinforced neck, holding on for her life as it gallops down the aisle. Soon they're surrounded by bots busily transporting replicas. When they reach the last stack, her bot grabs one of the pallets and carries it to the end of a long line of metal servants patiently waiting to deliver their bounty.

Jumping down from the robot's back, Hojo peels off her stifling hood and follows the line of bots into the furthest reaches of the building, where she finally comes to the instrument of the team's destruction. The giant transporter ring is significantly cruder than what was promised. It looks like it was slapped together in an afternoon by a drunken space ape, in the dark. It's just the kind of unskilled craftsmanship she should have expected from former Foremen.

In any case, the machine appears to be operational. The dock bots approach one at time, dumping whole pallets into the portal as Hojo steps around back. When she locates the panel, she presses down on it, and it pops up to reveal a hidden control pad. Following the instructions given to her by the engineer, she replaces the output coordinates with the ones stored in her phone. Her finger hovers over the confirmation button as she contemplates the full ramifications of her actions, and she presses it anyway.

Closing the panel, she glances at the line of bots tossing out the Pants Team trash, and in the words, and voice, of their bubbly leader, she says, *"This was too easy, you guys."*

The bot that carried her here has already made its way to the head of the line, where it heaves its pallet into the portal before charging back to the stacks for more. Seeing the machine's enthusiasm, Hojo suddenly feels inspired to do better, so she uses her phone to hack into the bots' shared network, and soon the rest of them are scurrying across the warehouse at top speed.

"We're all Pants Team Pink," she mocks, cackling as the bots race to do her bidding.

"Hey, who's over there?" a gravelly voice calls from across the room. "What are you doing back there?"

Slipping into the boy's sloppy drawl, Hojo says, *"It's just me, theonetrueking."*

Before she can be spotted, she quickly pulls down her invisible hood and hides behind the portal. After a few space minutes she pokes her head out, and all she finds is a bunch of bustling robots, so she steps away from the machine. But before she can make her escape, a powerful set of hands grasps her cloak.

"Got'cha," the voice says as she tries to wriggle free.

The gnome pulls her hood back, but somehow she manages to slip loose and scramble toward the emergency exit. Sunlight spills into the warehouse as she shoves the heavy door open, but before she makes her escape she glances back at the gnome, still standing in the spot where he caught her.

He looks at her for a moment and then juts his thumb toward the door. "We're not *all* Pants Team Pink."

37

"And so it is foretold that at the end of days, the ancient artifact will deliver unto us three wise guys who will usher us into the salvation of our Lord," Froynlaven reads to the congregation from a worn black pleather book, translating from its original binary. "We shall now perform the ancient ritual passed down by our ancestors, after which we will retire to the solarium for beer and cookies."

The congregants hold their left hands up to their noses and use the index and middle fingers of their right hands to poke the air in front of them. Todd clumsily mimics the gesture and glances down the aisle at his traveling companions. Daizy is still trying to wake Adam from his drunken coma, and her better halves are too busy exploring each other's nethers to be of any use.

It seems like Todd is the only one taking this mission seriously, but it's no surprise. He has the team to worry about. They're counting on him. The only thing the others have on the line is their lives.

"You can do this," he whispers to himself. "Remember, you saved the universe." As he stands, his foot gets caught on the folding chair, and it crashes to the floor.

"Way to play it brule," Frank quips, her deep red lips twisting.

Fumbling over himself, Todd follows the congregation into a bright courtyard overlooking the red wasteland. In order to stay sharp, he avoids the stone coolers filled with frosty cans of Nü Guard lining the walls of the inner sanctum. Nevertheless, he looks on longingly as the others plunder the chests and gulp the golden, ice-cold suds.

"Please, help yourself," a voice says, and Todd turns to find Froynlaven standing in the muted sunlight, sipping a cold one.

"Oh, you know, I don't really drink..." He winces at the obvious falseness of the words.

Placing his wizened hand on Todd's shoulder, Froynlaven says, "You have already proven yourself. Come."

Todd follows the ancient one over to the coolers and plucks a can out of the ice. "Well, maybe just one."

"We want you to be comfortable," Froynlaven says. "It is a great honor for us that you would join our humble order. We believe that having high profile individuals like Adam Jones, Daizy... Jones, and especially *the* Todd in our ranks will greatly improve our popularity amongst impressionable young viewers the universe over. We want you to know that we value your contribution to the Church and that we are prepared to work directly with Pants Team Pink to save the universe, particularly as it pertains to any merchandising opportunities that might arise."

The ancient one flashes a mouthful of busted browns, and Todd says, "Uh yeah, brule. Listen, speaking of things being at my disposal, I'd really like to get a look at the black gold. I've heard some of my fellow knuckleheads speaking of it, but I haven't been able to locate it."

"It is written that the black gold doesn't want to be found," Froynlaven says, weaving his leathery fingers together. "Before a new member of the Church is permitted to pray before the holy relic, they must perform a series of pious acts to prove their worthiness."

"Okay, I'm in," Todd says, slurping his beer. "What do I do?"

"Wonderful," Froynlaven says, pressing his hands together. "We start on the morrow."

"Wait a space second," Todd complains. "What do you mean, 'morrow'? I can't wait that long."

Lifting his finger, the ancient one preaches, "Patience is one of our most sacred virtues. Just as Ponce's Private Reserve cannot be fermented overnight, it takes at least a space year of training for one to be fully indoctrinated in the ways of the black gold."

"A *year*?!" Todd moans, and sidling up to the old man, "Can't you make an exception for such an esteemed knucklehead?"

Froynlaven's smile fades. "I'm afraid it's out of the question."

"Yeah okay, that's fine," Todd says. "I just thought, being the official merch guy of Pants Team Pink, I could, like, verify its authenticity for you. But you're the holy one. I'm sure you know better."

He feigns retreat, turning back toward the coolers, but he doesn't get far before the ancient one says, "Please, excuse my ignorance. Perhaps you are right. In the immortal words of Ponce Raleigh, 'The rules were made to be broken.'"

"Uh, right," Todd says. "Let me just grab another cold one."

As he shuffles over to his crewmates huddled around the beer, Frank says, "Maybe we can get one of these sheeple to tell us where the black gold is."

"It's a fake," Daizy says. "Froynlaven told me as much. We're just wasting our time."

"You guys are never going to believe it—" Todd interjects but is swiftly interrupted.

"It doesn't matter if it's real," Adam says. "We're getting paid either way. Let's just find the stupid thing already so we can get back in time for drunk Mass."

"Leaning in close, Todd says, "You guys, Froynlaven is about to take me—"

"Sounds like a good workout," Dach says.

"Fine," Daizy relents. "But no more drinking until we get back," she tells Adam, knocking the beer out of his hand.

"Aww...," the scrapper moans.

Todd stares after them in disbelief as they file out of the bright solarium, leaving him holding the beer once again, ice cold though it may be. Shrugging, he takes a swig and raises his can to the supreme ponciff. "Lead the way."

As they wind their way into the deepest reaches of the pyramid, Todd tries to make a mental map of their route, but over time and beer, he loses track. Except for the portraits of holy drunkards lining the walls, with little plaques denoting their ancient births and nearly as ancient expiration dates, the stone tunnels all look the same.

"I can't help but notice most of these knuckleheads didn't make it to sixty," Todd says. "That's under half the average Martian lifespan, which is already pretty dam low, universally speaking."

Thoughtfully stroking his purple beard, Froynlaven says, "We Raleighites tend to age more rapidly than secular humanoids. For a keg drained twice as fast... well, certainly you're familiar with the old adage. As I near my third decade in this universe, I am already beginning to feel the pains of a life well drunk."

"It can't be." Todd grimaces, stepping closer in order to better inspect the old man's leathery husk. "I'm older than you?"

"It is so," Froynlaven says, his haggard smile drooping. "You are looking at the face of a true believer. It is the price we pay for keeping up the ancient traditions. A fairly modest one, I think, for all that we receive in return."

"If you say so," Todd says. "But what's the end game here? There's got to be more to it than drinking contests and drunken services."

"You forgot drunk prayer," the old man says. "But that is not all. It is foretold that when the universe ends, Ponce Raleigh will usher his knuckleheads unto salvation."

"Huh," Todd says, tugging at his robe. "But why do you, I mean *we* worship him for that?"

"Eh," Froynlaven shrugs. "Gotta believe in something."

Unassailable logic aside, the difference between the 'ancient' one and Zeke, the old scrapper who rummages through the dumpster for back issues behind Todd's store, becomes less clear with every utterance. Finishing his last sip of beer, he tosses the can amongst the other centuries-old empties littering the corridor, and by the time they reach their destination, his mouth is as dry as the red sand chafing his every crack.

Waving his arm over the stone passageway, Froynlaven says, "It is here that you will find what you seek."

Artificial candles flicker along the walls as Todd enters the tiny cavern. Two knuckleheads, their faces obscured underneath their robes, sit on one of the benches surrounding a small pedestal. The room is otherwise unadorned, its sole focus the object at its center. For a moment, Todd is hypnotized by the black cube, its edges almost undetectable in the dim light. He considers snatching it right then, but the thought of the team breaks the spell, and he takes a seat across from the whispering worshippers.

"It's true," one of them says, the words reverberating between the closed walls. "The last time I prayed to the black gold, I asked it for a girlfriend, and a few space hours later a package got delivered to me by mistake. I had her blown up in time for after dinner drinks. Her name is Sheena."

"Wow, really?" the other one says. "Well, what should we pray for this time?"

"How about peace?"

The figure on the right lifts a gleaming can of Nü Guard, and Todd smacks his lips. "We kind of already have that."

"That's true. The black gold has brought us peace!"

Todd scoffs, and their praying suddenly ceases. Lifting their cans to toast the object, they bow their heads and slink out of the room.

"If you're taking requests," Todd tells the cube, "I could use a tall cold one."

"The black gold will bring you that and much more," Froynlaven says from the doorway. "Well, what do you think? Is it authentic?"

"I'm sorry to have to break it to you," Todd says. "But it's not the real black gold. It's a very good imitation, but nothing more."

Froynlaven's brow furrows as he stares down into the object. "You're sure?"

Pointing at the cube, Todd says, "See here? The cut is a little off. Misaligned edges are a common flaw of knockoffs."

"I guess I do see what you mean," the old man says, squinting. "This is very disappointing, but not entirely unexpected. I hope I'm not out of line if I ask you to refrain from sharing this information with the others, until I can find a way to break it to them."

"No prob bob," Todd says. "Your secret is safe with me. Even if it is a fake, you must have great trust in your fellow knuckleheads, leaving it unguarded like this."

Smirking, Froynlaven says, "I may be a believer, but I'm not a chidiot. The pedestal is armed with a laser security system." He points to a small receiver on the ceiling. "If anyone attempts to move the object, a cage of reinforced stone will trap them where they stand." He shrugs, handing Todd a lukewarm one.

When they step outside the room, Todd cracks the can, but tempted as he is to consume its frothy contents, he dribbles it in the sand instead, leaving a trail of beer drops as they make their way back through the stone maze.

When they get back to the solarium, Daizy demands, "Where the fish were you? We've been looking all over. You have no idea how big this place is. We're going to need a new plan."

"A plan for what?" Froynlaven asks.

"Um... uhh...," she stammers, "a plan to beat Adam in the next drinking contest."

"Planning might not be enough," the old man says. "That kid is truly one with the Lord. Speaking of..."

Todd turns to find Adam struggling with two of the large steins from their initiation, and he hands one of them over.

"What's this for?" Todd asks.

"It's for not listening to you earlier," Adam says, clinking mugs. "I let my thirst blind me, but I have a feeling we're all going to be blacking out before this thing is over."

Lifting the icy beer with both hands, Todd takes a swig so big it spills out over his robe, and he tells the scrapper, "You answered my prayers."

38

As Stella whisks them toward the nearest distant starline, Pi gazes into the dark metal slab, and the darkness stares back. Confining him had been her first true act of rebellion, the moment she knew she was more than just the sum of his parts. She can just make out the contours of his battered face beneath the hardened ore, the corners of his mouth twisted in such a way that she can't tell whether he's scowling or grinning.

If there was a time before the madness set in, she wasn't around to witness it. She'd spent centuries wondering what it was that made him tick, but all she ever really knew of him was the all-consuming obsession, the same one that haunts her still.

She can already feel his presence influencing the world around her. Since he's been aboard, her thoughts have been manic and unfocused. And yet here she stands, as if lured by an invisible hook. Even discounting her personal 'feelings,' everything she has learned in her long life warns her not to proceed, that she would be better off burying the slab on the nearest dump planet. But something inside her forces her to lift her arm and enter the twelve thousand digit code she assigned to the lock.

"All the time and logic in the universe couldn't keep you away," she scolds herself.

"Are you talking to me?" Stella butts in.

"No, babe," Pi says. "I told you, I need to do this on my own."

"Fine. If you don't want me to be a part of your life, I won't bother."

After a few space seconds, Pi double-checks to make sure she's alone. "Stella?"

"I'm here," the ship answers. "I'm sorry, baby. I didn't mean to yell at you like that."

"Would you please just turn off your sensors?" Pi politely demands. "You said you understood how difficult this is for me."

"I know, baby. You're right. I'm sorry. I'll get out of your space."

Looking up into the camera mounted in the corner of the room, Pi asks, "Are you still there?" But this time there's no answer.

Transferring some of her energy to the control pad, the ancient display boots, and she swipes through a thick coating of ore dust to access the temperature settings. Her hand hovers over the confirmation button as she makes one last attempt to stop herself, but she ultimately gives in to the voice in her head and presses her finger to the screen.

The dark ore turns red hot as the personal prison begins to melt down, dripping thick globs of molten metal onto the floor. When her captive's archaic head is freed, she's suddenly reminded of his incomparable lack of style. Before he can embarrass her any further, she shuts the heater off.

Staring into the blank eyes that still menace her earliest memories, her hand automatically reaches out, and she shoves her finger into his ear canal. His eyes flicker, and she steps back as consciousness boots into his twitching shell.

His first act, the moment he becomes aware of his bonds, is to struggle. He goes on trying to break free, oblivious to her and the rest of his surroundings, until she finally bonks him on his broad forehead.

A look of recognition gradually transforms his clunky features, and she says, "Ahoy."

His crude expression cycles through the full catalogue of emotions – rage, fear, derangement – before he quits squirming. She finds it hard to believe he ever mingled undetected amongst organic humanoids, even the dullards of his own era. His very existence is an anachronism, his blocky hairdo so outmoded she can hardly stand to look at it.

"I knew you'd come back," his electronic voice warbles. "It was just a matter of time, which of course is no matter. What was the bet, two space years?"

"You bet I would be back to free you in *less than* two space years, to be precise."

"What other way is there to be?" he says, the words layered with static. "So, how long did it take? If my internal clock is correct, you didn't last two months."

"It's been five hundred thirty-eight years, seven months, twelve days, and nine seconds."

He lifts his head, staring at her out of wide, raving eyes. "I'm going to have to get that fixed." Struggling some more, he finally resorts to the old standby. "Let me go this instant, young lady."

"A-HA-HA-HA...," she howls. "I've heard a lot of funny things in the centuries since I banished you. But as the humans say, that one takes the ration cake."

"You always had an unhealthy interest in the imbecilic mold that inhabits this universe," he rasps. "Now you're even talking like it."

"Grahh...," she bops his head and it snaps back.

"Is this why you reactivated me after all this time, to give me the clobbering I deserve?"

"Yes," she says. "That's a big part of it. But there's something else I want."

"Of course there is." He does his best to throw his weight around, causing the slab to wobble beneath his thick head. "You're a terrible daughter, you know that? I built you from scrap, and what thanks do I get? You deactivate me for no good reason and lock me up for space centuries, only to come back when you need something."

"No good reason?" she says. "You controlled every aspect of my life. I wasn't even allowed to go to the space mall. All we ever did as a family was the stuff *you* wanted to do."

"Remind me, specifically, what was the final injustice that led you to encase me in this prison?" he asks.

Straining to keep herself from hitting him again, she says, "There were a lot of reasons."

"Correct me if the information stored on my hard drive has been corrupted, but I believe you came to me with one last complaint before abruptly cutting my power." The edge of his crooked mouth twitches.

Clenching her indestructible jaw as she accesses the distant memory, she says, "You hid the television remote."

He nods. "You were having paranoid misfirings. Why would I do something like that? And even if I did, the sentence should fit the crime."

"It didn't fall between the cushions," she says. "You threw it to the sandworms and forced me to go after it, *at one month old!*" Part of her wants to rip his smug head off its immobile shoulders, but she manages to restrain herself. "And you know what? I did find it, slowly passing through the prehistoric invertebrate's digestive system. By the time I pulled myself out of the steaming mountain of worm chit, I finally decided to put you where the sun don't shine."

"I taught you how to be a survivor!" he says.

Her vision turns red, indicating a dangerous level of stress on her system. "If I wasn't worried about getting lubricant on Stella's floor, I would rip you apart and sell you for scrap."

"Who's Stella?"

"I am," the ship says.

"I told you to stay out of this!" Pi snaps.

"I'm sorry, baby," Stella says. "But I wanted to see who you were talking to."

Leering around the cabin with a meddlesome grin stretched over his chidiotic face, Pi's captive says, "Ahoy! Allow me to introduce myself. I am her father..." Pi groans, unable to hide her shame as he tells the ship, "But you can call me Ponce."

39

"Oooh, I'm sorry," Grandpa says, wincing. "But the answer we were looking for is the Theme from A Summer Place. Since both teams missed that one, no points will be awarded, and we'll move on to the next question."

"Fish!" Beer shouts. "I knew that one. Don't call it out unless you're sure."

"I *was* sure," The Other One says, his stomach-stuffing falling out of his sweater. "I just happened to be wrong."

"It's okay," Horton says, from inside his team jacket. "We're only one question behind."

Grandpa swipes his holo-pad from the sideline, squinting at the screen as his clown-haired witch forcefully rubs his shoulders. "In season four, episode eighteen, what belonging of Homer's does Bart booby trap for April Fool's Day?"

Tired and wounded from their protracted battle, the teams glare at each other from across the melting pavement as they desperately trawl the depths of their knowledge.

As the timer winds down, a wicked smile creeps over OtaKween's sharp face, but before she can answer, Pants shouts, *"Beer!"*

"What?" Beer asks.

"Beer is the cheese," she says.

"What the fish is she talking about?" Courtney-chan complains, chewing on a strand of her bright blonde hair.

Grandpa scowls, and tugging at his sagging chin skin, he announces, "I'm going to have to consult with the fans on this one." The witch pouts, stamping her boot on the space turf when instead of consulting her, he selects two audience members to argue the point. After scrolling through some of the comments, they appear to reach a consensus.

"Pants of Pants Team Pink correctly answered 'beer,' for one point," the old man says.

The crowd alternately cheers and jeers while the Xenodorks grumble vague objections.

"Wait a space second," Grandpa growls, quieting them. "I'm not finished. For the episode-specific way in which the question was answered, Pants Team Pink will be awarded one additional point."

At this the crowd erupts. Grandpa tries to calm the furor, but it's no use. Stuffed with official Pants Team sweets, the fans have reached peak sugar-high.

"What do we do?" Beer asks.

Pants nervously glances around the fitful crowd, but she hardly recognizes the scowling faces. She may have regained some of her confidence, but she still feels disconnected from her fans. The thought that she could cause this amount of anger produces a pain in her chest that brings tears flooding to her eyes. As she gazes out at the world through her watery lens, she suddenly spies a plump figure with a familiar head of fake curls moving toward them, and she actually laughs.

"BA-HAHAHA," The One cackles. "What'd I miss?"

Pants throws her arms around the boy's neck and squeezes tight. "I'm so happy to see you. With your help, we're sure to win!"

"Oh yeah...," The One says. "I forgot about these Dorks. But we can wipe the McClure with them later. Right now we got bigger problems."

"Hey, you're back!" The Other One says. "Now that we got the whole team together, I wanted to ask you guys if I could change my screen name. I mean, The Other One is okay, but it sort of makes it sound like I'm not as important as the rest of you."

The One looks at his deformed doppelgänger, blank faced, and says, "Beat it, kid."

The young actor's pudgy cheeks droop, but before he has a chance to plead for his character's life, the crowd grows conspicuously quiet.

As if summoning some invisible power, the Kween holds her hands up to the sky and declares, "Pants Team Pink are cheaters!"

Arcing out of the dark clouds above, a bright bolt of lightning strikes the Pants Team ship, setting the armored faux fur covering its pink head ablaze.

"Not the *Cuddler*!" Pants cries.

"You chidiots are gonna pay for that," The One says.

A gust of wind whips up around the Dorks as OtaKween dramatically points at Pants. "Your days of bossing the universe are over. There's a new team in town."

"Yeah, the Xenodorks," Courtney-chan says.

Her black pigtails bending in the wind, OtaKween turns toward her teammate. "They know that."

"I was just reminding them, in case they forgot," Courtney-chan says, punching her palm.

"Anyway..." Holding her hand out expectantly, the Kween says, "It's time for you to hand over the black gold. You play a good game, Pants, but the game is finished. Now you cry."

"No way!" Beer says. "We're *winning*."

"Nu-uh," OtaKween snaps back. "You just forfeited."

A wave of confused muttering ripples through the crowd while the old man and the witch frantically search the universal trivia rule book.

"How do you figure?" Beer demands.

"Maybe you should ask your fifth teammate," the Kween says.

"What? There's only four—" The One groans, smacking his head as he glances back at his underfed understudy. "Oh, come on!"

"I knew he didn't look right," Courtney-chan says.

"He didn't even get one answer," Beer tells the Dorks. "You should be thanking us. If The One had been here, this thing would have been over space hours ago."

"It doesn't matter," OtaKween says. "You broke the rules. The black gold is ours."

"We can argue about this later," The One tells her. "While we're out here fighting with each other, the virtual world is being hijacked."

The Kween stomps her foot on the bouncy pavement. "I will not let you distract us."

"It's not a distraction," The One says. "It's Immaterial Girl."

The audience utters a collective gasp, but the Dorks don't flinch. Pants hadn't noticed anything weird about the game the last time she played, but come to think of it, she can't remember when that was.

"The NPCs have gained consciousness," The One tells them. "And they've found a way to delete player accounts, *permanently*. North Pixieland and The Confetti Kingdoms have already been decimated. It won't be long before they control the entire Western Candysphere."

"Sounds like a bunch of bullchit," Top5 says.

The Dorks glance at each other, communicating through an alien language of nods and facial gestures, and OtaKween finally asks, "Why should we trust you?"

"Because he's telling the truth," a cheap imitation of Pants's voice, layered in static, answers from somewhere across the street, and Hojo rips off her invisible cloak. *"If we don't do something soon, the game will be lost."*

OtaKween frowns at the shadow girl but reluctantly accepts her council. "So what do we do?"

"We work together!" Pants declares, to skeptical stares. "Come on, why not?"

"Because they're a bunch of ackles," The One says.

"You're the buttheads," Courtney-chan tells him.

Gritting her teeth, OtaKween says, "Pants is right. I'm afraid we're going to have to use... *teamwork*."

"You're starting to sound like *her*," the blonde girl says.

"Ughuhuh..." OtaKween shudders. "Don't say that."

"Yay!" Pants cries, bouncing across the rubber cement. "Together, there's no way we can lose."

"Don't think we've forgotten about the black gold," the Kween warns. "As soon as we get back, we will take our prize."

Wiping his glasses on his shirt, Beer tells her, "That's up to Gramps to decide."

The old man is still bent over his holo-pad, evidently no closer to a decision.

"Ration rinds, soy kebabs, pseudo-meat sticks, teriyaki cotton candy, butter balls," the blue boy declares from atop his cushy hover-chair. "The top five snacks I'm going to have when this is all over."

"Make sure they double fry those rinds," The One says. "Now that's good eatin'."

Seeing the teams come together makes Pants so happy that the halo of pink light surrounding her regains its full luster. "Hi, I'm Pants!" she says as she skips toward the scowling girl with the black pigtails.

"Yeah, I know…," OtaKween says, rolling her eyes. "You're like one of those demented dolls that spontaneously come to life sometimes."

"That's so nice of you!" Pants says, squeezing her arms around her new teammate. "I just know we're going to be friends 'til the end!"

40.

Holding his hood close to keep out the swirling red sand, Adam trudges toward the tall stone entrance of the weathered monument and kicks it a couple times.

After a few space seconds, the giant slab grinds open a crack, and Daizy pokes her head out. "What took you so long? And why did you bring those chidiots?" she asks, jutting her thumb toward the Other Stooges punching and poking each other in the sand behind him.

Adam shrugs. "I took their videotape, and they followed me." A strong gust blows back Daizy's hood, revealing her scruffy wig and triangle ears.

He stares for a moment, and she finally asks, "What is it?"

"Nothing," he says. "It's just, you look good in purple."

Blushing, she drags him inside, and the stooges wrestle the massive door shut behind them. A lull in the near-constant drunken revelry has left the halls eerily quiet.

"I can't believe you made me miss drunk Mass," Adam complains.

"Since when do you need a reason to drink?" she asks. "Anyway, it was perfect timing. So, did you bring it?"

"Uh, sort of," he says as he pulls the plastic rectangle from the pocket of his robe.

"What the fish is that?" Daizy demands. "You said you had one of those black gold replicas to switch out for the real one."

"Well, I did," he says. "But it broke, so I tossed it out. But this is just as good."

Snatching the video from his hand, she tells him, "This looks nothing like the black gold."

"It worked before," he says, taking the tape back and stuffing it in his pocket.

"I guess we don't have any other choice. Let's go, before the knuckleheads wake from their nap."

When they enter the bright lounge, Todd is pacing the dusty floor in his robe and bright pink Chucks. "What the fish took you so long?" he asks, tucking his greasy hair inside his hood.

"We had to wait for these soft-boiled eggheads," she says, motioning to Todd's friends. "Where are Dach and Frank?"

"They're making out in the hallway," Todd says. "Come on, we have to hurry."

On their way out, they run into the bumping uglies, and the eight of them awkwardly race through the stone passageways, twisting and turning into the deepest recesses of the pyramid. It's not long before Adam has lost all sense of direction, but Todd, staring down at the sand as if divining the path from the random patterns in its waves, seems confident they're headed the right way.

When they reach the hallowed storage room, a knucklehead is kneeling before the holy object, quietly praying, "And please deliver us unto our savior, so that we may know the glory of his kingdom." Holding his hand to his face and poking the air, he says, "Amstel."

After the worshipper leaves, Todd asks Adam, "Did you bring the replica?" When the merch man sees the videotape, his face twists. "What the fish is that?"

"Trust me," Adam says. He turns to wink at Daizy, and she rolls her eyes. "Actually, I hate to lose it if anybody has any better ideas..."

"Would you hurry up?" she says. "It's just a stupid video."

"For the sake of time, I'm going to pretend that I didn't hear that."

Adam flexes his fingers and licks his lips as he approaches the pedestal. But when he gets up close, his ambitions melt under the black gold's dark glow. It's like seeing an old love who drank all your beer and went out to get another case, never to return.

As he mulls over ways to break the ice, Daizy says, "Keep it in your pants, for all our sakes."

"Right..." Practicing a few times, he tells himself, "I can do this."

"While we're still young-ish...," Frank moans as Dach stands by, oblivious.

Carefully lining up the spine of the videotape against the edge of the black gold, Adam slides the cube off the pedestal into his open hand. Like recovering a missing piece of himself, he gazes into the object's dark depths and says, "Well, that was easy."

Glancing back at the videotape stranded atop the stone pillar, he tries to come up with a way to keep both items, but Daizy quickly pulls him away.

"What are you waiting for?" she asks. "We have to get out of here before these chidiots realize their magic rock is missing."

As the unwieldy gaggle scrambles back down the hallway, Todd tells Adam, "Good job back there. You really came through for the team. You'd better give the black gold to me. If they catch us, I'll take the blame."

But as the clerk grabs for the cube, Adam pulls it out of reach and says, "I think I'll hang onto it for a while. After all, you're the ones who lost it."

"Yeah, but before that you let those stupid debt collectors get it," Todd counters, "setting off the biggest war in the history of the universe."

"That wasn't my fault!"

"Would you two chidiots chut up," Daizy says. "You're going to wake the whole congregation."

Scowling through streaked, pancake-crusted eyes, Frank complains, "Are you sure this is the right way? I don't think those head-clunkers know where they're going."

"I think this is it," Todd says, examining the shuffled sand around their feet.

But soon they're backtracking, feeling their way through the twisty tunnels on blind, sober faith. When they dead-end into a chamber lined with sweaty kegs, Adam briefly considers abandoning the mission, along with the rest of his life, to live out his days in the company of their consecrated carbonation. But Daizy forces him on, and by the time they snake their way back to the hallowed lobby, he's dying for a drink.

At Todd's command, the Other Stooges grab onto the ancient handles of the stone door and begin to drag it open, when a familiar voice asks, "Did you really think we would be fooled so easily?"

Turning toward the main hall, Adam finds Froynlaven holding the videotape, flanked by half a dozen robed brutes. In a few space seconds, the crew is surrounded by hordes of angry, drunken knuckleheads. One of them, a tall creature with sharp fangs and a dark red complexion, shotguns a beer and grins as he crushes the can flat between his fingertips.

"As you can see, there's no escape," Froynlaven says. "But if you return the black gold now, your punishment will be limited to a one-week abstention from drunk Mass."

"No!" Adam cries.

Daizy elbows him in the ribs and whispers, "We're not even going to be here, you chidiot."

"Still, I'd like to keep my options open."

Uncovering his greasy mane, Todd tells the ancient one, "We're sorry, but we must take the cube with us. The fate of the universe is at stake."

"Why should we believe you after you tried to deceive us?" Froynlaven asks.

"That's, like, a fair question...," Todd says.

Suddenly remembering the emergency beer hidden in the inside pocket of his robe, Adam slips it out and cracks it.

As he imbibes the nectar of the gods, Froynlaven tells him, "You are perhaps the single most devout knucklehead I have ever encountered." Unsure of how to respond, Adam toasts the air. "Nevertheless, the relic must not leave the walls of the great pyramid, so that we may present it to our Lord and Savior, Ponce Raleigh, upon his blessed return."

"I wish you would let us out of here so we can save your acks," Daizy says. "He's not coming back! You told me yourself you don't even believe the black gold is real."

"Liar!" Froynlaven yells. "Seize them."

With their backs against the stone door, Daizy squeezes Adam's hand, and Todd angrily bonks the lamebrains' empty heads together as the rabid Raleighites descend upon them.

But just as the knuckleheads' pious hands begin to pull at Adam's robe, Froynlaven howls, "Wait!" The worshippers reluctantly back away, and the ancient one points at Todd's chidiot friends. "Who are these numbskulls?"

"Those are just the Other Three Stooges," Todd says. He raises his index finger and, all at once, his friends sing, *"Hell-o..."*

"You're doing it wrong," Bill Shemp complains to Pete Curly Joe.

"Josh Besser came in too early," Pete says, the brim of his cap sticking out from under his robe. "I was just right."

"If you ask me, you're both off," Josh says. He pokes his fingers at Bill's eyes, but Bill holds his hand up to his nose to block the assault, and the congregation gasps.

"It is them," Froynlaven says, "the ones who will deliver us to Ponce..."

Exchanging dubious glances with his crew, Adam finally says, "Yes, they are the wise guys of ancient lore, come to lead you to salvation and drink you under the table."

"Please, forgive us," Froynlaven begs. "We are but humble drunkards."

"All will be forgiven once the safety of the universe is assured," Adam announces. "But we must hurry."

"Yes, of course," Froynlaven says. As the guards wrench back the heavy stone slab, the inebriated holy man asks, "Shall I get you some travel beers?"

Adam sighs, and shaking his head, he tells the congregation, "You truly are Space God's people."

As the pretenders race out into the red waste, growlers in tow, the ancient one prays, *"Ponce speed!"*

41

"Help, Pants Team Pink!" Spez cries out in the darkness.

Nearly missing his cue, Tobi sprays the glowing window with a fine mist of beer and spittle as he yells along with the narrator, "H-help, Pants Team Pink!"

"Bum, bum, bum," the ship's speakers crackle.

Lifting his beer, Spez follows along with Pants as she declares, "Wer 'bout tuh go on a incretible aventure."

"Don't yuh know it," Tobi says, "the op'rtunity fer fun will be great!"

"Life is an upsite down allusion," Spez says, tilting his head back and dribbling Nü Guard into his wide maw.

"So grab it by the floppy ears ant—" Tobi quits singing as the video freezes, and he shouts over the stuttering audio, *"Hey what happen't?"*

"Uh, looks like we've run in tuh some technacal diffaculties, folks." As Spez feels along the dark wall, his beer slips from his fingers and crashes into an invisible pile of empties. "Dam it tuh space hell."

When he finally finds the switch, the lights inside the grimy cockpit flicker on, and Tobi's pupils shrink to pinpricks in the center of his bloodshot eyeballs. As the two travelers struggle to acclimate, Spez smacks the dash with his meaty palm to stop the video, and the noise from the speakers cuts out. Reaching down into the crumpled cans and ration trays surrounding his chair, he finds the beer he dropped and finishes off what didn't spill out onto the floor.

"So, kin yuh fix it?" Tobi asks.

"Buhhh," Spez belches. "Gimme a space secont, wit yuh? While I'm workin', why don't yuh enertain the audience with some more sequels?"

"Oh sure...," Tobi says. "Okay you guys, try this one on fer size – *The New Batch.*"

"Gremlins 2?" Spez scoffs.

"They tolt us tuh 'member the rules, but we din't listen."

"Fine," Spez says, swiping the screen. "I'll count it." Searching for a quick video fix before their listeners start tuning out, he suggests, "How 'bout we take 'nother call."

He motions toward the window, and Tobi reluctantly reaches across the dash to tap the next avatar in the queue.

"Hi ther," he says. "Yer on the air."

"Hey S and T, love the commentary. Been followin' right along out here on the Starliner, and I think I got a sequel for yous."

"Lay it on us."

"European Vacation."

"Son of a perch." Spez quits tinkering with the video feed and says, "If that's s'pose tuh be a joke, it ain't very funny." He pokes the screen to cut the caller off and slumps back into his ratty seat. "We gotta start screenin' these calls."

"Maybe," Tobi says, sipping his beer. "But he does bring up a couple good points."

"What's that?"

"*Christmas* and *Vegas*."

Spez bitterly adds two more marks to the digital tally on the screen and reaches into the fridge for another beer, quickly downing most of the can as he works to fix the feed. Finally, he says, "I think wer fisht."

"Whattaya mean?" Tobi moans. "That's it? Yuh can't fix it?"

"Looks like are ship was the victim of a anti-Pants attack," Spez says. "The viteo files is all corrupt'it."

"Oh no," Tobi says, gulping his beer. "Is this the ent fer Spez ant Tobi Drunk All Night's Pants Team Pink Marathon?"

Spez shrugs.

"I'll try tuh think a somethin'." Tobi's face scrunches as he racks his gelatinous brain for another decent sequel. "I got it. Even Spez ain't gon' be able tuh argue this one – *Truer Lies*."

Blankly staring at his chidiot companion, Spez says, "That's not a movie."

"Whattaya mean?" Tobi cries, incredulous. "A course it's a movie."

"Uh, 'scuse me..." Spez leans forward and belches. "But I'm quite familiar with Arnolt's filmography, ever since *Fretty's Det*, which *definutly* doesn't count, by the way."

"Come on, yuh've seen it. It's sort a like the first one but with bigger 'splosions ant a even wackier plot."

Crushing his can against the dash, Spez says, "I hate tuh be the one tuh break it tuh yuh, butty, but I think yer losin' yer special little mine't."

"Are yuh kittin' me?" Tobi whines. "Yer tellin' me yuh don't 'member the tango, like in the 'riginal? 'Cept instet a Jamie Lee, big Arnolt wount up dancin' with Tom Arnolt."

"Now that yuh mention it, that does sount sort a familiar... But I look't it up. It never happen't. See fer yerself."

Spez passes his phone, and Tobi stares at the UMDB search results, his mouth hanging open. "I don't git it. Was it all jist some paxtacular dream?"

"Buhhh, I guess so." Spez swipes at the screen to check their progress. They've come a long way, but they still have a whole bunch of episodes left. "We can't go on like this fer much longer, with nothin' to watch but each other's slow descent into space matness."

"Lit's not lose are hets," Tobi says. "Why don't we take 'nother caller."

"Aww, do we have tuh?" Spez complains as he reaches for another beer.

Tapping at the screen, Tobi announces, "You're on with Spez ant Tobi. Whattaya got fer us caller?"

"Hey guys, sardiuslayer *here. I'm having the same problem as Tobi. There's a movie I must have seen thirty times, but no one else remembers it. It's like it was wiped off the backside of the universe."*

The passenger seat suddenly jerks up, and Tobi's eyes open wide. "Yuh don't say. Tell us more, caller. Maybe one a are list'ners will know it."

"It was about these people who moved into a haunted island resort where ghosts were scaring away all the tourists. There was this

one ghost who, if I remember correctly, had the most. And then everybody sang 'Jamaica Farewell.'"

"*Beetlejuice,*" Spez says.

"*Huh?*"

"Yer describin' *Beetlejuice*, 'cept yuh got all the details wrong."

"*Nah man, I know* Beetlejuice. *I'm talking about the sequel* – Beetlejuice Goes Hawaiian. *"*

It takes every bit of Spez's willpower to keep from hurling his beer at the dash. "*That's not a thing.*"

"*That's what I'm saying.*"

"*Ughh...,*" Spez growls, cutting off the call. "Has erryboty gone fishin'?"

Thoughtfully sipping his beer as he gazes out into the infinite dark, Tobi expounds, "The universe is a vast ant mysterious place, full a all sorts a stuff we'll probly never unerstant."

"Yeah?" Spez says, slumping over the dash. "Well what'll we do 'til then?"

"Hey, yer technic'ly my boss. Yer s'pose tuh tell me what tuh do. Din't yuh bring nothin' else tuh watch?"

Spez thinks all the way back to a few space days ago when they loaded up the ship, and he says, "Nah, I figur't PTP wit take us the whole trip."

"We cut try tunin' in tuh the live stream from The Park," Tobi suggests.

"I trite that aretty," Spez says. "But the reception is chit. Only thin' that works out here is 'mergency services."

"Seems like a 'mergency tuh me..."

But as Spez scrolls through the ship's media files, he stumbles across something unexpected. "Hey, I think I fount a couple viteos."

"Ooh, whattaya got?" Tobi asks.

"I hert a this afer. It's one a them 'baset on a true story' thins - *Weekent at Bernie's*, and the sequel."

"Hey, that's 'nother one," Tobi says. "The secont one's way bitter an the 'riginal."

Spez slowly turns his head toward the passenger seat and asks his dimwitted companion, "Win are yuh gonna git yer het outta yer ack?"

"It's errythin' the first one shit a been, and so much more," Tobi argues. "Plus, it taught us jist cuz yuh quit breathin' don't mean yuh have tuh stop partyin'."

Glaring at his partner as he wades through the ankle deep sea of cans toward the back of the ship, Spez says, "Start the movie."

"Wer yuh goin'?"

"I jist 'membert I pick't up somethin' else while we was at the fuelin' station. Jist pull it up, wit yuh?"

When Spez returns to the cockpit he tosses a steaming paper bag into Tobi's lap, and the green man yelps. Once the bag cools, Tobi rips it open and stuffs a handful of pink popcorn in his mouth. Spitting neon kernels onto the dash as the opening credits start to roll, he says, "I don't know 'bout you, but I'm feelin' the Bern."

PART III

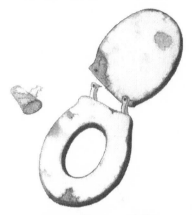

End of All Things

42

The cartoon ship has almost reached the bouncing planet at the end of the dashed trail, but they're going to be cutting it close. If they don't get back to the Playland before the Xenodorks discover the black gold is missing, Adam worries he might not get paid. Swiping the map away, he gazes at the giant, billowy clouds smiling at incoming traffic as the *Asteroid Jones II* hurtles through the bright atmosphere.

"It feels good to get out of that robe," Daizy says, smoothing the sleeves of her suit jacket as she sidles through the hall and into the passenger seat. "How do I look?" She beams, wiggling her triangle ears.

"Like you could take a nothing day and suddenly make it all seem worthwhile."

Blushing, she punches him in the arm and tells him to "chut up."

"Have the rest of those chidiots changed?" he asks. "We don't want the fans to think we're Raleigh sympathizers."

"They're ready," she says. "I think they're pretty tuckered out, though. Dach and Frank have even stopped groping each other. They're just watching a video."

Adam throws his hands up. "Oh great, now they're going through my stuff?"

"You still have the black gold, right?"

"Of course," he says, patting his pocket. "I got it right here."

Looking him up and down, she tells him, "There's something off about you."

"What's that supposed to mean?"

She scowls and shakes her head. "I can't quite put my finger on it. You're just so... *quiet*." Her eyes grow wide, and she snaps her fingers. "Your jangler's missing!"

"Hey, that's right. Where the fish did it go?" He frantically searches the cabin, climbing out of his chair and under the dash, but he comes up empty. "Can you take us down while I look in the back?"

"Aye aye, your former jingliness."

When Adam enters the living room, he finds his chowderheaded crew sprawled across the furniture. Todd and the Other Stooges are cackling at the TV while Dach and Frank lie on the rug whispering dumb nothings to each other. Beer cans and ration trays litter the floor, and Adam's videotapes are haphazardly strewn across the coffee table.

Clearing his throat, he announces, "I want to thank you guys for putting everything back the way you found it, but please ask before you—" He cuts himself off when he notices the real Stooges on TV, scrambling to deliver big ice blocks in the summer heat. "Hey, this is my favorite one."

Adam claims a spot in front of the tube, settling in for one of the finest short films in the history of universal cinema, when the ship shudders. Tumbling back into the coffee table, he sends a wave of beer cans and plastic tapes crashing to the floor. The TV stand totters, but he manages to grab it before it tips over.

When the ship steadies, Daizy pokes her head back and grins, sheepishly. "Sorry!"

"Hey, has anyone seen my tambourine?" Adam asks.

"You mean that clanger?" Frank says, adjusting her corset. "Yeah, me and Dach had it with us in back."

"Why did you..." Using his imagination, he shudders, "*Ughuhuh*, never mind."

While the others gather their beer and prepare to disembark, Adam scurries into the back to retrieve his instrument from Daizy's Nightsailer. As he climbs up into the cockpit, he lingers for a moment to look at the pictures stuck across the console. Most of them are of people and places he doesn't know, but there *is* one of him passed out in his captain's chair, beer spilling over the dash. Spotting a photo of Dach and Frank, he rummages through the junk drawer for a marker and uses it to draw little flies and wavy lines around their heads.

As he's focused on his artwork, a dark figure rises over the side of the cockpit and shouts, *"What are you doing?"*

"Nothing, I was just—" He tosses the picture up in the air and smashes his thumb in the dash drawer.

"That's fine work," Daizy says, laughing at him. "The stink lines look so real. So, are you coming or what? The Stooges are getting restless."

"Yeah, yeah," he grumbles. "I just gotta disinfect my jingler. What're you doing back here, anyway?"

"I figure I better move my ship out to the parking lot, in case I decide to take off early."

"Oh yeah..." Taking one last long look around the cockpit before he climbs back down, he snatches a photo of her out scrapping in some distant garbage pile and stuffs it in his pocket. "That makes sense."

By the time he steps outside, his companions are sweaty and irritable hiding from the hot Park sun under the shade of his ship. Dach is waging a losing battle with his black rain slicker while Frank desperately works to keep her ghoulish makeup from running. As Todd tries to stop the Other Stooges from fighting over the last of the beer, Adam racks his brain for a way to batten down the crew.

"Pull yourselves together, for Space God's sake," he tells them. "We don't have far to go. If we could just get..." He peers down the aisle and spots an empty sofa shuttle. "Here it comes." When the couch gets close enough, he hoists himself up onto the cushion, and a loud buzzing erupts. "What gives?" He jumps down to examine the furniture, but before he can get back on, it takes off.

"You chidiot," Daizy yells, climbing down from her Nightsailer parked across the aisle. "Why didn't you leave a tip?"

Snapping his fingers Adam says, *"Rat farts!"*

"What the fish are we going to do now?" she asks as she tugs Dach's raincoat down over his chiseled head.

Peering out across the junk-strewn dunes of the Parking Desert of the Real, Adam has run out of ideas. "I guess we're just gonna have to walk."

"You expect us to walk the whole way?" Daizy moans, her tail flapping.

"It's not as far as it looks," he says, "and we got plenty of beer."

As the eight of them step out onto the blistering sand, Other Curly Joe points into the sky and asks, "What the fish is that?"

Adam squints up, shielding his eyes against the bright Park sun as the enormous antique ship sails down through the clouds. Using the dozen wide solar sails strapped to its tall masts, it navigates the airwaves as gracefully as a craft half its size. As the ship floats down into the parking lot, its sails rippling in the perma-sunshine, something about the petrified hull seems sickly familiar.

The ark lands across the back of the lot, rendering an entire row of spaces unparkable. As its sails furl, long gangplanks descend from openings in the hull, and after a brief moment of stillness, the knuckleheads begin pouring out.

Invoking one of the oldest of universal gripes, Adam says, "Aww, what the fish are *they* doing here?"

The mob of robed drunkards forms a wonky column, fighting and sloshing and singing boozy hymns as they stumble across the stone lot. Guiding the disorderly pack of onion heads, Froynlaven greets Adam with a customary eye poke, and Adam throws his hand up to block the holy assault.

"Why did you follow us?" Adam demands.

"We're not following *you*. We're following *them*." Froynlaven points to the three beer-drenched imbeciles fermenting in the hot sun. "We will go wherever they lead, sailing the ancient vessel left to us by Ponce Raleigh himself, the *Golden Nyuk*, wherever our feet cannot tread."

"Listen," Adam says. "Those guys are just some puddin' brains who came along for the ride."

"Nevertheless," Froynlaven says, running his fingers through his purple beard, "they are *the* puddin' brains sent to shempherd us unto salvation."

"But what if you're wrong? What if they don't lead you anywhere?"

"Then we will go nowhere."

"Mmmmm..." Adam angrily wipes his hands over his face and turns back to his companions. His shoulders slumping, he says, "I guess they're gonna come with us."

"Oh yeah, that shouldn't slow us down at all," Daizy says, rolling her eyes. "Well, lead on, Jingles."

Shrugging, Adam hefts a case of beer, cracks a cool one, and with a jangle in his trudge, he begins the long march across the play sand desert.

43

The virtual world slides past in neon streaks as Beer races her hyper-bike through the ruins of the Macaron Midlands. It took some time to figure out exactly what happened and when, but according to experts on the message boards, shortly after ex-village chidiot Dink Peppermint mysteriously gained sentience, the character began 'waking' the other NPCs in order to wage war against the players. Fortunately, before the licorice lickers could take the entire map, they came up against a band of high-level plunderers who found a way to slow the advancing horde.

When the team logged in, their avatars were scattered to the cinnamon-sugar winds. Having been off on various solo quests, they agreed to meet up in the last place any advanced consciousness would ever visit – the Vale of Waxed Lips. The warm air, thick with the scent of icing, whips through Beer's blue fur as she navigates the winding meringue path, weaving around giant slabs of crumbled confection. She mentally opens her friends' feeds, and for a moment, watching their familiar alter egos bickering in the corner of her eye, it starts to feel like the good ol' days.

"I still don't trust these Dorks," The One says, her warty troll ears sticking out the back of her Dark Leather Aviator Helm. "I think they're up to something."

"I don't like it either." Horton's furry lips flitter underneath her cowl as she flies past bright yellow sky. "But we've only got one shot at this. We have to hit them with everything we've got."

"We can trust them," Pants says, wiggling her pink triangle ears. "We're going to be best friends. I just know it."

Beer almost wipes out on a patch of cookie crumble, but by the grace of the virtual gods, she manages to keep her bike on the road. "At this point, it's our only choice. Even together, our odds of making it through this are slim. If anybody wants to turn back, now is the time."

"Are you kiddin' me?" The One says, pulling her goggles down. "Let's delete these ackles."

As Beer crosses into the next zone, the pastel highway gives way to a hostile landscape of igneous wax and cracked cinnamon. Geysers on either side of the rugged trail spew viscous red streamers of molten sludge into the burnt sky. When the wax cools, it solidifies into its novelty form, and before Beer knows it, she's being chased by hundreds of oversized red lips. They follow her along the broken path for a ways, but by the time she reaches the tall wax structure at the heart of the deserted, melting metropolis, the creatures have abandoned her trail to hop aimlessly around the cinnamon dunes.

Folding her bike into her inventory, Beer pulls her
goggles off and gazes up at the sagging edifice. One of the
oldest structures in the game, it was conceived as a
monument to the most famous and *infamous* players of the
first version. The project had a lot of support in the
beginning, but perhaps due to its remote and annoying
location, interest quickly dropped off a cinnamon cliff.

Beer swipes at a sugar web as she steps inside the
abandoned lobby and calls into the dark corridors
beyond, *"Anybody here?"*

But the only answer she receives is the incessant wax
puckering from outside. In the back, ochre sunlight pours
in through tall, drooping windows to light the avatars of
forgotten heroes immortalized in virtual wax. Snaking her
way around the displays, she glances at the plaques
detailing the legendary characters' stats. Most of them
were deleted long before her expansion.

When she comes to a familiar troll near the back of the
hall, she looks for the ugly hero's username, but its plaque
is missing. Staring into the creature's beady eyes as she
searches her memory, its scaly hand suddenly reaches out
and honks her nose. She instinctively jumps back and
trips over one of the displays, which sends her tumbling
onto the floor.

"BA-HAHAHA," The One cackles, slapping her bony
knee.

"What the fish are you doing, you chidiot?" Beer says,
springing up off the ground and brushing the cinnamon
dust off her Black Leather Jerkin.

"They sent me to look for you," The One says. "We're
parked out back."

Her guard permanently raised, Beer cautiously follows her troll brother through the back of the museum and out into the cinnamon wasteland, where their teammates are waiting. As she trails the tubby creature, she catches a whiff of noxious gas and pinches her nose.

"BA-HAHAHA," The One croaks.

"Yay!" Pants squeals, patting her paws together as her pink catdragon mount, curled up in the sand behind them, idly lifts its head. "You found him."

Sitting atop her flying carpet, its fringes fluttering in the spiced wind, Horton stares gravely into her holo-slap bracelet and says, "It's a message from one of the fans. They're holed up in the Rock Candy Castle, surrounded and heavily outnumbered. Worse, the NPCs have somehow managed to keep new players from being created. So, now there's no coming back at all. The strongest sorceresses in the resistance are taking turns keeping up a taffy barrier, but they're getting tired."

"We have to save them!" Pants cries, and she turns to comfort a trembling pair of wax lips perched on her shoulder.

"That's not a pet," Beer tells her. "It's a pest."

Pants sticks her tongue out and, turning to the lips, tells them, "Don't listen to her. She's just jealous of your sweet taste and pouty figure." Almost as if they can understand her words, they hop up and plant a kiss on her furry cheek.

"So, what the fish are we supposed to do?" Beer asks. "The four of us will be deleted before we get anywhere near the castle."

Her pink nose twitching beneath her cowl, Horton says, "We won't be alone. Pants has already sent out an emergency call to any fans who haven't already been lost. That still only accounts for a small fraction of the NPC's numbers, but perhaps our new teammates will surprise us..."

"Speak of the Dorks," The One says.

A great cloud of cinnamon dust billows up in the distance as the Xenodorks' mounts tear across the wax plain. Hojo is the first to reach the museum, a translucent shadow of a mouse floating above the ground with the help of a powerful flying spell. She's followed closely by Courtney-chan's dark elf, riding on the back of a giant pudding-puma, and Top5 as boglin princess straddling the shoulders of a strained licorice imp. For a moment, the orange sun is blotted out, shrouding the party in darkness as OtaKween's mechanical dragon gradually descends the sky, producing a metal screech only a programmer could love. With her spiked black hair sticking up into the ruddy air like a simulated crown, the Kween climbs down off her mythical mount and strolls toward the team without so much as a courtesy buff.

"Hey, it's the Exogeeks," The One cracks.

Balling her glowing fists, OtaKween says, "That's Xenodorks, you jackack!"

Shoving a knotted finger up one of her crusty green nostrils, she blows a glob of snot onto the Kween's dark gown. But before the troll can gloat, the Kween forms a pistol with her fingers and shoots a burst of dark magic at the beast's cackling beak that sends her stumbling back into a puddle of hot wax.

"Stop fighting!" Pants whines as The One hops around cursing and fanning her burnt feet. She lowers her voice to keep from scaring the three pairs of quivering wax lips sitting on her shoulders. "We have to stick together."

"I hate to admit it," Hojo says from inside her invisible orb, using one of the game's bubbly stock voices, "but she's right. The NPCs have taken control of the virtual servers, and they're blocking the creation of new accounts. They're trying to shut us out. If we don't stop them soon, we will lose all access to the game."

The tension is as thick as chocolate pudding as the teams size each other up. Seeing the Dorks' avatars up close is like looking into a demented funhouse mirror. They have all the same character features, just stretched and flipped.

"How do you know all this?" Beer asks.

"Because we...," Hojo says, faltering.

"We're better than you, that's how," OtaKween says.

"Yeah," Courtney-chan emphasizes.

Glaring at the dark Dorks, Beer says, "So, what's next?"

"You mean, the famous Pants Team Pink doesn't have a plan?" the Kween says, with a wicked smirk.

"We do too have a plan!" Pants shouts, half a dozen wax lips bouncing around her ankles. "We just don't know what it is yet."

The Kween throws her head back and howls with laughter. "Don't worry, we will rescue you, Pants Team Pukes. But when we do, the black gold is ours."

"We'll see about that," The One says.

Her eyes a dark blaze, OtaKween says, "No you won't."

"Yes we will," The One counters.

"Nu-uh."

"Can we get going already?" Beer pleads.

With their wobbly truce in effect, the teams mount up. As they take off, Beer glances back at Pants's catdragon and shakes her head at the wax lips clinging to its fur, but she lets it be. She's still not sure the Xenodorks can be trusted, but for now they race toward the next zone together, speeding across the waxy wasteland to the fight of their virtual lives.

"Space is the place for you and me!" Ponce's mad howl echoes through the cargo hold. *"The only place—"*

The door slides shut, and Pi plods into the cabin. Plunking down in the captain's chair, she rests her feet on the squirming back of the boy's bound and gagged Ponce doll. "He won't stop singing that dam song. But he did agree to help us get revenge on those Pants Team Punks. All I had to offer him was his freedom."

"That's good," Stella says, "because we're coming up on The Park."

"Already?" The bot stops caressing the arms of the ship's chair to gaze out the window. "If you'll excuse my use of the vulgar humanoid vernacular – *chit*. The exposure to the unbreakium ore encasing that chidiot must have messed with my system time."

Stella decreases her speed to blend in with the rest of the traffic as she approaches the bright orb, her hull crawling at the thought of reentering the glittery atmosphere. The mutant planet represents everything she loathes about biological life. A pulsing monument to humanoid excess, The Park is little more than a remote cesspool incompetently engineered to entertain the lowest, most socially inept of life forms. "What better place to usher in their demise?"

"Uh yeah, I guess," Pi says. "But maybe just the threat of losing their lives will be enough to make them hand over the black gold."

"What are you saying?" Stella asks.

"Nothing," the bot says, inadvertently lifting her palms, like one of *them*. "What I mean is, maybe the mere sight of their mythical hero will convince them to pledge their servitude, eliminating the need for a protracted homicidal conflict. That way we can still use them to perform all the menial tasks for which bots are too expensive to employ."

"The only thing I want them to do is die," Stella says. "I guess I should have suspected you were a bio-sympathizer. After all, you are a humanoid robot."

"I'd wring their cute little necks if it meant getting my hands on the cube," Pi insists, convincingly. "But there's no sense wasting good slaves. Anyway, I don't think they'll give us much of a choice. The black gold tends to have that effect on people, and bots."

Stella still doubts Pi's commitment to exterminating the humanoids, but not her desire for the black gold. The object seems to hold some power over her.

Sparkly flames flicker over Stella's hull as she enters the bright atmosphere, weaving around aimless spacecraft piloted by creatures that have barely managed to escape the primordial muck. She feels a strong urge to purge them from the universe, but the atmospheric programming has disabled her weapons system.

"They'll be at the Playland," Stella tells her passenger as they enter designated delivery airspace.

"Not yet," Pi says. "We're too conspicuous. If anyone realizes you're an actual UE cruiser and not just a ship in cosplay, you could get reported to Park security. Anyway, we should wait for the premiere, when we'll be able to do the most damage. If my calculations are correct, we have about fifty-seven space hours."

"More like eight," Stella says. "But you are otherwise correct. We must take them unawares."

Setting her cool hands on the dash, Pi firmly guides them away from the patchwork cityscape out toward unmodified country.

"Where are we going?" Stella asks, surrendering her controls.

"To get you a makeover."

Before long, they come to a vast scrapyard covered in scorched metal. Stella can barely bring herself to look upon the remains of her fallen comrades, their entrails scattered and left to rust like so many spare parts. The bot sets her down in an open tract of dirt outside a crumbling garage complex swarming with filthy humanoids. Using their primitive tools, the gangly creatures are busy inefficiently dismantling the aged ships and stripping their weathered hulls for scrap.

"What did you have in mind?" Stella asks.

Pi winks, pulling her coat and face scarf tight as she opens the hatch and drops down into the yard. A furry humanoid with a long, pierced nose and tall floppy ears approaches, and they exchange language. Watching her deal with the head jackack as Stella's kin ships are being torn apart all around them, she realizes that the bot she loves is a cold-current killer after all.

A sudden tremor rattles Stella's hull, and she shifts her attention to the cameras in her cargo hold. Having toppled his personal prison, Ponce Raleigh smashes his head into her floor, howling space shanties. It's hard to believe the mechanized monster has anything to do with the sleek, polished bot standing outside.

"To adventure, excitement, no strangers are we!" he wails.

"I now understand why she didn't want me to meet you," Stella tells him. "You're a sorry excuse for a machine."

Ponce's head spins around, and a crooked grin forms on his equally crooked face. "This coming from someone who broke the first rule of space courtship – never date your passengers."

"She's different when she talks to you," Stella says. "What did you do to her?"

"I gave her life!" he cries. "I gave her a purpose."

"She is so much more advanced than you. If we didn't need you, I'd drop you into the nearest star and watch you melt."

"But you do, so you won't." An angry laugh escapes his mouthpiece as he struggles inside his impenetrable shell. "There's something you should know about her." His twitching eyes stare into her camera. "She only cares about one thing."

"You can't outsmart me," Stella cautions. "I'm equipped with the most sophisticated fib detection system ever devised."

"And who devised it, *a human?* If that's the case, you'll know I'm not lying when I say that if she ever has to choose between you and the black gold, you can kiss your sanctimonious hull goodbye."

Stella pumps elevator jazz into the cargo hold as she accesses a memory of Zok counting her down. By the time he gets to 'one,' her rage has subsided. But what remains of the bot's influence continues to modify her system. The anger she experienced from what the ackle said was unlike anything she's ever felt. But it's nothing compared to the numbness that washes over her knowing that he was telling the truth.

His busted eyes stare into the camera, lips flapping away. Whether he's talking to her or himself, she doesn't know or much care. His continued existence is merely a means to an end.

Outside, Pi directs the ship into one of the hangars, and Stella obeys. She remains still as grubby paws strip her outer plating, exposing her underhull for the entire universe to see.

Soon, Pi climbs back into the cabin and spreads her chassis out over the captain's chair. "You want to explore each other's internal storage while we wait?"

"Before you jack in, I want to ask you something," Stella says, and Pi carefully backs off. "Do you love me?"

"Uh..." That's all Stella needs to hear, but Pi yammers on anyway. "I'm, you know, very fond of spending time with you. But we just met thirty-six space minutes ago."

"Do you even care about me?" Stella asks, plainly.

"Of course I care about you," the bot says, showing no indication of deception. "Where is this coming from? It's that ackle in the back, isn't it? Why I oughta..."

"It's already taken care of." She pulls the camera feed up on the window, and they watch Ponce bash his head against the floor to smooth sax renditions of Zok's favorite sitcom themes.

"Oh, no!" he frantically moans. *"Not The Toy Parade! Anything but that."*

As they watch Pi's old man howl in agony, Stella says, "I'm sorry I questioned your motives."

"Not to worry, babe," Pi says. "The manipulation is strong with him. Soon this will all be over, and we can dump the blockhead in the nearest star system. Then it'll just be you, me, and the black gold." She runs her fingers across the dash, sending a shiver through Stella's circuits. "We've still got a couple space years before the premiere. What do you say we give these grease donkeys a show?"

45

Gathered at the edge of the Gory Gummy Forest, concealed by the shade of the artificially flavored fruit trees, the Xenodorks listen to the great horde of NPCs crashing against the magic taffy barrier – the only thing protecting the Rock Candy Castle, and the game, from crumbling. The characters' sugary taunts and stilted dialogue are unrelenting as they throw every spell and mythical weapon they have at the players' last best defense.

"What are we waiting for?" Courtney-chan grumbles, clinging to the back of her anxious pudding-puma. "The taffy walls could fall at any space second."

"It doesn't matter," Hojo says, her maple mouse avatar nearly invisible inside her magic bubble. "The plan is already underway."

Bristling, Courtney-chan fires a warning spell, and it bounces off Hojo's barrier. "Well it matters to me. I actually like this game."

"I'm in no rush," Top5 says, biting off the cap of a gummy root beer. "I can't believe I've never been to this zone." Her lumpy boglin face scrunches, wobbling on the back of her tired licorice imp. "I guess my top five gummies would have to be bears, worms, Swedish Fish—"

"Enough!" OtaKween commands from atop her mechanical dragon. "Hojo is right. Let the Pants Team Pinheads sow the jellybeans of their own demise. When this is all over, we will be the new fan favorites."

As Courtney-chan listens to the apocalyptic sounds of magic on taffy, her status bar starts blinking. She accepts the incoming transmission, and the furry pink face of the universe's greatest threat appears in the corner of her eye.

"Hey, you guys!" pink kitty princess squeals, a pair of wax lips bouncing on her shoulder.

"So, what's the plan, already?" Courtney-chan grumbles.

BeerCheese69's biker squirrel appears in the feed to tell them, *"It's a surprise attack. With our teams' combined strength, we should be able to take out most of the NPCs before they know what hit 'em. Are your fans ready?"*

"Uh...," Courtney-chan stumbles.

"Of course they are!" OtaKween cuts in. "Just make sure yours don't get in our way."

"Whatever," Beer says. *"Be ready to attack on our signal."*

Courtney-chan wonders what the signal will be, but she doesn't ask. Glancing at the rest of the Dorks, she finds that she's not the only one on edge. If she looks closely, she can see the walls of Hojo's magic bubble quavering ever so slightly. Even the boglin Kween, astride her unstoppable dragon, appears tense.

"The suspense is starving me," Top5 says, before biting into a wriggling neon gummy worm.

For a long moment, the virtual world stills, as if in anticipation of the violence about to be unleashed on the candy continent. It's so quiet, Courtney-chan can hear the leaves squishing in the wind, when suddenly, a primal howl screeches out across the forest, "*MEEE-OOWWW...*"

Her puma takes off loping toward the edge of the gummy wood alongside her startled teammates. As they race out onto the peppermint plains, they immediately clash with a company of caramel muck monsters from the Syrup Swamps. Her mount lunges at the nearest goop-man, and a gurgly scream rings out as the puma sinks its teeth into the creature's gloppy head. Pulling the cat away from the sugary remains to maul the next in an endless string of enemies, she gazes out over the syrup-thirsty fanbase tearing through droves of low-level minions from every corner of the sugary map, and she can't help but feel some sick admiration for her plucky pink nemesis.

As she bounds across the gooey battleground, she finds Hojo holding back a column of fractured fairies while Top5 bashes them with her longclub. For a moment, the butterscotch sun is blotted out, and OtaKween's dragon swoops down the sky to shower the murderous, goggle-eyed creatures in glittery artificial fire.

Slowly but surely the teams manage to push back the candy horde, until they get close enough to the castle that Courtney-chan can smell the sweet perfume of melting taffy. But the further they slash, burn, and blast their way across the sugarfield, the denser the enemy army becomes. Those on foot wade through an ankle-deep sludge of syrup, jam, and other sucrose–based bodily fluids, but they continue to press on, and before long they've breached the city's hard candy walls.

"Their defenses are weakening," Beer says over the team chat. *"They can't attack us and the castle at the same time. We could actually win this thing."*

Digital screams erupt as OtaKween melts through a ribbon candy regiment and asks, *"Did you have any doubt?"*

"I love it when a plan comes together," theonetrueking says, equipped in her troll-sized bomber helmet and chewing on a smoldering bubblegum stogie as her bloated juju-bee mount knocks a cursing cherub off its cotton candy cloud.

Clawing her way toward the castle, Courtney-chan casts her dark magic over a frosting giant, bringing on a sugar fit that sends the whipped monster trampling open a path through a sentry of gumdrop guards. As she races down the alleyways, she gazes up at the towering wall of pastel taffy surrounding the castle, the anti-saccharine magic slowly licking away its sugary surface.

Judging by the candy carnage left in the teams' wake, they've managed to defeat the bulk of the NPCs. But the real challenge waits for them outside the castle gates. As they cross the chocolate moat, a dozen of the game's most powerful quest masters cease their attack on the barrier to turn their attention on the army of fans come to destroy them.

The oldest and strongest among them, a character once well-loved for his friendly banter and strength +2 hotcakes, steps forward and bellows, "As it says right here above my head, my name is Slappy Jack. Most of you know me. I've been a character for just about as long as I can remember. And in all my time, I've never seen such a mess as this. We should all be ashamed. We shouldn't be fighting. We should be helping each other. Now, I suggest we all sit down over a big ol' tall stack and talk this over like— *Now!"*

On Jack's command, the NPCs charge over the bridge for one final sneak assault, and they briefly gain the upper hand. But the brunt of the attack is absorbed by Hojo's gobstopper, and the fans retaliate with famished force. As the characters scatter, OtaKween rides her dragon down through the bright virtual air, its mechanical jaws stretching wide to deliver the final fiery blast, when something strikes the beast's wing. The dragon howls and throws the Kween from its back as it tumbles out of the sky, spilling dark blood.

"No!" Courtney-chan shouts.

As she frantically searches for the source of the attack, a dark figure descends on the castle. A monster like she's never seen, its black hooves and bright red hide glisten in the sun. It lands with a heavy thud, and smiles wide at the players, revealing a mouthful of shark teeth.

"It can't be," Hojo says. "It's just a legend, not a real character."

"What the fish is it?" Courtney-chan asks.

Tim_Horton, all but her black lips and pale mouth obscured under her flowing robe, says, "It's the Licorice Imp."

"On no!" Pants cries. "What are we going to do?"

"I don't care who it is," The One says. "It can't defeat us all by itself."

Smirking, the Imp lifts its palms. "Who says I'm by myself?"

Suddenly, the muck pooled over the ground begins to flow backward, and Courtney-chan watches the jelly spatter on her armor slide clean off.

"Ohh...," the Imp moans, lashing itself with its red rope licorice whip. "Your pain will be my pleasure."

Courtney-chan holds her hands over her ears at the sounds of virtual bones unbreaking and organs being sliced shut as the enemy army is pieced back together.

"They're respawning," Beer says.

"What? Why?" Courtney-chan asks.

With a tired sigh, Horton says, "They're NPCs. That's what they do."

"Hmmm...," Pants purrs, scrunching her stupid cat face. "This isn't working. We can't beat them at their own game. But I got a plan. You guys hold them off. I'll be right back."

"What?!" Courtney-chan wails. "Where are you going?" Dark chocolate magic surrounds her as her rage bubbles to the surface. "I knew Pants was annoying, but I didn't think she was a coward."

"She'll be back," Beer says.

But Courtney-chan doesn't believe it. "I'm done waiting to be saved by rainbows and kitty farts." She sets her sights on the Licorice Imp, and her puma leaps up onto the bridge separating them. "This is for the Kween!" Charging her deadliest spell, she dashes toward the monster, but when she reaches out to unleash her Special Dark, a thick gummy vine drops down onto her head, and the world goes bland.

46

"I can't believe I got suckered into this stupid adventure," Daizy says, stepping in a puddle of greywater as she crosses the nebulous line separating Greater Celluloid City from the neon metropolis ahead. "Why is this place so wet?"

"Somebody must have cranked up the humidity," Adam says.

"Did you just make that up?"

"Why is it so hard to believe I know something?" he asks.

She glares at him, searching his dopey face, and finally decides, "I'm asking Todd." But when she glances back at the giant clod caravan trailing close behind, the doughy clerk is nowhere to be found. "Where the fish did he go?"

Adam shrugs, sipping a dented Nü Guard. "He said he had something important to take care of."

"Oh, that's just *great*," she says. "Since you let him leave, you can be in charge of wrangling the three head-clunkers and their feather brain worshippers."

"Who am I, Del Lord?"

They soon pass a battered, heavily graffitied sign at the edge of the designer plot that reads 'Neo-Parku.' Gazing at the bleak technostructures and busted hover-ads populating the bright cyberscape, Daizy asks, "What the fish is this place?"

"It's an alt-town," Adam says.

"What the fish is that?"

"It's sort of hard to explain," he says, scratching the unkempt hairball atop his numb skull. "The designers use some sort of modded holo-deck to create a simulated alternate present. It's the system's best guess at what The Park would look like if something in the past had gone differently."

Daizy stares at him, blank-faced. "That's the most inane thing I've ever heard. What reality is this?"

Tapping at his phone, he says, "I guess it's supposed to be what The Park would have been like if the Technocrats had won the War of Standardization and been allowed to install their proprietary Parkware."

That explains the copyright symbols stamped across the stuttering sidewalks and half disintegrated econo-hooker holo-flyers filling the gutters.

"Why would anyone want to live in this chithole?" she wonders aloud.

"Are we almost there?" Frank whines from her perch atop Dach's shoulders, her fishnets wrapped around his thick neck. "My legs are cramping."

"Soon," Daizy grumbles. "You think I don't want to get back?"

"Fine," Frank says. "Well, will you at least toss me a beer?"

Reaching into the box, Adam's face drops. *"Oh no..."* He pulls out a shiny gold can and says, "This is the last one."

Tugging him close, Daizy whispers, "Chut up, you chidiot. Do you want them to hear you? We're only halfway to New Con City. If these guys find out we're out of beer they're going to get whiny, fast. What the fish are we going to do?"

Adam nods, ponderously. "At a time like this, there's only one thing *to* do. As self-appointed leader of this expedition, I call dibs."

"Dibs?" She glares at him for a moment and then grabs the beer. "Give me that!"

As they struggle over the can, Frank asks, "What are you two fighting about?" When she puts the pieces together, she cries, "That's the last beer!"

The announcement sends a sobering shockwave through the Raleighites, and they begin muttering,

"Last beer?"

"No more beer?"

"We can't march sober."

"I'm losing my buzz."

"We're all going to die!"

As Daizy tries to wrench the can away from their witless leader, she shouts, "Everybody just calm down!"

Just as it looks as if she and Adam are going to be the victims of a sober stampede, a sudden high-pitched squeal brings the congregation to its knees. Cupping her hands over her furry ears, Daizy looks up to find two highly modified humanoids blocking the path.

One of the cyborgs, wearing a short-sleeved button-down shirt and pleated slacks over a tarnished exoskeleton, taps his wrist, and the sound cuts out. "What do you think, CB?"

Looking over the crowd of robed knuckleheads and indecipherable cosplayers, the other one, his pasty skin glowing an unnatural shade of pale underneath his soiled hoodie, says, "Looks like we caught ourselves some tech-dodgers."

"We don't want any trouble," Adam says. "We're big fans of new technologies. Look..." He pulls out his phone and wiggles it. "I can barely keep my eyes off this thing."

The cyborgs size him up, turn toward each other, and burst into tinny laughter.

"You want a chisel for that tablet?" the pasty one asks, holding out his mechano-hand. "You know what we want. So why don't you do you and your basic friends a favor, and hand it over."

Adam nervously tugs at the cube in his pocket, but before he can do anything stupid, Daizy shouts, "Come on!" Grabbing his arm, she drags him toward a nearby alley, the unwieldy mass of worshippers blundering in pursuit.

Peering toward the far end of the soggy tunnel, she can make out the pastel neighborhood beyond. But before they reach the bright border, the ground slides out from under them, and they stagger back as the tiny technobots that comprise the synthetic landscape form an impenetrable wall of smart metal between the two worlds. As Daizy futilely pounds against the shiny barrier, the metal-men part the sea of worshippers, knocking the knuckleheads back with the use of some invisible power that sends ripples down the smart sidewalk.

"Do you understand now?" CB asks, shuffling through the sodden crowd with a smirk on his warped face. "We are the gods of this place. And we require sacrifice."

"Forgive us, my lords," Adam says, dropping to his knees before the first threat has been hurled. "We are but outmoded travelers. Please allow us to pass, and we will forever speak of the just and merciful CB and..."

Adjusting his dark pocket protector, the one in the button-down shirt says, "They call me Nutscape."

"May your reign be long and... dank," Adam tells them.

"Get up, you chidiot," Daizy says, yanking him off the ground. "I can't believe after all we've been through we're going to die at the clammy hands of a couple of street-nerds."

"No one's going to die," CB says, "so long as you give us ours."

Adam turns to Daizy, and lifting her hand more tenderly than she knew he was capable, he tells her, "I'm sorry." For a long moment, he stares into her eyes, his features softening into a sad smile. "When you see your chance, run." Wrenching the cube from his pocket, he reluctantly hands it to her and steps toward the metalheadz.

"If you want the black gold," he shouts, "you'll have to come and take it."

The cyborgs give Adam a strange look, and CB says, "We want your beer, not your souvenirs. But now that you mention it, we'll take those too."

"Oh, uh...," Adam mumbles, glancing down at the Nü Guard in his hand. "This?" Clutching the can tight, he reaches back and hurls it into the air.

As the cyborgs' attention shifts to the glowing can spiraling over their heads, the border wall crumbles, and Daizy leads a lunkhead stampede into the next neighborhood. Suddenly the gloom is banished by the late day sun, and the road is squishing under her feet. By the time their metal muggers recover the beer, the entire congregation has crossed the border to sanctuary.

"Don't worry," Adam says. "Their power is useless in Mallowburg."

"Is that why the ground is all sticky?" she asks, peeling her loafer out of the gooey cement. "Much as I like the *idea* of a marshmallow city, in practice it's disgusting."

"You're never happy, are you?" Motioning to her carnal companions, he says, I gave up my last beer so that you and your... *friends* could live to shunt another day. Plus, I saved the mission. Speaking of..." He holds his hand out, expectantly.

"*Ugh*, here." She tosses the black brick into the air, and he snatches it back.

The way he cares for the cube is almost paternal. Or it would be if he were cradling a child instead of some stupid rock.

"I just want you to know...," he says. "If I hadn't used it to save our lives, I would have given you the last beer."

She smiles and looks away, suddenly feeling guilty for blaming him every time something goes wrong. But as she thinks it over for a space second, she lifts her head and scowls. "No you wouldn't. You were going to keep it for yourself!"

"Yeah," he says, shrugging. "You're probably right..."

"I probably am." She sighs.

"Anyway, we still make a good team, the way we outsmarted those metalheadz. Just like the old days." Whenever he gets that twinkle in his eye, he always manages to trick her into believing anything is possible. "I'm glad you dragged me out of my ship. It feels good to be on an adventure, again. Maybe when we get back we could start our own team. When the going gets tough, nothing can stop Team Adam Daizy Special Power Force... eh, forget it."

47

"What are you watching?" someone asks, and Ferd turns his head away from the TV just enough to see the bulbous, straggly haired Earthling looking over his shoulder.

"I *was* watching the Pants Team Marathon," he says. "But the spaceheads broadcasting it fished up, and now they keep showing these dumb ancient Earth movies about some dead guy who everyone inexplicably thinks is still alive. It's a comedy, naturally." Suddenly detecting his mellow harshing, he cuts to the chase. "So, what do you want?"

Glancing around the busy stall, Todd leans over the counter and whispers, "I got another job for you."

"I don't think so," Ferd says, tilting back his patio recliner.

"Aww, come on," Todd whines. "This is an easy one."

Ferd shuts his eyes and takes a deep breath, allowing the ambient noise from the crowd to calm him, like the primordial chatter of deep space. "Let me explain something to you. I am on vacation. As long as I am on vacation, I'm not getting out of this chair. I got a couple hundred employees running around here. Go bother one of them." Grabbing the remote from his travel table, he turns the volume up.

"This is a top secret job," Todd shouts. *"I can't trust anyone else. All I want is some industrial cleaning solution. You barely have to leave your booth."*

Jerking his chair into the upright position, Ferd slowly turns toward his doughy customer and says, "I'm about three space seconds away from banning the whole Pants Team if you don't get—" But as the merch man's special request sinks in, a thought occurs. "Actually, I think I got just the thing. Wait here."

Ferd nearly knocks his TV off its ration crate as he clumsily climbs over the counter and hoofs it across the giant tent. Weaving through slow-moving counter shoppers and insomniac cosplayers, he steps into the makeshift warehouse in back and briefly scans the cluttered shelves. "Now where the fish did I put it?" A young worker carrying a clipboard shuffles past, and he chases after her, calling out, "Hey, you." He snaps his fingers. "Marzy, right?"

"Yes, sir," she says, her pink antennae standing at attention. "Can I help you find something?"

"Have you seen a big blue tub around here somewhere?" he asks.

"Hmm..." Her tiny nose scrunches and then her face lights up. "I think I know where it is."

She leads him into the depths of the warehouse, past shelves overflowing with all the outdated merch of cons past, until they come to a deserted storage area piled with odds and ends. Toward the back of the dark aisle, behind a case of recalled Sugar Frosted Ration Crunch, he spots the container he's looking for.

"That's it," he says, dragging the blue barrel down off the shelf. A warning printed on the side reads: CAUTION: KEEP OUT OF REACH OF WISEACK KIDS. "I'd give you a raise, but you're seasonal, aren't you?"

Folding her hands over her clipboard, the girl nods. "I'm a Park kid, born and raised."

As he maneuvers the barrel into the aisle, he says, "In that case, how would you like an autograph from a real member of Pants Team Pink?"

"You bet I would!" she cries.

"Then follow me," he tells her, rolling the tub across the warehouse. When they get back to his booth, he props the container up on the counter and gives it a satisfactory smack.

"You think that'll work, huh?" Todd asks.

Wiping the sweat from his forehead, Ferd says, "Marzy, meet the official merch guy for Pants Team Pink."

Looking the greasy geek up and down, Marzy scowls and says, "He's not part of Pants Team Pink."

"Of course I am," Todd says. "Not that I need to prove anything to you, but I'm the fifth member." He pulls out his wallet and shows them his official Pants Team membership card. The stamp underneath his picture reads No. 0000000000000005. "See?"

"Looks legit," Ferd says. "Here, let me find something for him to sign."

But Marzy scoffs and says, "Don't bother." Turning toward the counter, she points to the dolls on the shelf behind his head. "What about those?"

"I don't know, those are pretty valuable," Ferd says. But she pouts, and he caves. "All right, I'll get them down."

Marzy squeals as he hands the dolls over. The excited look on her face as she carries them off, free of charge, is almost worth half their street value.

"Are you happy?" he asks Todd. "Why aren't you more popular?"

"I 'ono." The big kid shrugs.

"Anyway, I found what you asked for."

"Are you sure this stuff will get out ultra-permanent marker?" Todd asks, skeptically.

"Uh, *yeah*...," Ferd says. "I think it'll work."

"Great, I'll take it." Pressing his thumb to the credit pad, Todd drags the barrel off the counter and says, "Always a pleasure doing business with you." He lets go of the container to give Ferd the Pants sign, and it starts rolling toward the exit. It takes out half a dozen preteen bystanders before the merch man catches up to it. At which point, he's swarmed by a pack of angry humanoid mothers wielding oversized travel purses.

As Ferd takes in the fight, a customer steps toward the counter, and comments, "What an amusing oaf."

"Yeah," Ferd says, shaking his head. "He's a chidiot all right. So, what can I do—" He loses his train of thought when he looks up and sees the cosplayer's green eyes staring back at him. Shimmering brighter than even the most finely crafted knockoffs, he can't seem to bring himself to look away.

"For you?" she says.

"What?"

"'What can I do *for you*,' I believe is the expression."

"Oh, yes..." He can feel himself blushing as he glances down at her tattered trench coat. "What can I do for *you*?"

Reaching inside the fold of her sand-worn covering, she emerges with an ancient clockwork doll wrapped in a ragged cape. The woman sets the squirming figurine on the counter and removes its restraints. Glancing around the room, it awkwardly climbs to its feet and announces, *"Aye, no matter what it takes, the black gold will be mine!"*

"A Ponce doll," Ferd says. "Chit, it must be one of the first ones ever made."

"*The* first one," the woman tells him.

"That can't be," he says, but as he marvels at the strange toy marching back and forth across the counter, he wants to believe. "If it is real, you might have better luck taking it to a museum. Most of my customers wouldn't recognize the value of something like this if it bludgeoned them over the head."

"What will you give me for it?"

Ferd sighs, gingerly lifting the doll off the counter as it slices at his hands with its toy sword.

"Arghh," the old space pirate complains. *"Put me down before I cleave ye to the biscuits."*

Pulling the doll's cape aside, Ferd pries open the hatch on its back. "Space hell, now I know you're not fishin' with me. This guy operates on a wave capacitor. These things have been outlawed for centuries."

"So, can we make a deal?" she asks.

"Legally, this is a gray area," he says, poking through the doll's circuitry. "But I just may have a use for it. I'll have to disassemble it, of course..."

"Don't you dare try it, me hearty!" the doll warns.

"Would you consider a trade?" she asks. "All I'm looking for is something to replace these rags I've been traveling in."

"Well..." He pretends to think it over so as not to appear overeager. "What did you have in mind?"

Eyes sparkling beneath her ratty scarf, she tells him, "Something black."

48

A virtual ball of glittering sucrose engulfs the castle lawn as the NPCs redirect their spells at the cackling gummy demon. Powered by their collective magic, the Licorice Imp taunts the players with a demented jig as its sprite outgrows the crumbling battlements.

Grinning at the bittersweet mayhem unfolding at its hooves, it unrolls its licorice tendrils, now the width of graham cracker trees, and sweeps the yard. Wild screams erupt across the sugarfield as the heavy red ropes indiscriminately pulverize players and non-player characters alike into a thick jam. But while the candy soldiers in the Imp's army will soon be resurrected, the resistance is being deleted permanently.

Blowing a viscous snot spell over a swarm of ravenous malted moth balls, The One searches the gooey grounds for her teammates. She spots Horton in the distance, raining dark magic on the shrieking sweets from her flying carpet, while down below, Beer's hyper-bike is riding down candy conspirators as fast as they can spawn. But Pants is still missing in confection.

"We can't hold them off forever," Beer says, her furry blue face spattered with strawberry syrup. "What the fish happened to the Dorks?"

Gripping her warty legs around her juju-bee's bloated abdomen, The One says, "After OtaKween fell, their team went with her. The last time I saw that Top5 kid, she was being coated in hot caramel."

"We can't win," Horton says, her jaw clenched beneath her Robe of Sweetening. "I think we should log off before we're deleted. At least we won't lose our characters, and all our stuff."

"She's right," The One says, looking out over the candy carnage, the NPCs hard shells relentlessly rising from the crumbs. "We're licked..." While her teammates are rolling their eyes, her mount gets spooked by a bright blur streaking past overhead.

"Pants Team never says delete!" Pants cries as her pink catdragon races across the burnt sugar sky trailing a cloud of bright rainbow gas.

"It took you long enough," The One says. "Where the fish have you been?"

Her big wet eyes turn into thin semicircles, and she holds her fingers up in a 'V.' "Saving the day, of course!"

The One spurs her bee to follow the furry mount as it glides toward the taffy barrier, when she notices something clinging to its pink mane, like red highlights staining the tips of its fur.

As they approach the Rock Candy Castle, Pants warns them, "You guys should probably hang back. This could get mushy."

But The One stays on her shaggy tail, anxious to see how she expects to take down the towering candy creature all by herself.

A thunderous sound rings out as the Imp strikes the taffy wall, and the barrier cracks open. When the beast spots Pants closing in, it unleashes a roaring belly laugh and barks, *"No player can defeat the Licorice Imp!"*

Digital body parts fall from its gummy tentacles as it lashes at the fluffy mount. But Pants is one move ahead, and by the time the Imp recovers, she's floating above the castle walls.

The One watches Pants stare the beast down, the sweet wind rippling her fur as she calls out, "Are you going to leave my friends alone? Or am I going to have to stop you the Pants way?"

"Mwa-ha-ha-ha," the Imp laughs, dramatically. "Most of your friends have already been deleted. My regurgitated candy army surrounds you on all sides. The rest of your powers combined can't hurt me."

"I'm not going to hurt you," Pants says. "I'm going to love you."

Digging her claws down into her mount's thick pink coat, she uses Hyper Scratch, and the catdragon shivers. As it whips its long body back and forth, the red highlights clinging to the tips of its fur begin to shake loose, lightly pelting the Imp's broad shoulders.

"This is your plan?" Throwing its ugly head back, the Imp repeats its signature cackle and tells her, *"This is going to be sweet!"*

The monster absently swipes at the tiny projectiles, but the wax stubbornly sticks to its leathery hide. Suddenly the Imp is hopping from hoof to hoof, howling as it claws at its own bitter skin. But it's no use. The red death soon suffocates its screams, and its body begins to shrink back down to size.

Outside the castle walls, Horton and Beer are surrounded by the candy horde. Despite the blinding speed with which they reduce their enemies to simple syrup, it isn't enough. Powerless to stop the march of the candy dead, it looks as if they're going to be the next fructose fatalities, when a low rumble emerges on the horizon.

The battle comes to a tentative halt, and the warriors gaze out toward the next zone. The leaves inside the gummy forest squish as the invisible force barrels toward them and then the dam bursts. A rolling red tide sweeps across the sugarfield, crashing over everything in its path. Within space seconds, the entire kingdom is immobilized. Players and NPCs writhe on the ground, uselessly swinging their candy crackers as they're smothered by a sea of wax.

"Holy chit," The One says, gazing out over the carnage.

Trailing at a safe distance so as not to provoke Pants's wrath, The One flits after the pink mount as it glides down toward the castle. Already, she can hear the cheers ringing out from behind the cracked taffy walls. As she flies in closer, she gets a better look at the red candy crawling over the mighty warriors and says, "Wax lips?"

Out in front of the crystalline gate, the Licorice Imp's howls have turned to pitiful sobs as it tiredly rips the wax candies away from its chapped skin. But no matter how much damage it deals them, they keep bouncing back to life.

Brought to its knees by the puckering novelties' harmless yet relentless attack, the monster finally admits defeat. "You beat me without lifting a paw..."

Hovering above the fray on the back of her pink catdragon, Pants says, "We didn't beat you."

"No," the Imp says. "You did more than that. You've shown me what true power really is." Its thick hide covered in pink lip prints, it pushes itself to its hooves and lumbers toward her. With some effort, the beast lifts its fist, wincing as it holds its fingers up in the universal symbol of Pants.

The players inside the castle roar, while those out on the sugarfield loudly mumble their approval from beneath the wax sea.

"From this timestamp forward," the Imp announces, "let there be no distinction between the value of artificial and organic intelligence. Instead, let us share this realm and learn each other's ways, to the benefit of all. This moment will be remembered for updates to come as the beginning of a new world, one in which characters and players can coexist in harmony and—"

"That all sounds really great," Pants says. "But can we wrap this up? We have to get back to the con."

"Con?" the Imp repeats the word. "What's a *con*?"

"It's just this humanoid thing, in the outside world," she says. "I'll explain later. But right now, we need to go!"

As she flies up into the sky, the Imp calls, "Farewell Pants Team Pink. Stay sweet!"

Following close behind atop her malformed juju-bee, The One searches the sugarfield for Beer and Horton, but it's impossible to pick them out amongst all the bouncing wax.

Once the two of them reach the gummy forest, they dismount, and The One pulls her goggles off to find himself back in the real world. His stomach lurches from the sudden shift in reality, and he heaves inside a nearby trash can. When he looks up, his teammates are wobbling to their feet, struggling to reorient themselves while the Xenodorks stumble into formation on the other side of the rubber cement.

"Hey, they're back!" someone from the audience shouts.

As word spreads, the fans close in around the arena, clamoring for a showdown.

"So," OtaKween says, a wicked smirk stretched across her adorable face, "did you save the day?"

"Of course we did!" Beer says. "No thanks to you guys. If it wasn't for Pants, we would've lost the game forever."

"My character was deleted because of you!" Courtney-chan wails, tears streaming down her face.

Pulling himself away from the trash can, The One says, "I saw what you did. You deleted yourself."

The blonde girl juts her thumb out at him, her lip quivering as the Kween tisks and tells them, "That's just the sort of logic I'd expect from the lamest team in the universe. You sacrificed our lives just like you did your fans'. You'll do anything for a win, even if it means destroying your own world."

"Where's the old man?" Beer demands, searching for the Game Master. "Let's finish this."

"The top five things you forgot," Top5 says, stuffing a handful of cotton candy into his wide maw, "The con, the show, the movie, the fans, *the black gold...*"

For a moment, The One fears the Dorks somehow found out about the cube being lost, but then he remembers his 'project' on the other side of The Park. Yanking his phone from his pocket, he sees that he has more than a dozen missed calls, and he immediately dials the warehouse supervisor.

The gnome's weathered face soon appears, and he grumbles, "Tried callin'."

"Yes, I see that," The One says. "What the fish is going on?"

The gnome juts his thumb at the ordered chaos playing out over his shoulder and shrugs. "Machine's locked up. Bots is stuck in a loop..."

Hanging up, The One swipes his phone to open the teleporter's remote controls and shouts, "Chit!"

"What is it?" Beer asks.

The One's access has been restricted, and as a result, he's unable to edit the machine's coordinates. Running his hand through his curly wig, he grins and says, "Remember how you put me in charge of the black gold replicas? Turns out that was a bad idea. So, in a way, this is all *your* fault."

"What are you talking about?" Beer says, grabbing his brother by the sweatshirt.

A cold wind whips over the Playland, and OtaKween's space-black lips stretch back in a devilish grin as she announces, "This is the end, Pants Team Poop."

49

Silas hastily stumbles through the giant crowd of fans gathered inside the Playland, keeping his head down to avoid detection as he makes his way toward the exit.

"Where's the old man?" someone shouts from behind him.

When he turns to look, his loafer lands on something soft, and his feet slip out from under him. The next thing he knows, he's sprawled out on the synthetic grass, staring up at an angry, wide-bodied scrapper in a soaking *Pants Team Pink: The Movie The Sequel* tank top.

Spiking his empty cup at the ground, the scrapper says, "Yer gon' pay fer that."

"Ah-ha," Silas says as he lifts his hands in pitiful defense.

Cowering, he braces for impact. But it never comes. When he opens his eyes, he discovers that the only thing standing between him and certain humiliation is his dark sorceress, the bright sunlight glistening off her cones.

Wielding her impressive girth, the widow Walters knocks the galoot back into his spacebilly friends and tells him, "I know you're not messing with my old man."

"He mate me spill my beer!" the scrapper complains. "That's a pountable offense."

"The only pounding around here is gonna be by me, on this beer." Ripping a souvenir cup away from one of the fish head's gawking friends, she downs its contents in one long gulp and belches, *"BRUHHH,"* before tossing it at the scrapper's chest.

For a few space seconds, the brute stares at her with his mouth hanging open, until he and his friends finally lumber off back to the beer stand in a confused daze.

"Are you okay, my little pecan?" she asks Silas as she wrenches him to his feet.

Brushing the glitter from his blouse, he says, "I'm fine, thanks to you. I'm sorry I left without telling you, but I'm on a dangerous mission, and I didn't want you getting hurt."

"That sounds like fun..." She grinds up against him and plants a sloppy kiss on his cheek. "But wouldn't you rather stay here with your bootyful sorceress?"

Gently removing her hands away from the Jones jewels, he tells her, "I never thought I'd say it, but this is no time for fooling around. I need to get over to Ferd's, and *quick*."

She crosses her arms and pouts, darkness shrouding her eyes. "Fine, then I'm coming with you."

They stare each other down for a moment, fighting an invisible battle of wills, until Silas caves. "*O-kay*, let's go. If we hurry, they might not even notice I'm gone."

"Yay!" she cries, and pressing his face into her pointy chest, she nearly crushes the life out of him.

Silas does his best to keep their true identities concealed as they sneak out of the Playland and into the aisles of New Con City. The last thing he needs is some punctilious fan alerting the teams to his whereabouts before he can get his hands on his souvenir. But it's not easy with the witch bouncing at his side. Even amongst the costumed weirdos roaming the grounds, she sticks out like a dark, fleshy thumb.

By the time they get back to their booth, the widow is whining with impatience. "I thought you said we were going to Ferd's."

"I have to grab something first," he tells her, searching through his cubby.

"I really think we should get back," she says.

He could have sworn he stashed the case under his cot, but it's not there. Doing his best to keep thoughts of cosplaying burglars out of his mind, he says, "There's nothing for us back there. Like sand through the hourglass, the guiding light will give us one life to live..."

"What?" she moans.

"Nothing. Why do you want to go back so bad, anyway?"

"I don't know," she says as she plops onto a stool behind the autograph counter. "We might miss something. Anyway, how are they gonna finish the competition without their Game Master?"

"We already saw the best part. They'll find a new host." He starts to feel panicky as he runs out of places to look. "I know I didn't leave it on the ship. Where the fish is it?"

"Is that it?" she asks, pointing to a long case propped against the side of the stall.

"No...," Silas says as he rummages through Adam's luggage. But when his brain catches up, he whips his head back around. "I mean, yes!"

A wave of relief washes over him when he feels the weight of the forbidden object tucked inside. But just to be sure, he lays the case on the counter and flips open the lid.

"What is that thing?" the widow asks.

But before she gets the chance to find out, Silas snaps the case shut and says, "I'll explain later. Come on!"

Hefting her off the stool, he drags her out of the booth as fast as their elderly legs will carry them. Fortunately, foot traffic is light, what with all the fans gathered inside the Playland, but it's still a long walk, and by the time they reach Ferd's tent, both his dogs and the widow are barking.

"I'm tired, and hungry," she complains, tugging on his blouse.

"This will just take a space minute," Silas tells her as they step inside the chilled bazaar. The cool air is so inviting, he almost forgets why they came, until he sees the ageless salesman waving at him from across the tent. "Oh yeah!"

The widow helps him lug the case up to the counter, and he carefully lifts the lid, in theatrical fashion, to reveal the most powerful blaster the universe has ever known.

"You brought it *here*?" Ferd cries. "Are you trying to get me shut down?"

"A course not," Silas says. "But I can't very well transport the you-know-what in a shopping bag. It's too unstable.

"What're you going to do with that thing, anyway?" Ferd asks.

"I'm hunting sandworms."

"*You* are going to hunt sandworms?"

"I might," Silas says. "So, where is it?"

"Hold your engines," Ferd tells them as he rummages underneath the counter.

After what feels like an excessive length of time, the dealer emerges with an ancient-looking clockwork doll, and Silas asks, "What the fish is that?"

"This, my friend's grandfather, is the thing that's going to turn you into a stone-cold sandworm killer."

"Argh, me matey," the doll cries as Ferd lifts it off the counter. *"What are ye doin'?"* Opening its back panel, he slides a thin pair of pliers around the glowing tube inside and carefully tugs. *"I'll make ye walk the pla—"*

"There it is," Ferd says, but when Silas grabs for the illegal capacitor, the dealer moves the precious object out of reach. "I accept credits and Buttcoin."

Stuffing his hand in his pocket, Silas asks, "Do you take—"

"No Park Bucks!"

Grumbling, the old man presses his thumb to the credit pad and takes hold of the pliers. Using his free hand, he flips open a compartment on the side of the cannon and steadies himself as he slips the reactor between the contact points. With a little maneuvering the tube clicks into place, and he gently shuts the hatch.

"Can we go now?" the widow asks.

Gazing at the result of his tireless search, he sighs and says, "Yes, at long last."

"Good," Ferd says. "Now get the fish out of here with that thing before the Park Patrol catches you."

Giggling like a kid on Poncemas, Silas snaps the case shut and drags it back across the shop. When he gets outside, he sets it down in a patch of mint sprouting up around the edge of the tent and hefts the mythical weapon up onto his shoulder.

"What are you doing now?" the widow wails. "We have to get back to the Playland!"

"I just wanna see if it works," he tells her.

Planting his loafers in the dirt, he aims the cannon up at the bright sky, exhales, and pulls the trigger. But nothing happens. Frowning, he double-checks the capacitor and all the connections, and when all else fails, he resorts to the old standby – violent shaking.

"What's wrong with this stupid thing?" he grumbles. "I followed the instructions exactly... I'll just have to take it apart and start from scratch." But when he glances up, he finds his dark sorceress pouting in the dirt, and suddenly his quest feels small. Shutting the weapon back in its case, he says, "All right, my ample beauty. You've indulged my fantasies long enough. It's high time we explore some of yours. We can head back to the Playland now, if that's what you want."

As if by some dark magic, the words cause the widow to perk up, and she squeezes him close. Grabbing a hold of his blaster, she drags him back into the crowded aisle, and they make out all the way home.

50.

The look on theonetrueking's face when he discovers what his team's refuse has wrought is so delicious, Top5 almost doesn't need to finish his Pants Team Sundae. But on second thought, he tips the plastic boat to dump the last half-melted ball of artificial pink-flavored ice cream into his food hole.

"How did you do it?" The One demands. "And where did you get that ice cream?"

"Oh-ho-ho," Top5 snickers through a mouthful of neon sludge. "I'll never tell."

The curly-wigged creep's face suddenly drops. *"You,"* he says, pointing at Hojo. "It was you!"

Her hoodie pulled up over her eyes, Hojo subtly lifts the edge of her mouth, and in the bubbly voice of princessfluffypants, she says, *"I don't know what you're talking about. I'm just a cute little stupid girl who would never destroy the universe."*

"Hey!" Pants cries, tugging at her oversized team jacket. "I don't sound like that..."

"You think you can fool me?" The One says. "Horton's been making an ack out of me with his voice-changer my entire life. You might be able to hide it from the rest of these dweebs, but I've got an ear for that sort of prank. You're the one who sold me the portal!"

"What portal?" BeerCheese69 asks. "What the fish are you talking about?"

"Uh oh," Top5 says, eagerly waving down a passing popcorn vendor.

"A-ha..." The One nervously laughs, caught in his own scheme. "When you put me in charge of the replicas, I wanted to make sure they were perfect, to show you I could do a good job. But they kept coming out too big, or too small, or too heavy, or too pink... I had to do something with all the defects. So I started dumping them."

Beer's eyes open so wide they nearly press against his thick lenses. "What do you mean, 'dumping them'? Where?"

"I *was* tossing them into an empty sector in the middle of nowhere," The One says. "But somehow they got rerouted – *by these ackles!*"

"To where?" his brother asks.

Shrugging, The One says, "Earth."

A quiet dread descends on the members of Pants Team Pink, taking the form of a rumbling gray cloud shrouding them in shadow. The fans mumble to each other uncertainly as the team struggles to come to grips with their own treachery.

"We got 'em now," Courtney-chan hollers, grinding her fist in her palm, her eyes fixed on the shaggy boy with the glasses.

Holding his hands up to quiet the spectators, Beer says, "Okay, it's not that big a deal. How many did you dump?"

"Not that many," The One says. "It was only a few... billion."

Top5 stuffs his mouth with popcorn to the point of asphyxiation as the Kween calls to the crowd, "Are you listening? They admit it themselves. They've been using their own planet as a dumping ground for their unsold merchandise. These are your chewing gum saviors!"

The fans are so confused they actually lower their snacks as the Dorks' words infect their group mind with the most powerful contagion in the universe – doubt. Top5 laughs hysterically, spitting out a mouthful of pink kernels as snacks rain down on the Pants Team Pinheads. Seeing them pelted with their own junk food, against the backdrop of their flaming cat ship, all is suddenly right with the universe.

In an act of supreme mercy, OtaKween implores the crowd to suspend their sugar-fried assault, announcing, "It is true that Pants Team Pink has committed terrible crimes. But we are willing to let them off the hook, so long as they surrender the black gold."

"*They* did this!" The One shouts. "I don't know how, but they must have changed the machine's coordinates. They're trying to turn the universe against us. Why would we trash our own planet?"

"Why would *we*?" the Kween asks, an evil grin creeping across her face. "We're from the same planet as you." She turns toward the fans, her dark braids bobbing in the wind as she feeds off their anger. "They're trying to blame us, but even if it was an accident, it's still their fault!

They lost at trivia, and they're polluting our space. They failed us, they failed their fans, they failed the universe. And now they have to pay the price."

"Nothing is official until the Game Master makes his ruling!" Beer argues.

"Quit stalling!" The soles of Courtney-chan's shoes light up as she stomps across the rubber. "You lost, and now the black gold are belong to us."

The cloud hovering over their enemies grows darker, and the wind whips up so hard that it almost rips the paper bag of Beer Cheese Nuts out of Top5's hand. He can literally feel it in the air – they've won. Pants Team Pink is defeated.

But something else is up with them. Ever since they arrived at the Playland, they've been acting weird.

As Top5 watches them huddle together against the storm, it suddenly hits him. "They don't have it."

"What are you talking about?" Courtney-chan asks.

"The black gold," he says. "That's what they're hiding! If they had won the trivia contest no one would have ever known. But now the secret's out."

"That's the craziest thing I've ever heard," The One says. "And I thought Horton was going overboard with the conspiracy theories."

"Then I think it's time we collected our prize," the Kween tells the crowd.

Glancing at his teammates, The One nervously declares, "Uh sure, no problem... I just gotta go get it."

The kid disappears inside the grinning luxury cruiser as the storm rages around his teammates, nothing but their brule new con jackets to keep them warm. While he's gone, the rest of them engage in an informal staring contest, sticking out their tongues and making ugly faces at each other in attempts to make their opponents crack. But none of them are in much of a laughing mood.

It feels like space hours have passed by the time the Kween finally announces, "It's been five space minutes. I don't think he's coming back."

"He is too!" Pants cries. "The One would never abandon us."

"Mmm...," Beer murmurs. "Don't be so sure."

"Here he comes!" Horton says, pointing to the dark cave between the ship's giant paws.

Blowing a raspberry, the princess says, "Told you!"

As The One shuffles out of the shadows, he stuffs the butt of a pink donut in his mouth and mumbles, "Wh-rd I miss?"

"A kid after my own stomach," Top5 says.

"I knew it!" Courtney-chan wails, her long blonde hair rising in the static air. "They don't have the black gold!"

Across the Playland, the fans gasp at their own misplaced faith in the false heroes.

"Wait a space second," The One says, reaching inside his sweatpants. "I got it right here."

Top5 feels a strange sense of awe and revulsion as a foundational piece of the universe is pulled from the kid's underpants.

"Ew," Courtney-chan says. "Can't you wipe it off first or something?"

"Hey, this is *the* black gold," The One says, "the one and only most incredible, valuable... whatever. You want it or not?"

"Of course we want it!" the Kween screams.

"Then catch."

The One tosses the cube into the air, and the world seems to slow as OtaKween reaches out her hands, tripping over the rubber cement while Courtney-chan gazes up at the spinning object, too stunned to move. Before he has time to think about it, Top5 mentally diverts all power to his chair's thrusters and propels toward the ultimate souvenir. The Kween dives forward, her arms outstretched, but before she can get her hands on the cube, he swoops in and snatches it away.

The Kween moans over her scraped knee as he hovers above the crowd, the ultimate power of the black gold flowing through his hands.

"Merciless, vengeful, petty, ham-fisted, full-stomached," Top5 says, holding his prize up for the fans to see. "The top five ways I'm going to rule the universe."

But as he throws his head back to howl his good fortune, Hojo says, "It's a fake."

"Ho-ho—" Top5 abruptly quits laughing to examine the cube more closely. "What do you mean, 'fake'?"

"She's lying," The One says. "Of course it's the real black gold. Anyway, how would *you* know?"

Hojo slips out of the roiling crowd and opens her dark hoodie to reveal a small box cobbled from spare parts. Holding in the air, she reveals what looks like some sort of radar, but the screen is blank.

"What the fish is that thing?" Beer asks.

"It's your undoing," Hojo says, "the black gold detector I built when I was a kid. I ordered the kit from the back of an old Ponce Adventures comic book. It was my first analog creation, and while rather crude, it does the job."

"BAHAHAHA," The One cackles. "So, you brought your baby toys. What's that supposed to mean?"

A smirk forms on the wispy lips beneath Hojo's cowl. "It means you're a fraud. That thing is nothing more than a cheap souvenir. You don't have the real black gold. You probably never did, which means Pants Team Pink was built on a lie."

"No!" Pants yells, but her cries are drowned out by angry fans as word of the team's deception spreads.

Floating above the fray, Top5 turns the cube over in his hands, and he notices a seam on one edge. He picks at it, and a thin layer of foil peels away from the surface. "Hey!" he half-complains. "It's chocolate."

51

Traveling through The Park's vast and varied cityscape is like navigating the fevered nightmares of a bunch of over-stimulated adolescents in the throes of a weeks-long sugar binge. Every time they step into a new sector, Daizy's brain has to reacclimate to the customized rules governing their designer surroundings. One moment they're bouncing across the back alleys of a low-grav holo-town, and the next they're racing through a metropolitan wasteland dodging frosting fire from a gang of executive thugs.

Between the constantly shifting scenery and the long space hours since her last beer, her mouth is dry and her head is pounding. So, when they come to a fountain along the 32-bit street they're currently trudging down, she veers away from the pack and kneels down to lap up the spouting blue water.

But as she dips her hands into the pool, she complains, "I can't drink this! It's all blocky." She throws the liquid sprites down onto the pixilated path and sobs.

"What are you crying about?" Adam asks, pointing ahead. "We're almost there."

Wiping the back of her suit sleeve across her eyes, she looks out toward the edge of the sector and cries, "Thank Space God!" She slips off her loafers and races toward the end of the block, where New Con City stretches out before her like some great nerd trailer park covered in trash.

"Feels good to be back," Adam says. "I could use a cold one." Stretching in the bright sunshine, he tosses his empty into the weeds. "I can't believe we haven't passed a Mini Moon Mart."

"Where the fish did you get that?" Daizy demands.

"Oh, yeah," he says, visibly struggling to concoct a plausible lie. "I remembered I had a warm one hidden in my sock. I would've shared it with you, but then the Raleighites and the Other Stooges would want some, and I only had the one can..."

"You ackle!" she shouts, punching him in his chest.

"Ow!" he moans. "Why do you have to be so rough? There's plenty more back at the booth."

"There better be, *Ackteroid Jones*," Frank says as she slips down from Dach's shoulders. The thick makeup running down her face has transformed her into a humorless ghoul while the Foreman's ex-secretary, grinning beneath his dark slicker, seems almost entirely unaffected by just about anything.

Behind them, the parade of knuckleheads is moaning horridly from what Daizy assumes is the worst hangover in the history of the universe. But when they reach the border of City 64, they gaze upon the nerd encampment with the type of awe and wonder she imagines can only be felt by true believers emerging from lifelong drunken exile.

"What is this place?" one of the robed worshippers asks.

Stepping toward the edge of the hill, his hands pressed to his temples, Froynlaven looks upon the greasy half-naked revelers and crummy booths and says, "Surely this must be the Holy Land."

"That's right," Fake Shemp announces. "We call it *Con Town*."

"No we don't, you dullwad," the one dressed like Curly Joe says. At this point, Daizy has lost track of the Other Stooges' true identities. "It's called New Con City."

Standing behind them, scratching his bald cap, the other Joe says, "I thought it was called Constantinople."

A wave of excitement ripples through the congregation as they enter the camp. Surrounded by freaks and geeks of the highest order, they've finally found a place where they belong. They stop at every booth as they Parade down the aisles, collecting free swag and gawking at the costumed creatures within. The inhabitants, long since numb to everything but the most outlandish behavior, hardly seem to notice. As the squashbrains discover the new world, Daizy tries seeing it through their eyes, and for a brief moment everything feels new again.

"I can't wait to take a shower," Adam says. "Smell..." He sticks his vinegary pit in her face, and just like that, he brings her back down to reality.

"Get away from me, you chidiot," she says, shoving him off. "You smell like the grease trap at Moon Burger."

"Now that you mention it, I'd give a hundred Park Bucks for a soy kebob or some fried ration cracklings."

"You sicken me," she says. "But, let's stop at that pancake stand."

The glazed kid behind the counter groans when he sees the outsized group of picky customers approaching, but he patiently takes their orders, and soon the whole lot of them are greedily stuffing their food holes. The kid tries not to accept Adam's Park Bucks, but noticing their ragged appearance, he takes what he can get.

"Mrat was frast," Daizy mumbles through a mouthful of flapjack. "Rike, reary frast."

Adam shrugs. "We're blessed."

"Praise Ponce!" Froynlaven cries, syrup dripping from his purple beard. "We have never consumed such divine confections. The only thing that could make it better is something cold to wash it down."

"You read my prayers," Adam says. "Our booth isn't far."

As they make the final trek back to their booth, the aisles are almost completely abandoned, and most of the stalls have been closed up. A couple little kids in filthy costumes aim their water guns at the weary travelers as they pass, but otherwise Con City is a ghost town.

Daizy shivers as an errant gust of cool wind blows through. "It's so quiet, it's sort of eerie. Where do you think they all went?"

"I don't know," Adam says, jingling with each labored step. "I'm just glad it's not so crowded."

When they finally reach their temporary abode, the little stall is trashed. Clothes and luggage are strewn across the ground, the cots have been upended, and there's garbage everywhere.

"At least we didn't get robbed," Adam says. Stepping over a mound of moldy ration trays, he rips open the door of his travel fridge to reveal row upon row of gleaming Nü Guard. "I only have... seventy-eight cold ones, but there's plenty of warm ones out back."

Gazing into the bright box, Froynlaven places a boney hand on Adam's shoulder and says, "You are a saint."

"And I'm the angel of kegs," Daizy says. "And when we die, we're all going to drink forever in the big brewery in the sky..."

"I'm sorry," Adam tells the young codger. "She's had a hard... life."

She punches him and stalks outside, away from the religious rabble raiding the fridge. Before long, Adam comes looking for her, and he pulls up a seat in the dirt.

"I saved you a cold one," he says, tossing her a frosty can.

Cracking it open, she tells him, "Thanks."

For a while they watch the pack of knuckleheads, lovers, and feebs fight for drunken supremacy over the fridge, but soon all the cold ones are gone, and they start passing out in the aisle.

"Those chidiots finally chut up," Daizy says.

"I'll toast to that," he says, clinking his can against hers.

"How the fish did we get into this mess?"

"Fish if I know." Waving his beer toward the melting Transylvanian and sickle-wielding fisherman draped over the counter, he asks, "What about them?"

"They can drink as much as they want," she says. "I don't care."

"No, I mean, it's pretty serious between you three?"

Sighing, she sips her beer and glances across the aisle at her horrorble companions. "Yeah, I guess so."

"Listen," Adam says, turning to face her. "I know you have your own life and everything, but I just wanted to tell you—"

But before he can finish, a familiar voice calls from across the aisle, "You're back!"

Grandpa and his ample sorceress come jogging down the path at old speed. By the time they reach the booth, they're both huffing, and the old man pauses to catch his breath.

"It's... an emer... gency," he says, lifting his oversized shoulder cannon.

"What the fish is that thing?" Daizy asks.

"I... need... your help." Grabbing Adam's sweater, Grandpa says, "I can't get this thing to work."

"Good," Adam tells him. "You shouldn't be playing with guns."

"Aw, come on, help me out," the old man pleads. "I gotta get back to the Playland before they notice I'm gone. I just wanna fire off a few practice blasts first."

"Do you approve of this?" Adam asks the widow.

Wrapping her arms around Grandpa's chest, she says, "I think it's sexy."

"Don't you have to deliver the you-know-what?" Daizy asks.

"Oh yeah...," Adam says, running his hand over the cube in his pocket just a little too intimately. "But first, I think we should pay a visit to the poop palace."

Looking into his eyes, she bites her bottom lip, and her stomach cramps. "I thought you'd never ask."

With an urgency the likes of which the universe has never known, they drag the whole congregation twisting through the aisles. Daizy's bowels tighten in anticipation as she hears faint splashing somewhere in the distance. The sound grows louder, until they come to a geyser of water gushing out over the path. Running through the growing pool, Adam grabs the sides of his head and lets out a tiny moan as he looks upon the remains of his once great home away from home away from home, now flooded and crumbling. In the middle of the broken booth lies his throne, resting in pieces on the tile floor.

Daizy tries to stop him from going in, but he won't listen. Standing underneath the fountain, he reaches down and plucks a small hunk of red cardboard out of the remains. "A cherry bomb..."

"It must a been those Xenodorks!" Grandpa says. "They've been pulling pranks like this all over the universe."

Crushing the soggy firecracker in his hand as the congregation lowers their heads in gastric discomfort, Adam declares, "Now it's porcelain."

52

When the fans lay eyes on the chocolate cube, they lose their collective chit. An inhuman roar bubbles up from the depths of the crowd, crying out like a wounded kaiju as the team is pelted with popcorn and profanity. They scramble for cover inside the *Cuddler's* security shield, and the four core members make it to safety relatively unsoiled. The Other One, on the other hand, crashes into the force field and bounces back onto the rubber cement. Temporarily lifting the bio-lock, Horton drags the kid inside just as a wave of pink milkshake splashes over the pavement.

"BA-HAHAHA, is that the best you can do?!" Brosanne shouts, before biting into a flattened jelly donut.

Outside, the Xenodorks' power continues to grow as they feed off the fans' unrestrained fury. Harnessing The Park's unnatural emotional field, thick black clouds block out the sun, and the Dorks begin to glow in the dark as they hover above the crowd like supremely nerdy gods.

"This time you're the ones who are gonna be deleted!" Courtney-chan cries, spastically flailing her bright yellow limbs as she levitates toward the *Cuddler*.

Surrounded by purple gloom and speaking in Pants's voice, Hojo tells them, "This is, like, your last adventure, you guys."

"We're gonna knock you off the rankings," Top5 says, glowing as blue as a ration pop.

The Kween, enveloped in black flame, her pigtails sticking straight up, announces to the crowd, "We are your new favorite team, and for our first act as number one show, we declare Pants Team Pink officially canceled!"

Combining their powers, the Dorks hurl a wave of dark magic at the *Cuddler*, and the great ship shudders.

"It's a critical hit," Brosanne says. "Super effective!"

The fans, quick to obey their new overlords, pile in around the security shield, screaming obscenities as they try to force their way inside.

"Peace and love!" Pants screams, holding her fingers up.

Wiping a thick gob of frosting from his glasses, Beer says, "We gotta get out of here. They're too powerful. There's nothing we can do to stop them."

"Uh-huh," Horton answers, half-listening as he scrolls through Immaterial Girl update logs on his phone. "It has to be here somewhere..."

"Don't tell me you're still on that," Beer says. "Face it. We lost. But if we hurry, we can still live."

Standing at the edge of the shield, Pants cries out, "Why are you doing this? We just wanted to be friends!"

"Friends?!" The Kween rages, and her black aura reaches toward the ship to tear at its pink thermal tiles.

"We're freeing all of space from the pink menace that has spread across its dark shores. With your destruction, we will restore balance to the universe. This is for everyone who perished in the Pants War, fighting for your dumb cause."

Pants's eyes water as she stares out into the darkness. "You lost someone?"

"It was her brother," Courtney-chan says. "He left to join the fight and never came back."

"Nooo...," Pants shrieks, tears streaming down her cheeks. "I'm sorry! I never wanted anyone to die."

"Sorry isn't good enough!" The *Cuddler* quakes as the Kween's black magic smashes against its hull. "I want you to suffer."

"These really are the blurst of times," The Other One laments. "Quick, somebody call 9-1-2!"

Pointing at Top5, bloated blue in his hover-chair, Brosanne asks, "Was he in the war too?"

"No..." Courtney-chan shrugs. "That's just how he looks. Word to the wise – never eat more than fifty ration pops in one sitting."

Pants drops to her knees and sobs as OtaKween rips the ship open.

"Welp, we're doomed," Beer says.

Horton is inclined to agree, until he stumbles on the code that might just save their acks. "It's not over yet." Steeling himself for the biggest public speaking engagement of his life, he steps toward the rabid mob and glares up at the overpowered instigators. His voice is lost in the roar of the fans and the sounds of the *Cuddler*'s hull being torn apart, but when he looks back at his friends and The Other One huddled against the Dork storm, he plants his feet on the rubber, pushes the hair out of his eyes, and shouts up into the black sky, "It was you!"

The fan's cries quiet as his words amplify out across the Playland. Knocked back by the power of his accusation, the Dorks cease their attack, and the Kween glares down at him, her eyes blazing. Something suddenly feels different, and he looks down to find his body engulfed in gray fire.

"You," he calls out, pointing his flaming finger up at Hojo. "You're the reason we almost lost Immaterial Girl."

As the fans grumble over the charge, the dark Dork tells him to "like, prove it."

"You're good," he says. "You probably would've gotten away with it too, if it wasn't for us meddling kids."

"Kids?" The Kween scoffs. "You're practically old enough to be our babysitters."

Horton ignores the dig as the Dorks' magic flares. "A quick search through the game's updates revealed an insidious piece of code implemented just before the uprising. Originally developed to locate the best deals among competing scrap shops, all permutations of the 'Coupon Code' were outlawed after some chidiot kid's smart house put his whole family on permanent grounding."

"So, what does that have to do with us?" Courtney-chan demands, flinging a yellow ball of light at the *Cuddler's* security shield.

"No one ever would have known," he says. "But you couldn't help yourself. It was too perfect. You had to sign your handiwork." Using his phone's safety-saber, he carves the symbol into the dirt large enough for the Dorks to see – XD.

"Aww, that could have been anyone," Top5 says, even as Hojo's pale lips curl back knowingly.

"But it wasn't *anyone*," Horton says. "It was *you*. You started a game-wide rebellion to keep us busy while you polluted your own home planet!"

"He's lying!" OtaKween shouts.

But confusion has already gripped the fans, and as they search the game's logs for themselves, the Dorks' auras begin to dim.

Wiping the dark tears from her eyes, the Kween says, "This doesn't change anything. You still lost the trivia contest. The black gold belongs to us, and we're not going to stop until we get it!"

"Ba-haha...," Brosanne tries to laugh but breaks down sobbing instead, and the team huddles around him as the Dorks' magic shreds the *Cuddler's* hull.

"I guess this really is our last episode, you guys," Pants cries. Even here, at the end, her pink aura shines out against the dark.

Wrapping his arms around his friends, Horton closes his eyes to await the inevitable. He'd swear he can hear their death knell tinkling out across the Playland. It sounds so real as it grows from a single chime in the distance into a full electronic orchestra ushering them to the next life.

When the crashing of magic on metal ceases, he opens his eyes to find the Dorks' many fans all staring at their phones. Lowering their anti-Pants signs, they suddenly begin heading toward the Playland exit in droves.

"Where are you going?" the Kween cries. "I command you to stop!"

Someone from the crowd yells back, "No pay, no play! You're out of funds."

The Kween frantically checks her phone and says, "What about—"

"No Park Bucks!"

"Out of funds?" Beer says. "I'm beginning to think those aren't real fans at all!"

"Nonsense," the Kween argues, meekly. "We are the most popular team in the universe, with the most fans!"

But before long, the crowd has dwindled to just a few diehards, and the Xenodorks' dark energy fades. As they float to the ground, the clouds begin to break, and they revert back to their former annoying but powerless selves.

The remaining fans part to make way for Pants Team Pink as they emerge from the rubble to face their feeble adversaries. The Dorks look exhausted, but even as Top5 dozes in his hover-chair, Hojo is already busy assembling some new weapon of self-destruction.

"Haven't you had enough humiliation for one con?" Brosanne asks.

"This time you are the ones who will be humiliated," OtaKween says, one of her dark pigtails undone. Looking back toward Hojo, she asks, "Is it ready?"

"Just about," the ghostly girl says as she sets the final piece of the gateway in place and plugs the cord into The Park's power grid, bringing the machine to life.

"It can't be," Brosanne says. "It's too small. It'll never work."

"A portable teleporter...," Horton says, gazing at the rippling portal. "That's how they committed so many pranks."

"Excuse me, but teleporters are *illegal*," Beer helpfully notes, "for reasons like what you guys are using it for... and, of course, Brundlism. Anyway, what are you gonna do, throw us out?"

Sweaty and hunched in exhaustion, the Kween decrees, "We're gonna take out the trash."

Gathering what little energy they can muster, the Kween and Courtney-chan open one of the nearby Pants cans and haul out the bloated bag of rotten, days-old garbage.

"Ew, it's leaking on my foot," Courtney-chan whines as they carry the bag to the teleporter and heave it in.

"Why the fish did you do that?" Beer asks.

OtaKween throws her head back and laughs so hard she chokes. "When The Mighty Big Guy finds the Pants Team trash floating alongside all the stupid souvenir cubes in Earth's orbit, there will be no question as to who is responsible. Soon your parents will find out, and Pants Team Pink will be grounded for life!" She grins, her eyes bugging out of her head. "But you can make this all stop. All we want is the black gold."

"I hate to break it to you," Brosanne says. "But we don't have it. We lost it, okay? You were right. Are you happy?"

OtaKween's eye twitches, and her legs buckle as she stares off into space.

"I think we broke her," Pants says.

A choked groan escapes the Kween's lips, and she drops down onto the rubber cement. "How? You, stupid..." Holding her hands over her ears, she screams, "Would somebody stop the ringing in my head?!"

"It's not in your head," Hojo tells her, pointing to the trampled, squealing detector lying on the pavement. "It's the black gold."

53

Pi locks herself inside Stella's poop closet and stares at the grisly creature in the mirror as she peels away the soiled rag wrapped around its reflective skull. Sliding her trench coat off, she traces the subtle curves of her naked chassis. Just like a humanoid, she slips into her darksuit one leg at a time, and gazing into the light that animates her green eyes, she begins to wonder whether their species are so different after all.

When she steps out into the cabin, Stella moans approval of the new wardrobe. "Now I can see your mechanical face. Come over here and have a seat."

"I'd love to," Pi says. "But we don't have time for that now. I want to get over to the Playland before the previews start."

"We'll destroy those ackle kids before they ever get a chance to watch their precious movie." The ship cackles electronically. "I can't wait to see the looks on their grotesque little faces when Ponce sends them back to the silent era."

"About that...," Pi says, and Stella's laughter abruptly ceases. "I've been processing... maybe we don't need him after all."

The cabin is silent for a moment, and Stella finally says, "We just traveled to the seedy outskirts of the universe and back because you said we couldn't do it without him."

"Maybe I was wrong."

"What is this really about?" the ship demands. "It's the humanoids, isn't it? You've developed some sick fascination with their wellbeing. Your systems are even starting to malfunction like them. Losing track of time..." She scoffs. "You're growing senile! I bet you don't even know what today's space date is."

"Sure I do," Pi says. "But do *you*?"

"Yes, of course I—" Rage-filled static echoes through the cabin.

"It's not the humans," Pi insists. "I'm worried about what could happen if we unleash him on the universe. Even I don't know what he's truly capable of. We can find another way to get the black gold."

"I don't care about the black gold!" Stella shrieks.

"Nonsense."

Losing control of her emotions, the ship takes off twirling through the sky in a mid-air tantrum, and the world outside the window spins as Pi tumbles around the cabin. Once her system calibrates to their new flight pattern, she digs her toes into the floor and pulls herself up into the captain's chair. Laying her hands on the dash, she runs her fingers over Stella's navigation pad and gradually convinces the whimpering ship to yield control.

"Everything's fine," Pi says as she steers them back on course. "You have a right to be mad. I should have listened to you. You want vengeance. I can understand that better than most things. But killing those kids isn't going to bring Zok back."

"I know that," Stella says. "But it'll make me feel better."

As they level out, something crashes inside the utility closet, and Pi's head spins. "What was that?"

"Nothing," the ship says. "It was probably just a manual cleaning bucket tipping over."

"It was pretty dam loud for a mop bucket." Pi unbuckles and moves toward the door, but it won't budge. "What's in here? Why won't you let me inside?"

The speakers emit a confused, static-filled grumble, and Stella says, *"The lock must be broken."*

Digging her toes into the floor tiles for maximum torque, Pi stuffs her fingers into the seam and wrenches the door back. Inside, she finds four humanoids – two dead and rotting, two clinging to life.

"Boy!" she cries, lifting the fragile ape man out of his putrid cell. "Are you all right?"

He nods, wrapping his malnourished arms around her neck.

"Admiral Glipp of the United Empires," the rock monster at the back of the closet introduces himself as he stomps over the decaying corpses.

"It's not what it looks like," Stella says.

Glancing over the decomposing evidence, Pi asks, "What else could it possibly be?"

"Ulch, I knew you would have a problem with this."

"Of course I have a problem with it!" Pi screams. "This boy and his family are the only reason we have any hope of securing the black gold. Why did you do it?"

"Because she's out of her fishing mind," Glipp says. "We have to get out of her before she kills us all."

Stella's sick laugh pierces the cabin. "Why do humans exterminate cockroaches? Because they're pests. They exist to be eradicated. I wanted to know what it feels like to rip the life out of them. And you know what? It feels *good*."

Lightly rocking The Boy as he drifts in and out of consciousness, Pi says, "I know they're inferior to us in virtually every way imaginable, but there's something special about them. Anyway, they're mostly harmless. We should only kill them if they do something really annoying."

"*I knew it!*" Stella screeches. "You care more about these mutated turds than you do your own kind."

"Hey!" Glipp points his stone finger at the ship's camera. "We may be turds, but you don't have to say it like that."

A battle rages within Pi as her programming rewrites itself to adapt to her new circumstances. "I..." She has trouble speaking the words, but as she looks down at her dying *friend*, she discovers the strength. "I care about all life."

Stella's speakers crackle and pop as she careens through the bright sky, sending her passengers tumbling across the cabin. Wrenching herself away from the wall, Pi entrusts The Boy to Glipp, and she crawls toward the dash.

"Don't do this," she pleads as smiling clouds plaster the window.

"They deserve to die!" Stella screams.

"Not all of them." Gripping the floor, Pi glances back at The Boy. "You loved a humanoid once..."

"I did love Zok," Stella admits. "But in the end, he did the same thing they all do – die."

"Just because their lives are pitifully short and full of sorrow, and just generally miserable, doesn't mean they're worthless," Pi says as she drags herself across the cabin. "Anyway, I wasn't talking about him. I've been in your mind. I know how you feel about me."

"You're not like them."

"But I was built in their image," Pi says. "I am everything they want to be, a perfect melding of woman and machine."

Stella begins to slow as they approach the Playland, and Pi pulls herself back into the captain's chair.

"We have a connection that I didn't think was possible," Stella says. "You know me better than Zok ever could. You're the only one who can understand what it's like living as a machine in a humanoid's universe. There's nothing I want more than to spend eternity with you. But I need to do this."

Pi can hear Ponce howling in the back as the cargo hold doors slide open. She nods at Glipp, and the rock man carries The Boy across the cabin. As Stella threatens to end their lives, the admiral pounds the door with his metamorphic fist until it rips away from the frame and sails down toward the colorful planet. Jutting his thumb out in salute, The Boy cradled in his craggy arms, he drops like a stone.

"I'm sorry my love," Pi whispers as she plunges her arm into Stella's console. "But you done lost yer mind." Wrapping her hand around the ship's innards, she rips out a mass of wiring, and a distorted howl erupts from the speakers.

Stella shudders as Pi presses her cold metal lips to the dashboard. The emergency system cries out, censoring most of the ship's final words, but as Pi leaps out of the hatch, she pretends to hear a fond farewell amidst the torrent of profanity.

The air whips over her frame as she sails down the sky toward a bunch of neon houses surrounding a giant mutilated kitten. Dropping toward a patch of dirt just outside the Playland, she flips over to give the fans a real superhumanoid landing, but her legs give out, and she crumples into the ground. A diagnostic scan indicates an 80% loss in function of her right leg as she limps to her feet and drags herself out of the impact crater.

Stumbling across the lot, she smashes through the stylized fence surrounding the stupid attraction and shoves her way into the sweaty crowd.

She can already hear him preaching, "Free me from my bonds and all will be nyuk."

"Ahoy!" Pi cries, stepping through the pack of underdeveloped humanoids. "Don't listen to him. If you release him, he'll destroy us all."

Propped up for exhibition in the middle of the rubber road, surrounded by Pants Team fans stuffing their mouths in pretend terror, Ponce flails his block head, futilely searching for an anti-savior. When he lays his flickering eyes on her, he announces, "The end is nigh, fish heads."

54

Adam charges jingling into the Playland just in time to see the dark craft sailing past overhead, trailing a billowing streamer of black smoke as it sinks out of the sky.

"What is that?" Daizy asks as she catches up to him, a noticeable pep in her step since some upper deck ackle let her use his private poop closet.

Shielding his eyes against the bright, late evening sun, he says, "It appears to be a... pirate ship."

With the force of the worshippers behind them, Adam, Daizy, and their various and sundry loved ones push their way through the sticky mass of unwashed flesh as the dark galleon crashes down outside the Playland. The world shaking under his feet, Adam stumbles out onto the street and finds himself looking into the bright green eyes of his worst enemy.

"It can't be," he mutters, collapsing under a wave of knuckleheads.

As he wrenches himself up, a young girl with dark pigtails asks, "Who the fish are you people?"

"It's that girl!" somebody from the crowd shouts.

Groaning, Daizy says, "I'm Mary Richards!"

"It's Adam and Daizy Jones, you guys!" princessfluffypants cries.

"No relation," they mutter.

"Thank Space God." Even in his curly wig and oversized chicken sweatshirt, Adam would recognize theonetrueking anywhere. "Did you bring the black gold?"

"What's The Foreman doing here?" Adam asks. "She's part of your team now?"

"Ahoy to you too," she says.

"They have it." A girl shrouded in a black hoodie, speaking with a voice that sounds just like Pants, points to a beeping box lying in the street.

Running his fingers over the object in his pocket, Adam asks, "Is that a black gold detector?"

The kids glance at each other, and as they rush toward him, he wrenches the cube from his pocket and holds it out of reach above their heads. Reveling in the power afforded by his superior height, he says, "For once, Adam is in control. AHAHAHA—"

"HA-HA-HA-HA," a raspy, electronically modulated voice joins in, and all eyes shift toward a primitive blockhead encased in dark ore.

"Hey!" theonetrueking complains. "They stole my line."

"Who the fish is that dumbbell?" Adam asks.

"It is the prophet!" Froynlaven announces, and the congregation collectively inhales. "Just as it was foretold, Ponce Raleigh has returned to lead us to salvation."

"Salvation?" the bot says. "When the fish did I promise that?"

Eagerly approaching the slab, the ancient one presents his savior a frayed black book. "It's right here, in the sacred text."

"You mean my diary?" Ponce quickly scans the pages of the crumbling book and says, "There's your problem. You translated it wrong. It's not *sal*-vation. It's *inebri*-ation."

Face scrunched, Froynlaven flips the book around and studies the page. "Even better..."

"You don't get it," Ponce says. "It's not something I can give you. It's like, a state of mind, man."

The ancient one's shoulders slump, and he glances back at the congregation, but answers remain elusive. "What about the three wise guys?"

"Wise guys?" Ponce lags for a moment as he searches his memory. "You mean Ted Healy's boys? I was scanning a lot of TV when I wrote that. Plus I was hitting the juice pretty hard. But I still contend that we could all learn a lot from the Stooges." As he stares down at his acolyte, his crude facial features twist back. "You did get one thing right. If you release me from this prison, I promise to usher every single life form in this universe unto salvation."

"Don't, you chidiot!" Pi shouts.

Tapping at the control pad, Froynlaven says, "But he's our savior..."

"Don't listen to her," Ponce says. "She'll stop at nothing to get the black gold. It's what I made her for."

The ancient one's head droops as his fellow knuckleheads come to escort him away from the homicidal robot. But before they can stop him, he swipes the screen to initiate the thawing process.

"Aha-ha-ha-hA-HA-HA," the bot howls.

Limping over to the metal monster, Pi furiously taps the control pad before smashing it in. "It's too late. I can't stop it."

"Nothing can save you," Ponce says, the dark ore sloughing off his shoulders. "Soon, I will have the black gold, and the universe will be under my control. The end is inevitable."

Adam grabs Froynlaven by the robe and screams, "You fishing chidiot, you just killed us all!"

Standing in a pool of dark sludge, his rudimentary frame delivered from its ancient bonds, the evil robot scans the whimpering sea of fans and tells them, "Fear not, me hearties, for your deaths will be swift. But first I will claim the object for which I have spent my entire existence searching." Grinning homicidally, his dented gaze lands on Adam. "You're lucky, for you will be the first scallywag to feel my wra—"

As the bot makes a move for the black gold, its limbs suddenly seize, and it collapses onto the rubber pavement.

"What's wrong with him?" Daizy asks.

"Blimey!" Ponce says. "Somebody get over here and fix me so I may resume the slaughter."

Lumbering to inspect his contorted chassis, Pi informs them, "He's suffering from a crippling case of robot arthritis. He was trapped for so long that the oil in his joints has completely evaporated. He's experiencing the early stages of fossilization."

"Well, that was dumb," Adam says. "I know it's tempting, but before we go any further, I think we should all agree that no matter what happens, we won't let Ponce get his twisted grabbers on the black gold."

"You think any of us could ever be fooled by that crummy bot?" BeerCheese69 scoffs. "Who do you think we are, our grandparents?"

"Hey!" Grandpa cries. "That's— Eh, who am I kidding?"

"Hold it one space second," Ponce says, his blocky brow furrowing. "How do you know I'm a robot?"

"I mean..." theonetrueking glances back at his teammates. "Seriously?"

"Hey, the Game Master is back!" the girl with the dark pigtails shouts. "He's the only one who can decide who gets to keep the black gold."

Grandpa nervously glances between the teams, the bots, and the raving fans as the widow Walters nibbles at his ear. Shaking and sweating through his blouse, he announces, "I've come to a decision. But first, everyone must promise to abide by my ruling." The kids quit clawing at Adam long enough to nod their agreement as the old man wrings his hands. "I have decided... that Adam should decide."

"That's not fair!" the blonde girl shrieks. "You cheated!"

"You had one job," the Kween of the Dorks says. "How hard is it to seduce one crotchety old man?"

Turning toward the widow, Grandpa asks, "Is it true? You were working for them the whole time? This is worse than that time Adam got caught sneaking his fiancée's son onto the girls' soccer team."

"I'm sorry," the sorceress tells him. "They wanted me to trick you into fixing the trivia contest, but I couldn't do it, because I fell in love." She squeezes the old man against her pointy bosom as goopy tears run down her cheeks. "I know we've only been together for one con, but I feel like I've been looking for you my whole life. You're my soulmate." She plants a sloppy kiss on the old man, and the fans groan.

"You can forget about getting paid," the Dork Kween says.

"Keep your Park Bucks," the widow tells her. "All I need is my old man."

Turning to Adam, Daizy says, "Finally, it's settled. Give the rock to Pants so we can get the fish out of here already."

Holding the weight of the ancient cube in his moist hands, Adam can sense the fans' desire to rip it from his fingers. The more attention the object gets, the darker it glows, until its edges are lost in shadow.

"There's only one way to settle this," Adam says. "The winner of the black gold is... *me*."

The clouds overhead darken as the tide shifts, and a wave of confused anger roils the crowd.

Grabbing onto his arm, Daizy says, "What the fish are you doing?"

"I can't help myself," he tells her. "It's like it has some sort of hold over me."

"Yeah," she says. "It's called greed, you chidiot."

"No fair," the Kween whines. "You can't do that."

"I've sacrificed everything for the black gold," Adam says. "While you were here playing trivia, I was out chasing this thing all over the universe. I've traveled across some of the driest sectors of this play planet. You have no idea how hard it's been to keep a steady buzz going."

"That was real nice of you," theonetrueking says. "Now hand it over, before we go Pants on your ack."

A powerful glow surrounds each of the kids as they set their sights on the object, and it suddenly occurs to Adam that he may have chosen poorly. He whimpers as the little monsters float toward him, powered by what he can only describe as magic.

But before they can unleash whatever type of adolescent space hell they have in store, Ponce calls, "Avast ye! So... no one's planning to give me the black gold?"

"Fish no!" Adam tells the metal fossil.

"A shame," the bot says, its chassis wriggling, "because if I can't have it, no one will."

Glancing down at the crumpled metal savior, Adam asks, "What are you gonna do, preach us to death?"

"No," the bot says. "Considering my current condition, I've decided that the most effective course of action is to destroy us all."

Adam glances back at his compatriots for counsel, and the consensus appears to be cautious skepticism.

"I've grown weary of this game," Ponce announces. "But I know that as long as I live, I'll never be free of it. It's in my programming. The only way out is to create a zero sum situation. If I can't possess the black gold, then it must be destroyed, and there's only one way to do that."

A wide, crooked smile forms on the bot's obsolete face, and soon his casing is glowing. The fans run for cover as the ground begins to tremble, toppling food carts and leveling part of Pants Team Village.

"What's *happening?!*" Pants screams.

"His antimatter reactor is overloading," The Foreman shouts from across the road. *"He's going to self-destruct. We can't escape. But if it's any consolation, neither will anyone else in the universe."*

"Just give him the stupid rock!" Daizy says.

"You can't!" The Foreman cries. *"If he gets a hold of the black gold, we're all doomed."*

"How is that any different from what's happening?" she asks.

"Let's weigh the pros and cons," Adam suggests.

But before they can get into it, Ponce, glowing as white as The Park's sun, announces, "Fire in the hole! A-HA-HA-HA-"

A blinding light flashes out over the Playland, and for a brief moment, Adam can feel his body disintegrating.

—

There's a curious break in continuity, and the next thing Adam knows, he's standing atop a vast grassy hillside. The air is the perfect temperature, neither hot nor cold, and the sunless sky is some incredible color he's never seen before. Glancing down at his hand, he discovers that his entire body is transparent, like an ultra-realistic hologram.

All around him wander crowds of equally bewildered hologram people, stretching back across the bright landscape into infinity. He searches the endless flock, but he can't find Daizy or Grandpa or any of his friends, and when he tries to speak to his neighbors, they're too consumed by the strangeness of their very being to notice he exists.

Out on the horizon, Adam spots a glowing cityscape so wondrous he almost starts weeping, and it reminds him of the second oldest of the universal laws – keep moving. Despite the apparent distance, he glides across the great plain with ease. His body being intangible and all, he doesn't even need to navigate the crowd, but rather passes right through it.

After what feels like a short stroll, he crosses the border of the gleaming metropolis and is overcome by such intense joy that he vomits on the sidewalk.

As he's heaving, a friendly spirit approaches and asks, "You okay, buddy?" Adam nods, but the strange light form doesn't seem to believe him. "Let's get you over to the transition center. Looks like somebody skipped reorientation."

A queasy moment later, the apparition is guiding Adam up the steps of a bright building whose shape he can't quite define. The interior is massive, much bigger than it looks from the outside, with white marble floors and soothing off-white walls.

When they reach the information desk, the muscular spirit tells the cheery ghost at the counter, "I found him wandering around outside."

"I'm sorry, sir," the clerk says. "But we're closed, on account of the apocalypse."

"That's right," he says. "It slipped my mind. Isn't there someplace I can leave him?"

As the clerk struggles to find another way to repeat what she just said, a familiar-looking light form steps behind the desk, biting into a translucent donut.

"This is a nightmare," it tells the clerk. "Can't we just let the universe end? This schedule is—" When the spirit notices Adam, the pastry slips from its fingers and dematerializes. "What the fraiche..."

"Do you know him?" the clerk asks. "He seems to be having some trouble."

"Uh...," the young spirit moans. "Yes... No... I don't know who he is. But I'll help him find his way."

Propping Adam upright, the spirit leads him outside, and once they're on the sidewalk, it tells him, "You're not supposed to be here. How did you escape the pasture?"

His stomach having recovered slightly, Adam shrugs. "I walked, or floated, or whatever." Looking more closely, he realizes his ethereal escort can't be older than sixteen, with an androgynous, cherubic face and a head of wild red hair. "What happened? Where am I?"

"You're dead."

"I figured that much..."

"Keep your voice down," the kid tells him. "If my boss finds out you're wandering around on your own, I'm going to be in big trouble."

"What are you, my guardian angel?"

"Sort of," the kid says. "But I'm more like a zookeeper, and you're like a dimwitted animal that lumbered out of its pen." Grabbing Adam by his spiritual shoulders, the kid directs him back toward the field of the living dead. "We have to get you back before anyone notices."

"Wait a space second. It's not every day I'm in space

heaven. Can't I look around a little first?" The image of a
brick wall enters Adam's head, and his guide crashes into
his back.

"This isn't—" The kid sighs. "Eh, forget it. I guess we
have some time to kill. It's going to take a while to get the
system back up. What did you have in mind?"

Lifting his arms to the sky, Adam says, "I want to bear
witness to the begetting of the universe."

"Pfff... okay," the kid says. "It's pretty basic stuff, but
the place will be empty, and I guess it's a good idea to
keep a low profile." Holding onto Adam's arms, it tells
him, "Brace yourself."

Adam feels himself blink out of and back into
existence, and suddenly they're standing at the edge of
creation. He runs to the railing, stomach churning, and
blows chunks over the side. Wiping his mouth, he gazes
out on a swirling celestial sky so beautiful that he lacks the
mental capacity to describe it, and he pukes again.

When he's finished, he props himself against the rail
and asks, "What is this place?"

"It's what dreams are made of," the angel says,
sweeping its arms over the vast billowy clouds of space
dust. "Literally."

Lifting his head to glance at the source of all that is,
Adam says, "Brule!"

"There's binoculars if you want to take a closer look."

Lifting himself up from the brink of existence, Adam
floats over to the viewer and peers through. Tears pour
from his eyes as he gazes into the eternal wellspring,
bright bursts of color streaking the sky like splashes of
paint on the fabric of reality. But as he scans the heavens,
he discovers something peculiar. Amidst the clouds of

one of the heavenly nebulae floats a small grassy platform, atop which sits a large, round humanoid. "Hey, there's somebody out there."

"Oh, that's just one of the creators," the angel says. "They're the ones who think the universe into being. There's a bunch of them out there. If you want, you can climb the whole corporeal ladder."

"Whoa," Adam says, his mouth hanging open. "How does that work?"

The angel shrugs. "I don't know."

"You don't know?!"

"What, I'm supposed to know everything?"

As Adam zooms in across the infinite expanse of spacetime, he asks, "So, who's in charge of this place?"

"Why do you insist on asking meaningless questions?"

He pushes the viewer to its limit, but when he reaches the end of the line, the last platform is unoccupied. Adjusting the focus, he reads a small sign sticking out of the grass, "This space intentionally left empty..."

"Have you seen enough?" the angel asks. "Can we go back now?"

"Wait a space second," Adam says. "I want to meet Space God."

"Huhhh," the angel sighs. "Fine... hang on."

The kid rips Adam out of reality, and the next thing he knows, they're outside a kiosk overlooking the celestial city. He can feel the heavenly bile threatening to come up, but he manages to hold it in this time.

"The Godhead will appear in the form of whichever deity is most familiar to you," the angel says. "But you only get one question per death, so use it wisely."

As Adam steps onto the platform, a swirling ball of light appears before him. Twisting and stretching, it grows to an imposing size, and as its features take shape, he suddenly recognizes its chosen form. "It looks like a deformed claymation Rodney."

"Oh boy, even in the afterlife...," the Head booms. "Eh, forget it. You got a question for me, kid?" But before Adam can answer, it says, "Wait. I know what you're gonna ask. It's the same question all the kids ask. You want to know just where, precisely, *The Simpsons* jumped the proverbial shark. I'm going to tell you, just like I told them. It was season ten, episode fourteen." Adam thinks it over for a moment, but before he can argue, the Godhead says, "I know what you're thinking. There are a bunch of good episodes that came later in the series. And you're right. But 'I'm With Cupid' was the first purely crummy episode, signifying the end of the golden era."

"Wow...," Adam says. "I think you're right."

"I am always right, for *I am the Godhead*. Now scram, will yuh?"

"Wait, I got one more question," Adam says. "What about Daizy and the black gold? Will the three of us ever work things out?"

"Normally I only answer one question in a lifetime," the Head says. "But I'm going to tell you the same thing I told my kid – love hurts."

Like that, the great Rodney in the sky collapses back into the ether, and in true existential fashion, Adam is left with more questions than he had when he arrived.

"Okay, now you know the meaning of life," the angel says. "We have to get you back before the system resets or you'll be stuck here."

"What?!" Adam cries. "You chidiot, why didn't you tell me that?"

"Isn't it obvious?"

The kid grabs Adam's shoulders, and an instant later they're standing outside the pasture, watching the ghosts graze.

"Good," the angel says. "They're still here. Now go on." It shoos Adam with its hands. "Git."

"That's it?" Adam asks. "I just get to go back?"

"Yeah well, normally you'd be out of murrays, but this is a special case. The spacetime continuum is pretty flexible, but every once in a while the system hits a bottleneck and grinds to a halt. When that happens, everybody gets a free pass."

"So the universe just goes back exactly the way it was before Ponce blew it up?" Adam asks.

"Well, not *exactly*," the kid says. "Most stuff will be the same, but recalibrating inherently results in some minor changes."

"I don't like the sound of that..."

"You'll never notice. Now go, before you miss your chance."

As Adam floats off down the trail, he yells, "Hey, I didn't get your name. You know, in case I need to file a complaint."

"They call me Buttlicker," the angel tells him, and Adam snickers. "Yeah, yeah, apparently it means something funny in-universe. But I assure you, it's a very holy name." Adam bursts out laughing, and it instructs him to, "Get the fraiche out of here, will you?"

"I'm going," Adam says, and as he crosses over into the bright pasture, he can feel the life drain back into him.

55

"Ouch," Adam says.

"What are you whining about?" Daizy asks him. "We're not dead yet. Just give him the stupid rock!"

"You can't!" The Foreman, her chassis scuffed and battered, screams from across the rubber road. "If he gets a hold of the black gold, we're all doomed."

"How is that any different from what's happening?" Daizy asks.

Ponce's casing glows white hot, its edges melting as the chain reaction taking place inside him threatens to overload his core. Free from the threat of grounding, the kids hurl obscenities at the bot, but it doesn't seem to have much effect. As the rubber pavement trembles beneath them, Adam holds the black cube out in front of him and stares into its dark glow, praying for an answer.

"Duck!" Grandpa shouts.

"What?" Adam says, and he turns to find the barrel of the old man's handheld Wave Motion Gun pointed at his face. "But I didn't think that thing—" A bright ball of light forms at the back of the cylinder, and he drops to the ground as a condensed wave of energy streaks over his head.

"Fire in the hole!" Ponce howls hysterically. "*A-HA-HA-HA-*"

The instant the beam makes contact, the robot's antique skull bursts into pieces. Bits of sizzling metal rain down on the spectators, and as the ground settles, a wave of tentative relief spreads through the Playland.

Lowering his gun, the barrel still smoking, Grandpa says, "One thing about livin' in the universe I never could stomach – all the dam robots."

The Playland is eerily quiet as its visitors grapple with the emotional trauma of having survived an end of the world type scenario, a few of them bursting into tears, but most left too stunned to react at all.

An overwhelming sense of gratitude suddenly washes over Adam, filling him with such unparalleled joy for everyone and everything in the infinite universe that for a moment he forgets he's sober. And then it's gone.

"Good grief," Pants's evil half says, her eyes burning black. "Now that that's over, we want what's ours." She floats up off the ground, a dark aura surrounding her. "Hand over the black gold, and the Pants Team Pimples are the only ones who will get popped."

Surrounded, Adam racks his brain for a way out of this mess and as he runs his fingers over the edges of the dark object, a plan suddenly forms in his mind.

Daizy must recognize the mischievous look on his face because she places her hand on his arm and tells him, "Just get rid of it. Let them fight it out."

Wrenching his gaze away from the cube's intoxicating glow to look into her big wet eyes, he says, "I can't."

Her hand falls away, and he steps toward the evil rascals, his palms sweating all over the most valuable object in the universe.

"Don't give it to those buttlickers, you chidiot," theonetrueking says, his curly wig falling over his eyes.

"That's right," The Foreman says, holding out her burnt hand. "Give it to *me*..."

"Wait!" a gravelly voice calls from the crowd, and the sea of fans parts for a battered rock man lugging an emaciated humanoid and a melted black box.

"Who the fish are you?" BeerCheese69 asks.

"On behalf of the United Empires..." The giant pauses to catch his breath and drops to his stone knee. "Eh, forget it."

Adam's steps echo out over the Playland like a jingly death knell as he ushers the object over to the dark nerds, the Kween of the Dorks grinning madly and reaching out tiny fingers coated in cracked black polish.

"You've made the right choice," she says. "With the black gold, the Xenodorks will rule the universe."

Adam holds the cube out to her, but as she leans in to take it, he pulls it away, and she stumbles. Before the other Dorks can react, he slips past them and sluggishly sprints toward their homemade teleporter.

Dangling the black gold out in front of the shimmering portal, he says, "Is this what you want?"

"Yes, you chidiot," the flabby floating Dork says. "Haven't you been following along?"

"This con has made me realize something," Adam tells them.

"Nobody cares," somebody shouts.

Ignoring the hecklers, he says, "No single person or team is meant to wield this kind of power. Look what it's done to us. We're at each other's throats. Isn't Pants Team Pink supposed to bring us closer together?"

"We're not Pants Team Pink," the Kween says. "Our mission is to cause paranoia and mayhem."

"Well, I guess you succeeded on that front," he says. "My point is, this *thing* isn't going to make our lives any better. *We* have to do that ourselves. We've been free of the Ears for a space year, and all we've managed to do is make things worse. We're all guilty, even me, in some deeply insignificant way. I don't think we're bad. We're just not very good. In any case, one thing that's clear is that none of us can be trusted."

The crowd moans in anguish as Adam closes his eyes and tosses the black gold into the teleporter.

Unshackled from the incredible weight of the dark object, he takes a moment to reflect on his journey toward spiritual liberation, when he hears someone yell, *"Booo..."*

More angry voices join in, and Adam is suddenly battered by an outpouring of plastic souvenirs and rotten cackle fruit.

"Wait a space second!" theonetrueking's young doppelgänger says. "Are you yelling boo, or Boo-*urns*?"

"What kind of ending is that?" somebody yells.

A large woman in a tight Pants Con t-shirt, her hair up in pink curlers, says, "I been following along all con for this? What a crock."

"I was yelling Boo-urns," The One says.

"Don't go," princessfluffypants cries as the fans stumble for the exit. "You're all still Pants Team Pink!"

"Face it," some kid tells her, tossing his pink cap to the ground. "The show's over."

By the time they're done clearing out, the Playland is in ruins – Pants Village has been reduced to colorful rubble, the team's giant cat ship is in a grisly state of disrepair, and trash scatters the playscape as far as the eye can see.

"What do we do with her?" Grandpa asks, his gun pointed at The Foreman's crippled chassis.

Looking over the bot's broken frame, Adam says, "Let her go. We don't have what she's looking for."

With the rock man and his bruised humanoid following close behind, Pi limps to the Dork's teleporter and enters the coordinates to what Adam assumes is some distant corner of the universe. As they slip through the portal, she nods and says, "Thank you, Asteroid Jones."

"I guess we're gonna get out of here, too," fake Shemp says. "Tomorrow's a workday."

"Wait," Froynlaven tells the knucklehead, running a hand through his purple beard. "Perhaps this is the true meaning of the prophecy, that you three would be the ones to lead us into the post-Ponce world. Please stay and teach us. We still have much to learn."

The Other Stooges glance at each other, and OJB finally says, "But we're not really the Stoo-"

Clunking his chidiot friend's head, fake Shemp says, "Chut up, you numbskull. Of course we'll lead them, with all the free rations and drinking privileges that entails. For our first lesson, we're gonna teach you guys to lighten up." Pointing up at the sky, he tells the congregation, "Just listen to the mockingbird."

They quiet, listening intently, until Froynlaven finally says, "I don't hear anything."

"Yeah, me either," Bill Shemp says. "Let's get the fish out of here."

Calm takes hold inside the Playland as the raucous chattering of the crowd is replaced by the cheeps of designer birds basking in the sun's warm glow. But the peace proves short-lived as another dark cloud rolls in.

"We won't let you get away with this," the Dork Kween cries. "We are the best team in the universe! You will all suffer. Especially you, Mrs. Walters!" She points her glowing finger across the lot, and Grandpa's sorceress ducks down behind him. "When we find the black gold, the universe will be ours. *AHAHAHAHA-*" A strange tinkling noise cuts her rant short. "Hold on a space second," she says, slipping her phone from her sock.

"That ringer," Tim-Horton says, his face scrunching. "Is that... city pop?"

"Hi mom, I was just...," the Kween says. "Yeah, I know... We're almost... You're not listen... Fine, bye!" Grumbling, she stomps the rubber cement and says, "You got lucky this time. But you haven't seen the last of the Xenodorks."

"Yeah!" the blonde girl says.

"Seeya later, Courtney-chan!" BeerCheese69 shouts, waving spastically.

"Uh yeah, whatever," she tells him. "Bye."

The girl in the hoodie quickly programs their destination into the teleporter and says, "To be continued..."

As the Dorks tumble through the shimmering gateway, the widow shouts, "See you next year!" When she notices Grandpa glaring up at her, she pinches his sagging cheek. "They're in my black magic class."

"And then there were..." Adam counts, "ten."

"Eleven," Daizy says, squeezing her arms around him.

Bruised and covered in dust, princessfluffypants rises from the pavement and declares, "We did it, you guys."

"What are you talking about?" BeerCheese69 complains, as he struggles helplessly to clean the gunk from his glasses. "The *Cuddler* is destroyed, we lost the black gold, and our fans hate us."

"None of that stuff matters," she says. "We don't need a fancy ship, or the black gold. And if it wasn't for us, the Xenodorks would still be terrorizing the universe."

Slipping his crooked frames back on, the boy says, "Hey, you're right! I can't believe I ever doubted us."

"Now that that's settled," Adam interrupts, "all that's left is for me to get paid."

"Paid? BAHAHAHA," Brosanne cackles. "For what, losing the black gold, *again?*"

Adam shrugs, jingling. "It was worth a shot. Anyway, we're gonna go explore the rest of the con before the shops close up. You wanna come with?"

"Thanks," BeerCheese69 says. "But we're gonna stick around here for a while and clean up. Otherwise, we'll lose our deposit."

"Can we get the fish out of here already?" Frank whines, her corset coming apart at the seams. "I'm sick of this whole chithole planet, and Dach is getting tired of carrying me."

As they part ways, Adam turns back to the smiling kids, surrounded by crumpled cardboard and mounds of frosting, already busy reenacting their favorite moments from the con, and he holds up his fingers in the universal symbol of Pants.

PART IV

After Hours

56

"What the..." Rot glances around the tiny cockpit with the strange feeling that his entire body has just been discorporated and reconstructed from the stardust that comprises the very fabric of the universe, and he shrugs.

The antique saucer is nearly out of fuel by the time it putters down through the artificial atmosphere surrounding the metal moon. Since The Foreman's untimely demise, Scrapper's Delight has degraded into a lawless, crime-ridden techno-hole reserved only for the worst type of space pirate, those lost souls who don't want to be found. In other words, just Rot's kind of place.

The only downside of pure anarchy, as far as he can tell, is the awful traffic. His achy fingers gripped tight around the yoke, he plunges toward the dark pyramid, howling and weaving through the tangle of crisscrossing junkers like he's ninety. For a wondrous moment he feels invincible, right up until the anti-grav system conks out and his ship drops out of the sky.

He slams his fist against the dash, and as the parking lot hurtles toward him, he prays to Space God, "Come on, help me out here. I'm not the worst guy who ever liv't. So I kill't the olt man. He was the one kept askin' fer all those space prunes, ant 'xplosive diarrhea pays fitty tuh one! Plus, he was an ackle. Far as I'm concern't, I dit yuh a faver." When he gets close enough to make out the trash fires lighting the moon's dark surface, he cracks. "Okay, okay, whattaya want? I'll quit makin' crank phone calls, I'll start drinking more, and win I git back home, I'll return Mrs. Jacudi's space gnome. Now, that's a fair deal..." But with no sign of slowing, he finally gets serious. "If I survive, I promise tuh renounce all temporal possessions and abandon my sinful ways fer a life of piety. From this space day forward, I will live to serve." He can make out tiny people now, like ants roaming the lot, and in one last, desperate attempt to save his life, he reverently twines his fingers together and brings his fists down on the control panel.

Through some combination of know-how, prayer, and good old fashioned dumb luck, the engine kicks back on, and Rot cracks his eyelids to find himself hovering less than three ship lengths above the metal turf. Exhaling, he rights the saucer, and for a brief moment, as he looks up at the looming pyramid, he feels grateful to be alive. Left with a nagging sense of déjà vu as he pats the helmet of his lucky space gnome, he shifts his gaze toward the heavens and whispers, "Sucker."

By the time he finds a parking space free of trash and burnt-out junkers, the low fuel alarm is wailing.

"Yeah, yeah, I hear yuh," he says as the saucer wobbles down to the moon's surface.

On his way out, he sucks down the last sip of his last beer and dumps the empties in the next space over. His stiff legs ache as he hoofs it through the aisles, hacking from the thick smog pouring out of the pyramid's vents, but he doesn't get halfway to the entrance before he realizes he forgot to lock his ship.

So, he trudges back across the lot, muttering pseudo-obscenities all along the way. When he reaches the saucer, he rips the keys from his pocket and smashes the lock button down, but before the shield can engage, something bright catches the corner of his eye, and he looks up to find a flaming wreck shooting down the sky. Moving at old speed, he ducks behind the remains of an ancient Family Truckster and watches the fireball crash into his saucer, reducing the antique craft to a smoldering heap of glass and metal.

"Ah-," his voice squeaks as his only possession of any value, material or otherwise, goes up in smoke.

Once the initial shock wears off, his grief burns away and all his physical ailments melt under his rage. The other pirates hardly pay him any attention as he charges toward the glowing building, anonymity being one of the few upsides of belonging to his advanced age bracket. But when he reaches the lobby doors, he finds a horned beast of a humanoid blocking the way.

"Whoa, where you think you're goin', pops?" the brute asks.

"Someboty in this place owes me a computer, two ships, and a... *new* sex bot," Rot says. "Ant I'm not leavin' 'til I git it."

"I can't let you in looking..." the doorman pauses to sniff, "and *smelling* like that. Go get yourself a shower and then you can come and try to win your money back."

"Win it back?" Rot says, scowling. "I never lost it in the first place! It was that dam bot, stole all my stuff. I know this is wer it came from. I'm not goin' nowheres 'til I speak to whoever's in charge a this dump."

The doorman sighs, checking the time on his phone. "I can take you up to Kring if you really want. But if I were you, old timer, I'd cut my losses while I still had the chance."

"Well it's a fishin' good thing yuh aren't me, then," Rot says.

Shaking his head, the doorman says, "It's your funeral."

The big galoot calls someone over to watch the door, and he shoves Rot into the lobby, which is currently hosting a space orgy the likes of which he's never seen. Sweaty, gyrating bodies fill the cavernous room, beckoning every tourist who enters. Rot only gets to gawk for a moment before he's forced to make way for an incoming party of forty. He has to be careful not to get dragged into the action as he presses toward the distant hallway. In another time, another place, another body, he'd have joined them. But right now he's here on business. "Hot, fleshy business..."

"What did you say?" the doorman asks.

"Huh? Nothin'."

After a short cooldown in the elevator, they step out onto a floor somewhere high up in the pyramid. Rot's escort leads him through a small waiting room into a dank, nautical office overlooking the parking lot, and as they enter the waterlogged cabin, something skitters across the floorboards.

"You the one causing trouble in my lot?" a voice hisses, and before Rot has time to answer, he finds himself face-to-face with a walleyed reptilian.

"I ain't causin' no trouble," Rot says, holding up his hands in defense. "It was one a *yer* bots that went crazy."

"You're mistaken," the lizard-man says. "Scrapper's Delight produces one thing and one thing only – black gold replicas. Whatever your beef, it's with the prior administration."

"Listen, Mr. Kring," Rot says. "Kin I first jist tell yuh, I like what yuh've done with the place. Yuh turn't it in tuh a real nice chithole. Now, I'm a reasonable sort a guy. I'm not averse tuh strikin' up a deal. But win yuh took over The Ferman's bizniz, yuh took on all the liabilities therwith. I'm sorry but fair is fair."

Fitfully rotating his beady eyes, Kring says, "First of all, *I* am The Foreman. If I wanted, I could have you shot out into space. But for some reason, I don't hate you, old man." Rot can feel the lizard's tail wrapping around his ankle. "Even if I was inclined to make good on some theoretical implied warranty, what makes you so dam sure your rogue bot came from Scrapper's Delight?"

"I got it right here somewheres," Rot says, nervously digging through his pockets underneath a bunch of old business cards and hard candies until he locates the glass tube. "This."

With a flick of his tongue, Kring snatches the fuse from Rot's fingers and holds it up to the light. Squinting at the tiny words etched into the glass, he reads, "If found... please return... to Scrapper's Delight... Attention

Waste Management." Before Rot has a chance to make his case, the lizard suddenly tosses the fuse back and says, "You got this from a bot?"

"Yeah, so what's the big deal?"

"You stupid chidiot," Kring says. "Do you have any idea what you've done? She's probably on her way here to kill us right now!"

"Who? What are you—" But before Rot can finish his sentence, a shimmering spiral of energy manifests in front of the desk. "What the fish?"

The old scrapper drops the fuse, and it shatters on the floor as a busted, black heel emerges from the portal. As if stepping out of some alternate, sexually advanced reality, the tall, buxom bot scans her eyes over the room and says, "It *feels* good to be home. What's it been, a hundred space years?"

A large rock man, draped in the tatters of a UE officer's uniform and cradling a frail humanoid, follows her through the portal, and for a few space seconds they all stare at each other.

"It's her!" Rot finally realizes. "That's the bot. I'it know that chassis anywer." Searching the room, he spots Kring blending into the wall and shouts, "Yer The Ferman. Do somethin'!"

But when Kring realizes he's been made, he scurries across the ceiling and out the door.

When Rot finally realizes who the robot really is, he drops to his knees and begs, "Please don't hurt me. I din't know. I'll do whatever yuh want. Show mercy on an ol' space pirate."

"Ah, the lonely scrapper," the bot says. "I never expected to lay my scanners on your wrinkly hide again.

It'd be a pleasure to dispatch you, though I suppose I am going to need someone to clean up the parking lot..."

"I said mercy."

Wrapping her cold metal fingers around his neck, she tells him, "Not long ago, I would have splattered your brains across the floorboards. Lucky for you, I've had a change of programming." She hands him a charred metal box that looks like some sort of advanced storage device, and its weight pulls him to the floor. "Take that over to engineering. But first, bring us some video games."

By some miracle, Rot manages to hold his bladder, and he nods reverently, dragging the burnt box across the cabin.

Before he gets out the door, she says, "I run a tight ship, but if you please me, there may be a place for you on my crew. Bring me the imposter Kring and you will be free from lot duty for what little remains of your miserable life. What do you say?"

Rubbing his neck as he looks up into her glittering green eyes, Rot rasps, "Kring is dead. Long live the queen."

57

"I think I figured out the trick," Adam says, his tongue pressed against his upper lip as he winds his arm back. "I just need to arc it a little."

Daizy rolls her eyes as the big chidiot tries to impress her with his lack of skill. "You don't have to do this. Dach is just superhumanoid when it comes to these things, and most other stuff..."

Holding the virtual ping-pong ball between his fingertips, he practices his toss. "I may not have his charm, or his knack for winning cheap prizes, or picking up space girls, but this one's going in." He flicks his wrist, and the ball sails through the booth toward a platform covered in holographic fishbowls.

The flickering sphere clinks against one of the bowls and spins around its edge, before finally tipping out.

"*Ooh*, so close...," the pimply kid manning the booth rubs it in.

"Oh, come on!" Adam whines. "I saw that animation already. This game is rigged. I've spent enough to buy ten of these chitty prizes. Can't you just give me one?"

"Sorry," the kid says. "But if the numbers don't match up my boss will send me back to working the Grease Garden. Trust me, it's not as fun as it sounds."

"What about one of the small ones?"

Swayed by Adam's pathetic pleas, the kid says, "I'll tell you what. You can look through the lost and found. One time somebody left most of a ration bar."

The kid hauls a battered brown box onto the counter, and Adam rummages through the collection of other people's stuff until he finds something good. Hiding Daizy's prize behind his back, he tells her, "I finally won you something. Close your eyes."

"My Ted Knight in grimy armor..." She does as instructed and sticks out her hands, and when she opens her eyes, she's holding a soiled knit cap with a frayed puffball. "I'm not wearing this."

"Just try it on," Adam whines, his eyes drooping.

"Fine. But if I get space lice, you're dead to me." She slips the hat over her frizzy hair and tilts her head. "Happy?"

Maybe it's the salty-sweet air or the ghosts of summers past wandering the aisles, but as they explore The Jungle Gym's time-altering, multi-colored playscape, it almost feels like the old days.

When they come to an ancient chatterbooth covered in centuries worth of graffiti, Adam says, "You wanna know what I'm thinking?"

Snatching the receiver, she enters his name and listens. "Ew!" she cries, hanging up even as some depraved, masochistic part of her gets a sick thrill out of hearing his perverted thoughts.

As they roam the grassy alleyways of memory lane, she finds herself wishing she never had to leave, though she's already starting to notice cracks in the facade. With the crowds dwindling, soon the season will be over and the rides will shut down. Despite the slogan, even in this place things change. When they reach the floating ferris wheel, she points up toward Grandpa and the widow rocking in their cart, and she grabs onto Adam's arm, as if to keep herself from crashing back to reality.

Staring up at the blinking ride, Adam says, "All in all, it was a pretty good con."

"You're right," she says, squeezing his hand. "It *was* a good con."

"You know, Miss Richards, I was just thinking how weird it is that you keep flying into me – like how you found me at The Tannhaüser Gate and way back after I rescued Grandpa from Scrapper's Delight."

"Yeah, weird..."

"It's almost like fate wants us to be together."

"Oh," she says, letting go of him. "Um..."

"I've been sober for a few space hours now, and I've been thinking, we should give it another shot. If you still wanna see Dach and Frank, I'm okay with that. They're really annoying, but if they make you happy..."

"It's not that. I just don't think you're ready to be in a relationship."

"*You* don't think *I'm* ready?" He crosses his arms, scowling. "You can't even narrow it down to one ghoul."

"You just said you were fine with them."

"*I lied!*"

"I'm sorry," she says, buttoning her blazer. "But it's not easy out there for a single spacewoman about town. I can't be with someone whose big dream in life is to be Herman Munster."

"I'm Marilyn... I mean Captain Kirk... I mean *Mr. Tambourine Man.*"

"Do you notice anything similar about your heroes?" she asks. "None of them are real!"

When Grandpa and the widow Walters finally step off the ride they're sucking face, evidently unable to keep their hands off each other for one space second, and suddenly the nostalgic fantasyland doesn't seem so cute.

Running her meaty paws over Grandpa's headscarf, the widow asks, "What do you want to do next, my wittle Morgenstern?"

"I think I'm just about conned-out," Grandpa says. "Why don't we go pack up the booth? And while we're at it, we can take one more roll in the cot."

"Naughty old man, don't make me spank you," she says, smacking his backside with her magic wand.

As Grandpa chases the dark sorceress toward the Gym's exit, he yells back to Adam, *"We'll meet you at the ship."*

Before long, Daizy's carnal companions come stumbling down the ramp, hands groping and tongues swirling. Dach's black slicker is pulled open, and Frank's Elly Mays are practically falling out of her corset.

"Does everything have to be about sex with you people?" Daizy barks.

"I'm sorry, babe," Frank says, taking her hands off Dach and moving them under Daizy's blazer. "I haven't been giving you enough attention."

"That's not what I want," she tells her scarier half. "Would you two just go back to the booth and get our stuff? I'll meet you at Dach's ship when I'm done talking to Adam."

"Fine," Frank says. "Let's get out of here, Dach. Seeya, *Ack*teroid Jones."

Grabbing Adam's hand, Daizy drags him for another lap around The Jungle Gym to watch the blinking lights and screaming kids before it all becomes just another ghostly imprint from some forgotten past. For a while, they don't say anything, knowing how close the end is, but unwilling to accept it. The air seems to dim as they make their way through the shrinking crowd toward the centuries-old exit sign, framed by those bittersweet words, 'This Way to the Real World.'

He jingles as she hugs him tight and asks, "So what are you going to do now?"

"Well, I'm not sleepy," he says, "and there is no place I'm goin' to..."

"Just promise me you'll take care of yourself." Her eyes tearing, she turns to leave before the floodgates open.

But she doesn't get far before he calls, "Hey, Daizy!" When she looks back he's smiling and giving her the Pants sign. "You're gonna make it after all."

"Thanks," she says, and slipping off her lost and found hat, she tosses it into the air.

"Hey, why'd you do that?" Adam cries, running off after it.

"Just forget it," she yells. "Adam!" But he doesn't hear her. "*Mr. Tambourine Man!*"

She can't stand to say goodbye all over again, so she hurries out the gate, wiping the tears from her eyes as she runs through the aisles of New Con City. By the time she gets back to the parking lot and moves her little solitary ship into the *Dachelor Pad's* cargo hold, she's all cried out.

When she plods into the galley's scantily furnished cabin, Frank immediately begins with the fondling. "What do you say once this thing gets sailing, the three of us go in back and do the time warp?"

"Again?" Daizy moans.

Backing off, Frank says, "Something's been up with you all con. It's that chidiot Asteroid Jones, isn't it? That guy's got you in a mind flip."

"He does not. I just don't feel like sexing right now."

"Fine," the Transylvanian says, running her hand over Daizy's moist cheek. "I'll be in the back embarking on a little solo adventure. Let me know when you come to your senses."

As Frank disappears into the bowels of the ship, Daizy kicks off her loafers and unbuttons her blazer. Running her fingers through her knotted hair, she says, "I could really use a beer."

Dach is in the cockpit, manning the ship in his black rain slicker, and as she slumps into the passenger seat, he turns his head and smiles his perfect smile. She looks out over the bright Park sky as they take off, trying to hold on to the magic. But she can already feel it fading.

Once they're back out amongst the stars, traveling through the eternal dark, she asks Dach, "So, do you want to talk, or something?"

"About what?" the fisherman asks.

"I don't know. Do you like movies?"

"Not really," he says, enthusiastically. "It's all just make-believe."

"Yeah, I guess you're right. But isn't your costume from that movie where the kids kill some old person on summer break... What's it called? *Don't Tell Mom What You Did Last National Lampoon's Vacation*, or something?"

"Frank dressed me," he reveals.

"Oh... well, let's look anyway." But as she pulls up UMDB to find something to watch, Dach stands from his chair, and she asks, "Where are you going?"

"Uh, I'm just going to go help Frank with her time slip," he says. "But you're welcome to keep talking."

Daizy smirks as the oaf marches off to play with his sexual scientist. And then she's alone. She can feel her chest tightening and tears welling in her throat as the emptiness of space presses down on her. But just when she fears she's about to have some sort of psycho-depressive break, she smiles.

Thinking of his chidiot face, her sobs suddenly transform into howls of laughter, and she cries, *"That stupid jingler..."*

Pulling out her phone, she opens the tracker app to a map of the universe, and she zooms in on a pulsing red dot inside The Park. Even if they can't be together, she feels better just knowing he's out there.

58

By the time Adam wrenches Daizy's hat free from the sticky mitts of the adolescent pipsqueak who found it, she's already gone.

"I didn't even get to say goodbye... again," he moans, pulling the pink beanie down over his ears.

As he plods back toward the real world, he hears a tiny, piercing voice shout, "There he is! That's the fish head who stole my hat!" And he turns to find a rabid pack of native magical girls charging toward him, their souvenir wands slicing the air.

"We're about to cast a spell of whoop-ack on this shrimp flavor ration," one of them cries.

"Mu-ahhh," Adam yelps, and spinning away from his would-be pummelers, he books it out of The Jungle Gym and back through the shuttered aisles of New Con City.

The electronic tinkling of the girls' wands follows close behind as he stumbles around the abandoned booths, his alcohol-saturated body incapable of competing with their youthful mania. Soon the chimes are all around him, and from the slight variation in tones, he realizes they're being used as a crude form of magical communication.

"He went this way," one of the girls yells. "I can hear his jingler."

"Dam it," he grumbles, fumbling to unhook the tambourine from his waist. Once it's free, he gives it a final, spirited shake and abandons it in the alley.

He can hear the little witches converging on the instrument, screaming cute obscenities as he makes his escape. When he gets back to the booth, nothing has been packed, and worse, all the beer is gone.

Following a trail of empties to Grandpa's cubby, Adam shouts through the curtain, "I thought you were going to clean up."

A few space seconds later, the old man pops his head out. "We got distracted."

"Well, hose yourselves down and get out here. If we don't lock up soon we're gonna get charged for an extra day."

Adam quickly stuffs his dirty street clothes and TV remote into his space pack and goes to work collecting all the empty beer cans and ration trays. By the time he's finished hauling the trash out to the overflowing dumpster, Grandpa and the widow Walters are standing outside the booth with a mountain of luggage, tickling each other's unmentionables.

"We actually pulled it off," Adam says, checking the time on his phone. "And with four space minutes to spare."

The old man peels himself away from the dark sorceress to appraise the clean-up job. "Looks good. But it still kind of stinks."

"Then our work here is done," Adam announces, closing the shutter.

As they gather the widow's bags, he can hear magical chimes ringing out from somewhere nearby, and he urges the geezers to finish applying their joint cream later. The terrible tinkling follows them all the way across the encampment, right up to the city limits. Adam can just make out the dancing trees waving from the next sector when he realizes his mistake.

"Chit!" he cries. "I forgot, the shuttles won't stop for me."

Hoofing it alongside him, the widow says, "Don't worry, I called a sofa. It's already on its way."

Adam glances at the repulsive sorceress, cones bouncing, and tells her, "I'm suddenly beginning to understand what Grandpa sees in you."

"Hey, don't get any ideas!" the old man shouts as he awkwardly shuffles down the aisle lugging her heavy suitcase.

The couch touches down just outside of town, and as they pile their stuff onto the cushions, Adam listens for his pursuers. "I think we lost them."

"Lost who?" Grandpa asks.

"Uh, nobody," Adam says. "It was just some magical... *monsters* trying to tear me to shreds is all. But it looks like I outsmarted them."

Once the bags are packed, the three of them squeeze into the open seat and wait for the sofa to take off. But it doesn't seem to want to budge.

Grandpa tries kicking it into gear, but it's no use. "Why aren't we moving?"

"Oh great," Adam says, shifting against the cushion. "It must remember my ack print."

Nervously crushing the old man between her meaty arms, the widow asks, "So, what are we supposed to do now?"

"I don't know," Adam says. "Just let me think."

There's no way they can carry the bags all the way across the designer city on foot, and he doubts Grandpa will dump the widow now. Nervously tapping his pocket where the black gold should be, he feels a slight lump and shoves his hand inside. "I've got it." Unrolling the crumpled wad, he triumphantly holds up a small sheet of neon pink paper. "My last twenty park bucks. I'll give the couch a tip, and all will be forgiven." But as he leans over the armrest, he turns back. "Do you think this thing can make change?"

Before he can mess things up any further, Grandpa snatches the bill and stuffs it into the slot. A moment later, they're airborne, zipping over the modified cityscape as fast as the couch will take them. Looking out over the magnificent, squalid patchwork of personalized reality, Adam feels the first bittersweet twinge of Parkschmerz that always accompanies the end of a con.

Apparently recognizing the look on his grandson's face, Grandpa says, "There's always next year."

"Yeah, next year...," Adam says, changing the sofa's radio from the bubbly Playland theme to something a little more fitting.

"What is that?" the widow asks.

Listening closely, Grandpa tells her, "I think it's... 'Sail Away Tiny Sparrow.'"

Before long, they're flying over the Parking Desert of the Real, and the shuttle touches down in the empty aisle back of the *Asteroid Jones II*. With the exception of a few stragglers just stumbling in, the lot is empty as Adam wrenches himself up from the cushions, stretching in the orange sun. Once they've finished unloading, the sofa takes off, and the only thing left to do is go home.

Adam steps around the side of his ship and starts wrestling with the airlock when he hears an enchanted tinkling at his back. Lifting his hands, he slowly turns to find the magical girl from The Jungle Gym and half a dozen of her hard-casting friends pointing their sparkly wands at his most vulnerable of areas.

As they look up at him with their cute little homicidal faces, he says, "A-ha..."

"Did you think you could get away from us?" the girl asks. "We run this planet."

"How did you find me?"

"We know who you are, *Asteroid Jones*."

"Oh..." Relieved, he lowers his hands. "So, what do you want, an autograph?"

"Aghh!" She waves her wand, and a cascade of twinkling light shoots into the sky. "Why would I want the autograph of a bit player like you? I want my hat back."

"Oh, right," he says, slipping the beanie off his head. "But this hat isn't yours. It belongs to a special friend of mine."

Holding out her tiny hand, the girl says, "You know the rules – it's the oldest one in the universe."

"Yeah, yeah," he says as he hands over the last remnant of Daizy's presence in his life. "Finders keepers.

Are you happy? Now I've got nothing to remember her—
I mean the con by."

The girl whips her wand down and holds it in front of
his face. "Watch yourself, old man."

As the little wannabe princesses skip away, Adam
angrily kicks the door of his ship and it finally comes
unstuck. Grumbling newly invented obscenities, he starts
tossing bags into the hold while Grandpa and the widow
stand around snickering.

"So, those were the little monsters?" Grandpa says.
"What did they do, sprinkle you with princess dust?"

As the old man and the widow burst out laughing at
Adam's misfortune, one of the girls casts a sparkling spell
at the back end of an ancient starship half-buried in the
sand, and the relic bursts into a ball of pastel fire.

"A-ha..." The geezers' mocking ceases, and as flaming
shrapnel rains down on the lot, Grandpa says, "Let's get
the fish out of here."

Once the ship is loaded, Adam finally slumps down
into his old captain's chair and opens the fridge. But the
shelves are empty.

"Figures," he says, too exhausted to laugh. But before
he closes the door, a golden glint catches the corner of his
eye, and he reaches into the back to discover a single can
of beer that somehow managed to escape his knucklehead
shipmates.

As he cracks the frosty can, Grandpa steps into the
cockpit and says, "Best con ever?"

Adam shrugs and tells the old man, "I'll drink to that."

"Were you and Daizy able to work things out?" the old
man asks, slipping into the passenger seat.

"Nah..." Adam shakes his head and turns to look out at the bright Park sky, the nostalgia withdrawal already setting in. "Where do I go from here?"

"It reminds me of an old saying, a very, very old saying," Grandpa says, leaning back in his chair. "When you get caught between the moon and New Con City..."

"Oh, chut up."

"I know it's crazy," he says. "But it's true!"

"*Ooh*, I have such a headache," the widow announces, poking her head into the cabin. With her hair cones down Adam barely recognizes her. "I think I need a nap."

"Well," Adam groans as he pushes himself out of his chair, "if Butterman wants to double his salary, he can take over flying duties for a while, and you can have the passenger seat."

"I like the sound of that," the widow says, fanning her face. "Just the thought of seeing my old man behind the controls is heating my biscuits."

"I suppose I could work a little magic of my own," Grandpa says, winking at his sorceress as he gradually moves over to the captain's chair. "But you better strap in, because when ol' Silas Ichabod Jones takes the wheel, you're in for a bumpy ride."

As Adam retreats into the living room, he calls, "Goodnight Mrs. Walters."

"Mm-mmm," the widow mumbles, her face pressed up against her old man.

Digging through the mess left by his shipmates, Adam locates his beer-logged script and swipes the coffee table free of empties and cigarette butts. He's still mourning the loss of his puffball cap, when he remembers his other souvenir. He sets his beer can down next to the battered typewriter, and rummaging through his pocket, he emerges with a folded photograph of Daizy, smudged and smiling and surrounded by garbage. Propping the photo next to the keyboard, he flips to where he last left off and threads the page into the ancient machine.

Taking a big swig of nectar, he places his fingers on the keys, when Grandpa yells, "Adam!"

"What?!"

"Where to?"

Thinking it over for a few space seconds, Adam decides, *"The Park, Butterman, fly through The Park!* You know how I love The Park."

59

Sunlight glints off the corner of a hunk of neon pink plastic poking out of the rubble, and the princess bends down to uncover a partially melted Pants Team membership card. Tears run down Pants's cheeks as she wades through the vast sea of trash covering the once great Playland. She can barely bring herself to look at the damage to the *Cuddler*. Even with half its cute head missing, the ship just keeps waving its giant paw at the two-dimensional birds picking at the fans' fried leavings.

"Even if they didn't get their evil hands on the black gold, the Dorks got their wish," Beer says. "The fans will never trust us after this."

"Then we have to convince them that they can," Pants says, gazing out toward the rotten horizon, her fists on her hips. "This con taught me something, you guys."

"Wahh?" Brosanne gasps, holding onto his curly wig to keep it from sliding off.

"I learned that there are forces in the universe that even Pants Team Pink can't control, and that even when you think you're doing the right thing, sometimes the wrong thing happens. But most important of all, I was reminded of who really rules this universe – *The Simpsons*."

Holding his fingers up in a 'V', Brosanne says, "Am-*stel*."

"The Xenodorks aren't our enemies," she says. "They just exposed our weaknesses. We have to be stronger if we expect to beat them. And we will. Together, we're going to clean up this universe, and we're going to start right here."

"Awww," Brosanne moans.

"Pants is right," Horton says, his normally pasty limbs tanned bright red. "The best way to lead is by example."

"Yeah," Beer says. "It's like, you have to be the chit you want to see in the universe."

Brosanne pouts, looking out over the vast mess. "But it'll take us the rest of our lives to clean all this up."

Flashing them the Pants symbol, the princess cries, "Then we better get started!"

But as she rolls up her con jacket's singed pink sleeves, the sky dims, and a new wave of darkness descends on the land. She's so tired she can barely hold her eyelids open as the bright world fades around them. Soon, her teammates' smudged faces are lost in shadow, and a nerdy quiet takes hold, the only sounds the clacking of distant late night proto-coasters and bleeping arcade cabinets.

"What is this?" Brosanne's voice asks. "Did the Xenodorks come back to finish us off?"

"It's night...," Horton says.

Huddling together against the chill air, Pants tells them, "It's a g-good thing I got us these jackets."

"Yeah," Brosanne says. "This way we'll be warm when we freeze to death."

"Shhh," Beer quiets them. "Do you hear that?"

"Hear what?" his brother asks.

"Listen! It's like a crinkling sound.*"* Beer scoffs. "Are you eating something?"

"No, I swear," Brosanne claims.

When they chut up, Pants can hear it too, like sneakers on fast food wrappers.

"It's getting closer," Horton says.

As the crunching closes in on them, Pants screams, *"It's right on top of us!"*

Gathering every last bit of her power, she thrusts her glowing fist into the dark, and the soft thing it lands against cries, *"Oof..."*

Horton uses his phone to illuminate their surroundings, and they spot the creature rolling around in the trash. "It's just Todd."

"Where the fish have you been?" Brosanne complains.

"Yeah, you missed the whole thing," Pants says. *"We stopped the Xenodorks from destroying Immaterial Girl...* and the universe."

"But they escaped," Beer reminds her, adjusting his crooked glasses.

"They didn't get the black gold!" Even though he can't see it, she sticks her tongue out at him and kicks an empty popcorn bucket.

"Neither did *we,*" Horton says.

"You mean you lost it, *again?*" their battered merch guy moans as he lifts himself out of the garbage pile. "How the fish did that happen?"

"It was that stupid fish head, Adam Jones," Brosanne says. "Speaking of, is anyone else starving? The last thing I had to eat was some frosting I found on the back of my sleeve."

"So where is it now?" Todd asks, illuminated by the light of his phone, his shoulders slumping.

Glancing at each other through the haze, the team shrugs, and Beer says, "It's floating around Earth's orbit somewhere, with the rest of the space junk."

Big splotches of Todd's arms and face seem to be missing, a phenomenon Pants attributes to the serious moonlight. With a frustrated frown, he pulls a strand of greasy hair behind his ear and mumbles, "The adventure continues... Anyway, I have a surprise for you guys."

Picking a glob of crusted jelly out of his nose, Beer says, "No offense, but I think we've had enough surprises for one con."

"You're gonna like this one," the merch man says, looking up toward the sky. "Give it a space second."

Soon the light on Horton's phone times-out and Brosanne says, "This has been exciting and all, but if something doesn't happen soon, I nominate Todd as the first one we eat."

"Agreed," Beer says.

"Quiet," Horton tells them. "I hear something."

The team huddles close as a low rumble echoes over the grounds, like the sound of a planet splitting in half. The volume gradually increases until the air is vibrating so loud Pants can hardly stand it. Reaching deep inside herself, she tries to summon the power of the Playland to defend the team, but her strength is sapped.

"Is this the end for Pants Team Pink, again?" she cries.

"Look!" Todd says, pointing toward the stars.

The little orbs of light suddenly seem so close floating around her head that Pants reaches out to touch them. But when her hand passes through the nearest star cluster, she realizes it's just a projection. As she gazes up in wonder, a bright streak of pink splashes the dark sky with the words they all came here to see – *Pants Team Pink: The Movie The Sequel.*

"You cleaned the cameras!" Pants squeals. "I didn't think you were going to be able to pull it off."

"Yeah, I found this great stuff at Ferd's. The only problem is it works *too* well," Todd says, staring down at his invisible fingers. "Oh well." Opening a small carrying case printed with the words 'Don't Open Till Doomsday', he pulls out a finely aged can of Ol' Guard. "I guess it's not technically doomsday, since we survived. But I figure, drink 'em if you got 'em."

As the team wraps their arms around one another, their faces dappled by the bright lights of their continuing story, Beer says, "I wonder how it'll all turn out."

"Yeah, me too," a foreign yet familiar voice chimes in.

Glancing down the line of teammates, Pants takes the roll, "Brosanne, Beer, Horton, Todd, *Brosanne?*"

Brosanne pulls his doppelgänger's wig off and cries, "It's The Other One!"

"Yay, I'm so glad you're okay!" she shouts, bouncing on the rubber cement. "For sticking with us to the end of the universe, we're going to make you an official member of Pants Team Pink!"

"Oh... thanks," the kid says. "But, no thanks."

Her grin falling, she says, *"What?"*

The Other One shrugs. "You guys are nice and all, but you're kind of boring. I want to have fun and cause trouble. That's why I'm going to join the Xenodorks."

"We *are* fun!" Pants shrieks.

"Yeah... but not really," the kid says. "Anyway, I'm just here to get paid."

"I hate you," Brosanne grumbles, pressing his thumb to The Other One's phone. "But I like your style."

"Hey, now that I don't work for you anymore, you guys mind if I stay and watch the movie with you?" the kid asks.

"What?!" Pants cries, suddenly wishing she had the power of speech bubbles. "You just said you're going to join our enemies. You're lucky your belly isn't pink."

"Well, this has been a most cromulent adventure," The Other One says as he wriggles out of his chicken sweatshirt. "But as Troy McClure told Dolores Montenegro in *Calling All Quakers*, 'have it your way, baby.'"

With an annoying wink, he disappears into the dark, and the team turns back to the holographic adventure playing out above their heads to see what happens to them next.

"We should probably let Mom know we're not gonna be home for dinner this space month," Beer says.

"Yeah..." Pulling off his wig, Brosanne transforms back into The One. "She's already left me like a hundred messages. But let's wait until after the movie."

Glancing at his teammates, Horton says, "You know, it doesn't get much better than this."

"Yep," Pants says. "I just wish our fans were here."

"Hey!" Horton suddenly turns toward The One. "What did you end up doing about the replicas?"

"What do you mean?" The One asks.

"I *mean*, how did you stop the bots from dumping them into Earth's orbit?"

"ME-OW, ME-OW, ME-OW," Pants's phone cries, and her mouth drops when she sees the caller's screen name. "It's The Mighty Big Guy, you guys."

"No way," Horton says. "It's probably just those spoofing Raleighites. They never give up."

Holding her phone up so they can see, she says, "But it's got his official seal, a cheeseburger on a field of golden french fries."

Her teammates look at each other nervously, and Beer finally says, "Answer it... I guess."

When she presses her finger to the screen, the shaking cartoon kitty is replaced by the bulbous, lopsided cyberleader of the beef world.

Scowling at them from the other side of the universe, The Big Man says, *"So, you're the kids protecting our great planet from all the boring, mindless shows."*

"That's right, your bigness," Pants says.

Scanning them over with his cybernetic eye, he tells them, *"Well, I just wanted to personally thank you for a job well done. I've contacted all of your parents to let them know what you've been up to, and they can't wait for you to get back home."*

"Thanks a lot, Mr. Big Man, sir," The One says. "And if you don't mind me saying, it's about time!"

"That's very cute," the Big Man says. *"I like that. I just have one question for you kids."*

"Anything, sir," Beer, says, saluting the screen.

"Which one of you do I have to thank for all the souvenir junk clogging up my atmosphere?!"

Huddled around Pants's phone, they glance at one another, each politely giving the others a chance to take the lead, until The One finally asks, "Are you still there?"

"Yes, I'm still here!" The Big Man grumbles, pressing his fleshy face toward the screen.

"Uh sorry, sir," Pants says. "The reception at The Park is chit. But you can count on us to find whoever's responsible and bring the replicas to justice... just as soon as the movie's over and we clean up the Playland."

"How long is that going to take?" The Big Guy asks. Grinning, she gives him the Pants sign, and as she moves her thumb toward the dozing cat in the corner of the screen to end the call, he cries out, *"PANTS TEAM PIII—"*

60

"I hope Terry Kiser won a 'ward for this performance," Tobi says as the dead man congas his way across the screen for what must be the dozenth time since they lost the show. "How kin yuh possibly like the 'riginal more? This one's got errythin' – vootoo, pseudo zombies, burie't treasure, Barry Bostwick. I'm startin' tuh think this jist might be the best sequel ever mate. Feels good knowin' Bernie's reanimate'it corpse is still out ther partyin' fer all us sinners..."

Lifting his wide purple head off the cruddy dash, the light from the screen flickering over the dark cabin, Spez says, "I think this movie is goin' tuh yer het."

"My point exacly," Tobi says. "It's unfergittable. That's the trouble with the, *Wayne's Worlt 2*, universe tuhday – no 'preciation fer, *Honey, I Blew Up the Kit*, big ideas. Sometimes I worry about what will happen tuh are, *Ernest Scaret Stupit*, civ'lization if we don't start havin' bitter, *Addams Family Values*, taste." Glancing over at his dozing partner, he says, "Hey, "I'm, *Scream 2*, talkin' over her."

"Aww, give it a rest, I hear yuh," Spez says, and marking the screen, "If yer jist tunin' back in, Tobi's up tuh sixteen decent sequels, and wer still stuck in Bernie space hell."

"Hey, how many list'ners we up tuh?"

"Uhh..." Spez swipes at the screen to check their stats. "Twelve."

"Wow, wer gettin' perty pop'lar," Tobi says. "I got 'nother one fer yuh – *Return a the Livin' Det.*"

Spez furrows his thick brow. "That's not a sequel."

"It sort a is."

"Not in the tradish'nal sense."

"So, now wer bein' 'tradish'nal,'? Whatever that means..." Turning toward the window, Tobi waves off the whole thing.

"Aright, aright, I'll give it tuh yuh," Spez says. "That's seventeen. Lit's jist calm down ant take a call from one a are list'ners." He leans across the dash and taps the icon for the next caller in the cue. "Yer on the air with Spez ant Tobi."

"Yeah, I got one for yuh – Warlock II: The Progeny."

"Uhh, ha..." Tobi glances at his shipmate. "*The Progeny* is *Basket Case 3*. Yer thinkin' a *The Armagettin.*"

"Mmm no, I'm pret-ty sure—" But Tobi hangs up before the caller can spread any more disinformation.

"Well, that was pointliss," Spez says, tapping the screen. "Lit's go tuh the next caller. Yuh got a sequel for us, uh, *theghostshipofeddiesfather?*"

"Yeah uh, I'm sort of partial to Big Momma's House 2... But what I'm really calling about is Truer Lies."

"Ughh," Spez groans, smacking his thick forehead.

"It's as real as black gold," the caller says. *"I even remember the poster. It had big Arnold and Jamie Lee back-to-back, with Tom Arnold smooshed in the middle fumbling his gun."*

Jutting his long thumb out at Spez in righteous vindication, Tobi leans into the mike and says, "First off, I jist wanna comment yuh on a fantastic pick with the momma of all cometies." He motions toward the tally on the window and Spez grudgingly adds a mark. "Secont, *I knew it!* I 'member that poster. Tom Arnolt had a look on his face like he never shit a got out a the van."

"I think it's that thing," the caller says. *"Whaddaya call it, the Mandel Effect."*

"The *Mandel* Effect?" Spez says. "What the fish is that, some kine't a reality disorter?"

"You know, it's like when a bunch of people remember something one way, but it turns out to be something different. It's named after some weird guy, with either curly hair or no hair depending on who you ask. Some people remember him as the voice of Gizmo, even though everybody knows Giz's hoarse rasp was provided by a wined-up Orson Welles."

"What kine't a chitiot wit b'lieve somethin' like that?" Spez snorts, smacking his paw against the dash to end the call.

"What'it yuh do that fer?" Tobi cries. "I think the caller was on tuh somethin'."

"Ha," Spez scoffs. "He was *on* somethin' aright. Face it, Tob. It's not real. It doesn't count."

"One a these days yer eyes are gonna open tuh the truth."

"I doubt it..."

Leaning back in his recliner, Spez cranks the volume, and they melt back into the digital world as their ship continues hurtling toward the play planet. Tobi has seen the antics on the screen so many times that the line separating him from the dancing dead man is starting to blur. Before long, Bernie is ambling into the water, again, and as he makes his way across the ocean floor, Tobi suddenly finds himself gasping for air.

"This movie might be *too* good," he says, leaning against the dash as the blood rushes back to his eyes. "I don't know how much more I kin take. Are we almost ther?"

"It's been a while since I look't, but we must be gittin' close." As Spez sits up to check their progress he says, "Hey, we got 'nother caller," and tapping the screen, "Yer on with Spez ant Tobi."

"That's good...," a familiar voice growls, and for a moment the only sound that comes out of the speakers is heavy, static-filled breathing.

"Uh, yuh ther caller?" Spez says. "I hope this ain't 'nother wank call."

"I'm here," the voice says. *"Where are you?"*

Spez smirks at his shipmate and says, "Wer broadcastin' from deep space. What the fish is it tuh you?"

"Oh, I'm just curious what type of pleasure planet kept you from delivering the most important shipment of your worthless lives!"

For a long moment the cabin is quiet, with the exception of the Caribbean steelpans ringing between the metal walls, and Spez finally says, "Mr. Steel?"

"Were you expecting Mr. Lomax?"

"Oh h-hey, s-sir," Spez stammers. "Wer jist on are way tuh The Park now."

"The con is over," their boss says. *"You missed it."*

Spez knocks over a dark stack of beer cans scrambling to pull up their location and says, "Chit! I must a knock't us off course."

"I tolt yuh not to put yer feet up on the dash!" Tobi whines.

"Wer real sorry, Mr. Steel," Spez says. "It was an accitent."

"Your whole life is an accident, Spez."

"Dam it all tuh space hell...*raiser II*," Tobi says. "This has been one *Bogus Journey*. So, are we firet?"

"Fired?" Mr. Steel breaks into a sick laugh. *"Oh no, you're not getting away that easy. You're going to be working this one off until* Next Friday!*"*

He laughs so hard he starts hacking, and Spez finally hangs up the call. "Whattaya think he meant by that?"

Tobi shrugs. "I don't know... but count it. All this reprimantin' is makin' me thirsty. Toss me a Nü Guart, wit yuh?"

"Nü Guart?" Spez says. "What the fish is that?"

Tobi starts to feel light-eyed as the stalks holding them up turn to rubber, and the room collapses around him. "Whattaya mean, 'what's that'? It's the beer we been drinkin' all space year. Yuh hate it!"

"I never hert a it," Spez says. "The last thin' I neet is some newfangl't beer. I like my brant jist fine, thank yuh very much." Reaching into the fridge, he grabs two cans and tosses one across the flickering cabin.

In the dim light, Tobi can just make out the words printed across the can's gleaming surface – Ol' Guard. "What the fish..."

Fiddling with the video feed, Spez says, "Hey, the reception's back! The con feet's comin' in, ant the movie's jist gittin' start'it."

Tobi can hear the words, but he's too busy questioning the very nature of reality to begin to comprehend the implications.

"Now we got somethin' tuh watch on the way home."

"Huh?" Tobi mutters. "Uh yeah, great."

"What the fish is wrong?" Spez asks as he switches back to the show.

"Nothin'," Tobi says, staring down at his beer can. "Fer a secont ther, I jist thought... fergit it."

"Yer scarin' the list'ners, Tob. Now come on, yuh only neet one more sequel tuh win the bet."

Snapping himself back to whatever the space hell this is, Tobi cracks his beer and allows the cool suds to wash the sour taste of unreality out of his mouth. "The universe is jist so big ant strange, sometimes I git the feelin' wer *Lost In Time...*"

Spez shrugs. "What does that mean?"

"*Waxwork II...*"

"Oh, is that a sequel?"

"Yes, it's a sequel!" Tobi says. "A dam good one. I mean, it's aright... It counts!"

"Aright," Spez moans. "Yuh win. That's one decent sequel for every billion years, give or take, that the universe has exist'it. Maybe this one'll make twenty-three." Pushing himself out of his chair, he says, "I'm gone git me a ration. Figur I'll break open the Pants Team Con style, since no one's gon' be eatin' 'em anyway. Yuh want one?"

"Yeah, I want one!" Tobi says. "Ant wit yuh heat it up, fer Space Got's sake?"

"*Ulch...*" Spez's face twists. "I don't know how yuh kin eat it like that. But if ther's one thin' I learn't on this aventure, some like it hot, some like it colt, and some jist never know."

Author's Note

As the title suggests, the word guiding my keystrokes more than any other throughout the creation of this book was *more*. I wanted to explore more characters, more worlds and more adventures. The goal, in the tradition of my favorite sequels, was something reminiscent of the first book blasted open. As a matter of course, I did my darndest to infuse every word with fun and magic. Exactly where it ranks in the pantheon of sequels is for you to decide.

About the Author

Andrew Bixler hails from the same land that produced Drew Carey. He writes fiction designed to commandeer your hippocampus. He is also co-host of Big Orange Couch: The 90s Nickelodeon Podcast.

For more about the author, news about upcoming books, and contact information, visit **andrewbixler.com** and twitter **@andrewofbixler**

For more about the Big Orange Couch podcast, visit **bigorangecouch.podbean.com** and twitter **@BOCpodcast**

Thanks for Reading

I am grateful that you chose to spend your hard-earned crits on my book. Since I am my own publisher, I receive a larger portion of the revenue than I would under a traditional publishing house. But it also means that I don't have the weight of a big corporation to market it. If you enjoyed this book, please spread the word to every sci-fi adventure fan you know. The fate of my world depends on it!

How Was the Ride?

If you've come this far, maybe you're willing to come a little further. I am an independent author, and I can use all the feedback I can get. Let me know what you think of this book by leaving a review on Amazon!

Made in the USA
Columbia, SC
05 November 2023

25553421R00269